Praise for international bestseller Harriet Evans

Love Always

"Marks Evans out as a writer of top-drawer popular fiction. . . . It's a dose of escapism that brings with it the promise of 'custard yellow' sands and hot summer sun." —*Independent* (UK)

"Written in the author's usual warm, witty style, this is perfect for a cozy night in." —*Cosmopolitan* (UK)

"Complex storylines, flawed characters and cupboards that positively rattle with skeletons. If you've yet to add Harriet Evans to your 'must-read' list, now is a great time to start." —*Daily Record* (UK)

"A modern romance and a delightful tale of second chances." —*Now* (UK)

"Heartwarming and hugely enjoyable." —*Closer* (UK)

"A broken heart and a forbidden affair are the compelling components of this poignant tale of self-discovery. . . . Wonderful." —*Marie Claire* (UK)

"[A] story of heartbreak and rivalry. . . . An effortless and deeply satisfying romantic tale." —*Glamour* (UK)

"An engrossing novel of jealousy and forbidden love." —*Woman & Home* (UK)

I Remember You

"A satisfying summer read."

—Library Journal

"A compelling story complete with mystery, unearthed secrets and longing for new adventures and old comforts."

—Romantic Times

"The perfect girly read."

—Cosmopolitan (UK)

"A fabulous feel-good love story of friendship lost and love regained."

—Woman & Home (UK)

"A moving and witty story of love, friendship, and self-discovery . . . and a great read for those cozy nights in."

—Closer (UK)

"Very touching, warm, and sweet."

—Heat (UK)

The Love of Her Life

"A heart-tugging tale. . . . Peopled with well-rounded characters and compelling dilemmas, the story will have readers sighing, hoping and finally smiling. A read both entertaining and emotional; tissues at hand highly recommended."
—*BookPage*

"Evans captures the essence of the young twenty-first-century career woman. . . . Delightful."
—Fresh Fiction

"A poignant twist on the usual tropes of chick lit."
—*Booklist*

"[A] page-turner. . . . An unputdownable, gripping story of life, loss and one girl's search for happiness."
—*Glamour* (UK)

"You will cry, guaranteed."
—*Company* (UK)

"A modern day love story, packed with hope, humor, hurt and happiness. I couldn't put it down."
—*Manchester Evening News* (UK)

"Brilliantly observed and emotionally charged throughout."
—*Daily Mirror* (UK)

"Page-turning escapism."
—*Woman & Home* (UK)

"If you are a fan of well-written chick lit, you will love this book. . . . The plot keeps the reader guessing right to the very last page."
—*Refresh* (UK)

"A touching story with a modern heroine you can relate to."
—*Woman* (UK)

A Hopeless Romantic

"A delicious romcom, surprisingly believable." —*Marie Claire* (UK)

"Hard to resist." —*Elle* (UK)

"Touching, engrossing and convincing . . . a rollicking ride of joy, disappointment, and self-discovery, which you'll want to devour in one sitting." —*Daily Telegraph* (UK)

"Harriet Evans has scored another winner . . . will warm you up like brandy on a winter's night. . . . Witty, entertaining, self-reflective, and full of characters you'll grow to love." —*Heat* (UK)

Going Home

"Fabulous. . . . I loved it."
—Sophie Kinsella

"A brilliant debut novel. . . . A delightful romantic comedy with self-effacing humor and witty dialogue."
—*Romantic Times*

"An engaging first-person recounting of a watershed six months in one young woman's life."
—*Booklist*

"A lovely, funny heart-warmer. . . . Evans's heightened comic style and loveable characters make it effortlessly readable."
—*Marie Claire* (UK)

These titles are also available as eBooks

By the same author

Going Home
A Hopeless Romantic
The Love of Her Life
I Remember You

Harriet Evans

Love Always

G

GALLERY BOOKS

New York London Toronto Sydney

G

Gallery Books
A Division of Simon & Schuster, Inc.
1230 Avenue of the Americas
New York, NY 10020

Originally published in Great Britain in 2011 by HarperCollins*Publishers*

First Gallery Books trade paperback edition June 2011

GALLERY BOOKS and colophon are registered trademarks
of Simon & Schuster, Inc.

For information about special discounts for bulk purchases,
please contact Simon & Schuster Special Sales at 1-866-506-1949
or business@simonandschuster.com.

The Simon & Schuster Speakers Bureau can bring authors to your live event. For more information or to book an event contact the Simon & Schuster Speakers Bureau at 1-866-248-3049 or visit our website at www.simonspeakers.com.

Manufactured in the United States of America

10 9 8 7 6 5 4 3 2 1

Library of Congress Cataloging-in-Publication Data

Evans, Harriet, 1974–
    Love always / Harriet Evans.—1st Gallery Books trade paperback ed.
       p. cm.
    1. Life change events—Fiction.   2. Family secrets—Fiction.   I. Title.
PR6105.V347L66 2011
823'.92—dc22   2011001533

ISBN 978-1-4516-3962-9
ISBN 978-1-4516-3964-3 (ebook)

For Chris
I. W. O.

We can never go back, that much is certain. The past is still too close to us. The things we have tried to forget and put behind us would stir again, and that sense of fear, of furtive unrest, struggling at length to blind unreasoning panic—now mercifully stilled, thank God—might in some manner unforeseen become a living companion, as it had been before.

—*Rebecca,* Daphne du Maurier

One crowded hour of glorious life
Is worth an age without a name.

—Thomas Osbert Mordaunt,
quoted by Mr. Justice Marshall
in his summing-up at the Stephen Ward trial,
30 July 1963

Love Always

Prologue

Cornwall, 1963

If you close your eyes, perhaps you can still see them. As they were that sundrenched afternoon, the day everything changed.

Outside the house, in the shadows by the terrace, when they thought no one was looking. Mary is in the kitchen making chicken salad and singing along to "Music While You Work" on the Home Service. There's no one else around. It's the quiet before lunch, too hot to do anything.

"Come on," she says. She is laughing. "Just one cigarette, and then you can go back up." She chatters her little white teeth together, her pink lips wet. "I won't bite, promise."

He looks anxiously around him. "All right."

She has her back to him as she picks her way confidently through the black brambles and gray-green reeds, down the old path that leads to the sea. Her glossy hair is caught under the old green and yellow towel she has wrapped round her neck. He follows, nervously.

He's terrified of these encounters—terrified because he knows they're wrong, but still he wants them, more than he's wanted anything in his life. He wants to feel her honey-soft skin, to let his hand move up her thigh, to nuzzle her neck, to hear her cool, cruel laugh. He has known a couple of women: eager, rough-haired girls at college, all inky fingers and beery breath, but this is different. He is a boy compared to her.

Oh, he knows it's wrong, what they're doing. He knows his head has been turned, by the heat, the long, light evenings, the intoxicating almost frightening sense of liberation here at Summercove, but he just doesn't care. He feels truly free at last.

The world is becoming a different place, there's something happening this summer. A change is coming, they can all feel it. And that feeling is especially concentrated here, in the sweet, lavender-soaked air of Summercove, where the crickets sing long into the night and where the Kapoors let their guests, it would seem, do what on earth they want. . . . Being there is like being on the inside of one of those glass domes you have as a child, visible to the outside world, filled with glitter, waiting to be shaken up. The Kapoors know it too. They are all moths, drawn to the flickering candlelight.

"Hurry up, darling," she says, almost at the bottom of the steps now in the bright light, the white dots on her blue polka-dot swimming costume dancing before his eyes. He clings to the rope handle, terrified once more. The steps are dark and slippery, cut into the cliffs and slimy with algae. She watches him, laughing. She often makes him feel ridiculous. He's never been around bohemian people before. All his life, even now, he has been used to having rules, being told when to wash behind his ears, when to hand an essay in, used to the smell of sweaty boys—now young men—queuing for meals, changing for cricket. He's at the top of the pile, knows his place there, he's secure in that world.

He justifies it by saying this is different. It's one last hurrah, and he means to make the most of it, even if it is terrifying. . . . He stumbles on a slippery step as she watches him from the beach, a cigarette dangling from her lip. His knee gives way beneath him, and for one terrifying moment he thinks he will fall, until he slams his other leg down, righting himself at the last minute.

"Careful, darling," she drawls. "Someone's going to get killed on those steps if they're not careful."

Shaken, he reaches the bottom, and she comes towards him, handing him a cigarette, laughing. "So clumsy," she says, and he hates her in that moment, hates how sophisticated and smooth she is, so heedless of what she's doing, how wrong it is. . . . He takes the cigarette but does not light it. He pulls her towards him instead, kissing her wet, plump pink lips, and she gives a little moan, wriggling her slim body against his. He can feel himself getting hard already, and her fingers move down his body, and he pushes her against the rock, and they kiss again.

"Have you always been this bad?" *he asks her afterwards, as they are smoking their cigarettes. The heat of the sun is drying the sweat on their bodies. They lie together on the tiny beach, sated, as the waves crash next to them. A lost sandal, relic of someone else's wholly innocent summer day, is bobbing around at the edge of the tide. The cigarette is thick and rancid in his mouth. Now it's over, as ever, he is feeling sick.*

She turns to him. "I'm not bad."

He thinks she is. He thinks she is evil, in fact, but he can't stay away from her. She smiles slowly, and he says, without knowing why he needs to say it, "Look, it's been lots of fun. But I think it's best if—" *He trails off.* "Break it off."

Her face darkens for a second. "You pompous ass." *She laughs, sharply.* "'Break it off'? Break what off? There's nothing to break off. This isn't . . . anything."

He is aware that he sounds stupid. "I thought we should at least discuss it. Didn't want to give you the—" *God, he wishes it were over. He finds himself giving her a little nod.* "Give you the wrong impression."

"Oh, that's very kind of you." *She stubs the cigarette into the wet sand and stands up, pulling the towel off the ground and around her again. He can't tell if she's angry or relieved, or—what? This is all beyond him, and it strikes him again that he's glad it will be over and that soon he can go back to being himself again, boring, ordinary, out of all this, normal.*

"It's been—" *he begins.*

"Oh, fuck you," *she says.* "Don't you dare." *She turns to go, but as she does something comes tumbling down the steps. It is a small piece of black slate.*

And then there is a noise, a kind of thudding. Footsteps.

"Who's there?" *he says, looking up, but after the white light of the midday sun it is impossible to see anyone on the dark steps.*

In the long years afterwards, when he never spoke about this summer, what happened, he would ask himself—because there was no one else he could ask: Who? His wife? His family? Hah—if he'd been wrong about what he'd seen. For in that moment he'd swear he could make out a small foot, disappearing back up onto the path to the house.

He turns back to her. "Damn. Was that someone, do you think?"

She sighs. "No, of course not. The path's crumbling, that's all. You're paranoid, darling." She says lightly, "As if they'd ever believe it of you, anyway. Calm down. Remember, we're supposed to be grown-ups. Act like one."

She puts one hand on the rope and hauls herself gracefully up. "Bye, darling," she says, and he watches her go. "Don't worry," she calls. "No one's going to find out. It's our little secret."

But someone did. Someone saw it all.

Part One

February 2009

One

It is 7:16 a.m.

The train to Penzance leaves at seven-thirty. I have fourteen minutes to get to Paddington. I stand in a motionless Hammersmith and City line carriage, clutching the overhead rail so hard my fingers ache. I have to catch this train; it's a matter of life and death.

Quite literally, in fact—my grandmother's funeral is at two-thirty today. You're allowed to be an hour late for dinner, but you can't be an hour late for a funeral. It's a once-in-a-lifetime deal.

I've lived in London all my life. I know the best places to eat, the bars that are open after twelve, the coolest galleries, the prettiest spots in the parks. And I know the Hammersmith and City line is useless. I hate it. Why didn't I leave earlier? Impotent fury washes through me. And still the carriage doesn't move.

This morning, the sound of pattering rain on the quiet street woke me while it was still dark. I haven't been sleeping for a while, since before Granny died. I used to complain bitterly about my husband Oli's snoring, how he took up the whole bed, lying prone in a diagonal line. He's been away for nearly two weeks now. At first I thought it'd be good, if only because I could catch up on sleep, but I haven't. I lie awake, thoughts racing through my head, one wide-awake side of my brain taunting the other, which is begging for rest. I feel mad. Perhaps I am mad. Although they say if you think you're going mad that definitely means you're not. I'm not so sure.

7:18 a.m. I breathe deeply, trying to calm down. It'll be OK. It'll all be OK.

Granny died in her sleep last Friday. She was eighty-nine. The

funny thing is, it still shocked me. Booking my train tickets to come
down to Cornwall, in February, it seemed all wrong, as though I was
in a bad dream. I spoke to Sanjay, my cousin, over the weekend and
he said the same thing. He also said, "Don't you want to punch the
next person in the face who says, 'Eighty-nine? Well, she had a good
innings, didn't she?' Like she deserved to die."

I laughed, even though I was crying, and then Jay said, "I feel like
something's coming to an end, don't you? Something bigger than all
of us."

It made me shiver, because he was right. Granny was the center of
everything. The center of my life, of our family. And now she's gone,
and—I can't really explain it. She was the link to so many things.
She was Summercove.

We're at Edgware Road, and it's 7:22 a.m. I might get it. I just
might still get the train.

Granny and Arvind, my grandfather, had planned for this moment. Talked about it quite openly, as if they wanted everyone to be
clear about what they wanted, perhaps because they didn't trust my
mother or my uncle—Jay's dad—to follow their wishes. I'd like to
believe that's not true, but I'm afraid it probably is. They specified
what would happen when either one of them died first, what happens to the paintings in the house, the trust that is to be set up in
Granny's memory, the scholarship that is funded in Arvind's memory, and what happens to Summercove.

Arvind is ninety. He is moving into a home. Louisa, my mother's cousin, has taken charge of that. Louisa has taken charge of
the funeral too. She likes taking charge. She has picked everything
that Granny didn't leave instructions about, from the hymns to
the fillings in the sandwiches for the wake afterwards (a choice of
egg mayonnaise, curried chicken, or cucumber). Her husband, the
handsome but extremely boring Bowler Hat, will be handing out
the orders of service at the funeral and topping up drinks at the
wake. Louisa is organizing everything, and it is very kind of her, but
we feel a bit left out, Jay and I. As ever, the Leighton side of the
family has got it right, with their charming English polo-shirts-and-

crumpets approach to life and we, the Kapoors, are left looking eccentric, disjointed, odd. Which I suppose we are.

Cousin Louisa is also in charge of packing up the house. For Summercove is to be sold. Our beautiful white art deco house perched between the fields and the sea in Cornwall will soon be someone else's. It is where Granny and my grandfather lived for fifty years, raised their children. I spent every summer of my life there. It's really the only home I've ever known and I'm the only one, it seems, who's sentimental about it, who can't bear to see it go. Mum, my uncle Archie, Cousin Louisa—even my grandfather—they're all brisk about it. I don't understand how they can be.

"Too many memories here," Granny used to say when she'd talk about it, tell us firmly what was going to happen. "Time for someone else to make some."

Finally. The doors wobble open at Paddington and I rush out and run up the steps, pushing past people, muttering, "Sorry, sorry." Thank God it's the Hammersmith and City line—the exit opens right onto the vast concourse of the station. It is 7:28 a.m. The train leaves in two minutes.

The cold air hits me. I jab my ticket frantically in the barrier and run down the stairs to the wide platform, legs like jelly as I tumble down, faster and faster. I am nearly there, nearly at the bottom. . . . I glance up at the big clock. 7:29 a.m. Like a child, I jump the last three steps, my knees nearly giving way underneath me, and leap onto the train. I stand by the luggage racks, panting, trying to collect myself. There is a final whistle, the sound of doors slamming further along the endless snake of carriages. We are off.

I find a seat and sit down. My mother doesn't drive, so I know the ways of the train. The key to a good journey is not a table seat. I never understand why you would get one unless you knew everyone round the table. You end up spending five hours playing awkward footsie with a sweaty middle-aged man, or surrounded by a screaming, overexcited family. I slot myself into a window seat and close my eyes. A cool trickle of sweat slides down my backbone.

This is the train I took every summer, with Mum, to Summer-cove. Mum would bring me down, stay for a few days and then leave before the rest of her relatives arrived, and sometimes—but not often—before she and Granny could row about something: money, men, me.

It was always so much fun, the train down to Penzance when I was little. It was the anticipation of the holiday ahead, six weeks in Cornwall, six weeks with my favorite people in my favorite place. Mum would be in a strangely good mood on the train down, and so would I, both of us looking forwards to diluting our twosome for a few weeks, away from our dark Hammersmith mansion flat, where the wallpaper peeled away from the walls, and in the summer the smell from the bins outside was noticeable. Bryant Court didn't suit summer. The noises inside and out got worse, scratching and strange, and the cast of characters in the building seemed to get less eccentric and more menacing. The hot weather seemed to dry them out, to make them more brittle and screeching. We were always eu-phoric to be out of there, away from it all.

Once, when we were on our way to Paddington and my mother was dragging me by the wrist towards a waiting cab, bags slung over our shoulders, Mrs. Pogorzelski hissed, "Slut!" at Mum, as she opened the door. I didn't know what it meant, or why she was say-ing it. Mum bundled me into the black cab and we sat there grin-ning, surrounded by luggage, as we rolled up through Kensington towards the station, both of us complicit in some way that I couldn't define. That was also one of the times Mum forgot her purse, and the cab driver let us have a ride for free after she cried. She forgot her purse quite often, my mother.

She is at Summercove already, helping Cousin Louisa sort out the funeral and the house. She is convinced Louisa has her eye on some pieces of furniture already, convinced she is controlling everything. Archie, Mum's twin brother and Jay's dad, is there too. Mum and her cousin do not get on. But then Mum and a lot of people don't get on.

* * *

The train is flying through the outskirts of London, out past South-all and Heathrow, through scrubby wasteland that doesn't know whether it's town or countryside, towards Reading. I look around me for the first time since collapsing into my seat. I want a coffee, and I should have something to eat, though I'm not quite sure I can eat anything.

"Tickets, please," says a voice above me. I jump, more violently than is warranted and the ticket inspector looks at me in alarm. I hand him my tickets—thankfully, I collected them at Liverpool Street, knowing the queues at Paddington would be horrendous. I blink, trying not to shake, as the desire to be sick, to faint, anything, sweeps over me again, and slump back against the scratchy seat, watching the inspector. He raises his eyebrows as he checks them over.

"Long way to be going for the day."

"Yes," I say. He looks at me, and I find myself saying, too eagerly, "I have to be back in London tomorrow. There's an appointment first thing—I have an appointment I can't miss."

He nods, but already I've given him too much information, and I can feel myself flushing with shame. He's a Londoner, he doesn't want to chat. The trouble is, I want to talk to someone. I need to. A stranger, someone I won't see again.

I haven't told my family I'm coming back tonight. Growing up with my mother, I learned long ago that the less you say, the less you get asked. The one person I would like to confide in is being buried today, in the churchyard at St. Mary's, a tiny stone hut, so old people aren't sure when it was first built. In the churchyard there is the grave of a customs officer, one of many killed by desperate smugglers. There is a lot about Cornwall that is still kind of wild, pagan, and though the fish restaurants, tea shops, and surfboards cover some of it up, they can't entirely conceal it.

Granny believed that. She was from Cornwall, she grew up near St. Ives, on the wild north coast. She saw Alfred Wallis painting by the docks, she was born with the cry of seagulls and the wind whistling through the winding streets of the old town in her ears. She loved the landscape of her home county; it was her life, her job. She lived most of her life there, did her best work there, sitting in her studio high at the top of the house, overlooking the sea.

There are so many things I never asked her, and now I wish I had. So often that I wished I could confide in her, about all sorts of things, but knew I couldn't. For much as I loved my granny, I was scared of her too, of the blank look she'd get in her lovely green eyes sometimes when she looked at me. My husband Oli said once he sometimes thought she could see straight into your soul, like a witch. He was joking, but he was a little scared of her, and I know what he meant. There are some things you didn't ask her. Some things she wouldn't ever talk about.

Because for many years, Summercove was a very different place, center of a glittering social whirl, and my grandparents were wealthy, successful, and it seemed as if they had the world at their feet. But then their daughter Cecily died, two months short of her sixteenth birthday, and my grandmother stopped painting. She shut up her studio, at the top of the house, and as far as I know she never went back. I learned from a very early age never to ask why. Never to mention Cecily's name, even. There are no photos of her in the house, and no one ever talks about her. I know she died in 1963, and I know it was an accident of some kind, and I know Granny stopped painting after that, and that's about it.

We're going past Newbury, and the landscape is greener. There has been a lot of rain lately, and the rivers are swollen and brown under a gray sky. The fields are newly plowed. A fast wind whips dead leaves over and around the train. I sit back and breathe out, feeling the nauseous knot of tension in my stomach start to slowly unravel, as a wave of something like calm washes over me. We are leaving London. We are getting closer.

Two

My grandparents met in 1941, at a concert at the National Gallery. When the war broke out, Granny was nineteen, studying at St. Martin's School of Art in London. She stayed there, despite her parents demanding she return to Cornwall. Not Frances, oh no. She volunteered to man the first-aid post near her digs in Bloomsbury, she was fire watch officer for St. Martin's, and when she had a spare hour, which was not many, she went to the National Gallery, around the corner from the college, to listen to Dame Myra Hess's lunchtime concerts.

Arvind (we have always called him that, Jay and I don't know why except he's not someone you'd ever think of calling "Grandad," much less "Gramps") was born in the ancient Mughal city of Lahore, in 1919. His father, a Punjabi Hindu, was a teacher at Aitchison College, an exclusive school for sons of maharajahs and landowners, so Arvind was entitled to a place there. Arvind was brilliant. So brilliant that the headteacher wrote to various dignitaries, and to people in England, and after two years of studying philosophy at Lahore's Government College (there's a photo of his matriculation on the wall of his study, rows of serious-looking young men with arms crossed and neat cowlicks), Arvind was given a postgraduate scholarship to Cambridge, and it was on a research trip to London during the height of the Blitz in 1941 that he wandered into the National Gallery.

I have a very clear image of them in my mind: Arvind, short and dapper, so politely dressed in his best tweed suit, his umbrella hooked over his arm, his hat clutched in his slender fingers, his eye falling briefly on the girl in front of him, watching the performance with total absorption. Granny was beautiful when she was old; when she was younger, she must have been extraordinary. I keep a photo of her from around that age in my studio: her dark blonde hair carefully swept into a chignon, her huge dark green eyes set in a strong, open face, a curling, smart smile, perfect neat white teeth.

Frances and Arvind were married three months later. Bizarrely for a man who has outlived most of his contemporaries, Arvind was told he had a weak heart and couldn't fight. He went back to Cambridge and finished his degree, where he and several other students were called upon to try a variety of code-breaking formulae. He also knitted socks—he rather took to it, he liked the patterns—and volunteered for the Home Guard. Granny stayed in London, to finish her studies and carry on driving the ambulances.

Though Granny and Arvind never said anything, I often wonder what her parents must have made of it. They were respectable, quiet people who rarely left Cornwall, with an elder daughter who had recently become engaged to a solicitor from a good family in Tring, and suddenly their wild, artistic younger daughter writes from a bomb shelter to let them know she's married a penniless student from India whom they've never met. This was seventy years ago. There was no one from France, let alone the Punjab, in Cornwall.

After Granny and Arvind were married, they rented a tiny flat in Redcliffe Square. Mum and Archie, the twins, were born in 1946 and then a couple of years later, Cecily. Money was tight, Granny's painting and Arvind's writing did not bring in much; he was writing his book for years, paying the bills with teaching jobs. The book became something of a joke after a while, to all of them, so the aspect of their married life that always took them by surprise, I think, is the money that came in when *The Modern Fortress* was finally published, in 1955. It argued that postwar society was in danger of reverting to a complacency and ossification that would lead to another world war of the magnitude of the one we had only just barely survived. It was translated into over thirty languages and became an instant modern classic, debated and argued over by millions, followed ten years later by *The Mountain of Light,* which initially sold even more, though it is now seen as the more "difficult" of the two books. When I was fifteen, we had to read *The Modern Fortress* for GCSE History, as part of the course was about post–WW2 Europe. I am ashamed to say I understood not very much of it, even more ashamed to say I didn't tell the teacher at school that Arvind Kapoor was my grandfather. I don't know why.

While *The Modern Fortress* was selling thousands of copies a week, Granny's paintings were becoming more acclaimed too and suddenly Frances and Arvind were richer than they'd ever expected to be. They could afford to buy the house they'd rented for a couple of summers in Cornwall for Frances to paint in, a dilapidated twenties art deco place by the sea called Summercove. They could send the children to boarding school. They could keep the flat in London and a housekeeper for Summercove, and they could have their nieces and nephews to stay, and provide a degree of largesse to all they knew that meant, for the rest of the fifties and the early sixties, Arvind Kapoor and Frances Seymour, and Summercove, were bywords amongst artistic and intellectual circles in London for an elegantly bohemian way of life, postcolonial poster children: the couple that seemed to have everything.

In Granny's bedroom at Summercove, there is a curved, dark wooden dressing table, with a beautiful enamel hairbrush set, old glass crystal perfume bottles, and two jewelry boxes. The dressing table has little drawers with wrought-iron handles on each side, and once when I was little and I'd crept upstairs to surprise her, I found my grandmother sitting at that table, gazing at a photo.

She was very still, her back straight. Through the long suntrap windows you could see across the meadow down to the path, the bright blue-green sea glinting in the distance. I watched her as she stared at the photo, stroking it with her finger, tentatively, as if it had some talismanic quality.

"Boo," I'd said softly, because I didn't know what else to do, and I knew it wasn't right to jump out at her now. I didn't want her to be angry with me.

She did jump though, and she turned to me. Then she held out her hand. "Oh. Natasha," she said, as I stood looking at her.

I adored my grandmother, who was beautiful, funny, charismatic, in charge of everything, always in control: I found her hugely comforting, thrilling too, but the truth is she was also a little terrifying. Compared to her happy, open relationship with Jay, I felt sometimes, just sometimes, she looked at me and wished I wasn't there. I don't know why. But children like me—with an overactive imagination and no one with whom to exercise it—are often wrong. And I knew that if I ever tried to talk to my mother about it she'd tell me I was making things up, or worse, confront Granny, and have a row with her.

"Come here," she said, looking at me, and she smiled, her hand outstretched. I walked towards her slowly, wanting to run, because I loved her so much and I was so glad she wanted me. I stood in front of her and put my hands on her lap, tentatively. She stroked my hair, hard, and I felt a tear drop from her eyes onto my forehead.

"God, you're just like her," she said, her voice husky, and clutched my wrist with her strong fingers. She twisted the fingers of her other hand over to show me the photo she was holding. It was a small, yellowing snap of a girl about my age; I was then around seven or eight. I wish I could remember more, because I think it was important. I remember she had dark hair, but of course she did, we all did. She looked like Mum, but also not: I couldn't work out why.

"Yes, you're just like her." Granny drew a great shuddering breath, and her grip on my arm tightened. "Damn it all." She turned, her huge green eyes swimming with tears, her lovely face twisted and ugly. "Get out! Get out of here, now!"

She was still gripping my arm, so hard it was bruised the next day. I wrenched myself free and ran away, feet clattering on the parquet floor, out onto the lawn, away from the dark, sad room. I didn't understand it, how could I?

Later, when we were having tea and playing hide-and-seek, she came up and gave me a hug.

"How's my favorite girl?" she said, and she dropped a soft kiss onto my forehead. "Come here, let me show you this brooch I found in my jewelry box. Do you want to wear it tonight, at supper with the grown-ups?"

I didn't know it then, but I saw a side of her that day that she rarely showed anyone anymore. She kept it locked away, like the photo, like her studio. I tried to push it out of my mind that summer, and when I got back to London. And now. It's not the way I want to remember her.

We are heading further and further west, the landscape is wilder, and though spring feels far away, there are tiny green buds on the black branches fringing the railway tracks. We go through southern Somerset, past Castle Cary and the Glastonbury Tor. I stare out of the window, as if willing myself to see more.

Oli and I went to Glastonbury last summer, because of his job— one of his clients gave us VIP tickets, with backstage passes. We were very lifestyle that weekend—I wore my new Marc Jacobs city shorts and some Cath Kidston polka-dot wellies, Oli was in his best Dunhill shirt: we felt like a low-rent Kate Moss and Jamie Hince. We saw Jay-Z, and Amy Winehouse, and the Hoosiers, who I love but Oli thinks are crap. It was great, of course, although I remember going in a camper van when I was nineteen with Jay and my best friend Cathy, the year of the legendary Radiohead gig, not washing for three days and being stoned the whole time, and that was better somehow, less complicated, no one in a mood, no one looking dissatisfied because there are only two free beers in the wanky hospitality tent where everyone's terrified they're less important than everyone else. Oli complained when they wouldn't give him another one. Oh, Oli.

I look out of the window, blinking back tears, and nod: there is the perfect little village with a beautiful house and golden-yellow church, plunked seemingly in the middle of nowhere, that I kept

my eyes glued to the window looking for every year when I was little. The fields are flooded; there are confused ducks swimming in the
water, not sure what to make of it. Up on the banks by the tracks,
cobwebby Old Man's Beard covers everything, the beautiful tracery
concealing the hard branches beneath. Thankful for the distraction,
I stare, wondering where my sketchbook is, anything to take my
mind off it all.

Granny loved jewelry. I'm sure that my interest in it stems from
the hours I spent with her looking at her pieces, holding them up
and thrilling to the sensation of metal and stone on my skin, against
my face. The two big jewelry boxes on that dressing table were neatly
stacked with all kinds of wondrous things: a chunky jade pendant,
worn on a thick silver chain, tiny diamond dangly earrings that she
bought for herself when she had her first show (it occurs to me now
that these were valuable; she kept them quite blithely with the costume jewelry), delicate strings of creamy coral, a gold Egyptian-style
collar necklace that she got from the Royal Opera House, a prop
from *Aida* which she used on a model for a painting, a large am-
ethyst ring that was her mother's, and finally the two that were never
in the box, because she was always wearing them. The thick gold-
linked bracelet studded with turquoises which Arvind gave her for
her thirtieth birthday, and the pale gold ring she always wore on her
right hand, of three sets of two intertwined diamond flowers, like
tiny peonies. It is a family ring: Arvind's father sent it from Lahore
when they were married. That was my favorite piece of them all, a
link with Arvind's family, the country he left long ago. Because I
vaguely remember Granny's father, but I never met Arvind's father,
nor any of his family. Two of his brothers died during Partition, and
his father stayed in Lahore. He never saw his son again.

So Granny's jewelry box was like an Aladdin's cave for me, and
now, when I sit in my studio, sketching out designs, working out
different ways to coat something with gold leaf, searching for an
enameler who won't demand payment right away, often I am reminded where I first got my inspiration from: Granny's jewelry box,
the almost terrifying pleasure of being allowed to look inside it.

Now, gazing at the bare branches black in the gray light, I let my mind drift. I think how lovely a silver necklace linked with tiny branches would look, and I wonder how easy—or extremely difficult—it would be to replicate the delicate, sugar-spun tracery covering them. I should make a sketch, in the ideas book I used to carry with me, always. I haven't drawn in it for ages. Haven't come up with anything for ages.

Five years ago, when I had a stall of my own and was making just enough money to afford the flat share in West Norwood and the occasional item from Topshop, life was simple. Now, we live in a trendy apartment off Brick Lane and I have a flashy website and a husband who earns enough money telling clients that their toothpaste's branding is too male-oriented to keep us both.

So really, it shouldn't matter that tomorrow I might lose my business, should it? Lose everything I've worked for and dreamed about, ever since the long-ago days when I'd climb onto Granny's stool and open her jewelry box, my mouth gaping in wonder. Strange, that the two things are so close together. Her funeral, my summons.

I shake my head, and the cold, clammy fear that, lately, always seems to be with me grips me again. No. I'm not thinking about that today. Not today, Granny's funeral, not today. They'll tell me tomorrow. I just have to get through today.

My phone buzzes and I look down.

Missed you again last night. When are we going to talk? Ox

Now I am going to be sick. No sleep, no breakfast, on top of everything else, and this time I know it. I stumble towards the lavatories, pushing open the rank, sticky doors, and I vomit, retching loudly, bile flooding out of me; it feels almost cleansing. People must be able to hear.

I'm trying not to cry at the same time, pushing my hair out of my mouth. I stand up and look in the mirror, tears running down my cheeks, because I feel so awful, so sad, every protective layer I cover myself with ripped off and suddenly the almost cartoon terribleness of it makes me start to laugh. Suddenly I remember Cathy saying to me, "Has anyone ever explained to Oli that when he signs off with his initial and a kiss he's writing the word 'Ox'?"

I smile, I look dreadful, lank brown hair hanging about my sallow face, dark brown shadows under my startlingly green eyes. People at school called me alien because of my eyes; I hated it. I hadn't thought of that for ages either and it makes me smile again. I wipe my mouth on a tissue. I will go to the canteen and get a coffee, a banana. I feel better, purged.

Slowly, I open the door, embarrassed in case someone is outside and has overheard, and I hear two voices, approaching briskly.

"My best guess is we'll be five minutes late, no more," the first, a male voice, is saying.

"I'll call Mummy. God knows she's got enough to do without us holding her up today."

I freeze. *No way.*

"Bloody good thing Guy's already there," the male voice says, languidly, but with a hint of menace I remember of old. "We need someone to sort through that house, make sure the valuable stuff gets treated properly. I mean, those paintings must be worth a bob or two. . . ."

Julius and Octavia. I shrink back against the door as they march past, catching only a glimpse of Octavia's sensible brown flat boots and gray wool skirt and her hand, clutching a twenty-pound note, as they stride purposefully past on their way to the buffet car, a Leighton phalanx of aggressive righteousness. I don't know why it surprises me—this is the only train from London that gets to Penzance in time for the funeral, but of all people Julius and Octavia are not who I would have chosen to bump into, post-vomit, outside the First Great Western lav.

They are Louisa's children, and so they are my second cousins, and though I spent almost every summer of my life with them, there is no emotional connection to show for it. If you knew Octavia and Julius, though, you might understand why. They have even been given Roman names, I think to reflect their parents' passion for discipline and order. I hear Julius's posh voice again. *"Bloody good thing Guy's already there."*

My skin prickles with silent rage. Guy is their uncle on their father's side. He is an antiques dealer. I never knew he was close to Granny, or our family. I grit my teeth at the thought of Guy going through Granny's paintings, her jewelry box, with Louisa standing behind with a clipboard, ticking stuff off on a list. They are very *definite* people, the Leightons. I love Louisa, she's kind and thoughtful, and she does mean well, I think, but she can be dreadfully bossy. The four of them, her, the Bowler Hat, Julius and Octavia, are all terribly—not hearty exactly, more—*confident*. The confidence that comes from living in Tunbridge Wells, being a civil servant, going to a public school, being a unit of four, a proper family. All things I am not.

I wait until their voices have faded into the distance and cautiously, I creep back to my seat, a little shaky still, and stare out of the window again. Two fat crows are picking away at the mossy roof of a disused barn. Above them, the skies are opening wider and wider, and birds wheel through the air. We're getting there, we are nearly in Exeter. My phone buzzes again.

> I can't keep saying I'm sorry. We have to talk. Thinking of you today. When are you back? Ox

Ox. I switch my phone off and close my eyes, turning my head to the window in case the others walk past, and, thankfully, I drift off to sleep.

Three

It's always been me and my mother. I don't know my father. Mum met him at a party, he was a one-night stand and she never saw him again. I found this out when I was a teenager; I had no idea where he was before that. When I was about ten, and impressionable, I saw *The Railway Children*, and it all suddenly became perfectly clear to me: my father was away, somewhere, but he would come back one day soon. He had been wrongly imprisoned, like Roberta's daddy, he was on a ship sailing around the world, rescuing people, he was a doctor helping famine victims in Africa, he was a famous actor in America and couldn't tell people about me and Mum. He was a person in my life, absent for the moment, but he would come back.

One summer, Granny drove me to Penzance; she said she had a surprise for me at the station, and I knew it then with absolute certainty, the kind of certainty that has got me into trouble my whole life. We were going to meet my dad off the train, and he would fling his arms open wide and smile, and I would run towards him, crying, "Daddy! My daddy!" He would hug me tight, and kiss my forehead, and come home with me and Granny, and then he would take me and Mum away from the damp Hammersmith flat to a beautiful castle in the countryside, and we would live—yes, we would—happily ever after.

Under my breath, the rest of the way there, I tried the unfamiliar words out on my tongue. Dad. Daddy. Hi Dad. By the time we got to the station, I was jiggling my legs up and down, I was so excited. Granny had a watchful, sparkling look in her eyes. She kept glancing at me as we waited for the train to pull in to the platform, holding my hand in hers as she was afraid I'd simply run off, mad with anticipation. She was right, I remember it, I felt as if I might.

When the train arrived and the teeming hordes of passengers had hurried off, when the platform was emptying and my neck was aching from craning forwards, desperate to see who he was, she finally squeezed my fingers.

"Look, there he is."

And there was Jay with Sameena, his mum, walking down the platform, also hand in hand, only he was straining with excitement to see me, and I just looked at him, my heart sinking, sliding my hand out of Granny's.

"He's come early," she said. "So you'll have someone to play with now."

I couldn't tell her she'd ruined everything, that I'd rather be on my own with dreams of my dad than playing stupid Ghostbusters with Jay. I couldn't explain how silly I'd been. How could I? She never knew, I never told her, but I couldn't ever think about that day again. How I tried to picture what my father would look like as he got off the train. From that day on I stopped looking for him. Like Granny's beauty, it became one of those things that's just a fact, rather than a changeable situation. The sea is blue. Granny has a scar on her little finger. You don't know your dad.

The sea isn't always blue though. Sometimes it's green. Or gray. Or almost black like tar, with roiling, foaming white waves.

The sound of movement around me wakes me and I look up, startled. St. Michael's Mount looms up in the distance, the battlements and towers of the old castle rising out of the water, glinting in the midday sun. When I was a child the holidays were one long effort on my part to persuade whomever I could to take me, walk across the glittering causeway to the castle at low tide, climb up to the turreted towers, and look out across the bay to Penzance or out to sea.

"Welcome to Penzance. Penzance is our final destination. Thank you for traveling with First Great Western. May we wish you a pleasant onward journey," a voice intones over the loudspeaker, and there is the usual rush around me as I rub my eyes, tasting something sour in my mouth. Still in a daze, I jump up, stretching, and climb off the train, nearly bumping into someone on the platform. I look up and around me. I am here.

You can smell the sea in the air. It is warmer than London, though it's still February and the wind is sharp. I huddle into my coat as I reach the end of the platform, wondering who's come to meet me. Mum said she or Archie would. People saunter past; there's no bustling and jostling like Paddington. It still does always remind me of *The Railway Children*.

"Nat?" A voice floats across the hordes of people. "Natasha!"

I glance up.

"Natasha! Over here!"

I look behind me and there is Jay, my beloved cousin. He is striding towards me, so tall, smiling sort of sheepishly. He folds me in his arms and I close my eyes, sinking into his embrace. When Jay is here, everything is always a bit better. He's one of those people who leaves a gap when he exits a room.

"It's good to see you," he tells me, dropping a kiss onto my head.

"You were on the train?"

"I looked for you, then I fell asleep. I had a late night, we were working through." Jay is a website designer; he works crazy hours, but he stays out crazy hours too. "I had to get some sleep." He squeezes me tight. "This is a sad day."

I nod and link my arm through his as we walk outside, into the fresh air.

The car park is next to the harbor, where ships and boats of every kind over the centuries have arrived and disembarked, spilling out silks and spices and foods and wines from the furthest corners of the world. The riggings clatter against the masts, tinkling loudly in the gusting breeze. Seagulls shriek overhead.

"Jay! Sanjay! Over here!" We look up to see my uncle Archie, leaning against his car, waving coolly at us.

I always forget when I first see him how much my uncle reminds me of those older male models, the kind you see in ads for cruises and dentures. Like my mother, he was very handsome when he was younger: I've seen the photos. Now, he's like someone from a bygone era; suave, international, at ease in any situation. Today he's in a dark suit but his usual uniform is a blazer, dark trousers, immaculate pressed pink or blue checked shirts with big gold cufflinks. He has a signet ring. His Indian father and English mother have given him a dual citizenship, also like my mother, with which he struggled when he was younger, but has now embraced extremely enthusiastically. It's almost his badge. He speaks with a posh English accent but at home his wife Sameena cooks the best Indian food you'll find in Ealing, a million times better than most of the ropey curry houses on the main drag of Brick Lane.

Jay and I are very similar, but I love how his dad and my mum, the twins, half Indian, went different ways. With me, my Indian heritage is hardly visible beyond my dark hair and olive skin, thanks to a mother who uses it in a lazy cross-cultural way when she wants to show off, and thanks to a father who I assume is white, although who knows? Whereas Jay goes the other way, the reverse of me. He is almost wholly Indian, and slips easily back into that culture, thanks to Sameena, then back into the world of Summercove, as if he's changing from one pair of comfortable shoes to another. I envy him that ability, and I love him for it.

Jay is waving back at his father. "Look at him," he says, as Archie sneaks a look at his reflection in the car window, staring intently at himself for a brief second. "He's looking more and more like Alan Whicker every day. Hey, Dad," he says.

"Aha, Natasha, my dear." Archie hugs me enthusiastically, gripping my shoulders. His moustache tickles my face as always and I have to tell myself not to shrink away. "It's wonderful to see you. Jay. Son." He gives his son a walloping great slap on the back. Jay rocks back against me.

"I'm sorry about Granny," I tell him.

"I am too," Archie says soberly. "I am too." He scratches the bridge of his nose vigorously, suddenly, and turns away. "Let's be off." His hand is on the boot of the car. "Bags?"

"No bags," I say.

Archie looks at me as if I'm insane. "No bags? Where are your things?"

I take a deep breath. "I can't stay tonight, unfortunately," I say.

He stares at me. "Not staying? Does your mother know? That's crazy, Natasha."

"I know," I say, trying to sound calm, collected. "I'm really sorry, but I've got a meeting tomorrow I can't get out of." I wish I could tell them why. But I can't. They mustn't know, not yet.

"I should have thought . . ." Archie mutters, trailing off. Jay, who is watching me intently, jumps in.

"The sleeper's much better and if you have to get back for a meeting, there it is." His father frowns at him, opens his mouth to say something, but Jay presses on. "Come on, Nat," he says, slinging his rucksack into the boot. "We're cutting it fine anyway, aren't we? Let's go."

Suddenly, I remember Octavia and Julius. "I saw Octavia and Julius on the train. I mean, *think* I saw them," I amend. "Should we—"

"Oh," Archie says, ruffled, he hates any interruption to his plans, to being told what to do by anyone except my mother. And indeed, our cousins are emerging from the station and looking around. "I'm sure they'll have made their own arrangements. . . ."

But they haven't, it turns out. Octavia and Julius are the kind of ruthlessly efficient people who expect others to be at their beck and call. They're like the answers to those survival guide questions: both of them could survive on a raft floating on the Indian Ocean with only a mirror and a comb for days, I'm sure. But they'd never think of getting round to booking a car or a taxi. They assume that someone else will have got the train down too and will furnish them with a lift. And they assume rightly, of course.

"I must say, it's extremely strange we didn't bump into either of you on the train," Octavia says, as Archie drives off along the harbor. "I suppose you two were sitting together." She makes it sound as if we were planning a high school shooting.

"No," Jay says simply. "Meeting you all is a lovely surprise on this sad day."

"Jolly sad. So," Julius, already red in the face, looking more than ever like a fatter, less patrician version of Frank, his father, asks, "what's the order of things today? Straight to the church? Or nosh first?"

Squashed next to Octavia in the back of the car, Jay and I dare not exchange looks. It's as though we're children again.

"Hrrr." Archie clears his throat, self-importantly. "The funeral is at two, so we're going straight to the church," he says. "Don't have time to stop off beforehand and we couldn't have it any later, some people—" he raises his eyebrows—"*some* people came down last night and are going back to London this evening." I nod politely.

"We'll meet the others there, then?" Jay says.

"Yes, yes," Archie says briskly, as though he's got it all under control and supplementary questions are ridiculous. "Father's going with Miranda to the church. Then we're all off back to Summercove afterwards, for some food."

"I know Mum's done an *awful* lot of cooking," Octavia says slowly. "She's been flat out all week, poor thing. It's been pretty stressful for her." She sighs. "And clearing out the house, getting *poor* Great-Uncle Arvind settled somewhere new—I mean, we all know he's a brilliant man, but he's not exactly easy, is he!" She laughs.

Don't let Octavia wind you up, I chant to myself. *She signed up for an Oxbridge-graduates-only online dating service and she fancies George Osborne. That is the kind of person she is.*

I would still quite like to smack her though. I hope the feeling doesn't stay with me all day. I wish I could. I wish I could get really drunk at the wake and start a fight, *EastEnders* style. Perhaps I should. Archie and Jay are silent. I make a noncommittal sound.

"Your mum's been wonderful," I force myself to say instead because it's the truth, despite being annoying to admit. Louisa is the one who gets things done, she always has been. She is the one who'd take me into Truro to buy me new socks and shoes for the autumn term at school, muttering all the while about how someone had to do it, mind you, but still. "Oh, Louisa, she is wonderful," is sort of her shoutline. That's what you say about her, in the absence of anything else to say.

We are climbing up and out of Penzance. Below us, the sea is frothing and churning. There are dark, restless clouds on the horizon. We drive in silence for a while, going further inland. Here on the south coast the country is wild, but lush, greener than the rest of the country, even though it's February. We pass Celtic crosses, their intricate decorations long worn away by the wind from the sea, and soon we are driving past the Merry Maidens, the ten girls who were turned to stone for dancing on a Sunday. They're all so familiar. It is so strange to be here when it's not high summer, but it is so wonderful all the same, and then I remember why I'm here. Granny would have loved a day like today, walking through the winding lanes and over the high exposed fields, a silk headscarf covering her hair, her eyes alight with the joy of it all.

In the front, Archie turns to Julius.

"So, Julius, how are the markets?"

"Weulllll—" Julius begins, in his low, blubbery voice. "Patchy, Archie. Patchy. . . ."

I am spared the rest of his answer by Octavia turning to me.

"How's your jewelry stuff going then?" she asks, curiously. As ever I grit my teeth at this question, which makes it sound as though I've been to the Bead Shop and threaded a few plastic hearts onto a string for a friend's birthday, rather than that it's my job.

"Fine, thanks," I say. "I'm just finishing a new collection."

"Wow, how great," Octavia says. "Where will you sell that, on a stall, or . . . ?" She trails off, almost embarrassed.

It has been about two years since I sold my jewelry on a stall, first in Spitalfields Market, then at the Truman Brewery nearby. I got lucky when one of my pieces, a gold chain made of tiny interconnected flowers, was featured in *Vogue* a couple of years ago, and a minor but quite trendy pop star wore it in a magazine, after which a boutique in Notting Hill and one just off Brick Lane started stocking my stuff. That's how it works these days. Someone I'd never heard of wore a necklace of mine and I ended up hiring a PR rep to promote myself and setting up a website. Now I sell online through the website, and through a few retailers. But Octavia, a bit like Louisa, still likes to think that I'm standing behind a stall wearing a hat, gloves, and change belt, shouting out, "Three pound a pair of earrings! Get your necklaces here, roll up, roll up!"

There's an implied snobbery there too which is hilarious. I made as much on the stall as I do now. In fact, often I'd sell more there in a day than I do in a month online. Plus the stall was a great way of meeting customers and other designers, seeing what was selling, talking to people, finding out what they liked. Pedro, who used to have a veg stall in the old Spitalfields Market and upgraded it to an upmarket deli stall in the new, updated, boring Spitalfields, has a house in Alicante, a timeshare in Chamonix, and drives an Audi TT. Sara, the girl whose stall used to be next to mine, bought her mum a house in Londonderry last year and paid for the whole family to go on holiday to Barbados. I thought taking myself off the stall would move me to the next level, and I suppose it did.

But increasingly I've come to wonder whether I was right. Things have been difficult, the last year or so. The recession means people don't want jewelry. And even though Jay designed my site for free, bless him, other costs keep mounting up—hiring the studio, paying for materials and for the metals and stones, the PR rep who I hired, the trade fairs which you pay to attend. . . . It adds up. I haven't heard of the pop star who wore my necklace since, incidentally. Perhaps that explains it.

A few months ago, it didn't seem to matter. We had Oli's salary too. Mine was "pin money," as he called it, which I found superpatronizing. But it's true. It used to be joyful, exciting, stimulating. Lately, it is almost painful. I'm no good. My thoughts are no good, my head seems to be blank. And it shows.

"On the website, through some shops," I tell Octavia. "The usual."

"Oh," she says. "That's good—well done."

I sink lower down into my scarf and look out at the dramatic, wind-flattened black trees, the yellow lichen, the startling green of the sea, crashing against the gray rocks, as the car bowls through the empty, muddy lanes, deeper into the countryside. I chew my lip, thinking.

I wonder if anyone has opened her studio since she died? I wonder, for the thousandth time, how Granny could have stopped painting all those years ago when I know how much the landscape around her meant to her, how it inspired her. But though no one ever says it, it's obvious something died inside her with Cecily, and it never came alive again.

Archie slows down, and all of a sudden we've arrived at the church, perched high on the edge of the moor. I squint, and see the hearse pulled up outside the door. They are unloading the coffin. There, twisting an order of service over in her hands, is Louisa, and next to her, ramrod straight, stands my mother. The pallbearers are sliding the long coffin out—Granny was tall—and it hits me again, that's her inside the wooden box, that's her. Archie turns the engine off. "We're here," he says. "Just in time. Let's go."

Four

Granny always knew what she wanted and so the funeral service is short and sweet. We slip into our seats and the coffin is carried in, my mother, Archie, and Louisa walking behind it. I stare at Mum, but her head is bowed. We sit and listen to the minister in the small chapel with big glass windows, no adornment, no incense, everything plain. Outside, the wind whistles across the moors. There are two hymns, "Guide Me, O Thou Great Redeemer" and "Dear Lord and Father of Mankind." The collection is for the Royal National Lifeboat Institute. Louisa reads from Exodus. Archie reads an extract from *A Room of One's Own,* by Virginia Woolf. At Granny's request there is no eulogy. That's the only thing that is weird. No one gets up and speaks over Granny's body, there in its oak coffin in the aisle of the church, and it feels strange not to talk about her, not to say who she was, how wonderful she was. But that was her instruction and, like all the others, it must be followed to the letter.

As we are all bashfully singing the second hymn, accompanied by a worn-out, clanging old piano, I look past my mother, to see if Arvind is OK. There's no space for his wheelchair in the pews, so he sits in the aisle next to the coffin of his wife. It is rather ghoulish, but Arvind doesn't seem to mind. He is the same as always; shrunken to the size of a child, his nut-brown head almost bald but for a few wispy black hairs. His eyes are sunk far into his head, and his mouth is pursed, like an asterisk.

He stares at me, as if I am a stranger. I smile at him, but there is no reaction. This is Arvind's way, I'm used to it. It was only when I was old enough to know that a "That coat is lovely on you!" means

"That coat is garish and vile" or a "Wow, I love your hair!" means "Good God, who told you you could carry off a fringe?" that I began to realize how lucky I was to have Arvind as my grandfather. He simply cannot dissemble.

Ignoring the hymn, he holds up the flimsy order of service and waves it at me. "Is it recycled?" he says, in his incredibly penetrating, sing-song voice, which still has a strong Punjab accent sixty-odd years since he came to the UK. "Is their carbon footprint reduced? This is *very* important, Natasha."

Separating us is my mother, in her sixties but still ravishing, in a long, black tailored coat with an electric blue lining, her thick, dark hair cascading down her back, her green eyes huge in her heart-shaped face. Now she looks down at Arvind.

"Be *quiet*!" she hisses.

"We must all recycle everything, every little thing," Arvind tells me, leaning forwards so he can catch my eye and speaking completely normally, as if it were just the two of us taking tea together. "China can carry on emitting more CO_2 than the rest of the world put together, but it will be MY FAULT if the world ends, because I did not recycle my copy of *PLAYBOY*." He finishes loudly, his voice rising.

"Dad, shut *up*," Mum grips the top of his arm in rage. "You *have* to be quiet."

"Father," Archie says, rather pompously, behind us. "Please. Be respectful."

"Respectful?" Arvind shrugs his shoulders, and waves his arms around in a grand gesture. "They don't mind."

I turn around, partly to see if he's right and catch my breath as I see for the first time how many people are here. I hadn't really noticed as we hurriedly took our seats, and more have arrived since then. They're standing at the back, three deep in places, crammed into the small space. They are here for Granny. I blink back tears. Who are they? A lot of them are rather advanced in years. I guess some are friends from around here, some are people down from

London, old friends from the golden days. I don't recognize many of them. They are all watching this scene at the front of the chapel with interest.

Around me, my relatives are unamused. Archie is furious. Octavia looks as though a nasty smell is troubling her. Louisa is flustered, staring beseechingly at Arvind; her lovely brother Jeremy and his wife Mary Beth, who have flown in from California for the funeral, are studiously still singing. The Bowler Hat is officiously, soundlessly, opening and shutting his mouth, like a minister for Wales who doesn't know the Welsh national anthem. Arvind catches my eye, winks, and goes back to the hymn. I stare at the sheet, unable to concentrate on the words, not sure whether to laugh or cry.

As the service ends and we process out to the churchyard for the burial, following Granny's coffin, I realize I am leading my mother who has Archie by the arm while Jay pushes Arvind next to us. Louisa, the architect of this, has respectfully dropped behind, and it is just the four of us, my cousin and our parents, who have their arms around each other. I don't know what we should be doing, other than following the minister. I grip Mum's arm, feeling strange, and wishing someone else was here with us. I especially wish Sameena were here, but she's in Mumbai visiting her sister who is not well, and she's not flying back till next week.

Well, really, it's Oli. I wish Oli were here, holding my hand. But of course he's not, because I asked him not to come.

The graveyard looms, our small family totters towards it, disjointed and odd, and behind us comes Louisa, the de facto leader of her branch of the family, clutching her brother Jeremy's hand.

"Earth to earth, ashes to ashes, dust to dust."

My mother sobs, loudly, a great shuddering cry. Archie hugs her closer. Jay is watching the hole in the ground, intently, as if it is moving. Arvind is gazing into space, he doesn't look as if he's here at all.

They lower Granny's coffin into the ground, and I look around

again to see the congregation now assembled behind us, scattered
in and around the lichen-covered gravestones on the edge of the
moor. Suddenly I think of Cecily. Where's her grave? I look around.
Wouldn't she have been buried here too?

Granny was from here. But we, my mother and uncle, my grandfather and my cousin, we are from many other places as well. With
a sudden flash of pain in my heart I long to be back in London,
walking through the cobbled streets round Spitalfields and Bethnal
Green, feeling the centuries of history in the city under my feet.

But now I'm away from it, now I see the emptiness of my life
there, in a way I haven't before. It is empty. A job I can't do, a marriage I might lose, a life I don't recognize. They are throwing more
earth into the grave now, it patters softly on the wood, like rain. I
feel my throat closing up.

When the crowd starts to disperse, gathering outside the church,
getting into cars that are clogging up the tiny lane, we are all left
around the grave. No one speaks. I look at their faces: Mum's is a
mask, smiling and staring into space; Archie has sucked his lips in
and is bouncing on his feet. Louisa sniffs, and puts her hand gently
to her mouth. Behind her, the handsome Bowler Hat has bowed his
head, his face serious. Next to him, Louisa's brother Jeremy looks
out of place. He is sleeker than them all, tanned, his hair is good,
his clothes are pressed, his teeth are white. He is standing a little
apart from his sister and cousins, holding Mary Beth's hand. I look
at them all, and then down at my grandfather. Arvind is staring into
the grave, and his thin fingers are gripping the plastic arms of his
wheelchair.

Something strikes me then: it's funny, but they look totally unconnected. There's no likeness between them all, no sense that we
are one big family gathered together for a funeral. My friend Cathy
and her mother and sister are like peas in a pod. Whereas Mum, Jeremy, Louisa, the Bowler Hat—they might have just met, you'd never
know they spent every summer down here, four and five weeks to-

gether at a time. I've seen photos—not many, I suppose because of Cecily they don't keep many here at Summercove. But Mum has a couple in her room at the flat, her and Archie, posing on the terrace, Archie like a young film star, raising his eyebrows, my mother Miranda pouting beautifully, Louisa and Jeremy smiling, their arms crossed. And there's one of Archie and the Bowler Hat, and Guy, gurning down on the beach. I suppose that was the summer the Bowler Hat and Guy came here for the first time. In Granny's room, she had a picture of Louisa and Mum, demure in halter-neck swimming costumes, lying on the lawn together when they were about twelve or so.

You'd never know it to look at them together now. They seem like strangers to each other.

Arvind clears his throat and the spell, whatever it was, is broken. The sun has gone in and it is very cold. I sway on my feet, a combination of grief, hunger, fatigue. Suddenly, an arm is wrapped round my shoulders, and Jay whispers in my ear, "Come on, let's go back to the house. You need a drink."

We walk in tiny steps towards the car, behind other mourners who are chatting and gossiping as they stand around waiting for us to drive off. Our progress is slow. Oli likes to collect sayings, things that you say and then realize afterwards are a cliché. "Is it just me, or are policemen getting younger and younger?" is one of his favorites—I said that to him without thinking last year. Now I want to say, "We are moving at a funereal pace." I look at Jay, but I know he won't get it.

"Everyone," Louisa is saying loudly, her voice floating across the ranks of mourners in the watery sunshine, "Frances's family would like to invite you all back to Summercove for some refreshments. Please, do follow us. Thank you."

With her pink and white complexion, her halo of graying-blonde hair and striped, padded jerkin over sensible countrywoman's attire, she looks like an organized angel. One of the admin assistants helping St. Peter at the Pearly Gates. People nod respectfully—you always do what Louisa says. They smile at her. My mother walks on ahead, and I notice the glances she gets in contrast. The curious stares, the sighs. Louisa follows Miranda, her beautiful, wicked cousin, and we make our way to the cars. We are going to Summercove.

Five

Without the setting, Summercove would still be a beautiful house. With it, it's—well, it's jaw-dropping. To me, at least. Maybe it's not to everyone's taste. I don't care. To me, it's the place I'd rather be, more than anywhere else. Always.

Off a small lane, covered in foliage in summer so green and dense it's almost dark, you turn down a driveway and suddenly the house is there, at the edge of a lawn that slopes gently towards the cliffs. There is a proper garden at the back, manicured grass, rows of lavender, rose bushes climbing up the side of the house, a table and chairs for tea or for lounging in. There are even palm trees—they grow everywhere in Cornwall. But at the front of the house is a terrace with simple stone steps leading to the lawn. At the other end is a beautiful tiny gazebo, like a glass carousel, where you can sit and look out to sea. Next to the house by the lane is a gate, which opens onto a tiny path with high hedgerows that in summer are smothered in orange kaffir lilies, ivy, brambles, full of noisily chirping crickets. The path gives way to grassy moors and stony rocks, from where the rest of the coast suddenly opens up in front of you, the foaming cerulean sea, the blue, blue sky, the wild flowers dotted all around, and if you're lucky and it's a clear day, you can see across to the Minack Theatre one way, and almost to the Lizard the other. You have to be careful as you clamber down, holding on to a rope chain, as the path has been cut through the rocks and is frequently slimy and damp. You must move slowly, surely, taking care not to slip. You climb down, down, down, and you're on the beach, where the sand is custard yellow and there are flat, black rocks to lie on. And there's no one else around. Just us, our own private beach, leading down from the house.

Summercove was built in the 1920s, for a millionaire's son who wanted to be an artist (along with roughly twenty per cent of the people who come to Cornwall). It wouldn't look out of place in Miami—a low square art deco house with round edges, studded with big, rectangular suntrap windows and gracefully settled in the incline of the land before it dramatically drops away to the cliffs. The sitting room has French doors which lead out onto the terrace, the bedrooms upstairs have wide window seats.

It is not a mansion, but it is big, and airy, and light, and always warm, built in concrete and brick to withstand the rough sea winds. My room, which I shared with Octavia for the week or so that our holidays coincided but usually was lucky enough to have to myself for most of the summer, was small and would have been pokey had it not looked out to sea. It was my mother's room when she was younger. The curtains were 1950s, Heal's, pale gray, tiny patterns dotted over in blue, green, yellow, red. The furniture is darling, two small beds with dark wooden frames, pale pink silk goose eiderdowns, a bookcase also in dark wood stuffed with my mother's books from when she was little: *My Friend Flicka, Swallows and Amazons,* the Narnia books, Jane Austen, and—my favorite of all—a tiny, low armchair on brass wheels, covered with a sturdy navy hessian studded with pink polka dots. It is worn in parts but still intact, and I used to sit either there or in the window seat for hours.

I was a dreamy, withdrawn child, extremely awkward, a sad contrast to my glamorous, confident mother. I don't have time for people who claim special privileges because they suffer from crippling shyness. We all do, I believe, we just learn to carry it off in different ways. My mother is, I think, also shy and awkward, but she gets past it by assuming a persona, that of the mercurial beauty. But I remember in particular that when I was twelve or so, and life seemed overwhelming—at my new scary secondary school, with my mother, with my growing awareness of my place in the world—my room at Summercove was an absolute refuge to me.

The Hammersmith flat was boiling in summer, freezing in winter, with paper-thin walls that meant everyone knew your business. Here, by the sea, it was private. Even for the brief time that Octavia and I were both there together, she'd spend most days outside, down on the beach and in the garden. Whereas I could sit in my room and sketch for a whole afternoon, or stare out at the horizon, or write terrible poems about how no one understood me, all the while flicking my hair from one side to the other, eyes filling with tears and sighing about the awfulness of my life. I was probably ghastly, I'm afraid to say.

Poor Octavia. I'm so sure I'm right and *she's* the ghastly one, it has never really occurred to me that it's most likely the other way round. I don't remember *her* ever having a tantrum or gazing moodily out of the window for hours on end.

Now, in late February, the branches are almost bare and so the lane leading to the house is lighter, though the road is muddy and full of mulch. The huge wheels of the car crunch as we turn into the drive and I crane my neck to catch a first glimpse of the house once more. A curving, white shape slips into view before us, and I see the green of the field and the blue of the sea beyond. I steel myself for what's coming.

"So, Natasha, what time is your train tonight?" Archie says loudly. He turns off the engine. "Have you heard this?" he says, looking at my mother.

Oh, God.

"Tonight?" my mother squeaks, climbing out of the car, one long leg at a time. She peers into the back where we are sitting with Arvind. "You're not going back tonight."

"I am, I'm afraid," I say, sounding ridiculously formal. "I'm sorry. I have to—I have a meeting tomorrow."

"Natasha! You can't!" Mum's mouth is pursed like a child's.

"We are here," Arvind says suddenly. "We are at home again."

"Yes, Dad," Mum pats his arm briskly, as if pushing him away. She is still pouting. "Natasha?"

"I know it's ridiculous," I say. "I'm so sorry. But I really can't miss it. The meeting." I know I sound as though I'm lying, and I can't help it.

"What, it's so important you have to leave your grandmother's funeral early?" she demands, her voice stringent and high. "You can't stay with us for just one night? Natasha, *honestly.*"

She's right, and I don't know what to say. I look away from her and up at the house, tears stinging my eyes. I should have canceled, I know. But if I cancel, that's my last chance gone, really.

If Oli were here . . . things would be different. Everything would be different if Oli were here, but he's not, because I asked him to stay away from Granny's funeral, screamed at him to, in fact, laughed at him for daring to make the request in the first place. If Oli were here I wouldn't hate myself, for wondering about money, for wondering what's gone wrong and where, for how I'm going to get myself out of it. The truth is, I'm not wondering about money so much as worrying about it, frantically, obsessively. If Oli were here with me I wouldn't need to. At our wedding, in a sunny garden by the Thames, the registrar asked us, "For richer, for poorer? In sickness and in health? Forsaking all others, till death do us part?" "Yes," we said. Yes to all of that, yes yes yes and I remember looking over his shoulder, at my mother, my grandmother, in shade under the canopy, watching with pride, and thinking, I've done it, we've done it. We're our own family now.

And now that Granny is buried, in the ground, the earth piling up over her as we stand here and talk, everything looks different. It is strange how often I've caught myself wondering if she'd like something I'm doing, these last two weeks. Makes me realize how much I wanted her to like it to begin with.

"It's for work. It's—" I can't tell her. "It's really important."

"More important than *this?*" Mum waves her arms around the car. I don't take her bait, though she's right to be confused, upset. My voice sounds childish as I say, "No, of course not, but I'm here, aren't I? I just have to go back early."

"It's bad enough Oli not being here as well," my mother says. "Now you're racing off as soon as you possibly can, and—" She drops her hands by her sides, as if to say, "This daughter of mine, what can I do with her?"

There is a pain in my heart. I wish I could tell her. I wish she was the kind of mother I could tell.

"Help me, Archie," Arvind tells his son, and this creates a diversion, as Uncle Archie gently helps him down from the car. They walk behind us, slowly, Jay following in silence, and we walk towards the open front door. The wind creaks around us, but there is no rustling sound from the bare trees.

Mum is still staring at me. She says slowly, "You know, Natasha, I'm really very upset with you."

I nod, unable to speak suddenly as we walk across the threshold. The lovely fifties Ercol sideboard has flowers on it, white lilies that are just starting to die; the smell is cloying. Granny must have bought them. Her presence is still here, the last tasks she performed still evident.

There are clanging sounds as we turn left into the kitchen; Louisa is already in residence, assisted by Mary Beth and Octavia, who are taking out trays, fetching glasses, spooning out hummus from plastic tubs into my grandmother's favorite porridge bowls. Again, it looks all wrong, this activity. Normally it would be Granny, pottering slowly but surely about her kitchen, calmly putting things together, in her domain. This whirlwind of activity is for her, for her funeral. I close my eyes.

"And there's another thing." Mum is still talking furiously. I am the one who has ignited the smoldering grief and anger she has been suppressing all day. "While we're on this subject, Natasha. How come your own husband can't even be bothered to come to Mummy's funeral, doesn't even write or ring to apologize? Doesn't he care at all?" She turns and faces me, her cheeks flushing dark cherry, her green eyes huge in her lovely face. I stare, she is so like Granny, so beautiful, always has been. *"At all?"* she repeats.

Louisa looks up. "Miranda," she says briskly. "Ah, you're here at last," as if Mum had stopped off for a facial and a manicure on the way. "Can you please unpack the nibbles in those cartons there?"

Mum simply ignores her; if this were a different situation I would love how much my mother and her cousin loathe each other, really so much that sometimes it's a wonder they don't simply take their shoes off and wrestle on the floor. Mum turns to me again. "Really, darling. I mean, he's your husband."

There is a rushing sound in my head again. I look up to the ceiling.

"He's not anymore," I hear myself say.

"What?" she says. "What?"

The rushing is louder and louder. "I've left him. Or rather he's left me. That's why he's not here."

They all turn to me. I feel myself going red, like a child caught doing something they shouldn't. It's weird. They look at me, Mum's jaw drops open and the silence stretches out till it is overwhelming, until Mary Beth helpfully drops a glass on the floor. It shatters, which at least gives us all something to do.

Mum flattens herself against the wall, away from the path of glass which has splintered closest to her, and pushes shards towards the center of the room with one velvet toecap. "Oh, my gosh," says poor Mary Beth, her hand flying to her mouth. "Darn it." She crouches on the ground and Louisa flies in with a dustpan and brush screeching, "Don't touch the glass! Careful!"

There's a brief moment's silence. I watch them, watch the splinters and the stem of the glass, rolling slowly around the linoleum on its side.

"Nat?" Jay is still behind me, I hadn't seen him. "You've left Oli? What? Why?"

"I don't want to talk about it," I say, and then helpfully, the floor feels liquid beneath my feet and is rising up to meet me. I step back, away from the glass, and shapes and colors swim before my eyes and it is almost a relief when gradually, everything goes black, and I sink to the ground in a dead faint.

Six

When I awake, I'm not sure where I am, or what's going on. It's dark. I sit up and look around me, blinking in confusion, and slowly, it all comes back to me.

The first thing I notice is that I'm in my old bedroom. The curtains are half drawn. They took me up here, Jay and the Bowler Hat lugging me up the wide staircase, and I fell into bed and fell fast asleep—a sort of narcolepsy, I could barely keep my eyes open.

I look at my watch; it is a quarter to five but I don't know how long I've been up here. I stretch and yawn, running my hands through my hair. I have a throbbing feeling, as if I don't have a headache but am about to get one. I run my fingers slowly, experimentally, over my skin. There is a plaster on my forehead, and underneath a swollen lump forming, hot to the touch. Perfect. A massive bruise should be there by tomorrow. Just in time.

Oh dear, I think again. I fainted like a lunatic. My elbow is very sore, from where I must have hit it on the way down. As is my thigh. I feel dreadful, as though I'm hungover and I've been beaten up, but more than that I am embarrassed, mortified, even.

I didn't want to tell my mother my marriage was over, not like that. She didn't deserve that—none of them did. At Granny's funeral too—I wince; it's awful.

There's a soft tap at the oak door. "Come in," I say.

The door opens slowly, and Jay's handsome face appears around it. "How are you?" he says.

"You want the truth? Pretty rotten," I tell him. I crane my head,

to see him better. "And sorry. I'm sorry, I didn't mean you to find
out like that."

"What the hell, Nat? What's going on with you?" he says, advanc-
ing into the room. He sits down heavily on the bed next to mine
and switches on the bedside lamp, his body casting a huge shadow
on the opposite wall. "You've left Oli? But you guys were—he was
your life!"

He is looking at me as if I've just killed his pet rabbit.

"Yeah?" I say. "Right."

"Yeah!" Jay says, almost angrily. "What's up with you?"

"It's not me," I say. I laugh. "Well, perhaps it is. He—he slept
with someone else."

It sounds so weird when you speak those words. They're such a
cliché but you never expect to be saying them out loud, and in rela-
tion to your own life.

"He what?" Jay looks blank, as though he doesn't understand the
words.

I swing my legs off the side of the bed. "She's a client. It was
after a conference." I am looking for my shoes. I can say it out
loud if I just disassociate myself from it, completely pretend it's not
happening.

"But . . ." Jay is frowning. "But it's you two. You're like my perfect couple. You can't split up."

"We're not a perfect couple." I want to cry. He looks bewildered.
I say gently, as though it's him I'm breaking up with, "Things . . .
things have changed. I don't know him anymore."

"But—you've known him forever, Nat. He hasn't changed."

I met Oli at college. He was the first person—the only person—
to tell me my green eyes in my sallow skin were beautiful. We were
already friends by then. It was in the student union bar; we were
both in Dramsoc, celebrating the end of our successful run of *HMS
Pinafore* with a themed nautical party Oli had organized. I think I
fell in love with him a little bit then, though we didn't get together
for years after that. Six years, in fact. I hugged him, when he said it.
He looked so pleased, he was easily pleased back then.

I have to remind myself of this now, but Oli wasn't a cool kid when I met him. Over the years, he transformed himself from an earnest young man from a small Yorkshire village with a spluttering manner of speech and a terrible habit of blushing. Now his enthusiasm is much more high-octane. He likes doing the deals, meeting the clients, pressing the flesh; he wants people to like him, I guess. He always did. I used to find that intensely endearing. Until the way he got them to like him turned into shagging them. *That* I don't find endearing.

"But that's just it," I say. "I don't think I do know him anymore. Even before he told me about . . . about it. Things haven't been right. With either of us."

Jay stares at me. He looks as if he's about to say something, and then stops. We're both silent, listening to the rumble of conversation from downstairs.

It seems such a long way away from here, that London life we have, full of expensive meals and hospitality suites, the cool flat with its seventies film posters on the walls and the bright red Gaggia espresso machine. From our disintegrating marriage and secrets that we—both of us—have been keeping from each other. Small secrets, biting the lip here and there, not talking, not telling the truth, the kind of secrets that grow and grow until they fester within you, and you can't go back and make them right. We started lying to each other too long ago for that. I see that now I'm here, far away from it all.

I draw my legs up and hug my knees. "Open the curtains," I say.

"It's getting dark, you know."

"I know."

The light is fading and the moon is just appearing, full and yellow. The sky is gun-metal gray, the sea an oily lavender-black. It feels too soon for it to be dark; we've only just got here. Suddenly I wish with all my heart I could stay, that I didn't have to go back to any of it, to tomorrow. We are silent for a moment, Jay sitting next to me, and above the voices downstairs I can hear the faint roar of the sea outside, like a shell against my ear.

"We should go down," I say.

"Sure, in a minute." Jay wrinkles his nose, and takes his watch off his wrist, holding it in his hand, an old habit of his. "What you going to do, then? Are you going to kick him out?"

"He's gone already, that was the night he told me." Two weeks ago.

"Seriously? And you didn't tell anyone?"

"He wants to come back, he didn't want to leave. He keeps saying how sorry he is, what a mistake it is." I drum my fingers on my forehead, and wince as they touch my bruised flesh. "I didn't . . . know what to do."

"You could have talked to someone about it. So—*no one* knows?" He looks incredulous. I take a breath.

"Cathy knows. And—well, Ben."

"Ben?" Jay makes a loud clicking sound with his tongue. "You told Ben but you didn't tell me? Or your mum?"

Ben has the studio next to me. He's a photographer, an old friend of Jay's from college, that's how I heard about the studio in the first place. We have tea most days. Ben wears woolly jumpers and loves Jaffa Cakes, like me; he's a very comforting person to be working next to all day, like a shaggy dog, or a nice old lady who runs a sweet shop. I cried all over him the day after Oli left.

"You should have told us about this, not *Ben*," Jay says. "Should have kept it in the family."

Jay does have a tendency to talk like a Corleone. "Oh, Jay, honestly." He is frowning. "I couldn't! And then Granny died, like, a week later. I'm hardly going to email everyone and go, 'See you at the funeral, and by the way? I'm separated from my husband, fill you in then!' "

Jay shakes his head. "You're mental." He gets up and stares out of the window, then turns to me. "Nat, it's me. OK? It's me. Of course you should have told me. I—I'm here for you, you know that?"

"Yes," I say. "I know you are. I just couldn't." My eyes are filling with tears. Jay squeezes his watch in his hands; I hear the links of the metal strap clinking together.

"Sometimes . . . I just feel like I don't know you anymore," he says, after a pause. "You're a different person these days, Nat. Quiet, subdued. You're not yourself."

I don't look at him. I don't want to talk about it, to acknowledge that he might be right, how wrong everything is. "I spend a lot of time on my own," I say, blankly. "In the studio, at home."

He shakes his head. "That's not it. I feel like you . . . you're sad, and I don't know why." He puts his finger under my chin. "Nat. What's the meeting tomorrow about?"

I'm silent. He looks at me, and the kindness and concern in his eyes are like pains in my heart. It's just easier if he doesn't care. If he leaves me alone.

"It's with the bank." I stare back at him, hugging myself. "It's not good."

"How come?"

My voice is croaky. "I've defaulted on my loans. They want to take me t-to court." Jay opens his mouth, shocked. "I'm probably going to lose the business. It's not working. Well—it's me. *I'm* not working." I swallow.

"Yes—yes, you are!" Jay says, in outrage. "You're brilliant, Nat!"

"I'm honestly not," I say. "Not anymore. Don't think I ever was. I haven't drawn anything for months."

"But you're always—you've always had your pencil going, sketching something—" he waves his hand round, indicating, *here, here*— "coming up with some design for a tiara when you were a kid, some earrings, a ring—you love that stuff! You're brilliant!" He says it again, and it just sounds hollow.

I touch his hand. "I can't do it anymore. I don't know why." I look down, I can't bear to meet his gaze. "I've got no new ideas. And the stuff that's out there already—no one's buying it. The business, me, it's all—" I take a deep breath, to steady myself—"it's screwed. Not that the website doesn't look beautiful, Jay." I want to reassure him of that. "It's just we're in a recession. People aren't treating themselves to a nice bracelet from some jewelry designer they've never heard of."

Jay looks bewildered. "But you're going places, you've had your stuff in magazines, that celebrity girl wore your necklace thing? I don't understand."

"That was ages ago. And I got too big for my boots," I say. I am trying to sound chipper, but I am very scared. This is my job. I don't know how to do anything else, and it terrifies me that I've let myself come so low. "Oli's been keeping both of us, the last couple of years," I say, and my eyes fill with tears again. "It was fine, at the start. We knew it'd take a while. I've had to buy gold, and materials, and pay for the business cards and the stationery and everything— and the rent on the studio. Plus the accountants and all that, to do with the company accounts. But . . . I'm about fifteen grand in debt." I breathe in. . . . I hate saying it out loud. I hate it all.

It's the look on Jay's face I can't stand, this is why I don't want to tell people, to see the disappointment, the surprise in their eyes. He shakes his head, as though he doesn't understand it, as though I'm an idiot, which I have been.

"I didn't know things had got that bad," he says eventually. "What will you do?"

"I have no idea," I say. "But I have to do something. I've known it for a while, and then Oli—Oli told me about the girl, and then Granny died, and it's all I can think about, how disappointed she'd be, how I've let her down. . . ." My throat is closing up; I don't want to cry. "I never used to think I'd find someone, or be able to do something I'd like. I thought I'd end up like Mum, you know? In a horrible flat, lying about everything and pretending she's in a film, not reality. I thought I'd got away from it . . . me and Oli, the two of us, my job, you know. . . ." I ball my hand into a fist and push it into my stomach. "Oh, God."

"Granny dying was always going to do this, unleash a lot of crap," Jay says. He puts his arm around me. "Oh, Nat. Man, I'm sorry." He squeezes me tight. "Hey, why don't you come and stay with me? I've got that little study, I hardly use it."

I smile. "That's really kind. No. . . . I hope—I don't know what's going to happen."

"You mean you hope he'll come back?"

"I think he wants to come back," I say. "He keeps texting, asking to talk about it some more, wanting to meet up. I just don't know if that's right or not. I don't know anything anymore." I look up at him. "What's going to happen, Jay?"

"It's going to be OK." Jay pats me on the back. "Come on," he says. "It's getting late. You need to show your face back downstairs, especially if you're running away in an hour or so."

"Yep," I say. "I'm sorry. I shouldn't have put all this on you now."

"I'm glad you did, Nat," he says. "You should have earlier. I've been worried about you. Look, you're talented, OK? This meeting tomorrow, it's going to go fine. And then you can talk to Oli, work things out . . . it's going to be all good again. Promise."

I nod. "If you say so."

"Trust me. Family." I give a mirthless laugh, pull on my boots, and we head towards the light, out of the dark, echoing corridor downstairs to Granny's wake. Arvind's chairlift is at the top of the stairs; he must be up here, having a nap. I hear a noise next to us and look round, half-expecting to see Granny in the shadows, standing behind the banister, coolly enquiring where we're off to, what we think we're doing? But she's not there. No one's there.

Seven

The gathering in the sitting room has a desultory, unreal air. There aren't as many people as there were at the funeral. I suppose most have gone by now. The large room looks odd; people don't usually stand around in knots, talking softly, politely. I scan the room, checking off the members of my family. When was the last time we were all together, in the same room? I honestly cannot remember. Her seventy-fifth birthday? It's been years, and even then infrequently. This—this formal, tepid tea party—it's not Granny. It's not anything.

This feeling of absence, of something being strangely wrong, is also because Granny's not here. Normally, you're waiting for her to come into the room. It wasn't that she was an especially gregarious person—she wasn't. More that you felt she and the house were linked, in a fundamental way. Without her, knowing she won't come in, ever again, is sad and unsettling, too. I look around, touching my hand to my throbbing forehead.

In the old days, back when Summercove was a mecca for the young and bohemian, it wasn't like this either. I look around, wondering, "Are they here, any of those people, today?" They'd be old, too, if they were. There are several people I don't recognize along with my family, all the varying parts of it. Mum's cousin Jeremy and his wife Mary Beth stand in the furthest corner, as if they've backed away from everyone else as far as they can and ended up there. They look tired, weary of this long, strange day. By the French windows, my mother and her brother also stand, talking intently to each other, as ever. They don't look at each other, they never do when they talk.

My mother is staring into space as Archie hisses closely into her ear, and her gaze sharpens, focusing on me. She looks me up and down, nodding as Archie talks, and holds up a hand to me, questioning. *What's going on with you?*

Octavia and Julius are talking to an older man in glasses who seems vaguely familiar. Over by the buffet, their mother is collecting up empty bowls and used plates loudly, so that the china clanks together. My mother and uncle turn to her, Mum with an imperious expression on her face, but all that's visible is Louisa's sturdy, wide bottom, clad in its crepey black bias-cut skirt. The Bowler Hat stands by the fireplace clutching a glass of wine, his still-handsome face a mask of polite boredom. Though he's watching his wife he seems impervious to her, clearing away next to him, tucking her graying blonde bob, which keeps falling in her eyes, behind her ears. Again, I remember and it occurs to me that Louisa was lovely when she was younger in the photos I've seen. Now, she's . . . I don't know. I suppose your life doesn't turn out the way you'd expected, that's all, and I should know.

A couple comes up to say goodbye to Louisa. She raises her head from wiping the table and smiles briefly at them. They are old, around Granny's age, and they smile back, kindly, at her. As they are leaving, the wife nudges her husband, and whispers something, pointing at my mother and Archie. I see the queer, sharp look she gives my mother, this old woman whom I've never seen before. I hear her voice, hissing.

"That's the daughter," she says. "The *other* daughter, dear. You remember?"

"Oh . . ." says the old man curiously. He stares at my mother who I know can hear them but is pretending not to. "Yes. The one they—"

"Shh," his wife admonishes. "Come on, Alfred. We're *late*," and she practically pushes him out of the room. I watch them go, and rub my eyes.

"Natasha, dear," another old lady says, handing me a glass of champagne. "It's so wonderful to see you. Now, let me tell you a story about one of your necklaces. I bought it in London. A lovely silver flower on a chain, dear, do you remember that one?"

"Yes," I say, nodding politely, trying not to look over her shoulder at Mum.

"The clasp didn't work properly. And I took it back to the shop—because, dear, I did want to support you, and I was so glad to have bought it—and do you know what they said?"

"Oh, Jeremy," I hear Louisa say behind me to her brother. "Do you have to go already? Oh, dear."

"Well, let me know if they don't give you a refund," I say as the old lady pauses for breath, as if I've listened to and understood every word she's saying. "Excuse me, will you?" I make my way over to the table, and grab some crisps. Jeremy is hugging his sister, Mary Beth is kissing the Bowler Hat.

"Ah," Jeremy says, as he turns and sees me. "Natasha. I'm so sorry I haven't had a chance to talk with you today." He squeezes my shoulder and nods, his kind face creasing into a smile. "But you look well." His eyes rest on the plaster on my forehead and he hesitates a little. "And—er, I hear all's good with you, you and Oli, and the business, that's really great."

"Um—thanks." I don't know what to say. Louisa gawps a little, and the Bowler Hat just smiles urbanely at us all—I want to hit him.

"Jeremy," Mary Beth says, at his side. "They just split up." She kisses me on the cheek. "I'm so sorry, dear. We're worried about you. Are you feeling OK? How's the head?"

"Um—" I begin again, willing myself not to cry, it would be too awful. Mary Beth is pretty, with fluffy brown, bobbed hair with bangs, as they say in the States, and she is dipping her slender hands into her pockets. She stands next to her husband, slightly tense. I can't read the body language.

"Oh, my goodness, I'm sorry," Jeremy says, looking taken aback. "I had no idea—well, gosh, I'm not back very often, I suppose, I hadn't heard."

"It just happened, don't worry," I say to him. His forehead crinkles up, like concertinaed folds of paper. "Are you—are you really off? I haven't seen you at all."

He nods. "I'm awfully sorry. We have a crazy early flight from Heathrow and we're staying in a motel close by tonight." I'd forgotten, because I haven't seen him for a while, how he has a curious turn of phrase, a combination of British time-warp gent and regular American guy. But he says things people here don't say anymore, like Austin Powers. "Need to get there and get some sleep, I guess," he says. He looks around the sitting room, his eyes scanning the paintings, the people, the old familiar things. "Lovely to be back here again, even if the reason's a sad one." Mary Beth pats his arm.

"How long's it been since you were here?" I say. "Erin and Ryder were still at school, weren't they?"

Jeremy glances round. "Oh, about five years," he says. "Just been busy, you know? And now my mum and dad are both gone, have been for ten years now, there's been less reason to visit Franty and Arvind. It's just Mary Beth's family's in Indiana. We spend time with them in the summer. It's so far to come, when we don't have much vacation."

"Of course," I say.

He looks relieved that I understand. "Well, yes. That's the way it's been. Very sadly."

I can't help it, I give a ragged sigh. "There's nowhere quite like Summercove, is there? It's paradise down here, especially in summer. Oh, I'm going to miss it so much. I expect you will too, now it's going."

Jeremy looks quickly from left to right. "No," he says. I'm not sure what he's saying no to. There's a silence and then he says, "Actually, I don't really think about the old days, if truth be told. It was all a long time ago." And then he takes Mary Beth's hand, clutches it hurriedly, wincing as if he's getting a headache. "So, we're going. . . ." He kisses his sister again. "Bye, love," he says, and he hugs Louisa, hard. "Thank you . . . thank you for everything, Lou. You're wonderful."

He nods briefly again at me. "Lovely to see you, Natasha." Mary Beth raises her hand, and they are gone.

Louisa stares after them. "Oh, dear," she says, and her eyes are full of tears.

I go to her, put my arm round her. "You'll see him soon," I say stupidly.

"I won't," she says, her smile sad. "He never comes back anymore. Especially now Mummy and Dad are dead, you know."

I nod. Their mother, Pamela, was Granny's sister, a rather starchy old lady. She died about seven years ago, her husband before that. They'd come to Summercove, not as much as Louisa, but they were there.

Louisa's face creases. "He only came back this time for me. Darling Jeremy." A tear rolls down her cheek. "Oh—oh, this is awful," she says.

My arm is still around her. It feels weird. Louisa is the mumsy, organized one. Seeing her cry for the first time is wrong. Like everything else today.

"Oh, Louisa, I'm sorry," I say. Her head is bowed and she is properly crying now, tears flowing easily down her crumpled face. She looks up at me then, and almost flinches. And then she blinks.

"No, I'm sorry, Natasha dear," she says, moving away, so that my hand falls to my side again. She presses the Bowler Hat's arm. He kisses her on the head, briefly, tenderly and pulls her against him, and she looks up at him, gratefully happy. I watch them with interest—I see the Bowler Hat so rarely, and any interaction between long-standing couples is fascinating to me at the moment. I turn away, to pick up some more crisps from behind me.

"She looks so like her, doesn't she?" Louisa says, her voice still a bit wobbly. "I'd forgotten."

"Cecily," says the Bowler Hat, slowly, not troubling to keep his voice low. "Yes, she does. You're right."

No one ever mentions Cecily. It's like a bullet fired into the conversation.

Perhaps I would have pretended not to hear Louisa, but the

Bowler Hat's voice is loud. "I look like Cecily?" I say, turning back with a bottle in my hand.

Louisa is facing her husband, plucking at a piece of fluff on his jacket. He meets her gaze, briefly, and then looks back into his drink again. I can't decide if he's uncomfortable, or simply tired. They ignore me, it's as if they're in a world of their own. "She gave you your name," Louisa says. "Don't you remember?"

He nods, his chin sunk onto his chest, I can't see his face. "Yes. She did, didn't she?"

I close the gap between us, by reaching forwards and filling the Bowler Hat's glass, and they both look up at me. "I didn't know that," I say. I've never really thought about it, strange to say. That's just how he's always been referred to. "Really, that's how you got the name?"

He nods and switches his wine glass to his other hand. There are smeary finger marks on the glass. He pulls at his collar.

"Yes," he says, and he smiles. "You know my brother Guy?" I nod. "He and I came here for the summer, that was the first time I met the rest of the family. 1962?" He turns to his wife, and for a second he is younger, his craggy strong face unlined, his colorless hair blond again, a still-handsome, strapping young man.

" '63," she says quickly. " '63."

"Of course. Profumo—the trial had just started when we arrived." He smiles. "Yes! We got the train from London. Read about it on the way down. And after we'd arrived, Cecily took one look at me and said I looked like I should be wearing a bowler hat, not shorts. She could be very funny." He shakes his head. "Tragic. So sad." He is silent, Louisa is looking down at the floor.

I never hear them talk about when they were younger, probably because of Cecily. Never heard anything about the summers down here when they were children. It's hard, now, to believe they hung out together for weeks on end, had picnics, swam together, lay in the sun. Sure, there's the odd photo, and the odd reference—"That was the year Archie broke his arm, wasn't it?" But that's it. Louisa comes—came—for a week to Summercove every year with the children, that's how I know them better, but the Bowler Hat never really came, he'd stay up in London, working. Mum and I would sometimes be down here for Christmas, but not often. Mostly it was at home, or with Archie and Sameena in Ealing. We didn't make jolly family visits to Tunbridge Wells, and I don't recall Mum ever entertaining Louisa and the Bowler Hat to dinner in our tiny, damp Hammersmith abode. They don't socialize, when I think about it. They're so different now and there's no intimacy between them all. And apart from that photo of Cecily that Granny had and I saw only once I know nothing else about her. Cecily simply doesn't come up. What happened doesn't come up.

So the three of us stare at each other, unsure how to proceed: we've gone down a conversational dead end.

"Natasha's right, though," the Bowler Hat suddenly says, unbending. "It was like paradise, Summercove. So laid-back and free. That day we arrived, Guy and I, and you were lying out on the lawn in those great tight-fitting, black trousers, remember?" He smiles, wolfishly. "Yes, we were young then."

"Frank," Louisa says, through gritted teeth. "That wasn't me. My shorts ripped, remember? That was bloody Miranda."

"Your memory, dear," Bowler Hat says. "Incredible. Hah." He looks around him airily. *I will not be embarrassed by this mistake, don't try me.*

"Is Guy here? I haven't seen him yet," I say hastily. "Though it's been so long, I don't know if I'd recognize him."

"Oh, you would," says Louisa. "He was at Julius's wedding. Guy!" she calls. "Guy!"

Last year, Julius married a Russian girl, a trader he'd met through work. He was thirty-seven, she was twenty-three. It was a smart hotel in central London, in a huge room with gold paneling on the walls, and red-faced, huge-handed Julius and a stick-thin beautiful young woman in acres of tulle posing for endless photos. They had a huge row—at the reception—and she stormed off. Jay says he heard she ended up at the Rock Garden in Covent Garden with one of her bridesmaids, snogging a Russian guy. I don't believe him, though I'd love it to be true.

All I really remember about that night is that Oli and my mother got really drunk; they're a bad combination, those two. Oli managed to offend one of Julius's ghastly City friends: unintentionally, he can be a bit full-on when he's had too much to drink. I had to take him home. Julius's wife isn't here today. Neither's my husband, though.

"Ah," Louisa says. I turn around.

"Hi, Guy," I say, holding out my hand. Again I hear Julius's words on the train. *Bloody good thing Guy's already there.* I grip his hand, suddenly angry, and pump my arm up and down a little too hard. Guy is nothing like his brother, he is mild-looking and rather thin, wearing a tatty, checked shirt with a corduroy jacket. He smiles at me.

"It's nice to see you again, Natasha. It's been a very long time." He nods, his gray eyes kind.

"Hi," I say. I haven't seen him for ages.

"I was in a shop where they were selling your bracelets the other day," he says. "Nearly bought one for my daughter."

"I wish you had," I say. He stares at me.

"Guy's an antiques dealer," Louisa says behind me. She crumples a tea towel up in her hand. "We thought it'd be useful for him to come to the funeral, you know? Get started on the work ahead. Because of course, there's some interesting things in the house too."

Interesting. "Has anyone been into her studio yet?" I say. "It's locked, isn't it?"

"Yes," Louisa says, her face tight. "Your mother found the key and went in, a couple of days ago. She started taking things out, but I managed to stop her. Someone should be making sure it's all properly done."

"Arvind wanted to go in," the Bowler Hat says. "In fairness to Miranda."

"Well, fine," Louisa says crossly, but she doesn't seem convinced. "Anyway, it's all in there."

"Like what?"

Louisa is brisk. "A few paintings, which is wonderful. That's it though. And her old sketchbooks and paints. Why, what were you expecting them to find?"

I shake my head, feeling stupid.

"It's time we sorted everything out." Louisa narrows her eyes. "Is that Florian leaving? Yes." She turns to me. "I mean, they weren't wealthy in other ways, not for years now. But there are a lot of valuable paintings, letters, books, that sort of thing. And we need to decide what's best for them all. For all her work, and everything else they've got here."

I know about the signed first editions by Stephen Spender, Kingsley Amis, T. S. Eliot, which line the shelves rising from the floor to the ceiling either side of the fireplace. About the Ben Nicholson print in the hall, the Macready sketch with its white frame in the dining room: *Frances at the Chelsea Arts Club,* 1953. They lent that one for his retrospective at the Tate, a couple of years ago. It was the cover of the catalog. I hadn't thought about all of that. To me, they're a part of the house, as much a part as the doors and the taps and the floors.

It makes sense that there's some kind of trust to look after Granny's paintings, but I can't help feeling uncomfortable. I barely know Guy and I don't think Mum and Archie do, either. Sure, they all spent a summer together years ago but that doesn't really count. Does it? And I wish I didn't, but I object to the idea of him eyeing up these things in the house at the funeral. Poking around in Granny's studio. Picking up the pair of Juno vases on the mantelpiece, the Clarice Cliff teapot, and clicking his tongue with pleasure. I glare at Louisa, but she is oblivious, and so I glare at Guy instead. He smiles at me in a friendly way, and I want to hit him. Now is not the time to be picking over the house for the juiciest bits, like the carcass of a chicken.

"Where's your mother gone?" he asks. "I haven't seen her for— gosh, ages. It'd be good to catch up with her about all of this." He pauses. "And Archie too."

"They were there—" I look round for them but they've disappeared. Instead I see Jay in the corner, now talking to Julius. "They're probably in the kitchen. Excuse me," I say. "Good to see you again."

"Oh," Guy says, obviously surprised at my abruptness. "Right, see you soon then."

I reach Julius and Jay, who are standing against the wall, clutching their glasses, not really saying much.

"How you feeling?" Jay asks me.

"Fine, fine," I wave him away. "Hi, Julius."

"Er—" Julius scratches his face. He is looking bored. "Sorry about you and—er—Oli." I don't know if he's shy or if he genuinely can't remember his name. "So—what happened? He slept with someone else?"

"How did you know that?" I say.

Julius shrugs. "Good guess. That's usually why, isn't it?"

Jay, standing next to him, rolls his eyes. Julius is our relative, it's weird to think of it. He is kind of vile.

"Yes, he slept with someone else," I say. "But—"

But what? Exactly. I look over at my mother and bite my lip. I still haven't even talked to her about this, and it feels wrong. Not because I usually tell her everything, in fact, I usually tell her nothing, but she's my mum. I should talk to her first.

"Anyway." I change the subject. "I was just talking to your uncle. Do you think it's appropriate he's here?"

"Why shouldn't he be here?" Julius says, unperturbed by my question. "He was her nephew, you know. He flew all the way from San Diego for the bloody funeral, damn nice of him, considering."

"Not your uncle Jeremy," I say, annoyed. Julius flusters me. "Your other uncle. Guy. Your mother's brought him down here to—to basically do a valuation on all the stuff in the house. Just think it's a bit rich."

Julius doesn't even blink. "You've got to pay for the nursing home your grandfather's going into," he says.

"Come on," I say. "That's rubbish. There's—there's money. Mum and Archie can sort it out."

"With what?" Julius says. "With all the money each of them has floating around?" Jay stiffens and I frown. "There's nothing, they've spent it all," Julius says flatly. He sticks his thick, rubbery lips out, like a child, and like a child I hate him again. I am sharply reminded of how he would push me against the rocks down on the beach, and laugh, and my back would be grazed with a repeating rash of brown beady scabs, for the duration of our holidays together. In truth I didn't really know him or Octavia that well, we didn't see each other for the rest of the year and I wasn't used to aggressive, boisterous boys like him. He scared me, it wasn't the picture of Summercove I wanted in my head. I watch him now. He hasn't changed all that much. "You're bloody lucky my mother's sorting all your crap out for the lot of you, you know."

"What business is it of hers anyway, all this—" I wave my hands round, trying not to get angry. "She's acting like Granny was *her* mother, like it was *her* house, she's organized it all, it's completely . . ." I trail off, not wanting to go on, surprised at the force of the rage I'm feeling.

"Who the hell do you think would have done it if it wasn't for her?" Julius says, half angry, half laughing, aggressively. You stupid little girl, the tone of his voice says. "Your mother? Oh, yeah, sure. There'd be no funeral and your grandfather would be out on the streets, or dead in a couple of weeks after your mother forgets that he can't actually get up the stairs or buy food himself anymore." He is working up a head of steam, and he turns to Jay. "And hey. At least Guy won't try and sell the stuff himself and pocket the profit."

There is a terrible silence after he says this. What's worse is Julius doesn't look at all embarrassed by what he's just said. As though he knows he's right. Jay and I stare at each other, then at him. A dark red blush stains Jay's cheeks.

"Fuck off, Julius," he says. "You're really out of order. OK?"

Julius doesn't look abashed. "Come on. They've always been like that, the pair of them. Everyone knows it."

And he walks over to where Octavia is chatting to an old lady.

Jay and I are standing there staring at each other. Jay breathes out, whistling slowly. "Nice to see Julius again, isn't it?"

"Yes," I say. I put on a faux-serious BBC announcer voice. "And it's a sad day, but it's lovely to see the family again. All gathered together, reunited once more in the same place." I'm trying to sound jokey, but it's scary. This is what we're like now Granny's not here. It's all changed, and I don't know how, or why.

Eight

It's a while before the final cluster of guests starts to leave: old neighbors, a few artists who have retired down here, a magistrate, a well-known writer and her husband—they know each other and aren't in a hurry to get back anywhere. I stand at the door of the sitting room, watching people disperse, looking around, thinking. A draught of cold air whistles past my back and I shiver, turning to see Jay waving goodbye to Mr. and Mrs. Neil who live up the lane. They have been there for thirty years and will miss Granny as much as us, I don't doubt. They saw her every day which is more than I did. Yesterday, as I was trying to sleep, I realized I hadn't seen her for three months, since November, when she came up to go to an exhibition at the Royal Academy and we had lunch in the café, where other old ladies and gents gather for a cup of coffee before getting their trains back to the Home Counties.

I wondered, as we sat there, if any of them realized who this still strikingly beautiful old lady was, that she had exhibited here, was in fact an RA, a Royal Academician. That she was sort of famous, in her day, appeared in the *Picture Post* and *Life* magazine, the famous bohemian painter and her exotic husband in their house by the sea with their mixed-race children, though everyone was too polite to mention that, of course, and if they did, they said it was *terribly* interesting. I wonder if they knew, if Granny knew what Mum once told me in an unguarded moment, that before the train left every term, my mother would dash to Boots the chemist in Penzance to buy a pack of disposable razors, to shave the black hair on her dark arms.

* * *

Jay comes towards me. "Hey." He looks round the empty hallway, the dresser and table littered with paper plates and half-empty champagne flutes, and says cautiously, "Thank God, those people are starting to go."

We both look at our watches. It's seven and the sleeper leaves at nine. "How are you getting to the station?" he asks. "I'll drive you."

At this exact moment, as if she's been waiting for this conversation, Octavia appears in the hallway. She strides towards us, her heavy, sensible black shoes loud on the floor. "Are you talking about the trains?" she says. "I'm going back tonight actually too. I have a meeting at the Ministry of Defense tomorrow, just found out." She waves her BlackBerry authoritatively, her thick ponytail swinging out behind her head as she nods at us.

"Should you be telling us this information?" Jay says. "Won't we have to kill you now?"

"Ha," says Octavia, ignoring him and turning to me. "How are you getting to the station?"

"I've booked Mike the taxi," I say. "He's coming in an hour."

"I'll get a lift with you then," Octavia says. She adds, almost under her breath, "If that's all right." There is no way I can say, "No, it's not all right, I hate you and your horrible brother! I don't want you coming back with me!" Which is kind of what my eight-year-old self would want me to say to her.

I nod instead. "Of course," I say. "Have you booked a cabin?"

"Yes, just now," she says. "Don't worry, Natasha, I won't make you share with me like the old days," and she runs her hands awkwardly through her fringe and I feel a pang of guilt, for that is exactly what I was thinking.

"Well, that's great. I'm just going to find Mum then," I say, and I touch Jay on the shoulder and dash towards the kitchen. Mum is talking to Guy, the Bowler Hat's brother. Her hands are on her hips, she is leaning over him as if she's about to spit at him. They both jump as I stride in.

"There you are," Mum says, standing upright. Her jaw is set, her

green eyes flinty; she is staring at Guy with something approaching loathing and I know the signs. She's about to blow. She blinks,
rapidly, as if calming herself down, and she says, "Nat—darling, my
darling, how are you? We need to talk, don't we?" She winds some
hair round her finger.

I look suspiciously at Guy. "Everything OK?"

"Yes, absolutely," Guy says smoothly. "It's fine. I was just asking
your mother about the . . . stuff in the house."

"The stuff in the house," I say carefully, because I don't want to
be rude. "Look, I said this to your brother already, and please don't
take this the wrong way, but do you really think now's the time to
be poking around valuing things here?" He is turning red. "It's not
great timing." I'm surprised to hear my voice shaking. "Perhaps you
should come back another day."

Guy turns to my mother, who is staring at her feet. There is a
chicken vol-au-vent on the linoleum floor. "Why doesn't she know?"
he says.

Mum says nothing.

"Know what?" I ask.

"That's why it all seems rather abrupt, Natasha. Your grandparents agreed to it years ago, that when Frances died something should
be established in her name. A charitable foundation, or a gallery.
You know, she hasn't had an exhibition for years. It's a disgrace, a
painter of her stature. But she's never let them. There was a big show
planned for the autumn after Cecily, after she died." He stops and
collects himself, and I remember he must have known her too, that
summer. I hadn't thought of that before. "The country hasn't seen
Frances Seymour's work, apart from the two in the Tate Modern and
a few in America, for well over forty years."

I blink, trying to take it in. "So?"

"Now she's dead, the terms of her will say the foundation should
be established as soon as possible. Miranda," he says crossly. "You
should have told Natasha. She's one of the trustees, for God's
sake."

"Me?" I say. "I don't know anything about painting. I never saw her paint, anyway."

"It's nothing to do with that. She wanted you to be one of the trustees. You, your mother, and me—" He clears his throat, awkwardly. "I—I don't quite understand what I've got to do with it, but—"

"Look," says my mother, her throaty voice cutting across Guy's. "I get it, OK? I get the whole thing. All I'm saying is, Archie and I would also like to make sure that the house and furniture are sold in the right way. You know, we have got bills to pay out of all of this. And Arvind's nursing home." She twists the big jade ring she's wearing, and this seems to give her momentum. "You know, Guy, you've got a bloody nerve, showing up here, trying to tell *us* what to do, after all these years. I was going to tell Natasha, but you know it's been a busy day." She shakes her hair, pursing her lips and staring at him in fury, and she does look rather magnificent. "After all these years," she says, more quietly. "You should know that."

"Fine," Guy says. He holds his palms up towards her. "I understand. You're right. We'll discuss it another day." He looks up and chews his little finger. "Look, I'm sorry—I didn't think—"

"It's fine," I say, looking to Mum for confirmation. "Thank you, Guy." She is staring at me, but I interpret this as tacit approval of my actions. She's useless at confrontations, though she acts like a diva the whole time.

"Goodbye, Miranda," Guy says, turning to her. "It's been a sad day, but it was really lovely to see you again."

"Well—" Mum blinks slowly, her long, soot-black eyelashes brushing her smooth skin. There is a crumb of mascara on her cheekbone; I stare at it. "It was lovely to see you again. It's been a long time."

He nods, and bows his head at me. "Natasha, you too." He clears his throat. "Once more, I'm sorry if you've thought I've been inappropriate, or anything like that. Let me—" He fumbles in his pocket and takes out a card. "If you're ever up this way—"

GUY LEIGHTON
ANTIQUES & RARE BOOKS
CROSS STREET
LONDON N1

"I'm sure we'll be in touch, about the foundation at the very least." I take the card. "Well, thank you, Guy. Thank you." As if I am a dowager duchess whom he will never be fortunate enough to meet again.

"Goodbye, then," he says, and shuts the door quietly behind him, with one last apologetic look at my mother.

The room is silent. "Are you OK?" I say. Mum is blinking back tears.

"I am," she says. "I'm just rather tired. It's been a long day. Lots of memories, you know? And I'm worried about you, Natasha."

She says it quietly, without tossing her hair or rolling her eyes or trying to get something. She just looks rather beaten, and it hits me in the solar plexus. I put my arm round her. "I'm sorry, Mum," I tell her. "I wanted to explain about me and Oli, but it was . . . too hard. And then Granny died—I couldn't just drop it into conversation, could I?"

"So what happened?" she says. "Do you want to tell your old mum about it?"

Mum isn't very good at being a mum out of an OXO ad. She's better when she's just being a person.

"He's been sleeping with someone else," I say.

"An affair?" Mum's eyes are wide open now.

"No." I shake my head. "A girl at work. It was a couple of months ago. He says it's nothing. It's over."

"Ohh!" my mother says, her voice high, as if that's that then. "Right."

I look at her.

"That's absolutely awful," she adds. "You poor thing."

I can't believe I'm having this conversation with her; in fact I re-member one of the reasons why I dreaded telling her in the first place. Mum absolutely adores Oli. They get on really well. I often think they'd have a better time without me there. He thinks she's hilarious, wonderful, and she plays up to it, and they get drunk together and egg each other on, like old boozers in a pub, and I sit there, wearily watching them, feeling like a beige carpet in a Persian rug shop.

There's a frown puckering her forehead. I say, "I think he wants to come back, but I don't know what to say if he asks. I just don't know if I can trust him."

"Hmm," says my mum, one finger on her cheek as if considering this point seriously, and I remember the times I'd ask her when she'd be back home from a party or dinner with friends. "Hmm . . ." she'd say, finger on cheek, and after a long pause, "not late, darling. Not too late." And then, when I'd finally got to sleep, worn out by being terrified by noises inside the flat that I thought were rats or sinister intruders, and of being terrified by noises outside the flat that I knew were masked robbers or deranged psychopaths, in the dark still hours of the early morning I'd hear the creak of the door and the soft tap on the parquet floor as she crept past my room to her bed. "Hmm . . . I'm just not sure."

"I am," I say. "I can't trust him. I can't have him back if I don't trust him."

"He's your husband, and he looks after you, and you don't have to worry about anything," Mum says sharply. "I think you need to look at it like that instead, Natasha. I mean, he didn't *kill* anyone, you know. He slept with someone. He's a good husband."

"What?" I am momentarily stunned, as though this is a modern-day version of *Gigi* and I am Leslie Caron and should just put up with it. "He pays for our nice life, for my new boots, I should just shut up, right?"

She stares at me defiantly. "Sometimes, darling, I think you just don't get it at all. I'm just saying it's hard, being on your own."

I can't answer this, as I know she's right, but I can't agree with her without hurting her feelings. "I just don't know, Mum," I say. "I look at our life together and I—"

She interrupts me. "Relationships aren't perfect," she says. "They're not. You have to work at them. You were the first of your friends to get married, weren't you?" This is true, and I'm surprised she's aware of it. "Perhaps you just don't see your other friends in the same situations as you. And I've certainly not been much of a role model in that direction, have I?" She grimaces, blinking rapidly.

"He slept with someone, Mum. He didn't forget our anniversary. It's a bit different."

"Like I say. People make mistakes." She pauses. "Your grandparents are a good example. But they got over it."

"How? What do you mean?"

"I mean—" Mum begins, and then she stops. Her mouth is open, as though she's not sure how to continue, and then we hear a noise.

"Hello?" someone calls from upstairs. "Hello? I think your grandfather needs help." I push open the swinging kitchen door. An old lady is standing at the top of the stairs, peering out of the dark. "I just came up here to use the lavatory and I heard him . . . he's calling for someone."

I see Louisa breaking away from her husband and Guy and hurrying towards the hall. I step out.

"I'll go," I say suddenly, watching my mother's face. I can hear Arvind's voice, growing louder.

"Someone needs to come up here!" he is squeaking. "Immediately!"

"Thanks," I say to the old lady, who is waiting at the bend in the staircase. "See you later, Mum," I say, and I run up the stairs, my hands running along the smooth, dark wood of the banisters.

"I do hope he's all right," the old lady says, looking anxiously towards the closed bedroom door. I push it open and go in.

Nine

"Hello, Natasha," Arvind says. He is sitting up in bed, small as a child, bald as a baby, his hands wrinkled and lying on the crisp white sheets. The wheelchair is parked neatly in the corner; a metal stand is next to the bed. They don't go with the room, these metal hospital items. They don't match.

I love this room, perhaps more than any other in the house. But here on this dark February evening the heavy brocade curtains are drawn, and it is gloomy, with only the light from a lamp on Arvind's side of the bed. On Granny's side the sheets are smooth, and the bedside table is empty except for a blue plastic beaker; there's still water in it. I wonder how long it would take for it to evaporate all away.

"What's up, Arvind?" I say. "Are you all right?"

"I was bored," he says. "I don't want to sleep. I wanted to put some music on, but I was prevented by your well-meaning relative." He nods. His teeth are on the side, in a jar. His voice is muffled.

"Music?" I say, trying not to smile.

"I like Charles Trenet, so does your grandmother. When is a better time than at her funeral to play a compact disc of Charles Trenet? But that is not important." He taps the sheets with his fingers. They are etiolated and dry, dead twigs scraping the smooth linen. His mind is working away though, looking at me. He screws up his face. "Sit down."

I sit down on the edge of the bed.

"Do you know what the collective noun for rooks is?" Arvind asks.

"What?" I say.

"The collective noun for rooks. It has been annoying me. All day."

"No idea, sorry," I say. "A rookery?"

"No." He glares at me in annoyance. "I would ask your grandmother. She would know."

"She would," I say. I glance at him.

"It is sad," my grandfather says. His hands pluck at the sheet. He stares up at the ceiling. "So, how is the atmosphere downstairs? I must admit I was not sorry to have to retire. I was finding it rather exhausting."

"Most people have gone," I say. "But there's still a hardcore group left."

"Your grandmother was a very popular woman," Arvind says. "She had a lot of admirers. The house used to be full of them. Long time ago."

I say, trying to keep my voice light, "Well, you may find a couple of them sleeping on the sofas tomorrow morning."

He smiles. "Then it will be just like the old days, except they are all grayer and not that much wiser. Are you staying tonight?"

"No," I say. "I have to get back. I have a meeting with the bank. They want their money back."

"Oh? Why is that?"

"Well, I'm going out of business."

I don't know why I tell Arvind this. Perhaps because he is not easily spooked and I know he won't start wringing his hands or sighing.

"I am sorry to hear that." He nods, as if acknowledging the situation. "Again. Why?"

"I've been stupid, basically," I say. "Listened to people when I should have just done my own thing."

"But perhaps it will give you back some freedom."

"Freedom?"

"The ties that bind can often strangle you," Arvind says, as if we were chatting about the weather. "It is true, in my long experience. How is Oli?"

"Well—" It is my turn to start smoothing the duvet down with my fingers. "That's another thing, too. I've left him. Or he's left me. I think it's over."

Arvind's eyes widen a little, and he nods again. "That is more bad news."

I put one hand under my chin. "Sorry. I'm not doing very well at the moment." My throat hurts from trying not to cry. "I'm sort of glad Granny doesn't know. She was . . . well—she wouldn't have screwed everything up like this."

Arvind says slowly, "Your grandmother wasn't perfect, you know. Everyone thought she was, but she wasn't. She found things . . . hard. Like her daughter has. Like you." He gazes at the curtains, as if looking through them, out to sea, to the horizon beyond. "You're all more alike than you think, you know. 'The sins of the fathers shall be revisited upon the children.' "

I can't really see what he's talking about: Mum looks like Granny, but apart from that two more different people you couldn't imagine. Granny, hard-working, charming, interested and interesting, beautiful and talented, and my mother—well, she's some of those things I suppose, but she's never really found her own niche, her own place, the way her brother has. Granny was sure of her place in the world. Wasn't she?

A thick, velvety silence covers the room. I can hear faint noises from downstairs. A door slams, some murmured voices, the sound of crockery clattering against something. I wonder what time it is now. I don't want to leave, but I know I will have to, and soon. Arvind is watching me, as if I am a curious specimen.

He opens his mouth to speak, slowly.

"You look just like her," he says. "Did you know that?"

"Like Granny?"

"No." He shakes his head. "No. Like Cecily. You look just like Cecily."

"That's funny—Louisa just said that," I say. "Really?" A memory from long ago begins to stir within me.

"Oh, yes." Arvind scratches the side of his chin with two thin fingers. "I thought you understood. That's why."

"That's why what?"

"That's why your grandmother, she sometimes found it hard to be with you. She was so proud of you. Said you had her blood running in your veins. She loved your work, loved it. But she found it very hard, at times. Because, you see, you are like twins."

"I—I didn't know that," I say, tears springing into my eyes.

"It's not your fault." He wiggles his toes under the duvet, watching them dispassionately. I watch them too. "But you did look very like her. Perhaps her skin was darker, so was her hair, but the face—the face is the same. . . ." He gives a deep, shuddering sigh, almost too big for someone so tiny, and his voice cracks. "Cecily. Cecily Kapoor. We don't talk about you, do we? We never do."

He is nodding, and then he mutters something to himself.

"What did you say?" I ask.

"No, it doesn't matter. Here. Wait."

Suddenly, like an old crab, he shuffles over and pulls open the top drawer of his bedside table. He is surprisingly agile.

"It's right." He leans forwards and takes something out.

"What's right?"

Arvind moves back to his side of the bed again. I move forwards, to plump up his pillow, but he shakes his head impatiently. His face is alive, his dark eyes dancing. "Have this. It was your grandmother's. She wanted you to have it. I think you should take it now."

Like a magician, he opens his fist with a flourish. I peer down. It is the ring Granny always wore, twisted diamond and pale gold flowers on a thin band, Arvind's family ring, the one his father sent over for his son's new bride all those years ago. I know it so well, but it is still startling to see it here, on my grandfather's palm and not on Granny's finger.

"That's Granny's," I say, stupidly.

"It's yours now," he tells me.

"Arvind, I can't have this, Mum should, or Sameena, or Louisa—"

"Frances wanted you to have it, she told me quite clearly." Arvind's voice is devoid of emotion, and he's staring out at the thick brocade curtains. "You're a jeweler, she was very pleased with your work. She knew you loved this. We planned everything, we discussed everything. You are to have it."

I don't know what to say. "That's very sweet," I begin, falteringly. *Sweet*—such an insipid word for this, for him. "But I'd rather not take it from you."

"You are to have it, Natasha," Arvind says again. "She gave it to Cecily. Now it is for you. This is what she wanted." He puts it on my hand, his thin brown fingers clutching my large clumsy ones, and we stare at each other in silence. Arvind has never been the kind of grandfather who whittled toy soldiers out of wood, or mended your tricycle, or let you try the sausage on the barbecue. He is frequently obtuse and it is hard to understand what he means.

But while I don't know what his final aim is, in this moment, looking at him, I know each of us understands the other. I put the ring on, sliding it onto the third finger of my right hand, like a wedding. My granny had strong, large hands, so do I. It fits perfectly. The flowers glint gently in the low light.

"Thank you," I say softly. "It's beautiful."

"Would you be very kind and please open the curtains," he says, after a moment. "I would like to see the sea. The moon is also out tonight. I don't like to be shut in like this. They must understand this, in the new place. I want to see the moon. It will remind me of home."

I get up and draw the heavy fabric back. The moon is out and it shines, like the midnight sun, low and heavy on the black waters, golden light rippling towards the horizon. It is calmer now, but as a dirty cloud scuds across the surface of the moon I shiver. Something is coming. A storm, perhaps.

I open the window, breathing in the scent of the sea, fresh, dangerous, alive. The gold of Granny's ring is warm against my fingers. I stare into the water, into nothing.

"It's a mild night," I say after a silence.

"There's something brewing," he says simply. "I can smell it in the air. That's what happens when you're old. Peculiar, but useful."

I smile at him, and go back towards the bed. I notice the drawer of his bedside table is still open, and I lean over to push it shut. But as I do, I see something staring up at me. A face.

"What's this?" I say. "Can I see?"

I don't know why I say this, it's none of my business. But the idea that Louisa is going to go through this room, that everything is ending here at the house, emboldens me, I think.

"Take it out." Arvind glances at it. "Yes, take it out, you'll see."

I lift it out. It is a small study in oils, no bigger than an A4 piece of paper, on a sandy-colored canvas. No frame. It is of a teenage girl's head and shoulders, half-turning towards the viewer, a quizzical expression on her face. Her black hair is tangled; her cheeks are flushed. Her skin is darker than mine. She is wearing a white Aertex shirt, and the ring that is on my finger is around a chain on her slender neck. "Cecily, Frowning," is written in pencil at the bottom.

"Is that her?" I am holding it up gingerly. I gaze at it. "Is that Cecily?"

"Yes," Arvind says. "She was beautiful. Your mother wasn't. She hated her."

I think this is a joke, as Mum is one of the most beautiful people I know. I look again. This girl—she's so fresh, so eager, there's something so urgent about the way she is turning towards me, as if saying, *Come. Come with me! Let's go down to the beach, while the sun is still high, and the water is warm, and the reeds are rustling in the bushes.*

"Where did—where was it?"

"It was in the studio," Arvind says. "I took it out of the studio, the day after she died."

"You went in there?"

Arvind puts his fingers together. "Of course I did." He looks straight through me. "I never did before. She never went back in there, either. The day after she died, yes. I told myself I had to. She asked me to. To get what was in there. But it wasn't all there anymore."

"Get what was in there?" I don't understand.

I look at my grandfather, and his eyes are full of tears. He lies back on the pillows, and closes his eyes.

"I am very tired," he says.

"Yes, I'm sorry," I say. But I don't want to put her back in the drawer, out of sight again, hidden away.

"I'm glad you've seen her," he says. "Now you can see. You are so alike."

This is patently not true, this beautiful scrap of a girl is not like me. I am older than she ever was, I am tired, jaded, dull. I stand up to put the painting back. As I do, something which had been stuck to the back of the canvas—it is unframed—falls to the ground, and I bend and pick it up.

It is a sheaf of lined paper, tied with green string knotted through a hole on the top left corner, and folded in half. About ten pages, no more. I unfold it. Written in a looping script are the words:

The Diary of Cecily Kapoor, aged fifteen.
July, 1963.

I hold it in my hand and stare. There's a stamp at the top bearing the legend "St. Katherine's School." Underneath in blue fountain pen someone, probably a teacher, has written "Cecily Kapoor Class 4B." It's such a prosaic-looking thing, smelling faintly of damp, of churches, and old books. And yet the handwriting looks fresh, as though it was scrawled yesterday.

"What is this?" I ask, stupidly.

Arvind opens his eyes. He looks at me, and at the pages I am holding.

"I knew she'd kept it," he says. He does not register surprise or shock. "There's more. She filled a whole exercise book, that summer."

I glance into the drawer again. "Where is it, then?"

Arvind puckers his gummy mouth together. "I don't know. Don't know what happened to the rest of it. That's partly why I went into the studio. I wanted to find it, I wanted to keep it."

"Why?" I say. "Why, what's in it? Where's the rest of it?"

Suddenly we hear footsteps at the bottom of the stairs, a familiar thundering sound.

"Arvind?" a voice demands. "Is Natasha in with you? Natasha? I just wonder, isn't the cab going to be here soon?"

"Take it," he says, lowering his voice and pushing the diary into my hands. The footsteps are getting closer. "And look after it, guard it carefully. It'll all be in there."

"What do you mean?" I say.

"Your grandmother, she must have kept it for a reason," he says, his soft voice urgent. He drops his voice. "This family is poisoned." He stares at me. "They won't tell you, but they are. Read it. Find the rest of it. But don't tell anyone, don't let anyone else see it."

The door opens, and Louisa is in the room, her loud voice shattering the quiet.

"I was calling you," she says, accusatory. "Didn't you hear?"

"No," I say, lying.

"I was worried you'd be late for your train—" She looks at the open bedside table, at the painting at the top, the girl's smiling face gleaming out. "Oh, Arvind," she says briskly, closing her eyes. "No, that's all wrong." And she shuts the drawer firmly.

I slip the sheet of paper into one of the huge pockets of my black skirt and clench my fingers so she can't see the ring. "Sorry," I say. "I'm just coming." I bend over and kiss my grandfather. "Bye," I say, kissing his soft, papery cheek. "Take care. I'll see you in a few weeks."

"Perhaps," he says. "And congratulations. I hope that you can enjoy your freedom."

"Freedom?" Louisa makes a tutting sound, and she starts smoothing the duvet out again, tidying the bedside table. "It's not something to congratulate her on, Arvind. She's left her husband."

I smile.

"Freedom," he says, "comes in many guises."

My hands are shaking as I leave the room. I walk to the end of the corridor, to the staircase, past my room, which was also Mum and Cecily's room, down the end, to the alcove that leads to the door of Granny's studio. I stare at it, walk towards it, push it open, quickly, as if I expect someone to bite me.

It's all glass, splattered here and there with seagull crap. A step at the end. The faintest smell of something, I don't know what, tobacco and fabric and turps, still lingers in the air. The moon shines in through one of the great glass windows. The world outside is silver, green, and gray, only the sea on view. I have never seen the garden from this viewpoint before, never stood in this part of the house. It is extremely strange. There is a thin layer of dust on the concrete floor, but not as much as I'd have thought. A bay with a window seat, two canvases stacked against the wall and wooden boxes of paints stacked next to it, neatly put away, and right in the center of the room a solo easel, facing me, with a stool. A stained, rigid rag is on the floor. That's it. It's as if she cleared every other trace of herself away, the day she shut the studio up.

I look round the room slowly, breathing in. I can't feel Granny here at all, though the rest of the house is almost alive with her. This room is a shell.

Shutting the door quietly, trying not to shiver, I go downstairs, feeling the paper curve around my thigh in its pocket. There they are, gathered in the sitting room, the few who are left: my mother on the sofa next to Archie, the two of them sunk in conversation; the Bowler Hat, hands in his blazer, staring round the room as if he wishes he weren't there and next to him his brother Guy, also silent, so different from him, but looking similarly uncomfortable. On cue, Louisa appears behind me, pushing her fringe out of her face.

"All OK?" she says, and I notice how tired she looks and feel a pang of guilt. Poor Louisa.

I should just say, "Look what Arvind's given me. Cecily's diary. Look at this."

But I don't, though I should. It stays there, in my pocket, as I look round the room and wonder what Arvind meant.

Ten

Jay stands in the doorway of the house as Mike waits outside in his large people carrier, engine purring, and Octavia hugs her parents goodbye. "I wish you weren't going," he says. "Call me tomorrow and let me know how the meeting goes. And everything. Maybe meet up over the weekend? Get some lamb chops?"

"Sure," I say. I can't see further than the next five minutes at the moment; the weekend seems like an age away, there's so much to get through before then. "Lamb chops would be great."

We are both obsessed, perhaps because of the birthplace of our grandfather, with the Lahore Kebab House, off the Commercial Road. Neither of our parents will eat there—it's not posh enough for them. But we took Arvind once, when he was in London to receive an honorary degree, and he loved it. It's huge and opulent, full of lounging young men with gelled hair in leather jackets scoffing food, eyes glued to the huge TV screens showing the cricket. Jay often knows them. "Jamal!" he calls, as we sit down. "Ali . . . ! My brother!" And they all do those young-men hand clasps, hugging firmly, patting the back. They look me up and down. "My cousin, Natasha," Jay says and they nod respectfully, slumping back down into the chair to eat the food. Oh . . . the food . . . Tender, succulent, chargrilled lamb chops . . . Peshwari naan like you wouldn't believe, crispy, yet fluffy . . . Butter chicken . . . I can't even talk about the butter chicken. Jay jokes that I moved to Brick Lane so I could be near the Lahore. One week, Oli and I ate there three times. It didn't even seem weird.

As I stand outside Summercove, the wet Cornish air gusting into my face, the Lahore seems a long way away. "It would be great," Jay says. "I might have to go away for work but sometime soon, yeah? You're not . . . busy?"

"No," I say. Of course I'm not busy. I don't do anything much these days. I go to the studio and stare at a wall, then go back home and stare at a TV.

Octavia moves towards me and we stop talking. "Are you ready?" she asks briskly.

"Yep," I say. "Bye, Jay." I hug him again.

"Good luck, Nat," he says. "It's all going to be OK."

With Jay I feel calm. I feel that if he says it then it really must be true. It will be OK. This cloak of despair which I seem to wear all the time, it will lift off and disappear. Oli and I will work this out, and come through this stronger. The bank will extend my loan and I will have a means to live. Someone will give me a break.

And then I think about the diary in my bag. I frown. I nearly mention it to him, but I remember what my grandfather said. *Guard it carefully.*

Jay doesn't see, he doesn't know, how could he? He kisses me on the cheek, and I climb into the large vehicle. We're right at the back. It is dark and it's been raining.

"Are we ready?" Mike calls in his soft, comforting voice.

"Yes," Octavia and I say in chorus, and then someone thumps on the window and we both jump.

"Nat darling, bye." My mother is standing in the driveway, her hands pressed against the wet windows of the car, her hair hanging in her face, peering through at us. "We'll speak. Keep me posted." She is speaking much too loudly, and I wonder if she's drunk; she looks a bit hysterical. "I'm sorry."

I have already said goodbye to her, in the sitting room. I press my hand up to the glass so it mirrors hers. "Bye, Mum," I say. Behind her, Jay comes forwards and puts his arm around her.

"I'm sorry," she says again. "Take care, darling."

And the car pulls away as she stands there with Jay, watching us go. I can't see the house, it's too dark, and I'm relieved. I realize I'm glad to be getting out of there.

There's a silence, broken only by the ticking of Mike's indicator as he waits to turn into the main road.

"Is your mother OK?" Octavia asks, smoothing her skirt over her knees.

"What do you mean?" I say.

"She's been acting strangely all day, even for her."

I don't like her tone and I'm not in the mood for Octavia and her "my family grievances" corner. "It was her mother's funeral today," I say. "I think that's reason enough." And then I add, unwisely, "We're not all robots, you know."

"Are you talking about me?" Octavia says. She is facing forwards, doesn't look at me. "Do you mean my family?"

Oh, dear. I am too tired and my head's whirring with too many thoughts to keep ahold of what I say.

"We're all family," I tell her. "I just mean it's hard for her today, that's all. We should cut her some slack."

At this Octavia turns to me, her long nose twitching. It is dark on the quiet country road, and her face is marbled with moonlight, giving her a ghoulish appearance. I remember suddenly, I don't know why, that she played a witch in her school play when she was twelve. Jay and I found it hilarious.

"We're not family," she says.

"Er—" I say. "We are, Octavia. Sorry about that."

She smiles. "You have such weird ideas, Natasha. We may be related—our mothers are cousins, that's all. We spend the occasional holiday together. We're not proper family, I'm thankful to say."

I stare at her. "If you're not *proper family*," I say, "how come your mother's been bossing everyone around and drafting in people to value the house before Granny's even in the ground? If you're not family how come she dragged you down here every year to have a lovely holiday? I don't remember you complaining about it!" I am laughing. She's so stupid.

Octavia purses up her lips and sighs, but her eyes are glittering and I know, somehow, I know I've walked into a trap.

"Like I say," she says slowly, as if I'm an idiot. "We are not family, Natasha. My mother is very fond of—was very fond of her aunt. She—" She pauses. "She loved her. She felt Franty needed someone to look out for her, to take care of her after Cecily died. After all, no one else was. *Your* family certainly wasn't."

"They were—" I begin, but she holds up a hand.

"You're living in a dreamworld," Octavia says, icily calm. "Your grandfather lives in his own head. He doesn't notice half the stuff that goes on right under his nose. Your uncle pretends everything's a big joke and waits to see what his sister tells him to do, and as for her, as for your mother . . . Well. Your mother's the *last* person she'd ask for help."

I think of Mum's sad face, pressed up against the glass, of her defeated expression during our conversation about Oli, and I feel protective of her. It's so easy to paint her as difficult, as a flake, and it's not fine anymore, especially not today. "Look, Octavia," I say, as patiently as I can. "I know my mother's not like your mother—"

"You're telling me!" she says, with a cruel shout of mirth.

"Just because she's different, doesn't mean she's—she's evil."

Evil. Where have I heard that word recently? Octavia is still smiling with that patronizing look on her face and suddenly I get angry. I'm sick of her and her "family," with their smug we're-so-perfect ways, her boring bored father, her interfering uncle and her eager-beaver mother Louisa, sticking her nose in, trying to show us all up. . . . "Just because Mum didn't move to *Tunbridge Wells*," I say, as if it's the most disgusting place in the world. "Just because she hasn't worked in the same office her whole life, just because she doesn't have a stupid special *compartment* in her sewing box for *name tags*, OK? It doesn't mean she's a bad person, Octavia."

I'm shaking, I'm so angry.

"You don't get it, do you?" she says. "I didn't realize, you have absolutely no idea about your mother. No idea at all!" She stares at me, faux concern on her face. "Oh, Natasha."

"What do you mean?" I say.

"You all right in the back there?" Mike calls to us.

We freeze.

"Oh, yes!" Octavia says quickly, smilingly, and then she turns to me, lowers her voice, and hisses, *Do you really not know the truth about her?*

Her face is right next to mine. I shake my head, trying to look unconcerned.

"Whatever, Octavia. I'm not interested."

Octavia's face is pale, so close to mine. I can see her open pores, the down of hair on her cheek, smell her warm breath on my skin. Her voice is sing-songy. She says softly, "She killed her sister, Natasha. That summer."

At first I think I've misunderstood what she's saying, and I listen to the words again in my head. "No," I say, after a few moments. "That's not true."

Moonlight flickers into the car through the branches of the trees, as if a light is being turned on and off. I blink.

"Think about it," Octavia says. "Haven't you always known something strange happened?" And then she's silent, watching me, as I furiously shake my head. "Look, I'm sorry," she says, after a pause, as though she knows she's gone too far. "I didn't mean to—"

"I knew you were talking rubbish anyway," I say, thinking she's apologizing, that she's made it up to hurt me, but she says, "I didn't mean for you to find out like this. I thought you must know by now."

This family's poisoned. The diary's in my pocket.

"I don't think she planned it out," Octavia says. "It's not like she *poisoned* her or anything." Her voice is almost pleading, as though she wants me to be OK, as though she feels bad. "But—you know, they had a row about something—I don't know what it was. I don't think Mum knows. They had a blazing row and Miranda pushed Cecily, and she slipped on the path and broke her neck. That's what happened. Archie saw them. Ask—ask Guy," Octavia says suddenly, wiping her nose with her hand, very unlike her. "He knows it all. Your mother tried to seduce him. She tried to seduce my father too."

"Look, this is just so stupid—" I say. She ignores me.

"Well, he saw straight through her, they both did. That's why *no one* likes her." She gets out a tissue and blows her nose. "That's what the row was about." She sniffs loudly. "Everyone knows what your mother did, but they didn't want to upset your grandmother. They weren't even allowed to mention Cecily in front of her, were they?" I nod. We weren't—it was the only rule at Summercove. "But now Great-Aunt Frances is dead, well—things have changed, haven't they?"

The bubble is burst. It's cold in the cab and I squeeze my arms to my side. "I—I just don't believe you."

"Have you ever thought that explains quite a lot about her?"

"No," I say. "Absolutely not. And frankly, Octavia—"

"Maybe she didn't plan it, but she killed her all the same. Ask Guy. He was there," Octavia says again, flatly.

"That's such crap—how the hell do you know that's what happened?" I sit up, full of righteous anger. "How do they know? Why hasn't anyone ever said anything to me about it before? Why hasn't Mum ever said—"

"She's not going to, is she?" Octavia says, genuinely pitying. "But your mother—oh, I don't know what was going on that summer," she says. She scratches her forehead. "I don't think Mum knows, even. Just—all I'm saying is, your mother wouldn't tell anyone what the row was about, and there's no way of finding out, is there?"

"No," I say, and I think of the diary again, and then remember how thin the outline of it feels between my fingers, how childish. But I don't touch it again. I don't want Octavia suspecting anything. I look at her, and think how strange it is that I know her really well, and yet I don't know her at all. Never been to her house, don't know any of her friends, or about her romantic life, or her favorite books to read or anything. She's just always been there. I thought we were family, and it turns out I don't know her at all either.

She's right. I've been living in a dreamworld.

"Look," she says, as though she's regretting speaking so hastily. "I hope—I'm sorry, perhaps I shouldn't have said anything." She clears her throat. "But you had to know. I can't believe you've never heard an inkling of it before."

There's a lot I could say to this, but I don't. I raise my hand. "It's OK. Look, let's just not talk about it anymore."

We slide into an awkward silence for the rest of the journey, but I'm glad. I don't know what on earth we'd talk about.

Eleven

The sleeper train from Penzance has a special platform to itself, outside the main station. I like that; it accords it a proper position. In summer, it can be a trying experience. It is always crowded, frequently extremely hot (the air conditioning is temperamental), and it gets light so early that, as a child, I would wake at three-thirty and never be able to get back to sleep, lying there on the top bunk under the scratchy blue blankets, tossed about by the motion of the train.

Mum would come down again at the end of the summer to take me back to London, unless Granny was coming up herself, and I always hated it when Mum arrived because I hated leaving Summercove. It was like leaving a fairy-tale palace behind, a warm, airy, sweet-smelling palace where I was free, where my grandmother was always there so I never got lonely, and where the sun shone and Jay and I were together. Back in London we knew September would be racing to catch us, damp-drenched mornings when the sun rose later and colder, and winter lay just around the corner, putting me and especially my mother into a funk that would last till spring.

On the train back I would always go over the holiday in my head, committing it all to memory. The walk to Logan's Rock, and the terrifying winds that threaten to blow you off to the treacherous waters beneath. Sitting outside at the Minack Theatre, an amphitheater carved into the cliffs, screaming with laughter at *A Midsummer Night's Dream*. Jay and I clambering down through the rocks to the beach below the house; the astonishing green and blue of the water, the ginger beer that was sharp and sweet, at the same time, on your tongue. The warmth, the wet, the wildness, the knowledge that being in Cornwall is like being in a different country, and that every mile you draw away from it is like leaving a part of you behind. Yes, I thought it was like something out of a fairy tale.

After we've paid Mike and waved him off, Octavia and I stand on the blustery quayside, at the entrance to the station.

"Do you know what carriage you are?" I ask, my tone almost formal.

She shakes her head. "I have to go and pick my tickets up from the machine."

"Oh," I say. "Right."

We are silent. I look down at my black boots. I pulled them on this morning, at five-thirty, in the dark. It seems like a lifetime ago.

"So, I've already got my ticket," I say, waving the orange card at her. "I think I'll—"

"Yes, yes," she says, a touch too eagerly. "Well, it was . . ." she trails off. "Er, good to see you."

Someone hurries past us, dragging a suitcase on wheels. It crackles loudly over the tarmac. "Look, Natasha," Octavia says, after another silence. "I'm sorry. Perhaps I shouldn't have said it like that." She holds her hands up. Don't blame me. "I just thought you'd have heard. You know, everyone's always . . ." She trails off again, and crosses her arms defensively. "It's all water under the bridge, I suppose."

"It's clearly not though, is it?" I say. "It's anything but that. It explains a lot, anyway." I'm trying not to sound angry. "Look, your mum's always had it in for my mum and I've never known why, and now I do. That's why I'm not surprised."

"You understand why now." Octavia nods, as if to say, "Good. She's finally getting it."

"No, I don't believe it, Octavia. What I mean is," I say, breathing deeply, "I understand why you've always been so vile to us now. I mean, did your mother tell you this herself?"

"Not in so many words," Octavia says. "You don't sit down and explain something like that—we just always knew. Dad, too. And Uncle Jeremy. That's why he never comes back." She shrugs.

"Well, as you like. I don't believe for a second, a *second*—" and I raise my voice so I'm speaking as loudly as possible without shouting, and I can hear myself, high above the clinking masts in the harbor, above the train engine—"that my mother killed Cecily, or anyone. I don't know what happened, but I know that much." I sling my bag over my shoulder.

"Hey—" she begins. "That's just what they say. I'm just saying—"

"No," I interrupt. "Let's not go into it again, OK? I think I'm going to get on, now. See you around then. Thanks for—" I don't know what to thank her for, but since I've started I think I'd better finish. "Er—thanks for sharing the taxi fare with me."

Octavia nods back—what else can she do?—and says, "No problem."

I don't look back at her as I walk towards the train. I pray I don't bump into her again, but I'm pretty sure she'll steer clear of me this time. She thinks she's done me a favor. That's what upsets me most of all. Pointed out how stupid I've been.

In the summer the buffet car is always full; people arrive as early as possible to get a seat so they're not shut into their cabins, which are initially cute but soon become claustrophobic. In winter, the car is nearly empty, and after I have dumped my bag in the single-bed cabin and admired the free set of toiletries, I settle down into one of the single seats by the window, with a table and a lamp, and put my bag in front of me. I look around hastily again, but Octavia hasn't appeared. The diary pages are still in my pocket. I sit there, and the train pulls slowly away from the station, and I don't know what to feel.

There's a *Times* on the opposite seat—the guard obviously missed it—and I pick it up. I order some tea and biscuits, even though I'm not hungry, and I start reading the paper. The news absorbs me. I read about a cabinet plot to oust the prime minister, the flooding all over the country, the travails of a minor sportsman and his "celebrity" wife, what's happening in a reality TV show, which MP has tried to claim an antique rug on expenses. I feel as if I've been away for a long time, and I am gathering information to piece myself back together, bit by bit.

I know before I turn the page to the Obituaries section that I will see a photo of my grandmother, scarf in her hair, a broad smile curling over her perfect teeth, brush in hand, a mug of tea and painting paraphernalia—palette, brushes, rags, turps—cluttered around her, in the studio I was standing in over an hour ago. It looks completely different, crammed with canvases, postcards stuck on the walls, pot plants, a gramophone.

Something catches in my throat. She is smiling out at me. It's like Cecily's face, shining out of the drawer.

Frances Seymour

Highly acclaimed observer of Cornish landscape who never painted after 1963

Frances Seymour, who has died at the age of eighty-nine, was what one would call a star. Not for her the flamboyance, the tantrums and temperamentality, clichés of the artist: she was universally beloved, charismatic and beautiful, a magnet for men and women alike; her house, the beautiful Summercove near Treen in Cornwall, open to all and a haven for friends and family. She lit up every room she was in and her company was a rare gift.

Because of her charm and force of personality it is easy to forget, therefore, the gap Seymour created when she abandoned painting after the death of her youngest daughter Cecily, in a tragic accident. Frances never forgave herself for her daughter's death, and some have speculated this was her form of penance, for the events of that summer in 1963. This is not established. What it is important to

establish, however, is the role Frances Seymour played before that
in sealing the reputation of British painting in the mid–twentieth
century.

Frances Seymour was not a Cornish painter, or a female painter.
She was simply one of the most talented artists of the last century.

This was my grandmother, I want to shout. I want to wave the
paper out of the window, like the kind old gentleman in *The Railway Children*. Look how clever she was, how brilliant!

Tears come to my eyes, and I'm crying, I can't help it. I don't
understand anything anymore. I keep hearing Octavia's voice, and
when I close my eyes I can see her large gray eyes, her pointy noise,
looming at me in the dark, as she oh-so-carefully stabs my mother in
the back, over and over again. I want to hate her, to laugh at her, but
I can't. I ask myself why I can't.

Because, despite what I said to her only an hour before, I'm terrified that she's right.

I look out of the window, as if I expect to see someone's face
there. We have been going fast, through a blur of nondescript-
looking villages, but suddenly it is dark, a landscape with no lights
at all. I can see my own reflection in the window, nothing more. My
neck and the newspaper are both startlingly white against the blackness outside, the blackness of my coat and dress. I stare at myself; I
can't see the tears; I look like a ghost. In the black and white of the
light, I look like Cecily.

Carefully, I tear the obituary out of the paper and fold it. The
tearing sound is loud, and the couple at the table next to me look
up, curiously. I stand up and smile, backing away towards my room
and when I get there, I fall onto the familiar old scratchy blue
blanket and the smooth white sheets. I take the pages out of my
pocket and sit on the lower bunk, holding them in my hand, gazing
at them, at the scrawling black handwriting, my finger and thumb
poised to turn the first page. I close my eyes.

And now I can see myself, suddenly, back at Summercove. There are voices I recognize, but they're different somehow, thinner, higher. Bright sunshine is streaming into the living room, the smell of sea and grass and something else, something dangerous, almost tangible, rushing towards me. . . . And Cecily's face, as it was in the oil sketch. *Come with me! Come with me*, she is saying. And I do. I take a deep breath and I follow her, down to the sea.

The Diary of Cecily Kapoor, age fifteen.
July, 1963

St. Katherine's School for Girls
Denmouth
Devon
England

IF LOST PLEASE RETURN

Saturday, 20th July 1963

Dear Diary,

First day of holidays. That is — count it, my dears, count it —
SEVEN WEEKS of blissful beautiful no school!!!!
My summer project starts NOW.

I am writing this sitting on my bed at Summercove. On the
patchwork quilt Mary sewed me when we first moved here and I was
scared at night. One of Mummy's sketches is on the wall, of our little
cove down on the beach. There is a cupboard for our clothes built into the
wall with sweet little plastic handles dotted with stars. What else? There
are two shelves painted white with all my books on them (I share this
room with my sister Miranda. But she only reads Honey magazine).
I have everything from <u>My Friend Flicka</u> to <u>Pride & Prejudice</u> &
they are all mine.

Today is the first proper day of the holidays. I got home yesterday.
I love the luxury of the beginning of the hols, where time seems to stretch
out before you, for ages & ages. We go back 8th Sept. It seems a
lifetime away.

I have never kept a diary before. Two days ago, the last day of
classes, Miss Powell gave everyone in our class ten pages of paper, tied
together with string and our names on, and told us to keep a record of
our summer holidays: she said to write down what we did, who we saw,
and what happens. Everyone groaned when Miss Powell said it, but I
was glad. I want to be a writer when I grow up & this is good practice.

No one else was that excited about it, only me really. Annabel
Taylor, who can barely write in joined-up writing, looked completely
appalled. I have laid a wager with myself. It is that she will write 2
pages over the summer, and those will be about the boys she knows.

(that is not very nice of me.)

Miss Powell says she will not look at our diaries herself, but she
wants us to read some sections out to the rest of the class when we come
back in the autumn. She says, in years to come, we will find them and
read them and remember the summer of 1963. She says it is a year we
will want to remember. I thought she meant because of Mr. Profumo
and the scandal. We're <u>absolutely</u> not allowed to talk about it at school.
Still, I hoped she might mention it. She just said something instead
about the wind of change blowing. I like Miss Powell. She is younger
than most of the teachers, and she has fantastic cropped hair, and she
likes <u>Bonjour Tristesse</u>. Rita dies for Miss Powell, she cries about
her at night. Anyone's better than Miss Gilchrist, say I. Awful woman
with meaty hands, I'm sure she used to be in prison. Miss Powell isn't
like that.

Anyway, enough of silly school. It's hard sometimes, to get back
into the swing of life here after being away at St. Kat's for months on
end. One's head is full of drear things like plimsolls and kit bags and
hymnals. I'm back now. It's over! (for a while).

So what shall I tell you, diary? I shall start by describing where I am
and what's happening.

It is after tea & the house is quiet, but there are sounds, all dear
& familiar to me after months at school. Mary is in the kitchen,
cooking supper; I can hear her feet on the floor & the pans clattering.

Dad is humming in his study. It sounds like wasps, buzzing.
Dad is a famous sort of writer. He wrote a book people always
want to talk about, called <u>The Modern Fortress.</u> I haven't read it.
But lots of people have. It is an IMPORTANT BOOK.
Miss Green, our headmistress, said that to me last year.
"IMPORTANT BOOK CECILY." That means she
hasn't read it, I absolutely bet.

(must be kind & what if they do read it even though they said they
wouldn't?)

My cousins Louisa & Jeremy arrived today. They are playing with Claude, our dog, on the lawn. Louisa is wearing a beautiful striped bathing costume, I covet it. She has a new lipstick and she is terribly pleased with herself, for she has been offered a scholarship to Girton, and she is dreadfully ambitious and clever. Jeremy is at medical school in London. Jeremy is my favorite cousin, there are only two of them that I know, I don't know my cousins in Lahore, in Pakistan, but perhaps I would like them more than Jeremy. I doubt it. He's awfully nice.

Jeremy has been for a swim & carried the table outside for supper after the rain. That's enough about them for the moment.

My sister & brother (Archie & Miranda other way round) are gossiping in their secret annoying way, about who knows what as they walk round the edge of the lawn together, like Jane Austen heroines taking a turn about the garden. They are twins, 2 yrs older than me. They have just finished at school. Though Archie is staying on an extra term, to do the exam for Oxford and Cambridge, he says he won't go. Miranda is not doing that exam. She is not doing anything.

~~They are strange, the twins. I am not sure if~~

My hand hurts already. But I must go on!

Finally Mummy. Mummy is painting. She is in her studio, down at the end of the corridor. She is a famous painter. "Famous painter" — I am not sure if that is a good thing or not, but it is how she is always referred to by people. <u>The Picture Post</u> did a spread on us a couple of years ago. "Famous Painter at Home with her Family." As if her fame is as important as her painting. I wonder if it annoys her. Mummy has an exhibition this autumn & she is making me sit for a portrait. I don't like sitting for her except we talk, which I like. I sat for her this morning. The exhibition is soon & she is painting furiously, she is behind. She is short with Dad, but he doesn't notice. She smokes & looks out of the window a lot, & I hear her pacing up & down in the studio when I'm in my room. She's doing it now.

Anyway, I will write more about them all I am sure. We are to be joined in a few days by Frank and Guy Leighton, Frank is a schoolfriend of Jeremy's & he is Louisa's boyfriend. Guy is his brother. Mummy loves having people down. I do too, it's more fun when there are more around.

There are so many things I want to read & see & do, so many thoughts I keep having. I want to write it all down, to experience things I haven't (please excuse me Diary, I will try & write as much as possible). I want to broaden my mind, & summer holidays are the time to do something about this, & I undertake it in earnest. I shall read the papers & comment on them so this diary is also a well-informed record of the times.

For example, I was interested to see that the memorial service of the Rev. Cuthbert Creighton took place yesterday near Worcester, & that Miss BP Hards (that is a funny name) has got engaged. Also that the Duke of Edinburgh will be attending a lunch of the Heating & Ventilation Engineers next Tuesday at Grosvenor House in London.

The bell for dinner has not gone yet. So here is some more information, this time about me.

Name: Cecily Ann Kapoor
Age: 15 (16 in November)
School: St. Katherine's School for Girls
Favorite Subjects: English!, Drama, Art, History, Latin.
Best Friends: Margaret, Jennifer, Rita. (NB: I should like Linda Langley to also be my friend but she is not, as she is the year above.)
Favourite Teacher: Miss Powell
Favourite Book: Bonjour Tristesse, Françoise Sagan
Favourite Poem: The Prisoner, by Emily Brontë
Favourite actress: Kay Kendall RIP. Jean Seberg in Bonjour Tristesse the film. I want my hair cut short like hers, so chic & gamine but Mummy says NO.
Favourite actor: Stewart Granger in Moonfleet, SWOON! Gregory Peck in To Kill a Mockingbird DOUBLE SWOON, also Dirk Bogarde & Rock Hudson.

Favourite film: It used to be <u>Moonfleet</u> but it's a bit babyish for me now. <u>Bonjour Tristesse</u>, I LOVE that film, & the book, it is all so ~~chic~~ glamorous. And <u>To Kill a Mockingbird</u>, which is a marvelous & extremely wonderful evocation of the Deep South & its problems.

Favourite song: NOT The Beatles, everyone likes them & it's so dull! Miranda & Louisa practically weep every time they come on the radio. They play "Please Please Me" <u>every day</u> on the gramophone. They only like them because they are boys & from Liverpool ie <u>dangerous</u>, according to my Aunt Pamela, Louisa's mother, but she thinks the bin man on her road is a dangerous communist because she once saw him reading <u>the Tribune</u>. Miranda & Louisa are silly when it comes to BOYS anyway. I don't like boys (apart from Gregory Peck & Stewart Granger & they are men). I am concentrating on becoming an interesting & accomplished person because one day I want to be a writer & writers don't become writers by sitting around listening to Please pleaseZZZZZZZZZ me. Or Frank Ifield. Can you believe it, Louisa actually has an album by Frank Ifield. ZZZZZZZZZZZ again.

Anyway my favourite song & album is Juliette Greco. I also like the Four Seasons, & the Beach Boys. She is French, they are American, & I like that, it is something different. Not boring old England, all the time. Sometimes you would think it was the only country in the world.

Other interesting things about me: My father is from what is now Pakistan. My skin is darker than the other girls at school & so I don't need to lie in the sun to tan, which is good. Some of the girls like Annabel Taylor make me feel awful about it & say nasty things, I wish they wouldn't, I am as English as them. Mrs. Charles, the Deputy Head, called me a clumsy little wog when she was cross after I dropped all the blackboard dusters & made chalk cloud fly in her face & make her cough. I asked Archie what it meant & he was very cross with me.

Dear diary, the truth is I really don't like writing about this, but they are worse to Miranda, her skin is darker than mine. I feel sorry for her but I don't tell her, she gets cross. We are the only girls like it in our school. Dad came with Mum to drop us off last year & I don't know why he did, he barely knows we exist. I shouldn't say this diary but

I was embarrassed of him. He is small & quite eccentric & doesn't make sense when he talks, because he talks in riddles. Even though he is a famous writer, the girls at school don't know that, or at least they don't care. I wish they did, but they don't.

Thank god for Mummy. She looks like a film star, always has done. She is very beautiful, I'm sure Miranda & I are a sad disappointment to all who gaze upon our visages. Mummy has "it" — I don't know what "it" is, but she can put on her overalls or an old shirt & look stunning. I just look like a boy.

No dinner bell yet, what's going on? I'm ravenous.

Sometimes I wonder about where Dad came from too, I imagine palaces made of gold & the burning heat & markets with silk & exotic foods, like in <u>The Horse & His Boy</u> by C. S. Lewis. Dad says it is a bit like that but not really. He is from Lahore. It is a fortress town, Akbar lived there, he was one of the greatest Indian rulers, we did him in school & I could say that was where Dad came from. It was in the Punjab, now it is in Pakistan. It is because India is not ours anymore. I love the idea of it, the Mughal emperors & the forts & bazaars. I want to go to India. I will one day, when I am grown up & a famous writer. I shall have a scarf from Liberty, & smoke those Russian cigarettes, and do my hair like Juliette Greco —

We have been called for supper, I must go. I have been writing for well over an hour, it is nearly seven & my left hand hurts, a LOT.

I will add my exercises after I have done them tonight.

Bust exercises: 30
Nose-squashing exercises: 5 mins.

Love always, Cecily

Sunday, 21st July, 1963

Dear Diary,

After yesterday's writing marathon my hand STILL hurts so I will
be brief. I feel we have made a good start. It is lovely being home but it
is funny how the things you forgot about that are always there start to
come back after a few days. It is even funnier, reading them as you write
them down. Perhaps I shouldn't, but if I didn't record what happens and
what I think about my family I wouldn't be being truthful, would I?

I was out all day at the beach & then went for a long walk with
Jeremy to Logan's Rock. Very tired now. We talked about his walking
holiday in Switzerland, it sounds most interesting. I tried to sound
like an interesting person back, but I have never really been anywhere
and done anything, and it's hard. I expect Jeremy is all the time with
wonderful, interesting girls up in London. I rather hate to think about it.

Had another sitting with Mummy this morning. We are in her
studio, I never go in there so it's interesting only from that point of
view. It's very white & quiet & she wasn't like my mother when we were
in there. I can't explain it. She is much more . . . <u>definite</u>. Tells me how
to sit & what to do. Doesn't care I'm her daughter. She asks questions
to be polite, like Sandra, the hairdresser we go to in Penzance. It is
uncomfortable after a while, staying still like that. I like it because I get
to wear the ring I love so much round a chain on my neck. It is Mum's
ring, she let me take it to school last year and look after it. She says I
can have it one day, if I'm good.

The only thing I should record is that Mummy kept asking about
Miranda. If there was anything I thought we could do about her that
we weren't doing, as she has left school & has nothing in sight. I don't
know what to say as it's been decided that Miranda is a "problem."
By Mummy. (I don't think Dad has noticed any of us is actually
back from school, let alone that M has actually finished school & needs
something to do). They think she ought to know what she's doing, but
to be fair to Miranda they've never asked her before, I don't know

why they're worried about it now. I said they should make her join the French Foreign Legion. Mummy didn't laugh.

She plays jazz up there, Chet Baker & John Coltrane & she smokes while she paints, which is strange because she doesn't anywhere else. And she is different. I can't explain it.

Very tired & not making awful lot of sense so going to bed or as Jeremy always says, Off to Bedfordshire. Oh Jeremy. xxx

Bust exercises: 5

Must try harder with this & all things. Tomorrow!

Love always, Cecily

Monday, 22nd July 1963

My dearest Diary,

I hate Miranda. Sometimes I think I would like to smash her face in, carve my nails down her skin till it bleeds. She is ugly & nasty & I HATE HER. She makes me feel stupid and tries to make me look like a baby. She is the stupid one. I HATE her. Today, she stuck a leg out while I was coming back from my bath, just because I told her what Mummy had said yesterday. I was trying to help! I tripped over, and fell in a sprawl on the floor, & she just sat on the bed and laughed at me, and then called me a baby for crying. She is always saying I'm a baby for my age. I'm not, I'M NOT. I'm just not a vamp like she is.

Oh thinking about her puts me in such a bad mood. She makes me not like our family, or being here, she makes it all rotten. She doesn't like it here. She hates the holidays. She wants to leave home and go to London. Well I wish she would.

Anyway.

I left off my proper favourite book off my list. It is very important. Emily Brontë is amazing. This summer term, we read <u>Wuthering Heights</u> at school. It is a most wonderful novel, full of insight into that most miraculous of emotions — that of <u>human love</u>. (I must say though, if I met Heathcliff I would just hide in a cupboard. He is frightening). The story is terribly, terribly sad, & I felt, when he saw her lifeless, dead body, that I should cry so much my heart would break.

It's much better than <u>Jane Eyre</u>, I thought Mr. Rochester was boring & I wanted more descriptions of how the first Mrs. Rochester drooled & everything.

After my bust-up with Miranda I didn't do very much today, swam by the sea & read, sat for Mummy again. We talked about our favourite films. She loves Gregory Peck too. It was a bit better today but she still snapped at me when I scratched my arm and goodness gracious me, I'm allowed to scratch my arm, aren't I?

We had jam roll for tea today which was delicious. I read about the autumn fashions in the papers outside while the others went swimming. I do not want to wear a hat shaped like a cone, whatever anyone says. Miranda has some nice clothes this summer. I don't know where she got them from, but she's started trying them on in our room. Mummy hasn't noticed yet, but she will. It's funny. They're expensive, and they're grown-up, and they . . . I think they suit her. Miranda gets them out when she thinks I'm not looking. Where did she get them from? There's a black gros-grain dress I am particularly in love with, she's hung it at the back of our wardrobe but she keeps opening it to stare at it. She is pretty stupid.

Yesterday was the sixth Sunday after Trinity. I wish it wasn't like this anymore. I am starting to think everyone is in an awful mood this summer, apart from Jeremy.

Bust exercises: 45!
Nose-squashing exercises: 5 mins.

Love always, Cecily

Tuesday, 23rd July 1963

Dear Diary,

I fear I did not make a good beginning to this journal. There is too much silliness and feeling sorry for oneself in it. I need to show everyone eg Miss Powell, Jeremy, Miranda, & others that I am a grown-up young woman, because sadly <u>some</u> people still treat me like I am five years old and when I am dead & they read this I want them to know how wrong they were.

It is a bit like that at our school, but not as bad, because everyone is nearly the same age. I don't actually mind school, Miranda hates it. I like English, Drama, & History. Also I can't wait to see Miss Powell again in September because she treats you like a person. However I am also dreading having to listen to awful Annabel Taylor's descriptions of her ghastly family's holiday in St. Tropez or wherever it will be. She is such a show-off. Miss Powell says one should never advertise one's wealth or status & I agree. I don't go around school boasting that my father is an OBE & writes extremely important books, & lectures at the Sorbonne, & that my mother has had an exhibition at the Royal Academy in London, do I? No, I do not. AT is so vulgar too. What matters to her is how blonde your hair is, or whether you have a tennis court at home & are allowed to drink champagne by your family. She calls me & Miranda names too, because of the fact our skin is darker than hers. She has thick, dark blonde, beautiful hair & huge green eyes with thick, black lashes & pink cheeks & sweet little freckles, it's fine for her at a school like ours.

AT really is horrible. I shall refer to her as 21 (A is 1st letter of alphabet, T is 20th, add them together) through the rest of this diary, bc I can't bear to write her name.

And there is a secret about her & Miranda & even though we row terribly, the Kapoor sisters do stick together about some things:

Miranda is in awful trouble because of 21. Mummy & Dad
don't know it, but Miranda nearly got expelled this term because
of 21. She lost her temper with her, two weeks before we broke up.
Miranda was changing the water for the flowers, it was her turn.
We had just heard from Mummy in a letter that these two strange
boys would be coming to stay at Summercove & we were giggling about
them, talking about the holidays, for once having a good old chat.
"Maybe one of us will marry one of them and be very rich & have
lots of children," Miranda said. 21 walked past & heard Miranda.
She called her a horrible name again & said her children would be like
monkeys. Out of the blue.

Well Miranda just went potty. It was so strange. She said, "I've
had enough, I've had enough." She put her (21's) head in a desk &
banged it up & down on her, so hard I honestly thought 21's skull would
crack & her brains spill out onto the floor. 21 was screaming, "Stop it,
stop it!!" & Miranda just kept shouting, "I don't care, I don't care!"
& her teeth were gritted in between speaking. Her eyes were huge, she
was flushed, she almost looked like she was enjoying it. 21 had to stay
with the nurse for the night. She had bruises on her cheekbones for
weeks. And ringing in her ears.

Miss Stephens, the headmistress, had Miranda in her office
for ages. She was going to be expelled, I was sure of it. They said
they were going to send M home early but she somehow persuaded
Miss Stephens not to. I will never know what she said or how she did
it. 21 never bothered her again, she didn't like people knowing she'd got
beaten up like that.

I don't like thinking about it much, because it scares me. I am glad
she did something, I was proud of her in a very strange way. But
Miranda scares me, if I'm honest. She has a weird streak. Vicious.
And I can say it here but I do think she & Archie are strange, they
look like me, but I don't get them.

When Mum was upstairs working this afternoon I went into the
living room & read the <u>Times</u> with no one looking, because I knew

from Archie & Jeremy talking about it at breakfast that something juicy was happening in the Profumo Scandal case & I am very curious.

This is the trial of Dr Stephen Ward, who they say caused the whole thing. Well I must say I hope I am a broad-minded young person but good grief. It uses the word "intercourse" ten times. Every time they ask Christine Keeler if she had intercourse with someone, the answer is always "yes." I'm not even sure what that means, I think sex, but the whole way or just a part of sex? (feels weird to write that word). . . . Darling diary, I wish you could tell me. Dinah Collins at our school has had sex with her boyfriend, in his car at Christmas. She is such a slut. No one talked to her for all of the spring term when they found out. I don't know why. I wanted to ask her what it was like, does it hurt, isn't it embarrassing? It seems such a strange thing to do, when you think about it. People walk along the streets all smart & suave wearing new suits & yet they do <u>that</u> in the evenings with each other. . . . I don't understand it.

My hand hurts! I have been writing for an hour. The bump on my finger from writing in exam time is coming back. I feel very virtuous. It is supper soon & I should go & change, or at least comb my hair. We are having fish pie for supper; Dad says that's stupid in July & we should float the pie back out to sea where it belongs.

Bust exercises: 25
Nose-squashing exercises: 10 mins.

Love always, Cecily

Wednesday, 24th July 1963

My Darling diary,

I reread what I have written so far of this diary once again, & once again it makes me want to blush. I am a horrible person with a base mind. Also, I don't hate Miranda. Well, some of the time I do. She is just a bit difficult sometimes. She doesn't really have a weird vicious streak. I was going to tear these pages out & burn them, but I want to be a writer & you have to be truthful. So I will keep them, to remind myself, & then burn them maybe later, because GOSH I WOULD DIE if eg Jeremy knew I loved him or what I have been thinking about. I have nearly filled up these pages. I don't want to stop now. The boys haven't arrived yet and I want to write about them too. It's exciting. I must get an exercise book from Penzance so I can carry on writing for the rest of the summer.

President Kennedy has signed a nuclear test-ban treaty & he has promised to change the US immigration laws — but I don't know how, I only read the headline because Archie took the paper. I like President Kennedy, & he looks a bit like Jeremy though he is not as handsome as Jeremy (though he is still handsome).

I want to be a better person than I am. I want to look better too. I am so ugly, my nose is too big. I spent a long time in the bathroom yesterday doing my exercises: I squash my nose down so it doesn't stick out as much. I don't know if it works, like doing "I must increase my bust" fifty times a day, but I am doing them in case. It is awful to have a small bust. I hate it. Mummy says it will grow, but I hate talking about all that with her. She always wants to, & she is always wanting to have convs. about being a "woman," it makes me want to be sick. Sometimes I think I am a disappointment to her; I don't ever know what Mummy wants.

Anyway, today I said please could this painting be the last time I sit for you. She said, "Why?" I said, "Sorry Mummy I just don't like it very much." She was quite cross. Miss Powell says women should stand alone & fend for themselves, like Elizabeth I, but I'm not good at saying to Mummy what I want. Mummy can stand alone & fend for herself though that's for sure. "Though I have the body of a weak & feeble woman, I have the heart of a king, & a king of England too." Miss P made us declaim this at school this summer. I absolutely love it. Here are my top-ten list of favourite pieces to read out loud:

10. "Make me a willow cabin at your gate" from 12th Night
9.
8.
7.

Thursday, 25th July 1963

Dear diary,

Sorry I was called for tea & then we played games. I will finish the list soon.

Today was a funny day. Frank and Guy Leighton are here now and everything feels different. I don't know why. Because I feel confused. Louisa said something on the way to Penzance to get them. She said my brother is a peeping Tom. He watches her get undressed. I'm sure it's not true. It's disgusting if it is true. I don't know. . . .

But I am racing ahead and I should tell the day as it happened. In the morning I sat for Mummy & we talked about Profumo. I went into Penzance with Louisa and Jeremy, to pick the boys up. And I bought a new exercise book from Boots, so I can write as much as I please, which is good, I'm on the last page as you see!

Silly Cecily. Perhaps this holiday is going to be all right after all, I am glad that the others are here now anyway. Help — I am about to run out of space! I have written far too much already. Now I transfer to my beautiful new bk and I can carry on from there

Love always, Cecily

Part Two

July 1963

Twelve

"So, what time does Louisa's new *boyfriend* get here?"

"He's not my boyfriend, shut up, Cecily."

"He is! You're going to kiss him on the lips! And Miranda's never kissed anyone before. Doesn't that make you feel sick with envy, Miranda?"

"Honestly, Cecily, you're such a baby. You're fifteen. When are you going to grow up?"

"Poor Wardy. It doesn't look good for him. Filthy old bugger. I say, Archie, have you read this morning's *Times*?"

"I went straight to that page, naturally. I must say, she's a real goer, that Keeler girl. No better than . . . Well, anyway. Fruity stuff, isn't it?"

"You're disgusting, Archie."

"Louisa, don't talk about my brother like that."

"I will. He's completely disgusting, and he knows why."

"Why, what do you mean? What's fruity?"

A melodious voice spoke from the end of the table. "Jeremy, Archie, please. Not at breakfast."

"Sorry, Franty. It's nothing, Cec. Have you got the lime marmalade? Jolly nice stuff, Franty."

"Thank you, Jeremy."

I'm going to scream. I'm going to scream. Yes, I am.

Frances Seymour looked around the room, trying to keep calm.

Lately, the old feeling had started to come back. She had kept it at bay for many years now, she had thought the house in Cornwall was the answer, but increasingly it was as if she was not in control: of her children, of her home, of her own mind. She wished she were anywhere but here, presiding over breakfast with this loud, mucky troupe of young people, being the grown-up, sensible one. It was wrong.

There was a lot on. Too much, perhaps. She had a portrait of her youngest daughter, Cecily, to finish, for a big upcoming show in London. She had three teenagers of her own, two more staying with her, and two more on their way at this very minute, as well as a husband who didn't care whether you looked after him or not; she had once found Arvind absentmindedly chewing a piece of paper, and when she'd asked him why he'd said, vaguely, "I was hungry. I thought I would try the paper. I don't need it anymore."

The neighbors had just arrived for the summer, she should visit them, and the damn church fete was the week after, and Mary kept asking her what she wanted her to make. Didn't the woman realize she didn't care? She simply didn't bloody care?

Frances pressed a cool hand to her forehead. Then the Mitchells were coming to stay the week after, she'd have to get a fun crowd up for them, lots of booze in, Eliza needed constant entertaining and young men to look at. The crowds were descending: only a few days before the children came back from school, she'd just said goodbye to a huge party—some old friends from art college, Arvind's publisher, and two couples from the old Redcliffe Square days. She loved entertaining, loved seeing old faces, loved the praise, the company, the conversation, the stimulation—Frances had to be stimulated in order to be able to paint. She couldn't do it unless there was something burning within her, stoking her thoughts, firing her up.

And yet daily life had to go on too, and she was the one who made it go on. There was Cecily and Miranda's room to turn out—Cecily had grown so fast this last term, there was plenty the charity shop could have. She needed to take them both into Penzance, or maybe even Exeter, to get some new clothes; Mary never got it right. Cecily could have Miranda's cast-offs, but Frances, a younger child herself, always thought it was unfair she never had anything new, she deserved a party frock of her own, some shorts, a few summer shirts.

She frowned again and looked at Miranda, wondering where she'd got that rather nice cream linen top she was wearing; had she seen that before? It suited her; that in itself was unusual, Frances thought, and then felt guilty.

I don't care about their damn clothes.

There had been a time when she had worn new clothes, put her hair up, slipped into satin heels, nursed a glass of champagne as she laughed with handsome young men at the Chelsea Arts Club, or drank long into the night in some underground shelter, thick with cigarette smoke. There had been a time when she was young, desirable, with the world at her feet, and now . . . She sighed. She had become staid. Boring. *Ordinary.* A staid wife and mother of three, a painter of staid, boring, repetitive landscapes. And so the old, furtive unrest was beginning to creep over her again.

"Leave me *alone!*" Miranda squawked loudly. Frances looked up, startled, as Cecily smirked in triumph at some childishly won point and Miranda slumped back down against the high-backed dining chair. Across the table, Arvind carried on eating his kipper, staring into space as if he were alone.

Frances smiled at him, but he didn't see. He never saw. That was one of the things for which she had always loved him. Arvind wasn't suspicious. He wasn't trusting either. He was just in another world most of the time, and they worked well together because of it. Frances could still remember the first time she saw him, at that concert in the National Gallery, quiet and neat in his tweeds, impervious to everything else around him except the music, his short frame tensing at the swelling rhythm of the piano. She had smiled slowly at him, but he had focused shortly on her and then back on the music again, looking straight through her as if she weren't there. In years to come, Frances would always wonder if that was when she was hooked: he'd looked past her, not at her. She wasn't used to that.

She watched him now, her gaze flicking from him to their son, Archie, a young Louis Jourdan: beautifully turned out, his hair carefully combed, his shirt immaculate. He made her uneasy though. She didn't . . . what was it? She didn't trust him? Her own son? He was peeling his apple, oh so precisely, with a small knife, looking as if butter wouldn't melt. There was something going on behind that charming smile; Frances didn't know what. Why was Louisa so furious with him? What had he done this time? Was it the old problem again? Or was it he and Miranda, up to mischief?

Miranda—Frances sighed. Miranda was being particularly vile at the moment, and she didn't know what to do. She never knew what to do with her.

She had been such a cross baby. She was thin and fed badly, a tiny, hairy thing, feet turned outwards, like a little monkey, her expression always stormy, and from the moment she could walk her posture was almost comical in its teenager-gait: defensive, shoulders hunched, eyes glaring, and, years later, she had barely changed at all. The funny thing was that Frances, with her painter's eye, could see that Miranda had an idiosyncratic kind of beauty all her own. She was gamine, boyish, her eyes were startlingly intense, and her dark, beautiful skin glowed. When she laughed her face lit up, but she seldom did, except with her twin, Archie.

Since Miranda had got back from her final term at school she'd been even worse than usual, Frances thought. She had no plans, unlike Archie who was staying on at school for an extra term to take his Oxbridge exams. Miranda was trying to drag him down, Frances knew it. She had taken A-levels, but wasn't expected to make any mark on them. She was always saying how much she loved clothes, and fabrics—Frances was sure it was true, but to what end? That wasn't a *job*. The one thing Miranda had expressed any interest in, only the day before, was a finishing school in Switzerland. Should they send her off again, pay some elite establishment to round off her rough edges a bit? She could certainly benefit from it, but Frances loathed the idea, it was so . . . oh, just ghastly. So suburban!

Frances knew her mind wasn't fully on the twins and it should be. When the show was over, then she'd have more time to think, be a better mother, think about what to do with them both. Soon.

Her eyes drifted round the room, to where her niece and nephew sat at the other end of the table. She stared at them, helplessly; it was unsettling to her, how much they looked like her, like her sister, like their parents. Her own children were Arvind's children—dark, intense, complicated—and they were moody. Arvind wasn't moody, neither was she, where did they get it from? Cecily aside, she often thought she could see nothing of herself in her children. But Louisa and Jeremy were blooming, hearty, firm, and lithe, like adverts on the side of packets of Force cereal.

Her head buzzing, Frances looked at her watch; it was after nine-thirty. She got up. "I'm going up to the studio." She looked at Miranda. "Darling, can you make sure the table's cleared?"

"Oh, why *me*?" Miranda sank down into her chair, scowling. "I was going to go to the beach."

"Because it's your turn. And besides, the others are going into Penzance," Frances said, trying not to scream. But giving two reasons with Miranda was always a mistake. "Get Archie to give you a hand."

"Why can't Louisa?"

"As I said, Louisa is going into Penzance." A great weariness swept over her. "Oh, my God. I don't care," Frances said crossly, turning away from the table. "Tell Mary to save me some chicken salad for lunch."

"Do you want someone to bring you up a tray?" Louisa said, collecting up the plates and putting them on the sideboard. Frances turned to her gratefully. "Yes," she said. "That would be lovely. Come on, Cecily." She looked at her youngest. "Off we go."

"Oh, *no*," Cecily said, slumping against the wall. "Please, Mummy, do I *really* have to?"

Frances shut her eyes, briefly, blinking hard. "Don't you want to?"

Cecily chewed her nail. "Well, you know. It's so boring, just sitting there for ages and ages, and it's *so hot* in your studio. I think I'll *die* sometimes, and you don't even care."

"No," Frances said. "I simply could not care less if you dropped dead in the studio because of heatstroke. It would not matter to me one iota." She batted her daughter lightly on the rear. "Come on, Cec. We're nearly there."

"Oh, but I wanted to go to *Penzance*!" Cecily said. "I want to meet Louisa's boyfriend!"

"You'll meet him at lunch," Frances said. "Come on."

Cecily's expressive eyes filled with tears, and her dark bobbed hair fell into her face. "But I have to get my new book out of the library and get a new exercise book from Boots—I want to spend my pocket money, Mum, you said I could buy that. I need it for the rest of my diary, I've nearly run out of space. Miss Powell says . . ."

At the mention of the sainted Miss Powell, Frances, wanting to scream, gave in. "They're not leaving for a while. Come up till then. Louisa will fetch you." Cecily jumped up, her eyes shining. "Is that all right with you, Louisa?"

"Yes, of course, there's room for her," Louisa said. She cleared her throat and said, going rather pink, "Aunt Frances, I hope I've said it already, but thank—thank you for having Frank and Guy to stay. It's awfully kind of you."

It must be easy, being Louisa, Frances thought, looking at her niece. Or pleasant, at least. A classic English rose, huge blue eyes, flaxen blonde hair, endless legs, and a big smile. Virtually guaranteed a place at Cambridge, wealthy parents, and a young, handsome boyfriend, son of an old family friend. All so correct and proper. Frances often thought Louisa was like the heroine from a novel. *Emma,* maybe. What a nice life. Purposeful. Hearty. Rooted in tradition. She thought back to herself at that age, eighteen and on her way to London. She smiled. She'd worked as hard as she could to *not* be like that, to throw off the shackles of this boring, complacent, English way of being. Sometimes she wished, however, she could be content with a life like Louisa's. Without the need to . . . feel, whatever it might be, danger, sadness, happiness. Without the need to feel everything, all the time. What was it? Frances didn't know, she only knew she had to keep it to herself.

"Our pleasure," Frances said, smiling at her. Out of the corner of her eye through the French windows she saw Arvind walking across the lawn. He was holding a jar of lime marmalade and talking to himself.

She was enjoying her sessions with Cecily, more than she cared to admit. Normally, Frances saw sittings as a chore: you had to do them to get the result you wanted, but it was tiresome, having to put the subject at ease. She was used to painting the landscape, marveling at the ways it could change, rather than getting someone to sit still for an hour.

But this was different. She loved talking to her younger daughter. Cecily's mind was like a waterfall, endlessly bubbling over with new ideas and thoughts and she had no filter, no sense that something was wrong or right. One day, she would be cured of this, be more self-conscious but for now, Frances loved it. Cecily was like her father in that respect: an original thinker, untrammeled by popular opinion. She was refreshingly, blessedly unlike her sister, in temperament, in ambition, and in looks.

This morning, they talked about the news. Cecily always wanted to talk about the trial of Stephen Ward. It seemed as if it was playing out, with hitherto unseen levels of lurid detail, as near-perfect summer entertainment for the whole country.

"What's he done wrong, is what I want to know? He just introduced the girls to Mr. Profumo. He's not the one who's . . . met with the girls and done all those things, is he? It's Mr. Profumo who did that. And he lied to Parliament, and he's not even on trial. And—" Cecily's voice lowered—"Mr. Profumo was *married*!"

Frances, seated at her easel, smiled. The sun was flooding through the large windows into the white room, illuminating her daughter's face and casting it into shadow as she talked. She'd long wanted to capture Cecily's mercurial quality, however fleeting.

"Cec, stay still for me, darling, just a few moments," she said. "Stephen Ward is a . . . scapegoat, I think. They accuse him of living off immoral earnings—don't move! That means making money out of girls who are prostitutes. Stay still."

"Well, he doesn't sound like a particularly sound fellow to me, I must say," Cecily said. "Very odd way to behave."

Frances laughed lightly. "How very censorious you are, Miss Kapoor!" She felt her heart beating fast; Cecily was so innocent in so many ways, had no idea what grown-ups could be like. When she thought of herself at that age, she wanted to laugh. "I simply don't think he's as guilty as they're making him out to be. Profumo, too—it's all a big storm in a teacup, really." She looked again. "Stay like that. Just a while longer, please."

They were silent for a few moments. Outside, the faint sound of the sea crashing on the rocks beneath the house, and desultory conversation between Miranda and Archie outside on the terrace. Inside, people were moving about the house, and Frances could hear humming. That meant Arvind was working; he always hummed when he worked. She smiled.

"Mum?"

"Yes, darling."

"What's proscuring a miscarriage?"

"What?"

"Proscuring a miscarriage. They had a man in the paper yesterday sent to prison for doing it to two ladies."

Frances sighed. She hated censorship, hated lying to children about the world they were growing up in. She couldn't stop Cecily reading the newspapers, therefore, but it was sometimes hard to explain things. Cecily was rather unworldly—she'd been at a convent boarding school for four years, after all—but it pleased Frances that she was showing signs of being surprisingly sophisticated about things too. So awful to have a bourgeois child, a Jeremy or a Louisa! "Procuring, not proscuring. It's helping girls get rid of a pregnancy they don't want. An abortion."

"Why don't they want it?"

"Lots of reasons, I suppose," Frances said, after a pause. "They're poor. It's the wrong time. There's something wrong with it. The man has run off and left them. The girl didn't want to have sex, sometimes she was forced into it."

"Rape?"

"Yes," Frances said. She glanced up at Cecily, but her daughter's face was impassive. "This is an extremely pleasant conversation for a Thursday morning, isn't it? Prostitution, rape, and abortion. Now, stay still. I'm nearly finished."

A faint voice floated high up to the sunny studio at the top of the house. "Cecily, if you want to come, we're leaving in a couple of minutes."

"Fine," Cecily called, her long legs twitching on the stool, swinging wildly from side to side. "Coming."

"You know, because I really don't want to be late for Frank," the voice continued. "Cecily?"

"Yes!" Cecily yelled back. "Oh, Mum," she said softly to Frances. "I know I shouldn't say this, but Louisa is turning into a real *bore.*"

Frances hid her face so her daughter couldn't see her expression, and then she looked up reprovingly. "You can go, darling. Thank you. Be nice to your cousin."

Cecily jumped up, hitching down her blue Aertex shirt, and came and kissed her mother. "I am nice, Mum, I'm the nicest of the lot, honestly." She paused, and said dramatically, "Apart from Jeremy. Jeremy's *really* nice. I like him."

She opened the studio door and charged down the stairs, her shoes clattering erratically as she called, "Louisa, Jeremy! Don't go without me!"

Frances picked up a cloth and started cleaning her brushes, half-heartedly, the silence of the big glass and concrete room echoing in her ears. She looked down at her tanned, slim hand; there were flecks of vermilion paint drying on her arm. She picked them off, her fingers tracing the smooth, freckled skin, up and down. Frances closed her eyes, enjoying the sensation of her own touch, feeling the whorls of each fingerprint lightly brushing the hairs on her arm. . . . She breathed in. It was hot, and she was tired, that was all. There were new people coming this afternoon. That'd help. Two young men, to vary the party a little, add some excitement again, push the feeling of being trapped here in this glass studio away again. . . .

She stood up and went over to the window, gazing out at the garden, down at the gazebo, where her husband sat reading a book. She stared at him. She was forty-two, but she felt as if she could be twice that age. She was tired of it all. One day, she promised herself, she'd leave them behind and just walk down to the sea by herself, slip into the clear, cool water, and swim away.

She gave a snort of laughter as she heard the car drive off. One day.

Thirteen

"Archie's been looking at me again," Louisa said, as Jeremy's blue Ford Anglia (for which he had saved for two years and of which he was inordinately proud) trundled slowly away from the house, towards the less direct coastal road that led to Penzance. They were taking this road at Cecily's request, bowling through the rolling green countryside with its hedgerows full of orange kaffir lilies, blooming pink and purple rhododendrons in every garden and driveway, and palm trees visible in the distance, down towards the sea.

It was hot in the car, and the engine made an ominous spluttering sound which shook the frame.

"What's happened with Archie?" said Cecily, from the back.

In the front, Louisa ignored her. "What shall I do? He's disgusting, Jeremy."

Jeremy eased the car around a treacherous bend. He was silent for a moment; Jeremy was often silent. "Are you sure?"

"Sure about what?"

"Sure he's been . . . peeping."

Louisa laughed. "Of course I'm sure. I caught him at it once. I can hear him. And he smiles at me. These disgusting smiles, like he knows I know. As if it's our little secret." She shuddered. "Horrid . . . I hate him."

"What are you talking about?" Cecily demanded. "I can't hear properly in the back. What's Archie doing?"

"Archie's annoying Louisa," Jeremy said loudly. "Nothing to worry about, Cecily."

Louisa's sharp, pretty face appeared suddenly between the seats.

She said viciously, "Your brother kneels on the floor outside my room and looks through the keyhole to watch me while I'm . . . getting undressed. I've caught him doing it twice now. And when I'm getting changed to go swimming."

"Oh," said Cecily quietly. "Oh." She paused. "That's not very nice of him."

Louisa ignored her again. "It's the way he looks at me, Jeremy." She lowered her voice even more, and Cecily made an annoyed sound. "That's what I can't stand. Can you *do* something? Have a word with him? Especially with Frank and Guy arriving." She sighed and bit her little fingernail. "I have to say, I always forget how jolly odd they all are, but it's worse this year. Arvind's mad and darling Franty's in a strange mood this summer, I don't know what's up. I don't want the Leightons thinking we're part of it. Don't you agree?"

"Er . . ." Jeremy paused. "Sort of. Look," he said, trying to sound cheery. "Don't worry. Archie's been away at school for too long, he hasn't seen enough girls. He's just . . . well, he's a curious chap."

Cecily, watching Jeremy, opened her mouth to say something, and then shut it quickly again. Louisa made an exasperated sound.

"You can say that again. He's a—a *pervert*."

"I mean he's curious about the world." Jeremy blinked. "Perfectly natural. But yes, you're right. Shouldn't be spying on people, sneaking around. It's not on."

"You shouldn't be talking about people behind their back," said Cecily loudly. "Especially when you're guests in their home. I'm going to put it all in my diary."

"Oh, shut up, you little idiot," said Louisa. "What do you know? Nothing." She wound down the window and adjusted the metallic side mirror, so she could see her reflection.

"Here, I say," said Jeremy. "I can't see what's coming if you do that."

"Just for a second, Jeremy." Louisa took out a rose pink lipstick and expertly applied it, winding a stray blonde curl around one finger as she did. She pushed the mirror back into place. "There," she said, leaning back in her seat and closing her eyes. "Gosh, this day is exhausting already. I'm quite nervous, I must say."

She was young and beautiful, reclining in her seat, and she knew it, the wind rippling through her hair, her lightly tanned, smooth skin, her long, slim thighs clad in apple-green linen shorts.

Cecily was watching her. She said admiringly, "You do look lovely, Louisa."

"Thanks," said Louisa, who knew this to be true.

"Like a princess—hey, look at the Celtic cross!" Cecily shouted suddenly, and Louisa winced. "Someone's hung a garland on it, isn't that strange? Jeremy, can we get out and see?"

"No time, Cecily, not if you want to get your book and go to Boots," Jeremy said, as they drove through a little green valley and the turn-off to Lamorna Cove, busy with day-trippers and cars turning in towards the beach. A car hooted at them as they passed by, people waving gaily. The weather was infectious.

"Some people," Louisa said, annoyed, as if modern civilization were on the verge of collapse.

The fields off to their left marked the beginning of the stark, wilder moorland of northern Cornwall, rich in tin and coal. In the distance was a chimney stack, a remnant of the once-great tin-mining industry that was all but extinct these days.

Cecily sighed, drinking it all in. She was her mother's daughter, the landscape of the county was thrilling to her, no matter what the time of year. She settled back and gazed out of the window as Jeremy turned to his sister and said, "Between you and me, sis, it's Miranda I'm sometimes not sure about."

If Louisa was surprised at this sudden confidence from her brother, she didn't show it. "She is rather a funny old thing, isn't she," she said casually. "What do you mean exactly?"

Jeremy took one hand off the wheel and scratched his head in an unconscious Stan Laurel gesture. "I don't know, really. Feel she's out to cause trouble."

"That's Miranda for you," Louisa said with some satisfaction. "She's always been the same."

"That's just it, though," Jeremy said. "She—well, she's different this summer."

"How?"

Jeremy was lost for words. "I don't know. More—grown-up, in some ways. But worse, if anything. She stares at you, as if she's got a message for you."

Louisa misunderstood. "*She* stares at me too? Oh, goodness gracious."

"No, not—sorry, sis, wasn't being clear. She stares at *one*," Jeremy explained. "As if she had a message for *one*."

"Oh," Louisa said, running her hand over her hair again. "Yes, of course."

"No one likes Miranda," Cecily said. "It's just awful. No one likes her at school, either. It's because she's so moody," she added informatively. "The girls at school know how to wind her up. She got into real trouble—" She clamped her mouth shut suddenly.

"For what?" Louisa, alive to any possible scandal, turned round, intrigued. "What did she do?"

"I can't say," Cecily said.

"Oh, I bet it was nothing, and you're just making it up."

"I'm not, it was very serious," Cecily said furiously. "Very. I promised I wouldn't say. They nearly chucked her out—gosh, I mustn't say more. Mind you," she added, as if trying to be fair, "she isn't very nice. I, for example, don't like her. And I'm her sister."

There was a silence from the front of the car. "Oh, dear," said Louisa lightly, curling a blonde lock around one slim finger, secure in her position as family member adored by all. "Oh, dear. You shouldn't hate your sister, you know."

"I can't help it," Cecily said. "Oh, look, the Merry Maidens, I love them. Do look. I always mean to write a story about them. I might start it later. After I've written in my diary, of course."

She sighed, and was silent again, as they approached Newlyn. Louisa raised her eyes at her brother, but he did not respond. Already Cecily's diary was turning out to be a wearisome feature of the holiday, with pointed references to one person's inclusion or not in its pages, the lists it contained, and its role as a worthy receptacle for Cecily's world view. Last night, over fish pie, she had treated the table to a lengthy description of some girl at her school and how one day, she would definitely be sorry for being mean to her, Cecily.

"Why, Cecily?" Arvind had asked. "Why will this girl be so terribly afraid of your diary?"

The others around the table were surprised. Arvind normally didn't speak at meals. Cecily had turned to him, brimming with excitement. "Because, Dad, one day I'll be a writer and this diary will be famous. And she'll be *so sorry* she was mean to me. And called me names."

Louisa and Miranda had snorted loudly in unison, and looked up, surprised, at each other.

Now Louisa said to her brother, "We should plan some things for the boys. For the chaps. Ask them what they want to do."

Jeremy nodded. "I thought we could go to the Minack Theatre one night."

"Yippee, yes, please," Cecily shouted from the back.

"Oh, do we have to?" Louisa sighed. "Theater's so incredibly boring."

"But the Minack is great," Jeremy said, laughing at his sister. "They're putting on *Julius Caesar*. We can walk to Logan's Rock, they'll like that. Go to the pub for lunch, maybe. And I wondered if Aunt Frances would let us have a midnight picnic on the beach, cook some food on a campfire. It's the last year we'll all be together for a while, you know. Seems a shame not to make the most of it."

"What do you mean? The last year? Summercove's not going anywhere, is it?"

Jeremy was looking in the mirror. He didn't reply immediately. After a while he said, "Just—I just sometimes think, it might be different next year. We'll all be off doing different things. And Franty won't want us coming down every year." He looked uncomfortable. "Just don't know if we'll go there every year."

Louisa looked slightly alarmed. "I can't imagine us not coming down here every year," she said. "I love it." Cecily's face appeared again between the seats.

"I used to think that, now I don't," Jeremy said. "That's why I want to make the most of this summer."

Cecily opened her mouth and shut it again. Her eyes were huge. But Louisa was watching her brother, who never expressed an opinion about anything. She patted his arm.

"I think the Minack's a great idea," she said. They were on the outskirts of Penzance now, every other house a B&B or a café. Holidaymakers were walking along the harbor front, carrying buckets and spades. The outdoor seawater pool behind the harbor was in full swing, girls in bikinis and perfect hair demurely dangling their feet into the water. A group of boys lounged against a few motorbikes, parked up by the boats. They were smoking, in black leather jackets, their hair slicked back, and they stared at the car as it shuddered past them. Cecily stared out at them, fascinated.

"Mods are so passé. Honestly, Penzance is so out of date," said the worldly Londoner Louisa, glancing scornfully at them as they drove past. "Bet they've never even *heard* of *Bazaar*." She smoothed her hair behind her ears, anxiously, as Cecily watched in fascination. "Come on, Frank. Hurry up." She corrected herself. "Jeremy, sorry."

Jeremy laughed, and his brow cleared. "Don't worry. Look, here we are now."

Cecily got out early while Jeremy parked the car. Louisa was by this point actively anxious, looking at her reflection in every window they passed, even the glass of the ticket office at the end of the platform, much to the bemusement of the bulbous-nosed ticket officer who stared at her. It was a hot day, hotter in the station than outside, where there was a cooling breeze from the sea.

"It's strange being in a town on a boiling day like this, after a few days at Summercove," said Jeremy, running his forefinger around the collar of his shirt. "Actually does make you realize how lovely it is to be there."

"I know," said Louisa. "It is the most beautiful place. And we are lucky. I shouldn't be rude about them. I do love Franty. I love being there. Joining in—all of that."

"Such a little homemaker," Jeremy said, nudging her. "Love it when everyone's all together having a wonderful time, don't you? Even when they're not?"

Louisa put her hands on her hips. "Be quiet, Jeremy. That's rubbish. I just like . . . I like the idea that we're all together. And then we get here and . . . it's not how I expected." She shrugged. "But hey-ho—let's go onto the platform, shall we?" she said, squinting at the train track.

They waited in the covered station until the train chugged slowly into view, past St. Michael's Mount in the distance, the granite castle out to sea glowing strangely gold in the midday sun.

"There it is!" Louisa cried. "There it is!" She stared at the black engine moving into view, as if she expected Frank and his brother to be standing on top of it, waving placards. "I can't see them!"

"Of course you can't, you ninny," Jeremy said, shaking his head at his sister. Goodness, girls were such idiots about chaps. There was Frank, a perfectly decent sort, nothing wildly eccentric or unusual, and Louisa was completely gaga over him. It made him almost uncomfortable, he didn't know how to talk to her about him. She'd even used the word "marriage"! Louisa, who he'd always thought was a sensible sort of girl, the kind of sister one didn't mind having, the sort who got scholarships to study sensible things like biology . . . And it turned out she was just like all the others, obsessed with weddings and babies after all. Jeremy didn't know what Frank would think about that at all. Yes, girls were odd sometimes, even one's sister.

The plumes of thick white and gray steam cleared, the doors opened, and there was mayhem. Porters scurried to help the first-class passengers, elderly gentlemen in tweeds and their immaculate county ladies in neat hats and gloves carrying crocodile travel cases. Cross, important-looking City gents in bowler hats, their starched collars wilting in the heat, clutching furled umbrellas and briefcases.

Louisa and Jeremy peered past them as the first-class section gradually dispersed, but then instead of two young men came endless hordes of families, struggling with battered, heavy suitcases and screaming children, lots of boys with Beatles-style mop-top haircuts, sweating in polo necks, girls in pretty cotton dresses and low heels, cardigans draped over shoulders, housewives in headscarves, carrying their shopping in wicker baskets, farm workmen, officious men in suits with efficient moustaches, lounging men, old men . . . but no sign of Frank and his brother.

As the masses subsided into a trickle, and then to nothing, so that the platform was empty once more, Louisa and Jeremy looked despondently at each other. "Perhaps they missed the train?" Louisa said, her mouth turned down. "But wouldn't they have at least telephoned, to let us know?"

"I should have thought so," Jeremy said. "Not like old Frank to leave us waiting."

Louisa glanced desperately down the platform once more. "Perhaps they're . . . perhaps they're chatting with the driver."

"Lou, I don't think so," said Jeremy. "They'd know we'd be waiting. Old Frank wouldn't leave us hanging here while he swapped horror stories about Dr. Beeching with some railway bod. Perhaps their old man's been taken ill again, he wasn't well before Easter, I wonder if that's it. . . . Hullo! Who's that? Frank!" he said with relief, as someone poked him in the ribs. "Oh, dammit, it's you. Hullo, Cecily."

Cecily's face fell as she saw his expression. "Hello, Jeremy," she said in a small voice, blushing to the roots of her hair. "I got my book and my new diary. Look." She held up a Georgette Heyer in one hand and in the other, a simple red exercise book, with a stamp on the front: Name, Class, Subject.

"*The Toll-Gate*," Jeremy read aloud. "Right. Sorry, Cec. Thought you were Frank," he added, not seeing the look of anguish on her face. He turned back to his sister. "I'll just check with the chap at the ticket office. Perhaps there's a message for us, but I doubt it. Wait here."

Louisa's keen eyes missed nothing, and she nudged Cecily after he'd gone. "I can't believe you're blushing, Cecily. You've got a pash for Jeremy. Ha!"

"I haven't!" Cecily cried, hitting her on the arm furiously. She stamped her foot, her face still red. "Shut up, I haven't!"And she crossed her arms, blinking back tears of mortification, like every other teenager before and since.

"Sorry, Cec," Louisa said, feeling guilty. "That's your new diary, is it? Gosh, you've written a lot, to be getting a new one already. Are you enjoying it?"

"Yes," Cecily said, standing up straight again. "I love it. This new bit will be even more private, I can say what I like because I've finished the school project." She hugged both books to her.

"No sign," said Jeremy, appearing again. "I must say," he repeated, "not like him, leaving us high and dry. I thought old Frank—"

"Oh, shut up about damned old Frank," said Louisa, turning on her heel. "They're not coming. Let's just get back home, for God's sake."

"Yes," said Cecily, imitating her with a flounce. "I want to go home too."

Jeremy sighed and followed them.

Louisa was silent on the journey home. Jeremy took the quicker main road through the open countryside, driving fast because he was hungry now, and he'd heard Mary mention chicken salad for lunch.

"I don't understand what happened," Cecily said, equanimity restored, sticking her head between their seats. "Why wouldn't they have come?"

"Perhaps we got the wrong time. Or the wrong day," Jeremy said.

"Perhaps they just changed their minds," Louisa said. "I bet they did."

"Frank wouldn't do that," Jeremy said. "I've known him for eleven years, he wouldn't just not turn up. Guy either."

"How do you know him?" Cecily said. "I thought he was Louisa's *boyfriend*."

"Honestly, Cecily," Louisa said through gritted teeth, "if you say that again, I will ram this down your throat." She turned around, brandishing a battered, old *Shell Guide to the Roads of Britain* with some force. Her lipstick was slightly smudged, her hair out of place.

"We were at prep school together," Jeremy said. "Known him for years. Lives near us. We used to play tennis together, the three of us. And Guy. You'll like Guy," he told Cecily. "He wants to be a writer too."

"I bet he's not as nice as you," Cecily said quietly.

Jeremy didn't hear her. "They're good sorts. They like playing tennis, swimming, joining in with things, all of that." He turned the car off the main road, onto the dark, leafy lane above Summercove.

"Well, if they're such bloody good sorts, why—oh, *hell*!" Louisa cried. "This stupid car, Jeremy! The spring's come through the damned seat, look, it's torn my shorts! My beautiful shorts . . . oh, God." She squirmed around in the car.

"Maybe if you put the *Shell Guide* over the spring it'd stop it tearing anything else," Cecily offered helpfully. Louisa shot her a look of pure loathing.

They drew up outside the house. "I'll put the car in the garage, if you want to hop out," Jeremy said, and the girls got out. Cecily opened the gate while Louisa, still grumbling, followed behind her.

Cecily breathed in as they walked across the lawn towards the house. "Oh, it's lovely to be back on a day like today, isn't it?" she said. "I can smell the sea, I can smell the sea. . . ."

Voices drifted across to them from the terrace on the other side of the house. "I expect they're having lunch already," Louisa said ruefully. "Bet they didn't wait."

They walked around the side to the garden, and Louisa let out a cry.

"Oh! Oh, my goodness." She stared in amazement across the lawn.

There, kneeling on a blanket, in slim, black trousers, a white

T-shirt and a black cardigan slung over her shoulders, a white ribbon tying back her dark hair, was Miranda and, with her, two young men, one in meticulously pressed linen shorts and a navy polo shirt, a cricket jumper tied round his neck, the other in jeans and an open-necked shirt. They were laughing at something Miranda had said. She looked up.

"Oh, here!" she said, her cat-like face breaking out into a smile as the girls walked towards her. "Louisa's back from the station! I'm sure she can explain what's happened. Louisa, look!" she said sweetly to her cousin. "Frank and . . . it's Guy, isn't it?" she added shyly. "They wired yesterday to say they'd be down early, but it obviously never arrived. Isn't that strange?"

Frank and Guy sprang to their feet as Louisa and Cecily, on the edge of the lawn, stood there, mouths open. "Hello!" Louisa said, desperately clutching the flap of material on her bottom. "My goodness! What a lovely surprise! We'd quite given up on you two. How strange!"

"Are you all right?" Miranda asked, watching her cousin anxiously. "Is something . . . wrong?"

"No, no," Louisa said hastily. "I tore my shorts, that's all. Very annoying!" she added heartily, one hand still holding the ripped material. "Hello, Guy, Frank—" She patted both of them awkwardly with her free arm, bowing her head in mortification.

"Hello, Louisa," Frank said, kissing her on the cheek. "Very— very nice to see you."

"Oh, we *are* glad you're back," Miranda said. She unfurled her legs from underneath her and stood up gracefully, stretching her long arms, and Guy gave her his hand to help her up.

"Wow," said Cecily, in admiration. "Miranda, you look pretty today."

"Thanks," said Miranda. She tugged at her ponytail and looked sympathetically at her cousin. "Poor Louisa!" she said, in honeyed tones. "You'd better change your shorts before lunch, it's in five minutes. Guy, Frank—are you all settled in? Do you want a wash and brush-up?"

"When did you get here then?" Cecily asked. "How strange that we never got the wire!"

"About an hour ago," Guy said. He smiled at Cecily. "We got a lift from a fellow who was going to Sennen Cove. Very decent of him. We were a bit stuck, we didn't know what to do. We weren't sure which bus would take us to Summercove, and a taxi would have wiped us out." He leaned forwards. "I'm Guy," he said, shaking Cecily's hand.

"Hello," she said, pleased.

"Hello, Cecily," Frank said, also stepping forwards. "I'm Frank, I'm Jeremy's friend." He cleared his throat. "It is a pleasure to meet you."

Cecily stared at him. "Hello, Frank," she said.

He nodded. "Ah, yes," he said awkwardly. He pointed to his shorts. "We're all kitted out for a summer holiday, as you can see."

She didn't say anything, just kept looking at him.

"It's funny," she said after a while. "You don't look like you should be wearing shorts."

"Aah. I am not that used to them, it's true," Frank said.

"You look more like you should be . . ." Cecily paused. "Wearing a bowler hat."

There was a silence.

"Cecily, that's rude," Miranda said, pushing her. "Say sorry."

But Frank laughed. "No, it's not rude. She's right." He fiddled with some imaginary cufflinks, a smile on his handsome face. "I'm usually more happy in more formal attire, it's true."

Cecily rubbed her cheek. "I'm sorry," she said. "I didn't mean to be rude, Mr. Bowler Hat."

Guy gave a shout of laughter and Frank joined in. Louisa, however, looked mortified.

"I'm sure we passed you on the way," Frank said to Louisa. "We got our friend to sound the horn, and we pulled over, but you didn't seem to spot us."

"Oh, my goodness," Louisa said. "Of course. I remember now. . . ." She bit her lip, annoyed, and then clutched her bottom again. "I really should go and change," she said, blushing. "Sorry. Will you two be OK out here while I go off?"

She looked at Frank, but he was listening to Miranda, who was saying, "How wonderful you're here. Ah," she said, turning towards the house, "there's Jeremy. Now we're all present and correct." She sighed and smiled happily at the new arrivals, coiling her hair around one finger.

Suddenly a shadow passed over her. "Hello there," said a voice behind her, and Miranda and the two boys turned to see Frances walking towards them, her hand outstretched.

"I'm Frances Seymour," she said, pulling the headscarf that had been tying her hair back off her head. She shook her honey-colored hair out, scratching her scalp. "What a terrible welcome you've had." She smiled at them both, eyes sparkling, her clear, tanned face glowing with pleasure.

"Not at all," said Guy, shaking her hand, clearly taken aback. "It's wonderful to be here."

"Yes," said Frank, wiping his hand on his shorts and then holding it out to her. "Thank you, Mrs. Kapoor."

Frances looked up at the tall, blond, godlike Frank, and smiled, almost in amusement. "Frances, please," she said.

"I'm Frank," he replied. "Well, so that means we've got almost the same name!"

"Ye-es." There was a look on her face that he found rather disconcerting. "Well, let's get you a drink." She laughed, her green eyes glinting in the sun, and patted Miranda on the shoulder. "Stand up, darling. Isn't this wonderful? I feel as if the holidays can properly start now."

Fourteen

"More tea, vicar?"

"Tea? Ha—very good. Yes, please, Louisa."

"Guy, more champagne?"

"Thank you, that's very kind."

Louisa turned to her aunt. "Franty, is there anything else I can do?"

"No," said Frances, smiling. "You've been wonderful. Sit down and enjoy yourself, darling."

They had gathered on the lawn at the front of the house for drinks before dinner. There was no wind, not even the faintest breeze from the sea. The scent of lavender and oil from the lamps outside hung in the still air. "My One and Only Love," and John Coltrane and Johnny Hartman floated out to them from a gramophone.

Louisa, resplendent in mulberry-colored silk, was making the rounds with champagne, but it was Miranda who was the star of the show that night. She appeared after everyone else had gathered on the terrace, in a black gros-grain cocktail dress, extremely simple and obviously expensive, with a tulip skirt and tight bodice which clung perfectly to her gamine figure.

"That *is* a beautiful dress, Miranda," Louisa said generously, handing her a glass. "You look like Jackie Kennedy."

Miranda flushed, her olive skin mottling red.

"It *is* a beautiful dress," Frances said, curious. "Where's it from, may I ask?"

Miranda turned her face to her mother. She was glowing. "I didn't tell you, Mother. So please don't be cross. But Connie sent me a postal order to school. For ten pounds. I bought this in Exeter. And some other things." She was pleading.

"She gave you *TEN POUNDS*?" Cecily screeched. "I didn't know it was that much!"

The shirt that morning. The lovely blue pumps she'd been wearing yesterday. Of course. Frances nodded, appraising her daughter again. She definitely had style, she'd give her that much.

Not for the first time, Frances regretted making her old school friend—married to a wealthy industrialist and without children of her own—Miranda's godmother. She was absentminded but very generous—when Miranda was ten and a half she bought her a pearl necklace from Asprey's—but it wasn't fair on the others.

"Feel how gorgeous it is," Miranda said, taking her mother's hand and running her fingers over the thick, beautiful fabric, her eyes sparkling with excitement. "The capri pants today, too—the cut! It's so perfect. They're the nicest things I've ever owned."

Frances didn't know what to say. Funny, what a difference the right clothes and a sparkle in the eye made to the girl. All these years of struggling to make Miranda happy, and it turned out she should have just taken her to Harrods and bought her some nicer clothes.

She didn't know whether to laugh or cry. Even as she chided herself she looked again at her daughter, laughing with Cecily for once instead of snapping at her, tucking her shining black hair behind her ear, eyes shining. She hadn't seen her like this for a long time. She, Frances, as much as anyone else, was responsible for making Miranda feel small, and she was suddenly overcome with guilt.

Miranda turned back to her. "Is it really all right, Mummy?"

"Did you write and thank Connie?" said Frances, taking a sip of her champagne.

"Of course I did." Miranda stared at her mother, her green eyes unblinking. "I wrote her a really long letter telling her all the lovely things I could buy for ten pounds. And then she sent me another pound in the post, just like that! In case I went over it."

Frances sighed. How very Miranda. "Darling, that's awful of you." But she couldn't help smiling at her.

Cecily sipped her champagne, gingerly holding the stem of the flute. It was a special night, so she was allowed a glass. "Mm," she said, wrinkling her nose as the bubbles tickled her. "It's so fizzy."

"Don't get drunk and make a fool of yourself," Archie told her. He was himself beautifully turned out, his dark hair gleaming with brilliantine like a matinee idol. Next to his sister, they made quite a pair.

"What, like peeking at people while they get undressed?" Cecily said sharply, turning away from him.

Archie's expression darkened and he stammered. "What?"

Cecily's face flushed, but she was saved from responding by a clinking sound. "Welcome, all of you," said Arvind, addressing the assembled group, much to their surprise. He took his wife's hand. "We are glad to have you all here."

"Yes, cheers," Jeremy said, raising his glass. "Thanks, Uncle Arvind. We love being here."

Next to him, Miranda rolled her eyes. Frances, seeing her expression, tried not to smile, shaking her head at her instead. Dear, staid Jeremy.

Arvind gave Jeremy a polite smile. "Your good health, all of you. You are the future. I salute you."

He stepped forwards, raised his glass, and then frowned, as if he was surprised he'd spoken.

"Daddy is pretty eccentric," Miranda whispered loudly to Guy, who was standing next to her. "Just ignore him."

Guy nodded. "Excuse me a moment, would you? Sir—" he said, moving determinedly towards Arvind and leaving Miranda standing alone. "I'm extremely sorry to bother you with work, but I felt I couldn't stay here and not tell you how much I enjoyed *The Modern Fortress*."

"You enjoyed it?" Arvind said. "How extraordinary."

Guy was nonplussed. "Well, perhaps *enjoyed* isn't the right word." There was a silence. "I—er, it's a very interesting book, anyway."

"Thank you," said Arvind, staring at him through his small, round glasses. "You wear glasses too."

"Yes, I do," said Guy equably. "Sometimes. For reading."

"What do you do?"

"Er—me?"

"Well, yes, you." Arvind looked around as if there was someone else there.

"I'm up at Oxford," Guy said. "I'm doing PPE."

"Of course."

"What's PPE?" Cecily, who had materialized next to them, asked softly.

"It stands for Philosophy, Politics, and Economics," Guy told her.

"That sounds pretty dire," Cecily said. "I mean very interesting. Sorry, Dad."

"Ah," Arvind said. "The child rejects the parent. Very disappointing."

"The child rolls her eyes at the parent," Cecily replied gravely, but her eyes were twinkling.

Watching them with surprise on his face—in most of the homes of his contemporaries, you called your father Sir and you certainly didn't call his work "dire"—Guy coughed. "You're nearly taller than your father," he told Cecily, flushing slightly as he couldn't think of what else to say.

"Thank you, young man, for pointing out my lack of inches," Arvind said. He jabbed Guy in the stomach and smiled, and Guy laughed, his nerves suddenly gone.

"Sir, I wonder if you read Dr. King's Letter from Birmingham Jail?" Guy asked hurriedly. "Because there are several points in it which you touch on in *The Modern Fortress*. How oppressed people cannot remain oppressed forever. It is not possible. The desire for freedom always manifests itself and works its way through, even though it may take a long time."

"Ah—" Arvind said, his eyes lighting up. "The danger of the white moderate, greater than the white extremist. Yes, I found that very interesting."

"What are they talking about?" Miranda whispered to Cecily.

"Really boring stuff. Someone called Dr. King."

"Martin Luther King, that is," Archie said. He was standing next to them, one hand casually resting in his blazer pocket. "The head of the NAACP. He's a great man."

"NAACP?" Cecily said.

"National Association for the Advancement of Colored People," Archie said, enunciating each word. He took a sip from his drink, turning his handsome profile away from them, towards the setting sun.

"How do you know who he is?" Miranda asked scornfully. "You don't know anything, Archie."

She looked at her brother crossly, as she always did when Archie showed any signs of having a different opinion from her, or an opinion about which she knew nothing.

Archie licked his lips as if he were nervous. "I know all men were created equal. But we're the only different people we know," he said suddenly. He looked around; his father was engrossed in conversation with Guy, Louisa and Frank were laughing together on the edge of the terrace, and Jeremy and Frances were sitting on the bench by the steps. "And I get called a Paki at school and told to go home by boys whose parents can barely read or write, when my father's one of the cleverest people in the world, and his family lived in a palace in Lahore." There were bubbles of spit in each corner of his mouth. "You're stupid, Miranda. You don't stand up to those girls who bully you because your father's Indian. You should tell them you're better than any of them."

"They don't bully me," Miranda muttered, hanging her head, her hair falling in her face. "Shut up, Archie."

"They do bully you," Cecily said softly. "They're horrible to her," she told Archie. "They call her horrible things."

"We don't talk about it," Miranda hissed, grabbing Cecily's arm. She was bright red. "Remember?"

"We never talk about it!" Cecily said loudly, wrenching her arm away. Frances looked over at her three children, questioning. They huddled back together again, mutinous but quiet. *Don't break the pact.*

"There's nothing to talk about anyway," Miranda whispered. She stood up straight again. "All right? So shut up."

"Anyway," said Cecily. "I don't think it matters if Dad grew up in a palace or not. He could have grown up in a hut. They shouldn't do it in the first place."

But Archie wasn't paying attention. "Dad went to one of the best schools in India. With maharajahs and—and English boys," he said. "Much posher than the pit I go to."

"Only because his dad was a teacher there," Cecily pointed out. "That's what I mean, it doesn't matter either way. Just tell them they're bigots."

"No," Archie said. "I don't want to do it like that. I want to show them I'm better than them. That I'll make more money than any of them, be more English than them, beat the faggots at their own game." He nodded, as though he was talking to himself. "I've got a plan, you see. We have to have a plan." His eyes rested, briefly, on his twin. "You have to understand that, both of you. They're not going to help you. That's all."

The other two stared at him blankly, like he was speaking another language. And through the open window inside the house somewhere a tinkling, silvery bell rang suddenly, as if signaling the end of something.

"I think that means it's time for food," Frances said.

Miranda turned away from her siblings. She put her hand gently on Guy's arm. "Guy, would you like to go in to dinner?" she said in a husky voice.

Guy turned. "Oh, hello, Miranda," he said. "Yes, I'd love to. Shall we?" he said, turning to Arvind.

"Well, if we don't," Arvind said, patting him on the back, "it'll go cold. Dinner, my friends. Let us eat."

"So, you've got two weeks," said Frances. "Is there anything you'd like to do while you're here? Beyond relaxing and having a holiday, of course."

Guy paused in the action of handing the salad bowl to Miranda and looked down the table at his brother, who was seated next to Frances.

"We don't really have any plans," Frank said, staring nervously into Frances's amused green eyes. "We'd like to go to the beach. Obviously!" He laughed, a little too loudly. Cecily, next to him, watched him in amazement. "Um—" He looked at his brother for help. He was nervous, he wished it would go away. Across the table, Louisa smiled gently at him, and he looked ruefully at her. *I'm not normally this much of an idiot.* He had hardly said a word since he'd arrived. He'd never been anywhere like Summercove before.

The windows were open, the curtains drawn, and it was a still night. Occasionally they could hear an owl hooting in the woods behind the house.

"I'd like to go to the Minack Theatre," Guy said. "I've always wanted to."

"Well, if we can get tickets," Louisa said, looking at Frank to see if he registered any interest in this activity. "But it's often booked up."

Frances waved her hand. "That's fine. I know them. I'm sure if we motor over tomorrow there will be some available. Terrific!" She looked pleased. "I love the Minack, Guy, I hope you will too. It's such a wonderful setting. So dramatic. You feel as if at any moment the whole thing could be swept away into the sea."

"Is it very dangerous, the sea around here?" Frank said.

"We've lived here for eight years, if you count when it was just our holiday home," said Archie sagely. "We're all pretty used to the sea."

"The rocks can be treacherous," Frances said, staring at her nails. "But you just have to be careful. Sensible."

Yes, be careful. Be sensible. Don't rock the boat. She smiled, her teeth gritted together behind her lips.

"Well, I'd like a picnic on the beach," Frank said suddenly. "With food."

"Yes," Jeremy said, pleased. "We thought we'd do that. At night, if that's all right with you, Aunt Frances?" He turned to his aunt, next to him. "Don't want to leave you high and dry without company for the evening."

"So we're not invited to the picnic on the beach, I take it?" she asked him, amused.

"Oh," said Jeremy, flustered. "Of course, if you'd like to—if you'd want to. How rude of me. . . . I just thought, when Mother and Father arrive, you'd want to . . ."

"I'd rather be on the beach," Arvind said.

Archie jumped in. "I say, Guy, Frank, have you been following the Ward trial?" he said. "Pretty juicy, isn't it?"

"Oh, yes," said Guy. "I can't believe they're serving it up like this, every day."

"Profumo lied to Parliament, he deserves everything he gets," Guy said. He drummed his fingers on the table. "The times are changing. You can't have this Establishment covering everything up as it suits them anymore."

Archie nodded, pleased. "What do you think, Frank?" Frances asked the silent man next to her.

"I'm afraid I don't really care much," Frank said, his handsome face set in a frown. "It's just jolly entertaining, that's all." He looked around, shamefaced. "Expect that's an awful thing to say."

"I think that's what we all feel," Guy said. "It's terrible, but I want to read it." He turned to Miranda. "Do you read *Private Eye*?"

"Oh, yes," Miranda said. "We sneak it in to school, I think it's awfully funny."

"That's rub—" Cecily began, but bit her lip suddenly as Archie, next to her, kicked her.

"Seems to me it's the only paper or magazine telling the truth. There's so much hypocrisy out there, in public life, it's disgusting." Guy's quiet face was animated. "L-look at the Argyll divorce case, it made me absolutely sick. We scrabble around to feast on the bones of these people, just so we can say how decadent and awful they are over our breakfast cereal, and then we bow and scrape when a lord or lady comes into the room." His voice rose as he came to an abrupt halt.

Silence fell as they all nodded politely, awkwardly. Frances looked at her nails again, and Guy sank back into his chair, embarrassed. Mary appeared in the doorway. "Shall I clear away?" she asked. "Ooh, there's not much left of it, is there?"

"Thank you, Mary," Frances said. "That was delicious." The others murmured their approval, smiling, and Mary looked pleased. "You can go up afterwards, if you like. We can make the coffee."

"Behold, the symbol of our bourgeois repressive regime," Arvind said to Guy, after Mary had gone into the kitchen. "Mary. She cooks Beef Wellington and cleans for us and we give her money."

"Sir, I didn't mean—" Guy began, looking mortified. "Please don't—"

Arvind waved his hand. "Please. I was making a joke. You are quite right, young man," he said. "Things are changing, and we are wise to recognize it. Only I don't think any of us knows how they will change, not yet." He looked around the table, at his son Archie staring into space, at Louisa gazing at Frank, at Miranda watching them with a curious fury, at Guy, methodically eating his cheese, at Cecily, carefully peeling a grape and looking across at Jeremy under her eyelashes, and finally at his wife. She nodded back at him, but a little frown creased her brow.

They retired one by one that night; Arvind went early, followed by Cecily then Jeremy. The others stayed up, sitting outside on the terrace, talking quietly over coffee. Guy was next to go up. He said he was tired, and he was followed by Archie soon after. Frances, Miranda, Louisa, and Frank were left, until Frances took the hint and got up, with a look at Louisa and Frank and at her daughter.

Frank leapt to his feet. "Goodnight, Mrs. . . . Mrs. Kapoor."

She held her hand in his, smiling at him playfully. She'd forgotten how touching these boys could be. How bloody pompous too. "Goodnight, Frank. And please. Call me Frances. It's like Frank. Not too hard to remember."

He gazed at her nervously. "Yes . . . yes, of course."

She turned to Miranda, and her gaze flicked lightly back to Frank and Louisa, who was gazing shyly down at the flagstones.

"You leaving these two to it, then, Miranda dear? See you to-morrow."

Miranda, defeated, shot her mother a furious look. She got up from where she'd been artfully sitting on the ground. "Yes, I'm off too. Night, you two. Don't be too long. It's dangerous for the rest of us, you leaving the front door open," she said, somewhat obscurely.

Miranda didn't come up immediately. Cecily was kneeling up in bed when she finally appeared, her diary beside her, and she was looking out of the window.

"Are you peeping?" Miranda said. "Watching what's going on with the young lovers? Are they still down there?"

"No," Cecily blushed, and shut the window hurriedly. "Oh, you smell," she said. "Is that where you went? Have you been . . . *smoking*? Urgh."

"Oh, shut up, you baby," said Miranda, flinging herself on the brass bedstead. "I'm eighteen, for God's sake, I'm a bloody grown-up." She stared at the wall. "Not that anyone like Mummy seems to appreciate that fact."

"That's because you don't behave like a grown-up," Cecily said automatically. "You don't have a plan, unlike Archie." Miranda ignored her, and began unzipping her dress. Her younger sister watched her. "What *are* you going to do now? Do you know?"

"I don't know," Miranda said. "So leave me alone."

"You must have *some* idea," Cecily said, but her sister held up a hand.

"Don't start on me, please, Cecily. I'm not in the mood. Archie's an idiot sometimes. A swot, with his ideas about making money and all that. It's so boring of him. I'll be fine. I'll work something out."

"Miranda," Cecily began. "Can I ask you something?"

"As long as it's not about me." Miranda was struggling with the zip of her dress.

"It's not." Cecily leaned forwards and tugged it down.

"Thanks. Go on."

"Do you think it's bad, if people . . ." Cecily stopped. "A man and a woman. Do they—" She flopped back against her pillows. "Oh, never mind. Forget it."

"A man and a woman?" Miranda was intrigued. "What?" she said. "Are you trying to spice up your diary? What?"

"Nothing," Cecily said firmly. "I'm going to sleep now. Goodnight, Miranda."

Fifteen

The next day, at breakfast, when Frank appeared at the table, tall and handsome in shorts and a slightly crumpled polo shirt, Louisa pursed her lips and looked down at her toast.

Frank cleared his throat. "Hello, Louisa," he said.

Louisa blushed, ignored this, and turned to Guy. "What do you want to do today, Guy?" She popped a strawberry into her mouth and smiled at him.

Miranda sat down at the table, shooting a sideways glance at Cecily, who was bright red and munching her toast furiously, as if it had done something to offend her. So that was what had been troubling Cecily last night. She smiled.

"Yes, Guy," she said, also ignoring the hapless Frank, who clutched his plate and sat down. "What do you want to do?"

Guy put down his knife. "I thought perhaps the beach? I don't know, really. Whatever anyone else wants." He looked at Cecily. "What do you like doing when you're down here, Cecily?"

"Me?" Cecily looked astonished that anyone should ask her opinion. "Um—I like swimming in the sea, and playing card games and reading my book." She stretched out her legs. "And not having to pose for Mum, which I don't have to do today, thank goodness."

"She's painting you?"

"Yes." Cecily glanced around, to make sure Frances wasn't near the breakfast room. "It's pretty dull," she confided.

"Your mother's a wonderful painter," Guy said. "Who knows, one day you could be hanging in the National Portrait Gallery."

"That'd be nice," Cecily admitted. "I just can't see anyone wanting to gawp at me, that's all."

"Nonsense, Cec," Jeremy said, walking behind her. He patted her head. "You're a looker, isn't she, Frank?"

As Cecily glowed, Frank, still watching Louisa, said, "Oh—ah. Of course. Yes."

"Frank . . . Franty, your name is just like Mummy's," Cecily said, flushing with exhilaration. "I think we should just call you Bowler Hat from now on. To avoid any confusion."

"Yes," Louisa said, looking up suddenly, giving a thin smile. "Bowler Hat's the perfect name. Because I've been thinking about it and Cecily's right. You *do* look as if you should be wearing a bowler hat. Shorts really don't suit you. Your knees are *awfully* thin."

Into the silence that followed this statement came Mary. "Now, does anyone want some more coffee?" she said, wiping her hands on her apron. "Eggs? Frank, how about you?"

"No—no, thanks," Frank said. He smoothed his hands nervously along his muscular arms. He looked too big for the small seat, the cozy dining room.

"We're calling him Bowler Hat now, Mary," Louisa said. She pushed her chair back from the table and stood up, her long legs clad in a pristine pair of shorts, this time pale blue. She languidly stretched her arms above her head. "Not Frank. It's too confusing."

"Bowler Hat, eh?" said Mary, collecting up the empty scrambled egg dish. "Right you are."

When Miranda and Cecily were cleaning their teeth in the little sink in their room after breakfast, Miranda said carelessly, "So, was Frank asking Louisa something a bit . . . rude, last night, Cec? Is that what you overheard?"

Cecily's mouth was full of toothpaste. She stopped, toothbrush in hand.

"Wha'?" she said.

"Something about sex." Miranda mouthed the last word. "Something she didn't want to do."

Cecily bent over the sink and spat, and when she stood up again her small face was red.

"I wasn't eavesdropping. Honestly. I wasn't."

"I know you weren't," Miranda said.

"I don't think the Bowler Hat's very nice," Cecily said.

"What did he do?"

"Well." Cecily spoke in a whisper, and turned the square tap so the water was running. "I was watching them, because I heard them say my name. I had the windows open 'cause I couldn't sleep. They were sitting on the floor, and he . . ." She paused. "Oh, my goodness."

"What?" said Miranda, nearly mad with curiosity.

"He . . . well, he put his hand on her . . . chest."

"Oh. Is that it?"

"Miranda!"

"Come on, Cecily. You're such a baby!" Miranda turned the tap off. "What did Louisa do?"

"She pushed him away," Cecily said. "Quite hard."

"What did he do then?"

"He asked some other stuff. I'm not saying." She was bright red now. "And he was angry. He said, 'For God's sake, Louisa. Don't be so frigid.' "

"Gosh," said Miranda. "The Bowler Hat is really Stewart Granger. Who'd have thought it?"

"He is *not* Stewart Granger." Cecily was furious at this impugning of her idol. "Stewart Granger is tall and handsome, and a gentleman. And Frank is . . . tall. That's it."

"Oh, he's handsome. And I think he's rather sweet, in a buttoned-up way," Miranda said, musing, looking out of the window. "And the brother too."

Cecily frowned. "Oh, goodness," Miranda said in irritation, turning round and catching her sister's expression. "Do grow up a bit, Cecily. You're such a baby. Life's not like bloody boarding school, you know. One of these days you'll realize it's normal for men and women to want to be with each other, you know." She looked in the mildew-spotted mirror above the sink and ran one finger carefully over a silken dark eyebrow. "It's going to be hot again today. Very hot. I hope the others don't get hideously sunburnt at the beach." She smiled at Cecily, and ran one hand over her smooth, coffee-colored skin. "Have you ever kissed a boy?"

"Me?" Cecily said pointlessly. "No." She turned away. "Stop making everything about boys and girls, Miranda."

"That's what life is about, Cec darling," Miranda said. "Look at Mummy, flirting with every man that comes her way. Look at Louisa, sticking her bum out at the Bowler Hat, like she's an ape in the zoo—even you, Cecily dear. It'll happen to you one day—"

"You're vile," Cecily said, pushing past her. "I'm not listening. Stop it."

She picked up her swimming costume and threadbare towel, and ran downstairs.

The path down to the sea from the house was narrow, impassable in winter. Every Easter, the overgrown brambles that threatened to strangle the high hedgerows were cut away. By late July, the brambles had crept back, tangled together with goosegrass, wild roses, and ivy and croaking with grasshoppers. Cecily led the way, followed by Guy and Frank. Louisa and Jeremy said they'd pack up the hamper.

"It's only eleven, and it's baking already," Cecily said. She jumped over a trailing bramble. "The sea will be gorgeous, it's lovely and warm but it doesn't get too hot. We went to Italy a couple of years ago," she added airily, "and already by now the Mediterranean is like a bath. So warm and soupy, it's disgusting."

"Where in Italy?" Guy asked. "I'm going in August, for a month."

"I love Italy, you are lucky," Cecily said. "We went to Florence, and Siena, and then on to the Tuscan coast. I wasn't actually there with friends, you know. Daddy was doing a lecture," she explained.

"I understand," said Guy gravely.

"But I want to go back one day. When I'm a student myself." She slowed down a little, and turned back to look at Guy. "I want to travel all over Europe. I've drawn a map of where I'm going to go." She stopped. "Here's the path. It's a bit tricky, so be careful."

The steps were only a couple of feet wide, through the cliffs. "Good God," Frank said, as they started climbing down. "I'm a bit unsteady." He looked back. "Will Louisa be all right, carrying that huge great hamper down the steps?" he asked.

"Oh, she'll be fine," Cecily said blithely. "She's been doing that walk since she was a toddler, Bowler Hat. Calm down."

But Frank said he'd stay back and carry the hamper with Jeremy, so Cecily and Guy carried on down.

"Ye gods and little fishes!" Guy exclaimed, when they reached the bottom. He rubbed his head. "This is all ours? You're sure?"

Cecily ran across the sand. "It's not strictly speaking our own beach, but who else comes down here? No one!" She grinned at him, holding her hair back from her face. "Isn't it wonderful?"

"It's great," Guy said, setting down his pack. "Everything here is great." He smiled at her. "I don't know how you can bear going back to school, when you live in a place like this." His gaze roamed back towards the fields. "And your parents are marvelous people too. So interesting, so relaxed."

Her smile grew a little more rigid. "I suppose. So what are your parents like?" she asked.

"Oh, you know." Guy sat down on one of the huge, black rocks. "They're more Bowler Hat than . . . than your parents. Very correct. Think Weybridge is the center of the universe. Very kind, rather strict." He grimaced, a bit helplessly. "We don't often see eye to eye, put it that way. They certainly don't watch *TW3*. And as for discussing the Profumo scandal . . ." He laughed. "My goodness, if they had a daughter like you and she knew some of the things you know I think they'd have a heart attack."

Cecily was picking up stones, but she stood up at this and looked at him. "Why?" she said simply. "What's wrong with a daughter like me?"

"Nothing," Guy said, shaking his head at her. "Absolutely nothing. You're not like most other girls, that's all. You think for yourself, not for others. It's great. Well, I think so, anyway."

"That doesn't sound very alluring," Cecily said, scratching her arm. "Girls don't want to be told they're a bit odd, Guy. I jolly well hope you don't say that to girls at Oxford. No wonder you've had to tag along with your brother for the holidays, if that's the way you normally speak to your hosts."

Guy gave a shout of laughter. "Come here, you vile child," he said, getting up and racing towards her. He grabbed her and tickled her, pinning her arms above her head while she screamed.

"Stop it!" she cried breathlessly, but he carried on. "Stop it, Guy, stop it!" Suddenly her mood changed, as if she wasn't finding it funny anymore. "Get off."

She leapt up.

"I'm sorry," Guy said, standing up, breathing hard. "Cecily—sorry, I didn't mean—"

"It's fine," she said, and moved away from him, towards the sea.

Louisa appeared at the bottom of the steps. "Here," she called, as Jeremy and Frank emerged behind her, gingerly carrying the hamper. They were followed by Archie, who was wearing tortoiseshell sunglasses. Louisa looked at Cecily and Guy in a rather disapproving manner. "You're making such a racket, you two."

Cecily turned away, biting her lip, as Frank lifted the hamper clear above his head and carried it the last few steps onto the beach. "Whew," he said, laying it down on the sand. "That path is pretty hair-raising."

"Thanks, Frank," Louisa said, glancing at him. "Now, what have we got in here?" She knelt down on the ground, and he gently pulled her head towards his crotch as she opened the hamper. Her fingers fumbled on the leather straps as Frank stroked her hair, softly, looking down at her flaxen blonde crown, his fingers working their way through her scalp. "Um," Louisa said, faltering. "Well—"

"Is there anything other than ham for lunch?" a voice behind her said, and Miranda stepped onto the beach, in a bathing suit of blue and white vertical stripes that accentuated every bump and curve of her body. She gave Archie a half-wave. "It's just I don't really like it, especially the way Mary cures it. It's awfully soapy."

"Yes," said Louisa, not blinking. "There's tomato, with some lettuce and mustard."

"Oh," said Miranda, her expression unreadable behind her large black sunglasses. She shrugged her shoulders. "Well, that's fine. I'll just pick out the tomatoes."

Louisa opened her mouth, but Jeremy said hurriedly, "Thanks so much, Louisa, that all looks wonderful. Anyone fancy a game of rounders before lunch?"

"Games?" said Miranda. She spread her towel delicately on the sand. "Oh, no, thanks. I'm going to sunbathe. And read my *Private Eye*." She lay down, leaning up on her elbows, and, making a tiny moue with her lips, produced a magazine from a canvas bag.

Cecily opened her mouth to speak, and then closed it rapidly again. Louisa gave a loud snort. "How amusing," she said. "Let me know if you need any explanatory notes. Or let Guy know, rather."

Frank cleared his throat. "Louisa," he said, placatingly. "Why don't we go for a walk along the path? We can play rounders later."

"Yes, please," Louisa said. She looked up at him and smiled. "I'd love that." She took his hand. "Let's go."

They disappeared up the steps. Miranda looked around. "Oh, has Louisa gone off to play with Frank?" she said, after a moment. "I was hoping she'd get me a drink. He's forgiven, I take it."

"Miranda," Archie said, under his breath. "Stop it." He turned to the others and rocked on his feet. "We can play rounders with four, can't we? Improvise a bit?"

"Of course," said Guy. He looked up at the path and then back at Miranda. "Sure you won't play, Miranda?"

"Oh." Miranda was rather trapped. "Um—no, thanks, Guy dear. I think perhaps later? I do so want to read my *Private Eye*."

"I feel sorry for Miranda," Cecily said, as the four of them moved across to where the beach was smooth. "It must be awful, being so bad at whatever it is she's trying to be."

"Shut up, Cecily," Archie said automatically. "You don't know what you're talking about." He spun the cricket bat around in his hand. "Hi! Leighton, Jeremy, what do you say we play cricket instead? I fancy trying out my new fast bowling technique. It puts Wes Hall to shame."

"Great idea," said Jeremy, whose bulky frame was better suited to rugby than cricket. "Cecily, do you want to bat?"

"Yes, I do," Cecily said. "Miss Moore said I was a great batswoman this term. I've really come on, apparently. Perhaps I'll play for England one day."

The three men were silent. She looked at them, smiling slightly.

"Oh, sorry, I forgot. I'm a girl. How ridiculous of me."

"Right," said Archie, handing her his bat. "Show us what you're made of."

A rather hilarious game of cricket ensued, as Cecily demonstrated on a tiny pitch that she was, in fact, a talented batswoman. The tennis ball landed in the sea so many times the game had an extra added spin to it, but this did not daunt Cecily in the slightest.

"My hand-and-eye coordination is excellent," Cecily said immodestly, when Guy congratulated her. She smiled at him. "I've often been told so. I'm remarkable."

"So I can see," Guy told her. He looked up at Louisa and Frank, back from their walk. "Hi, you two."

"Where did you go?" Archie asked, as Louisa opened the hamper.

"Oh, just around, up along the rocks," Louisa said. "There are loads of tourists on the beach behind us." She lifted out a large package wrapped in greaseproof paper. "Isn't this fun, a picnic like this on the beach?" She gave a great contented sigh. "Oh, it's lovely when everything's lovely. Here are the sandwiches," she said, suddenly practical Louisa again. "Frank, can you give them out?"

"Of course."

"We walked pretty fast," Louisa went on. "It's lovely, there's a good breeze when you're up on the path. I saw a lovely flower, quite unusual. What did we think it was, Frank?"

"You thought it might be a Meadow Cranesbill," Frank said.

"Wow," said Miranda, gingerly inspecting the pile of sandwiches Frank was offering her. "Fascinating. What japes."

After lunch, Jeremy, Frank, and Louisa lit cigarettes, and sat back. The occasional light spray of water hit them, but otherwise everything was still.

"I want to get as boiling as possible, and then dive into the sea," said Cecily, closing her eyes and stretching out. "So that my skin feels hot to the touch." She slid one slim leg across a smooth, black stone. "It burns!" she said.

"It's great," Frank said. "We could be in Greece. Or India."

"Or France, it gets jolly hot in France," Jeremy said.

"I want to go to India one day," Cecily said. "Go and see where Daddy's from. Except it's Pakistan now, Lahore."

"I want to go to India," Guy said. "Some friends of mine thought they'd go after they've gone down from Oxford."

The others were silent. "It's a long way," said Louisa eventually.

"Well, but we've got the rest of our lives," Guy said easily. "I want a bit of adventure before I settle down. In ten years' time, I'll be a boring old something-or-other. I want to be able to look back and say, 'Oh, yes. I did that.' Before I go back to sleep by the fire."

"You'll never be a boring old something-or-other, Guy," Frank told his brother. "I will be. Not you. You'll be living in a flat on the Left Bank, wearing a beret and smoking Gitanes, talking about the summer you spent with Arvind Kapoor."

Guy gave a short laugh.

"The Bowler Hat's right," Louisa said. "You'll be up at the Moulin Rouge every night, hanging out with cancan dancers and drinking absinthe—"

"I say, when is this?" Guy said, amused. "1890? Is Toulouse Lautrec my best friend?"

Louisa looked rather stumped. "Oh, I don't know," she said.

"Where will you be in ten years, then?" Guy asked her. "Not one of the cancan dancers, I'll bet, Louisa. Not you."

"Oh. I don't know. Where do you think I'll be?"

Guy put his coffee cup down and stared out to sea. "I think you'll be in New York, running the UN."

"Oh, Guy! Come off it!" Louisa said.

"He's right," Frank said. "I think you will."

"Yes," said Archie. "Hundreds of men underneath you. You'd like that, Louisa."

"Shut up, Archie, you little pig," Louisa said.

"I didn't mean—"

"God, you're vile, you really are." Guy and Frank watched her, puzzled. She turned her back on Archie and swiveled round to face Frank. "You don't think that, really, do you?"

Frank was still staring at Archie in confusion, but he stopped and wrinkled his nose. "Don't know, but I can imagine it, Louisa. You're a terribly organized girl. Awfully clever, much more than me. You're a real go-getter."

"Well, I don't know if I want to be a go-getter," Louisa said archly. She seemed a little disturbed by this. "Perhaps I just want to be at home. Have some children, look after them. Be a good wife."

"Urgh." Cecily made vomiting sounds behind her. "Please, Louisa."

"You could do both, you know," Guy said. Louisa looked at him blankly.

"What about you?" she said, gently nudging Frank. "Where do you think you'll be in ten years' time? What will you be doing?"

"Oh. Um." Frank looked uncomfortable. "Don't know." He picked at the embroidered logo on his polo shirt. "Sounds rather boring, if you say it out loud."

"Say it," Guy said quietly. "It's not boring, old man, not if you really want it."

Frank stretched his arms above his head, faux-nonchalantly, and said, "Well, it's not much, really. Think about having a nice house somewhere. With a little drive, some hedges."

"Hedges?" Cecily said, almost in disbelief. "Why—" Guy nudged her.

"And you know—I'd have qualified as a chartered surveyor. Be working at a good company. I'd get the train into town every day. Work with some nice chaps. I suppose, I never thought about it much. And—and well," he said, getting into his stride. "There'd be a . . . a family at home for me when I got back."

"You really are the last of the great romantics, Bowler Hat," Cecily said. "Who is this family, a load of gypsies you've welcomed into your home?"

Frank took Louisa's hand.

"No," he said, squeezing her fingers. "My own family. My wife, and our children."

There was a silence as the others digested this and Louisa's eyes shone.

"If she's back from work, of course," added Frank, breaking in again. "Er—she might still be working, of course. Perhaps we'd even get the train back together," he said, really into his stride now.

Cecily got up. "I'll buy you both matching bowler hats for the wedding," she said. "Goodness, I got you quite wrong, didn't I?" She stretched herself out, languorously. "What about you, Archie?"

"Don't know," Archie said simply. His eyes roamed round. "Here's Miranda." He called out to his approaching sister, "You going for a swim?"

"I thought so, yes. I'm boiling. Come in?"

"Sure," said Archie. "Miranda's a brilliant swimmer."

"She's pretty amazing, actually," Cecily told Guy. "She can do a somersault in the air off the diving board at school. She swims like a fish. It's—" She stopped as Miranda reached them.

"Are you talking about me?" Miranda said suspiciously.

"Yes," Cecily said. "Just saying what a great swimmer you are."

"Don't lie," Miranda said.

"We were! Weren't we?" Cecily said, turning to Guy.

"What about you, Miranda?" Guy asked. "Where do you think you'll be in ten years' time? What will you be doing?"

Miranda looked taken aback.

"I'm going to be running the UN," Louisa said. "Guy's going to be living on the Left Bank wearing a beret, Frank's going to be wearing a bowler hat and going into the City every day and Jeremy, we didn't do you, or you, Cec."

"Oh, I'm boring," Jeremy said. "I'll be a doctor. I know what I want to be."

"That's wonderful." Cecily looked at him with adoration.

"Archie, what about you?" Miranda asked her brother quickly.

"I don't know," said Archie helplessly. "I'd like to live in a hotel. You know, Monte Carlo or somewhere. Drive a fast car, see a bit of life." He crossed his arms. "But I'd be successful. Have my own business, selling cars or something. Studying's a waste of time."

"But you're going to Oxford, I thought," Cecily said.

"No, I'm not." Archie shrugged. "Don't see the point. Whole world out there full of fun and excitement, I'm not going to molder away in some old building for three years studying things people don't care about anymore."

"But—" Cecily's mouth dropped open. "Did you know that, Miranda?"

"He can do what he wants," Miranda said.

"But have you told Mummy and Dad?"

"Cross that bridge when I come to it," Archie said, turning his face to the sun and closing his eyes.

"So that's the plan," Cecily said, nodding at him. She looked at her brother and sister, from one to the other. "Right. Well, it's none of my business."

Louisa, ignoring this exchange, said, "What about you, Miranda?"

Miranda shrugged her slim shoulders. "Never really thought about it," she said, adjusting the rubber strap around her goggles which were on her head.

"You don't know what you want to do yet?" Louisa said.

Miranda turned on her, and said vehemently, "Oh, shut up, Louisa. Just because you're perfect and know exactly what's going on with your stupid, boring life. Leave me out of it. I don't know, I tell you. I'm not good at anything, and that makes it rather hard."

"You must be good at *something*," Guy said, not unkindly.

"Well, I'm not," Miranda said flatly. "I'm ugly. I'm too thin, too hairy, too stupid to go to university. The only things I like doing are buying clothes, and sunbathing and swimming, and last time I checked you couldn't do that as a job. I'm the lame duck of the family, and I know you all despise me. So—so just . . . just fuck off."

She spat out the last three words and stalked off towards the sea, leaving Archie to run after her.

"Poor girl," Frank said, watching her costume-clad figure as she slid into the blue-green sea.

"Oh, she'll be fine," Cecily said, with a sister's impatience. "She just wants to go to finishing school and learn how to get out of cars properly and she's furious Mum and Dad won't let her."

"How do you get out of cars properly?" Guy asked, intrigued.

"No idea but we're all doing it wrong apparently," Cecily said. "She'll learn, and teach us, and then she can marry a rich husband and spend all day in Harrods buying all the dresses she wants. I suppose that might make her happy." But she didn't sound sure.

Jeremy nodded. Louisa was silent. The little group was still, for a moment, watching the twins as they bobbed in and out of the clear water.

"What about you?" Guy asked Cecily. "What will you be doing in ten years?"

"Thank you for finally asking, Guy." Cecily pointed one foot delicately in front of her. "Working on the script of the film of my best-selling novel about Mary Queen of Scots," she said. "Living in Hollywood with Stewart Granger. Buying my second silver Rolls Royce because the first one will be worn out with driving me to film premieres and parties. And eating all the cream éclairs I want." She stood up. "OK?"

"Yes," said Guy, taken aback. "You've worked it out, haven't you?"

"Oh, absolutely," Cecily said pragmatically. "But I'll have time to go to India with you before, if you want. Come on, let's swim."

Sixteen

That night, at dinner, a party atmosphere set in. Perhaps it was because of the sun but it became clear, when they gathered on the terrace that evening, that there was something in the air. The holiday
was real, it was happening. It was theirs to enjoy.

Yes, they were all on good form that evening. Louisa, like Grace
Kelly in a blue Grecian dress, shyly touching Frank's hand; Frank,
tall and more assured dressed for dinner in a jacket, shirt, and trousers than he ever was in shorts, dutifully meeting Louisa's smiles.
Miranda, the last one down, eventually appeared modeling another
of her recent purchases, a crisp cotton black-and-white gingham
shift, with a sash tie behind, her hair pushed back with a black silk
Alice band.

Her mother stared at her, Frank and Guy swallowed, and Cecily
whistled.

"Wow, you look great, Miranda," Jeremy said. He stared at her
with admiration. "You look like a film star. Doesn't she, Franty?"

Frances nodded. "Absolutely. You're like a swan, darling."

Guy whistled. "Why, Miss Kapoor, you're ravishing," he said, in a
terrible American accent.

"Thank you so very much, darling," Miranda said, in a husky
film-star voice. There was a little throb in her throat, almost as if she
was nervous. "So very kind of you. So kind." She accepted a drink
from Jeremy. "You look lovely tonight, Louisa," she said in a loud
voice.

Louisa, visibly touched, still looked startled. "Oh, Miranda . . .
thank you."

"No one has complimented me on my dress," said Arvind, who was sitting in a chair on the edge of the terrace, admiring the sunset. "No one has said, 'How nice you look today, Arvind.' "

"Daddy, you look ravishing," Miranda said, wanting to bestow compliments on everyone now. "Mummy, you too."

"Very heartfelt, Miranda," Frances said drily. "I'm not quite ready for the bath chair and the nursing home yet, you know."

"Mother," said Miranda, in a wheedling tone. "Can I ask you a huge favor, please?"

"Er—" Frances said. "What is it?"

"Can we put on the Beatles? Please? Your record player's so much better than the one upstairs."

Louisa clapped her hands. "Oh, Aunt Frances, please. I think you'd really like it," she said. It was so far the only thing Miranda and Louisa had found they had in common.

"I know it very well," Frances said drily. "I've heard that dratted album wafting down the stairs about ten times a day for the past week. And over Easter. I'm sick of it."

"Oh, go on," Miranda pleaded. She drank some more of her gin and tonic. "Listen to it properly. Please. 'Please Please Me!' " she said, and Frances laughed, and unbent.

"All right," she said.

So they ate supper to the strains of "Please Please Me" playing on the old gramophone from the sitting room, and Louisa sang "Love Me Do" softly in Frank's direction, and even Cecily (who was secretly rather keen on John Lennon), sang along to "Twist and Shout." "Because they didn't write this one," she explained, when Miranda looked at her coolly and asked why she was singing, if she hated them so much?

Arvind and Frances were not censorious parents, and they allowed wine at the table, though Cecily was only allowed a glass. This night, perhaps because of the wine, or the heat coming off their sun-kissed skin, or the heady, late summer smell of lavender and sea and sun oil, the wine disappeared faster than it might have done.

"Another bottle?" said Mary, when she came in to put down the peach melba.

"Oh—" Frances, who had been working in her studio all day, was tired and rather drained. She waved her hand. "Yes, a couple more, please," she said. "My glass is empty." She looked around the table. "I do feel old," she said, to no one in particular.

It was still very hot outside, humid and still, and Frances went to bed after supper, pleading a headache, followed by Arvind. The younger generation moved out onto the terrace where they sat for a while, too tired to move, not really saying much. Frank and Louisa stood at the edge of the group, he with one arm round her waist, a glass of wine in the other. He was rather drunk.

"This time next week, your parents will be here," Cecily said into the silence. She smoothed a hand over her brow, to the scarf she had tied back her hair with, and stood up. "I'm going to bed," she said, as if realizing she was not in the right frame of mind for the party. "Goodnight, everyone."

With her departure, it was as if the spell had been broken, and the party was deflating.

"I'm actually quite tired," Louisa said, moving Frank's arm which was creeping up around her waist towards her breast. He drained his glass, and she moved away from him. "It must be all that sun."

"Well, I'm off," Jeremy said. "I'll take the glasses through."

"I'll help you," Louisa said. She turned to Frank, and kissed him on the cheek. "Night, Frank. See you—tomorrow."

"Oh." Frank blinked. "Yes, tomorrow. You're—going."

"Yes, I am," Louisa said.

Frank's lips drooped. "Oh, right then. I suppose I'd better be off soon as well. Night, Louisa."

He stayed on the terrace as, one by one, the others filed into the house, saying goodnight. He was swaying slightly, but after a minute he shook his head and looked around him, as if noticing for the first time that the party was over. He stared contemplatively into the darkness.

Someone appeared around the corner, making him jump.

"Mrs. Ka—Frances, hello," Frank said, his eyes widening. "I thought you'd gone to bed."

Frances leaned against the wooden table, her eyes dancing. "I was having a cigarette down by the gazebo. It's such a beautiful night, I couldn't quite bear to go inside just yet."

She hugged herself, wrapping her slim, bare arms round her black-silk-clad body. Frank stared at her.

"Do you have a cigarette, Frank?" she said, and held out her hand.

Befuddled by wine, but mesmerized by her, Frank gave his hostess a cigarette. She put it to her mouth and watched as he lit it.

"Don't worry," Frances said, her voice rich with amusement. "I won't bite you."

"We're having such a jolly holiday, Frances," he told her.

"I'm glad to hear that," she said, smiling in the darkness. "I hope there's more to come." She rolled her head from side to side, listening to the vertebrae crunch slightly. "Ouch," she said.

"You all right?" Frank asked.

"Just—it's been a long day," she said. "My back's stiff. You're lucky, you lot. You're young. You sleep well, you eat well, you have fun. . . . And then you become a proper grown-up. And it's different."

Frank, holding his glass at an angle, appeared to have realized he was a little too drunk for this conversation. "I'm sorry," he said.

"It's not your fault." Frances bit her lip, sat down on the terrace and was silent for a moment. "But that's for another day. I don't want to puncture the golden dreams of youth." She took a deep breath. "Ah, when I was younger, we used to come to this part of the coast for picnics, to swim. Pamela and I, and our friends. I'd see this house, up on the hill, and wonder about it." She brought her legs up so her chin was resting on her knees. "I always wanted to live here. And now I do."

"That's great, isn't it?" Frank sat heavily down next to her.

"Yes," Frances said softly. "Yes, it is. I'm very lucky. I have to tell myself that. It's just sometimes I wish I was anywhere . . . anywhere but here."

He was silent, as was she. Upstairs, a window opened quietly, but otherwise the house was completely still.

Seventeen

Over a week passed, but it could have been a year: time seemed to stop, wrapping them in a cocoon. The days were filled with warm weather, fresh cold seas, lazing, reading, listening to music. By night they watched each other on the terrace or over dinner, watched as they grew more tanned, more at ease, knew each other, for better and for worse. It felt as if it had always been like this, a kind of heightened reality where everything was more exciting, colors were sharper, people were more beautiful, life was there to be taken. But of course, it wasn't really like that. Perhaps it was the summer wind, blowing off the sea and through the house, sweeping them up in its path. But none of them was unaffected by it.

They left Summercove too. Frances got them tickets to the Minack Theatre and they saw *Julius Caesar:* sitting out in the refreshing night breeze on the theater at the edge of the sea. They ate pasties in Marazion, and Cecily and Guy walked across the glittering, silver causeway to the beautiful fortress castle of St. Michael's Mount.

Some of them went surfing in Sennen Cove; one morning the others stayed behind while Guy, Louisa, and Cecily went with Frances to St. Ives to see her dealer and talk about the London show. As they were leaving, Frances stumbled and stepped on Frank, who was kissing Louisa goodbye; she pierced his foot with her stiletto heel, and was horrified as he sank to the ground in agony. They bought him sickly pink sticks of rock from St. Ives to say sorry, the sweet candy already stuck to the striped paper bags by the time Frank returned that afternoon from the beach, hobbling and supported by

Miranda and Jeremy. One evening, they went into Penzance, to see *Doctor in Distress* playing at the Savoy. Guy took photos with his old box Brownie: Cecily on the beach, standing on a rock, her bobbed hair blowing about her face like a glossy brown halo; games of cricket, the ball flying into the sea; Frances at her easel (after he'd asked permission, of course); Frank (by now recovered, no more than an angry red stigma on his foot) snoring on the lawn like a slumbering blond god, the view of the path down to the sea blinding white in the midday sun.

It would seem from the outside as if they were in a blissful, untroubled holiday bubble. It would seem too as if the Leightons fit in perfectly with the household, though of course it was their very outsider status which gave the summer its frisson of excitement, of fun, of them—all of them—feeling as if they were watching themselves in a film, that it was unreal.

The longer their stay the hotter the weather became, night and day. Frank was happiest when he was outside, playing sports with Jeremy and Archie, trying to flirt with Miranda and Frances, and trying also—it would seem unsuccessfully—to seduce his girlfriend. His wandering hands became something of a feature, the fingers creeping across Louisa's well-upholstered, neat figure, only to be pushed briskly away, much to his disappointment. Guy, on the other hand, just seemed to get on with everyone. Everyone except Miranda.

"He's so damned pleased with himself," she said to Cecily one Friday, a week after the Leightons had arrived.

Cecily had just returned from sitting for her mother upstairs and was in a bad mood; she disliked being still for so long. She was slumped in one of the worn-out damask armchairs in the cool of the living room, flicking through a recent *Country Life*. "Look at this girl," she said, slapping the back of her hand in annoyance onto the page. "Lady Melissa Bligh. Why do they always have these photos of boring English girls with awful teeth?" She gazed longingly at Lady Melissa's black lace dress and swanlike neck. "Anyway, Guy's not pleased with himself," she added after a moment.

"Yes, he is," Miranda said, also flicking through a magazine. "He thinks he knows it all. What's wrong and right. He's *very* pleased with himself, if you ask me." She looked out through the French windows onto the lawn, where Guy was playing cricket with Frank and Jeremy, practicing his bowling action. "I don't like the way he acts as if he knows us all so well."

"That's what I like about him, actually," Cecily said. "I feel like I've known him forever."

Miranda rolled her eyes. "You would say that, because I said the opposite. Of course."

"I mean it, honestly," Cecily protested. She looked awkwardly at her sister. "Please. Don't let's row again," she begged. "Last night was so awful. I said sorry for it. You know I did."

"All right," Miranda said crossly. She touched the glowing red scratch on her cheek, and Cecily too; they were almost identical. "We're all right now. Let's leave it, for heaven's sake."

There was a silence. The magazine slid off Cecily's lap onto the floor; she ignored it. "Well, I don't like Frank," she said after a while. "I just don't."

"Why don't you go and play cricket, Cecily?" Miranda said icily. "Burn off some of that energy before lunch. Little girls need to behave if they're going to eat with the grown-ups."

"Well, I'm going to go and play cricket," Cecily said, as if her sister hadn't spoken. She shot out through the French windows, calling, "Hi! Can I play?"

"Of course," Jeremy said, smiling fondly at his youngest cousin as she ran up to them. "Do you want to be a fielder?"

"Oh," said Cecily. "Um yes, why not?"

"Cec," said Guy, handing her his bat. "I was about to go up and wash my hands before lunch, why don't you take over?"

Just then, there was a scream from upstairs. "Oh! Oh, my God!" There came a muffled thud. "Leave me *alone,* you vile, vile little shit!"

"What's that?" Frank looked up in alarm. "That's Louisa. Louisa? Are you all right?"

There was no answer. Frank began to run, fast, towards the house. "Louisa? Hello? I say, what's happened?"

Jeremy followed him. "Louisa?" he called, breaking into a sprint. "Hey!"

"Archie again," said Cecily softly to Guy, who was looking up at the house.

"Archie what?" he said quickly.

"He's a peeping Tom," Cecily said flatly. "Come on, let's go and see if she's all right."

But it was Archie who needed the attention when they reached the top of the stairs. Through the open door Frank could be seen with his arms around Louisa, comforting her while she cried. And on the landing, rocking backwards and forwards was Archie. Blood dripped from his nose onto the green carpet, staining it black. His carefully groomed hair was messy, the quiff bobbing loose over his forehead, and his beautiful white short-sleeved shirt had blood on it.

"What happened here?" said Guy. He leaned down. "Oh, my goodness. We need Jeremy, where is he? I think you've broken your nose."

Cecily ran back downstairs to fetch him, her eyes wild, staring at her brother.

"She hit me," Archie said. "Silly bitch." He shot Louisa a look of hatred, his hand clasped to his nose. "I was just walking back from the bathroom and she came out of her room and hit me. I've no idea why. She's hysterical. She's a hysterical bitch. Bitch!" he repeated, as if that was the worst thing he could say. He wiped one hand on his jeans, smearing them with blood, and swore again. That was what was almost as shocking, seeing him so disheveled. Archie never had a hair out of place, he never showed any emotion other than amused detachment or careful watchfulness.

Cecily reappeared with Jeremy, who grimaced. He put his finger under Archie's chin and looked at his cousin, who had blood pouring down his face into his shirt. "My goodness," he said. "How did you do this?"

"I'll tell you how," said Louisa, breaking away from Frank and coming forwards. "He spies on me, I told you, Jeremy! I was just changing out of my bathers, and I heard a noise again, and I looked towards the door. There's a gap at the bottom, you can see shadows moving. So I pretended to be going to fetch my hairbrush off the dresser." She swallowed. "And then I opened the door and—I shoved my knee right in his face. Hard." She came up to Archie. "You disgusting, disgusting little dirty bastard," she spat. "What is it with you? What's wrong with you, with you and your damn sister? You're both *disgusting!*"

"I didn't do it!" Archie cried, looking around for support. His gaze fell on Miranda, who had arrived and was standing at the top of the stairs, watching them. "Miranda, I didn't do it. You know I wouldn't do it." He looked imploringly at his sister.

Guy said quietly, "What were you doing there, then?"

Archie was silent.

"Exactly," Louisa said triumphantly. "Look at you."

Frank put his arms around her again. "Poor honeybun," he said into her hair. "Why don't we get you a drink." He looked at Cecily. "Where are your parents? You'd have thought they'd have heard."

"Mum's still upstairs working I think, she doesn't really hear anything when she's in the studio. Dad—oh, who knows. He probably didn't notice either." Cecily knitted her fingers together, as if the unconcern of her parents was an embarrassment to her. She turned to Guy. "What shall we do?"

"Why are you asking *him*?" Miranda said scornfully. Guy looked at Jeremy and raised his eyebrows questioningly.

"I'm going to take you into the bathroom downstairs and get you cleaned up," Jeremy said calmly to Archie. "And then let's have a chat."

"I'm going to tell your parents," Louisa said. Her expression was vicious, ugly. "I've had enough. This whole holiday, the two of you . . . if it's not your sister like a dog in heat, it's you."

"What do you mean by that?" Archie said.

"I mean, this house is . . . oh, God, I don't know!" Louisa threw her hands up in the air, almost in despair. "I hate it! The two of you together, you peering and spying, and Miranda, getting up to God knows what at nighttime, I've heard her, I know what's going on. . . ." She trailed off. "You should both be locked up, what is it with you two? Is it something in your blood? The *other* side of the family, I mean."

There was an awful silence.

"I wouldn't say anything more if I were you, Louisa," Miranda said, facing her cousin, her hands on her hips. "It's not your house, it's ours. You're lucky to be here."

"Don't speak to me like that."

"I'll speak to you how I like." Miranda was shaking, her voice low, bursting with venom. "You'll be sorry, Louisa. I tell you. Don't— don't cross me."

There was a silence, and they were all still, frozen to the spot, staring at each other, as if seeing each other for the first time.

Louisa broke the spell.

"I've had enough of this," she said in a shaky voice, and turned back into her bedroom, Frank holding her hand. "Of all of this." She shut the door, leaving the others on the other side of it, Archie still bleeding, Miranda gazing almost in astonishment at the closed door, and the other three standing there, unsure of what to do next.

The atmosphere was charged with tension, bursting out everywhere, as if it had finally found a release valve.

"Let's go," Jeremy said uncomfortably, handing Archie another tissue, and their strange procession trooped downstairs. "I think we should find—"

"Hello?" A thin, rather querulous voice came from the sitting room, and as they got downstairs a figure appeared in the hallway. "Hello? Is anyone there?"

"Oh, my God," Jeremy whispered.

"Jeremy? Is that you? My goodness, what on earth has been going on?"

"Mother?" Jeremy said, emerging into the hallway. "We weren't expecting you till teatime!" He strode forwards, a smile on his face.

Pamela James, Frances's sister, was standing in the hall, holding a pair of immaculate white gloves. She offered her cheek to her son. "We left earlier, to avoid the traffic. Hello, dear," she said. "Daddy's just parking the car. Where is Frances? No use asking for Arvind, I suppose."

She was like a figure from another world, in a deep fuchsia tweed suit and sensible black patent court shoes, her handbag tucked into the crook of her elbow. Her calm, rather distant gaze took in Cecily, Guy, and Archie, a handkerchief pressed to his nose. "Again. Can someone explain what has been going on?"

Jeremy took charge. He said, "Archie walked into a door. I'm just going to get him cleaned up now, Mother. Cecily, why don't you go and find Franty—Aunt Frances, I mean?" Cecily nodded and ran towards the back staircase to her parents' room.

"Well, it's good to be here, even if no one seems prepared for our arrival," Pamela said, putting her gloves down on the table and looking around, while Archie, Jeremy, and Miranda stood transfixed in the corridor. "It was a very long drive and I'm rather tired. Is lunch soon, do you know?"

"I think so—" Jeremy said, and just then, much to their relief, Frances appeared. "Hello, hello," she said, rushing towards her sister, pushing her hair back up into her headscarf. "Pamela, darling, how wonderful to see you. We weren't expecting you till tea! You have made good time!"

"Thank you," Pamela said. "Yes, we set out early. I hope this doesn't throw your plans off." She pronounced it "orf." "I did say we might be here for lunch."

Frances waved her hands. "No, of course not! It's wonderful to have you here." She linked her sister's arm through hers and they stood there, both tall and similar in looks, but utterly different people: Frances barefoot in cropped trousers and a billowing smock, a patterned scarf tying back her hair, glowing with sun and a smudge of paint on her shirt and her long, slim neck: and Pamela, perfectly dressed, not a hair out of place even after a six-hour drive.

"I'll go and help with the bags," said Guy, glad to have an excuse to disappear.

"We've been overrun with young people," Frances told her sister. "Absolutely overrun with them. I've been feeling terribly old and dowdy, and now you and John are here, we can redress the balance." She smiled manically at Pamela, as if she wasn't sure who she was.

"I hope the children have been behaving themselves," Pamela said. "That they've not been too much trouble."

"The children?" Frances tugged at a blue glass necklace hanging round her neck. "Oh . . . goodness, no. They're wonderful. Terrific to have them all here. And the Leightons are lovely boys. I think they've been getting along fine—I'm afraid we've been terribly lax hosts," she said, scratching her head and smiling vaguely as Guy reappeared, carrying two suitcases, followed by John James, who was taking off his driving gloves as he entered the house. "Ah, John, how lovely!" She kissed him on the cheek. "I was just saying to Pamela, I'm sure the children have been getting up to all sorts of mischief. It's a good thing you're both here, I'm sure!"

Only then did she catch sight of Archie, and she ran her hand rather helplessly over her brow. "Goodness, Archie, you have been in the wars, darling."

They were all silent. Pamela and John stood there, watching them. From upstairs came the sound of Louisa's weeping.

"Is that *crying*?" Pamela said, as if she'd never heard it before.

"Oh, dear," Frances said, looking almost annoyed. "What have you all been up to?"

"You really didn't hear, did you?" Cecily said quietly to her mother.

"No," Frances said. "Have you all gone wild? Started beating each other up? Is this *Lord of the Flies*?" She laughed, but it sounded odd, harsh.

"What have we let ourselves in for, dear?" John said, rocking on his feet. His face was stern; he was only partly joking.

There was no answer to this. The others were silent. Frances went over to the front door, pushing it shut. "Come in," she said, taking a deep breath. "I'll find out when lunch will be ready. I'm sorry. Welcome, welcome."

Eighteen

There would be no "Please Please Me" blaring out of the sitting-room record player into the dining room now that Pamela and John were here, that much was obvious. There would also be no smoking after dinner, and Cecily would not be given her customary glass of wine. And there would be no lazing around on the terrace afterwards. Something in the atmosphere had shifted that day.

When Pamela and John came into the living room that evening, Guy was saying to Frances, "The Stratford by-election is soon, isn't it? I bet old Macmillan must be terrified. The way things are going, that Monster Raving Loony party could win it, you know. They've certainly got my vote."

"I don't think that's a suitable subject for discussion," said Pamela, stopping in front of him. "And I don't think one should refer to the Prime Minister of one's country as 'Old Macmillan,' Guy."

Frances jumped up. "No, of course not," she said cravenly, shooting Guy a glance of apology. "Quite right. Jeremy, will you get your mother a drink? Pam, will you have a gimlet? Darling, that's a beautiful dress, you put me quite to shame." She patted her sister's arm and turned, catching sight of her daughters, who were looking bored on the sofa. "Miranda, Cecily, you look like vagrants," she said, her voice sharp. "Go and change, for God's sake."

Looking slightly surprised at her mother's harsh tone, Cecily said, "But Mummy, Guy and I were picking the blackberries, you said it was all right."

"Not like that," Frances said. "Look at you." She waved a hand, encompassing her youngest daughter's stained yellow shorts and crumpled white cotton top. Cecily's hair was in knots where the wind had caught it. "Guy changed, why on earth can't you?"

Cecily turned to her, mystified. "Mother, you are very, very annoying."

"Cecily!" Pamela said, scandalized. "You shouldn't talk to your mother like that."

"She *is* annoying," Cecily said. "In the mornings when she paints me she's always trying to get me to be more ruffled up and dirty, and when I am, she tells me to go and change! Come on, Miranda."

"I'm not changing," Miranda said. She crossed her arms and stared defiantly at her mother, thick hair tossed to one side, her rosebud lips pouting.

"Oh, yes you are," Frances said, her voice quiet.

Miranda squared up to her. "No," she said. "I don't want to. And you know you can't make me."

She carried on staring at Frances, her jaw set, her eyes blazing. Cecily watched them.

"Fine," Frances said eventually, turning away from Miranda, but not before she'd given her a cold, hard look, quite chilling. "How did you get that scratch on your cheek?" she said suddenly. Miranda covered her face with her hand, blushing.

"Did it myself," she mumbled.

"Where's Archie?" Frances asked.

"Early night," Guy said. "Still a bit shaken." Frances looked as if she would ask something else, but then a voice behind her came from the corridor. "Ah. So, the outsiders are inside." Frances turned around gratefully.

"He lives!" she cried, trying to keep out the harshness she could hear creeping into her voice. "Darling, hello. Get a drink. How's your day been?"

"Unpleasant," Arvind said. "Troubling. Disrupted."

He advanced gingerly into the room; he was uneasy around his tall, brash, far-too-English sister-in-law.

Frances went over to him, smiling suddenly. "Poor darling," she said. "Have a gimlet. Thank you, Mary."

"Welcome," Arvind said, raising his glass to Pamela and John. They nodded politely.

Silence threatened to engulf the room. "How—how is your work going?" John enquired, looking vaguely from Arvind to Frances, both of whose professions, if you could call them that, were a source of mystery to him. John was a solicitor of the old school. Philosophers and painters were outside his remit but, unlike his wife, he thought you had to ask to find out.

Frances and Arvind looked at each other, like naughty children caught by a teacher.

"You first," said Arvind.

"Oh, well. I'm preparing for a show, at the Du Vallon Gallery, in September," Frances said.

"How interesting." John nodded.

"Thank you." Frances smiled. "We're having a party! They're sending out invitations soon."

John nodded again. "Delightful."

There was an awkward pause.

"Did you—did you hear about Ward taking an overdose?" Miranda said. Her mother frowned.

"They say he won't make it through the night," Jeremy added.

"This whole case," John said, shaking his head. "The state of the country after this trial is over—the damage will be incalculable."

Pamela nodded. "Oh, yes. I agree. Some of the details—!" She shook her head.

Frances batted her husband playfully on the arm. "Go and see if Mary's ready for us, will you, darling?"

"Of course!" Arvind exclaimed with relief. "Excuse me," he said, exiting for the kitchen.

Guy was watching this exchange when a movement by the French windows caught his eye. Cecily had reappeared, in a simple black linen dress, her hair smooth and gleaming, her cheeks flushed. She was leaning against the door frame, staring at them, smiling, her eyes full of tears.

"Hey, I say." He went over and nudged her. "What's up?"

"Nothing!" she said quickly, brushing away something on her cheek. "I'm just a bit tired. It's almost too hot, isn't it? There's a storm coming, I think, there's no breeze at all."

Guy ignored this. "Cecily? What's wrong?"

She smiled. "Darling Guy. Nothing. They're so funny, my parents, that's all. I don't understand them. I look at them and I think I don't really know them at all. That must sound silly."

"You never sound silly," Guy said, his voice full of warmth. "Trust me."

"You're being nice." She turned to him, her face glowing, and Guy was taken aback; she was so beautiful in that moment, her clear coffee-colored skin covered with a smattering of dark caramel freckles from the sun, her green eyes so dark they were almost black, and the evening breeze ruffling her hair. He caught his breath; the smell of lavender from the bushes next to them was almost intoxicating. She breathed in too, with a shudder. "I sometimes think I'm too emotional. Most of the girls at school, they're quite happy to leave their parents and brothers and sisters behind, for months on end. And their homes. I hate it, you know. I love them and I love it here, it's awful being away. And then I come back and I forget . . . how things are."

He was touched. "Why don't you tell them?"

Cecily shrugged her shoulders. "Oh, it's good for me to toughen up, I'm sure. I just—I wish I didn't *feel* things so much. All the time."

"Such as?"

She stared at him. "I—I can't say." She gave a little laugh. "Oh, Guy, I wish I could. To you of all people, I wish I could. But I can't."

"It's a good thing, feeling too much, Cecily," he said. "It means you care. . . ." He touched her bare arm and was surprised when she jumped. "Sorry," he said. "I didn't mean to scare you."

"You didn't," she said. She caught her lower lip in her teeth, and raised her eyes to his, slowly.

"God. . . ." Guy heard himself saying. "You really are beautiful, Cecily."

They stared at each other, blankly, for a moment. He held out his hand—she held hers out too. For a split second their fingers touched, and then she stepped away, hastily, and Guy was left standing by the window, watching her as she picked her way towards her mother. Something strange, fundamental, was shifting within him. He called to her, in a low voice, "Cecily—"

But she ignored him.

He did not take his eyes off her until they were called in to dinner.

Louisa linked her arm through Frank's as they walked towards the dining room.

"I do hope Daddy isn't too boring," she said in a quiet voice. "He can be rather . . . old-fashioned. He's furious about the Profumo affair, I don't quite know why. He tends to expound, once he's had a glass of wine. It's rather mortifying."

"Oh, I'm used to it." Frank yawned, and nodded. "Sorry," he said. "Awfully tired. Don't mind me, Louisa. Not on very good form tonight."

Louisa squeezed his arm in jokey exasperation. "How can you be tired? You had a nap this afternoon while we were all swimming and picking blackberries, didn't you?"

"Perhaps that's the problem," Frank said. "Oh, too much sleep, I suppose. It's—I'm much better now, promise."

She looked up at him. "Are you . . . all right, darling?"

"I am." Frank squeezed her arm back. "Been on rather subdued form, I'm sorry. I am very all right." He kissed the top of her head. "Listen, I've been rather a brute this holiday, I know. Trying to persuade you to do something you don't want to. Will you come for a walk with me, after supper? Steal away when the grown-ups have gone to bed?"

"Frank?"

"There's something we need to talk about," he said. He took her hand and squeezed it tight and Louisa smiled, her eyes filling with tears.

There came voices from next door and suddenly her expression changed.

"Oh, dear," Louisa said. "I think I was right."

"About what?" Frank sounded alarmed.

"Right about Daddy."

"Absolute rubbish," John James was saying, as they sat down. "I tell you, the woman is a common prostitute, nothing more. The men she was associating with. Black men, in Notting Hill. That Edgecombe fellow, turning up and shooting people. Those are the people Mr. Powell is talking about and I for one can't blame him. What are we coming to? It's all very well, and yes, people must be allowed to come into the country, but when they set up enclaves like this. . . ." He waved his wine glass in the air. "Whole system starts to go to pot."

"What system?" Miranda was sitting opposite him, in between Guy and Cecily. She was examining her dirty fingernails. She barely raised her voice; it was the disdain in her tone that was most surprising of all. "The system of white men oppressing everyone else for hundreds of years? Or the system of raping countries and people so you can make money?"

All of a sudden, the atmosphere in the room was electric.

"Miranda—" Frances said, in a warning tone.

"There's coronation chicken and salad," Mary said in a bright voice. "If that's all—"

The others were all sitting still. No one got up. John said, "Young lady, you are confusing the argument. It's a question of how our own great country has been polluted, is being polluted, with the question of immigration, with this lax—lax behavior in public life. . . ." He trailed off, cleared his throat, and then said, "With all respect, I don't think you know what you are talking about."

"Of course I don't," Miranda said scornfully. "I'm just a girl, what would I know? After all, girls are pretty stupid, aren't they?"

"Miranda—" Cecily hissed desperately, next to her. Her uncle was watching her, imperturbable, one eyebrow slightly raised, cold gray eyes in a thin, sculptured face.

"I don't think," said Pamela, "this is appropriate." She turned to her daughter. "Louisa, have you been keeping up with your tennis? Frank," she said, "do you know that Louisa's tennis instructor says she's—"

"No," Miranda's voice cut through, biting and clear. "Girls aren't nearly as clever as boys, of course not. They're born with fewer brain cells, did you know that? They can't drive properly or do science or maths, you know? All they're really good for is . . ."

"Yes?" John looked disdainfully at his niece. "Do enlighten me, Miranda."

"Fucking and cooking," Miranda said, standing up and throwing her napkin on her heaped plate, which Mary had just set down. Louisa gasped, and Guy screwed his napkin into his fist. "That's all we're good for, wouldn't you say?" She stopped and looked round then, as if realizing there was no turning back, she took a deep breath and plowed recklessly on. "Even someone like me, though, that's the question? Me, and my sister, and my brother, and my dad, do you really want us, polluting the country?"

"*Miranda!*" her mother hissed furiously. "Miranda, apologize to your uncle!"

"Oh, don't you dare talk to me," Miranda told Frances, her eyes blazing. "You of all people, don't you dare! You're the biggest hypocrite of them all, telling me what's best for me, how worthless I am!" Frances looked as though she'd just been slapped. "Yes, we're in such an *honest* country too, aren't we?" Miranda's voice shook. "Not hypocritical at all, oh, no. Definitely worth preserving the old way of life. Essential." Her face was pale; her eyes were huge. "I wish Archie were here. He'd say it better. Oh, hang it all."

She took Cecily's hand in hers and gripped it. Cecily wriggled away, embarrassed. She could not bear to look up at her sister, as if she were a leper on the street.

Into the stunned silence a voice spoke from the end of the table.

"No, Cecily, take your sister's hand," Arvind said. "Well said, Miranda," he told his eldest daughter. "Very well said. You don't need to swear, but you are absolutely right in everything else you say."

Miranda looked from him to her mother, who was looking down at her plate, not meeting anyone's eye, and then back again at her father, smiling very faintly at him, almost in shock.

"Well—" Pamela began. "I must say—"

Frances put her hand over her sister's. "No, Pamela," she said. "You mustn't." She seemed to be wrestling with something inside herself. "This is all wrong," she said. She tried to catch Miranda's eye, but Miranda stared straight ahead.

"Let us eat," Arvind said, lifting to his mouth a huge serving spoon that had ended up on his plate. His authority was, as ever, absolute. "We will not discuss the polluting of this great nation in my house. We will give thanks for it instead. Enjoy your coronation chicken curry." His expression was grave, but his eyes twinkled.

They ate without noise, in the airless room.

Nineteen

It came to an end for them not long afterwards. The following day, Saturday, was hot and muggy, and over the next few days the winds seemed to drop as the temperature increased.

The atmosphere had changed inside Summercove too, since Archie was caught peeking, since Miranda's blow-up with her uncle. The cousins eyed each other with greater suspicion; they fell into their own ranks, only Jeremy on the sidelines. Louisa barely spoke to Miranda or Archie, and was extravagant in her affection for the Bowler Hat, who was himself perfunctory in the repaying of it. Miranda and Archie were together even more. They would barely speak to Cecily, whom they considered to be some kind of pariah. And Cecily—Cecily changed, suddenly, almost overnight. Something had got to her. Whatever it was, she wasn't the same in the days that followed.

On the Tuesday morning, four days after the James's arrival, the thermometer in the kitchen read ninety-one degrees, and Mary said it was the hottest she'd known it. At the breakfast table John did what he'd done since he'd arrived, taking first the *Express* and then *The Times* and reading them in silence, digesting every last dirty detail of Stephen Ward's death three days previously and his upcoming funeral, while the others waited, resentfully, for their chance to read, eventually giving up and going outside to sit in the relative cool of the morning shade.

Arvind had taken to having his breakfast in his study, these last few mornings. Guy had got up early, gone for a long walk, the

Bowler Hat said. No one had seen him. The others drifted outside, one by one, hoping for some relief from the heat.

Pamela passed her napkin delicately over her upper lip. "It is extremely close, isn't it?" she said to Frances. "Too close. I should have thought the breeze from the sea would provide a little relief, but no."

"I'm sorry," Frances said. She was drumming her fingers anxiously on the table; there were dark circles under her eyes. "Perhaps the cloud will burn off later, you know. It's still early."

"Hm," said Pamela. "It's getting to be unbearable," she said, standing up. She nodded at her sister as she left the room.

"I agree," Frances said mirthlessly. She turned to Cecily, who was sitting further down the table by herself. "Cec, darling, will you be ready to start at ten?"

Cecily was picking at her placemat. She looked up. "Oh," she said, in a small voice. "Of course, Mummy."

"You look rather pale, darling. Are you all right?"

"Ye-yes." Cecily stared back down at the bowl. "Yes, I'm fine. I didn't sleep very well, that's all. Our room's awfully hot."

"I know, I must do something about it. I'm sorry, darling. The studio will be baking too, I'm afraid. We could do it in the evening, when it's cooler. Why don't you and Guy go for a swim again?"

"No. Not Guy."

"What's wrong with Guy?" Frances stared at her daughter. "Cec darling, what on earth's the matter?"

"Nothing's wrong with Guy," Cecily said. "I didn't mean anything by it. Let's just get it over with."

She looked so wan and sorry for herself that Frances leaned forwards and put her hands together. "Darling, are you sure you're all right?"

Cecily looked intently at her mother. "Mummy . . ." she said after a pause. "You would love me no matter what I did, wouldn't you?"

"Of course I would," Frances said.

"And Miranda, and Archie. You'd still love us, even if we did something terrible." She glanced down, picking strips of raffia off her mat. "That's the way it works, isn't it? We have to love each other no matter what?"

Frances paused. "What's going on, Cecily?"

Cecily said, "Not sure." She looked wildly around the room. "I'm not sure anymore. Everything's changed."

Frances turned towards the open door. There was no one there. Out in the garden, Jeremy and Louisa were lying on the grass, *The Times* spread out like a huge sand and black colored towel, in front of them. They were reading intently.

"What's going on?" she said again. "Cecily?"

Cecily got up. She took a deep breath. "Nothing, Mummy. I'm just being silly. Look, can I go and brush my teeth and my hair? And write my diary up before that? I'll only be a few minutes."

"Of course," Frances said. "I'll go and set everything up." She took something out of the pocket of her embroidered top. It was the ring Arvind had given her, the ring his father had sent over from Lahore after he'd proposed. Cecily loved it. It was her favorite thing, and Frances had even let her take it to school last year. She had her wearing it on a chain around her neck in the painting she was working on. "Here, have this."

Cecily stared at it blankly. "What, put it on now, instead of later?"

"No," Frances said. "I want you to have it to keep. From me. Because . . . because I want you to."

"But it's yours."

"Now it's yours," Frances said. Her eyes filled with tears.

"Why?" Cecily said.

"You love it, don't you? You've always said you did."

Cecily stared at the ring, lying flat on her small palm. "Yes. But why do you want me to have it now?"

"I just do," Frances said. Her voice was thin. "I like the idea of you having something of mine, darling, some jewelry to wear of your own from me. Like a talisman." She smiled. "Why, you're practically a woman these days, it's time we thought about this kind of thing."

Cecily didn't even smile. She just said, "Thank you."

Frances didn't know what to do next. She came round to her and kissed her daughter's silky head. "I'll see you soon, my darling." She added, "It's going to be fine, honestly."

Cecily paused at the door. "Is it?" she said quietly. "I don't know that it is."

Frances watched her daughter go. She didn't know why, but she knew that Cecily had grown up in some way, that the lanky-legged teenager who ran ahead of the others down to the beach, chattering nine to the dozen, had gone forever.

Twenty

"What's for lunch?"

"I don't know." Louisa stretched out on the grass. "You're so greedy, Jeremy. It's too hot to think about that now." She turned on her side. "Do you know where Miranda and Archie went?"

"Think they've gone off round the cliffs."

"They might bump into Guy," Louisa said. "Gosh, everyone's in a bad mood today." She rolled her head from side to side. "I'm starting to look forward to leaving, you know. Like I'll be glad to get away from here."

"Oh, I don't know about that," Jeremy said uneasily. "Don't see why."

Louisa glared at him. "You're the one who said you didn't like it down here, before the Leightons arrived." She chewed a nail. "It's—I don't know. How's it ever going to be right again after what Archie did?" she said pragmatically. "I mean, he could go to prison. And Miranda—what she said to Daddy, I can't believe she hasn't been punished for it!"

"I think Franty and Arvind aren't such sticklers for discipline," Jeremy said diplomatically.

"Well, and look where it's got them," Louisa said tartly, but lowering her voice. She looked at her brother. "Don't you think Miranda went too far? I mean, I think she was awful, and no one's really done anything about it."

"Er—" Jeremy said. "I think she was a bit rude. But—well, I think she meant, well, what she was saying. P'rhaps she didn't quite say it right." He plucked at the lawn. "Dad's a bit outmoded. He doesn't understand the way things are these days. Or the way things are going, if that makes sense."

"I know," Louisa said. "I mean, we've got Indian cousins, we know what it's like."

"Er—" Jeremy said again. "I suppose so. . . ." He looked at his sister. "I'm just suspicious of Miranda's motives, that's all. Think she had a point to prove rather than moral outrage."

"Well, that's Miranda, isn't it?" Louisa said lightly. She leaned her head back, face held up to the sky. "It's so humid, I can't even see the sun. She's an awful drama queen. And she's been so much worse, the last few days."

"It's true." Jeremy rolled over. "It's all rather . . ." His shoulders slumped. "I'm a bit tired of her and Archie, to be perfectly honest. All that sneaking around together and whispering. Odd behavior. What Guy and Frank make of it all I don't know. Old Frank's a sound chap though," he added reassuringly.

"Ye-es." Louisa spoke slowly. "Yes, he is."

She didn't sound overwhelmingly sure and Jeremy was not the type to pry. He was silent, and a few seconds later Louisa said, "He's asked me to marry him."

"My goodness!" Jeremy said. He stood up. "Louisa, old girl, that's wonderful news! Where is he?" He looked around. "I say—!"

Louisa sat up and pulled him back down. "Oh, sit down, Jeremy, you big fool! Shut up a second!" She gripped his arm. "I said no."

"What?" Jeremy's mouth dropped open, and he appeared lost for the right thing to say. "You said no to Frank? Thought you were keen on him."

"Yes," Louisa said. "I was surprised, too. But—" She rolled onto her stomach and stared at the grass. "I just don't know if that's what I want."

They were both silent for a moment.

"Really?" Jeremy said. "Old Frank?"

"Frank, yes—well, no—" Louisa shook her head. "I don't know. He's been different, these holidays, rather off. But I do think I love him, I suppose. Before they came here, I was so sure." She looked at

Jeremy, her huge, blue eyes wide open. "I thought we had an unspoken sort of agreement, that we were to be engaged, even if it wasn't talked about. And now—I just don't know anymore."

"Why?" Jeremy asked softly.

"Something Miranda said, if you can believe that. About women, about us and what we can do with our lives. I—I do love Frank, but oh, Jeremy—" She hit the ball of her palm against her forehead. "Can you possibly understand? I don't know if you can, Jeremy. I think if I marry him, my life will be over."

"Oh, Louisa, come off it."

She shook her head, smiling, and stood up. "You don't understand, I knew you wouldn't." She put her hand out to reassure him. "Don't worry, it's me. I have to decide. Go to Cambridge, study hard, get a good job afterwards." She brushed her shorts down methodically.

"Can't you do both?" Jeremy stood up too, looking mystified.

"I don't think I can," Louisa smiled. "I rather feel that if I marry him, my identity, me, it will be gone."

Jeremy looked upset. "I don't—"

Louisa put her hand on his. "Don't worry, big brother," she said. "I don't expect you to understand."

As they turned towards the front door, Frances appeared at the bottom of the side staircase.

"Gosh, it's hot. Where's Cecily, do you know?" she asked. "I've been waiting for her for ages."

"She's with you," Louisa said stupidly. "Isn't she?"

"No," said Frances. "She was supposed to be, but she went to brush her teeth and write her diary up. That was half an hour ago. She's not in her room." She stared impatiently across the terrace. "Where on earth's she got to? I know she hates it, but it's so very nearly done."

And then there was a scream, and hollered shouting, from the path towards the sea. "Help! Help!"

"What on earth . . . ?" Jeremy darted forwards. "What's that?"

They ran to the bottom of the terrace. Miranda was running towards them, followed by Archie and another figure behind them.

"Help! Get help! Ambulance!" she screamed. "Get the . . . get the ambulance!"

"What?" Louisa said, running towards her cousin. "Miranda—what's wrong?"

Frances stood stock-still, as if frozen to the spot.

"It's Cecily, Cecily." Miranda was racing like a madman, her hair whipping round her face. Two circles burnt red on her cheeks. "She fell—she stepped back and she slipped. . . . Oh, God." She stopped and looked up at them imploringly. "What have I done?"

"You didn't do anything," Archie said.

Guy appeared behind them. "What's happened?" he was shouting as he approached them. "I heard screams—who is it? Where's—where's Cecily?"

"I'll get the ambulance," Miranda sobbed. "Oh . . . Cecily . . . oh, my God."

"What?" Guy stood still. Sweat ran down his forehead. "Cecily?"

Frances was running towards the sea. "Where is she?"

She was opening the gate, but Archie stopped her. He put his hand on her arm, blocking her path. "No, Mum," he said, his face unreadable. "I don't think you should go down there."

"Why?" Frances's voice broke. "Get off me. Why?"

Archie said very quietly, "I don't want you to see her like that."

They knew, then. As Miranda's voice came out to them: "Yes, Summercove. Parry Lane. It's the Kapoors. No, dammit, *Kah*poor. Come quickly!" Her voice was breaking. "Please, hurry up!"

"I'm going down there," Guy said, breaking away and running towards the gate. "I'm going. . . . She might still be all right, we have to do something."

Miranda, emerging from the house, her pale face stained with tears, just looked at him, and then at Archie, and shook her head.

"What happened?" Frances said, watching her daughter. "What did you do, Miranda?"

Her son tightened his grip around her. "Mum. Don't say that. She didn't do anything."

Miranda, who had opened her arms to her mother, let them drop to her side. She looked back at her, and sank onto the stone doorstep like a broken doll.

They brought Cecily's body back up from the beach late that evening, as the sun was setting and the gray moths were fluttering around the candles they had set outside to light the way, just as the storm broke and it began to rain.

The police came too, of course: they had to know what happened, had to see where she'd fallen, take measurements and photographs. And what happened, it would seem, is that Archie and Miranda were out walking when they bumped into Cecily, at the end of the path on her way down to the beach. Guy was walking in the opposite direction, towards the cliffs, and he heard raised voices, shouting, and then screaming. Apparently Cecily had turned and slipped, a little of the rock breaking away with her.

She had fallen down the steps, her neck broken in the fall. It had rained the day after the James's arrival, and even in the height of summer, the steps, cut into the rock and without any sunlight, were often dank and slippery. Arvind and Frances had been advised to get them resurfaced. It was one of those things they'd been meaning to do, but the pair of them—when did they ever do what they were supposed to do?

She should have taken greater care, even Cecily who knew the path, the steps, and the beach so well. She should have been more careful. She should not have died. And though no one said it out loud, and though at the inquest a verdict of accidental death was recorded, it wasn't enough to silence the rumors that all was not what it seemed, that it wasn't, in fact, an accident.

There was something in the air that summer, like a poisonous cloud, growing in strength. And when it broke, like the storm that raged all that night after her death, nothing was the same again. The day after Cecily's funeral, when they had scattered her ashes out to sea (Arvind's idea), and everyone had gone—the mourners, the rest of the family, a stunned Guy, a teary Louisa—Frances locked her studio door behind her, and went into her bedroom. Arvind was in his study, of course.

It was a dull, wet evening, mid-August. The nights were noticeably earlier. There was a chill in the air, a suggestion for the first time that summer was drawing to a close. She held the key in her hand, staring out of the bedroom window. She gazed at the gazebo where her son and remaining daughter sat, huddled together, looking out to sea. Her eyes narrowed as she watched them; hatred, she told herself it was hatred, squeezed her heart.

"It's over," Frances said to herself.

She clutched the key tightly and shivered. Then she opened her bedside drawer and dropped the key in, next to the ring she'd taken off Cecily's damp, cold finger a week ago. She shut the drawer and went downstairs, and sat in the big, empty sitting room until the light faded and she was alone in the dark. Miranda and Archie came in separately, and went to bed. Arvind too. None of them knew what to say to each other, so they didn't say anything at all.

Part Three

February 2009

Twenty-one

"So. Miss Kapoor. Thank you for coming today."

"Not at all," I say. "I'm as anxious as you are to sort this out?"

Unfortunately, I raise my voice at the end of this sentence so that it sounds as if it's a question, not an answer.

There is silence from across the gray plastic desk. I wipe my sticky hands on my skirt and I blink wearily; I've had not quite four hours' sleep. This is good for the sleeper train, where things fall onto the floor as the carriage jostles suddenly or drawers fly out as you round a corner, rousing you from your too-light slumbers. But it's still not much in the grand scheme of things and I am very tired. I can't escape the feeling that I'm still there, lying in a rocking berth. The office in Wimbledon—where my business account manager is located and thus where I have to go if I want to stop the bank calling in debt collectors—is warm and my eyes are heavy. The bump on my head from my Victorian heroine–style fainting fit is still swollen, and has turned an impressive purple color during the night. I haven't been home yet; I'm still wearing my funeral outfit, ironically appropriate for today as well as yesterday.

Yesterday seems like a world away. The pages of Cecily's diary are still in my skirt pocket. They make a crumpling sound as I shift in my seat. Ten pages, that's all, and then—what? Nothing.

When I climbed wearily off the train this morning, I wondered if I'd dreamed the previous twenty-four hours. It would make more sense, somehow. These scant pages in Cecily's scrawling, cramped handwriting, all too little an insight. I keep thinking of them all after the funeral, in the living room at Summercove. My family, standing around in knots, not talking to each other. The taxi ride with Octavia, the near-pleasure with which she thought she was telling me the truth about my mother. Was she?

I can't think about it now. I shut my eyes again.

Opposite, Clare Lomax, local business manager, stares impassively at me, her hands clasped neatly on the desk. Her suit jacket is slightly too big. It looks like a man's.

"So. We've been trying to contact you for a while about your overdraft, Miss Kapoor."

"Yes." I shift my focus back to the present moment. I nod, as though we're in this together.

"We've become extremely concerned about your ability to sustain a viable business. As you know. That is why we have decided to withdraw your overdraft facility and request immediate repayment of the amount in question."

"Yes," I say again.

Clare Lomax glances at her sheet. She reads, in a sing-song voice, "You are five thousand pounds overdrawn at this time, and you have defaulted twice on repayments for the loan you took out with us last year, also for five thousand pounds. I see you also have considerable debt on your credit card, also held with this bank. And despite several letters requesting repayment we have not been contacted by you with regard to these matters, which is why you've left us no other option, I'm afraid, Miss Kapoor."

"Yes," I say again, still nodding, so hard now that my neck is starting to hurt. It is such a huge amount, it doesn't seem real. How has it come to this? What have I been doing? And the answer comes back to me, clear, booming, Octavia's persistent voice in my ear. *Living in a dreamworld.*

"If we look at the company's bank statements—" a flick through the sheaf on her desk, before one almond-shaped pearlescent nail smoothly drags the offending sheet of paper into the light—"well, we can see what the problem is. Too many outgoings, not enough incomings. In fact the last payment into the company account was October 2008, for one hundred and thirty-five pounds."

Bless Cathy. Those were Christmas presents for her mother and her sisters. But I flush with shame that these were the last payments into the account: I am being propped up by friends, by my husband. There have been no website sales since then.

"Miss Kapoor." Clare Lomax shuts the folder with a flourish and puts her fingers under her chin. She stares at me. "It's not good, is it?"

"No," I say.

"And in the meantime—"the same nail scratches down a long list—"we've got payments coming out of the account regularly, driving you further into debt." I gaze down. "Website hosting . . . three hundred pounds . . . Two hundred pounds to Walsh and Sons, Hatton Garden?"

"They make tools. Er—pliers and things." It's the truth, yet I sound wholly unconvincing.

"Right. This payment here, for six hundred and forty-three pounds, in September, to Aurum Accessories."

"That was for materials."

"What kind of materials?"

My voice sounds high, like a little girl's. "Um . . . gold wire, earring studs, and clutches, that kind of thing?" I try to remember. "I've got the receipts in my folder here, I'll check." I've got every single piece of paper I could possibly need, neatly filed away, carried with me to Cornwall and back in preparation for today. I've documented the failure of my business meticulously.

"It's fine." Clare Lomax scribbles something on her pad. "Have you thought of using cheaper materials?"

"What, like string?" I smile, but there's a silence and I realize she's serious.

"I'm just saying there are some very nice necklaces and bracelets made out of waxy thread and beads. You know, you see them in Accessorize, Oasis. And so forth," she adds, pulling out the "th" of "forth" on her tongue, as if to give weight to it. "I'm just saying," she repeats. "You need to look at some other options, Miss Kapoor."

"I don't make jewelry like that," I explain. "I work with metals, enamel, laser cuts mainly, it's different—"

"Miss Kapoor." Clare Lomax raises her voice slightly and shifts her arms forwards and then back into their clasp. I see the flash of a tattoo on her wrist, quickly hidden again by her polyester jacket. I wonder how old she is. "We are here today to discuss your business and to work out a way to keep you from going bankrupt, which at the moment is looking likely." Her voice is clipped, brisk, precise. "You have defaulted on your loan repayments twice. You have refused to respond to us about your overdraft. If you want to avoid a consolidation repayment plan, where we charge you twenty per cent interest and demand repayment of the overdraft beginning now, we need to work out how you can change your working practice so that you don't accumulate debt." She gives a thin smile. "Otherwise, you will have no business. Is that clear?"

I nod. "Yes. It's very clear."

"Do you want to change the way things have been?"

She's staring at me. I sit up straight and meet her gaze. This woman, girl really, whom I've never met before, is calling me out, pointing out my flaws in a way no one else has, in a way I could never do. If she can see them, they must be pretty obvious.

I clear my throat. "Yes," I say softly.

"What?" She leans forwards.

"Yes," I say again, more loudly. "Yes. I really do want to. I want to change the way it's been. I don't want it to go on like this."

As I hear my voice, soft and tentative, saying these words out loud, it gives me a jolt, and I realize again how true it is. I nod, as if confirming it. To her, and to myself.

Clare Lomax folds down a small corner of one of the bank statements in front of her. "Right." She permits herself a small smile and I want to smile too. "Let's carry on, then. So—five hundred and fifty pounds paid out in November. To Aird PR Limited. There's a couple of payments to them last year. Who are they?"

"It's a PR firm. I hired them to publicize my jewelry." She looks at me blankly, as well she might. "They've worked with a few designers I know. People who have gone from having a stall or selling stuff through just a couple of shops to being featured in magazines, in blogs, so people write about you, look you out at the trade shows, and so on. It helps you to get a name for yourself."

"And have they done that for you?"

"No," I admit. "Not really. They got me a mention in the *Evening Standard*, but they got my website wrong. So I didn't really get any uptake from it."

Clare Lomax says, suddenly kind, "You have to ask yourself if your product is right for the general public. If there's more you can do. We see this all the time with small businesses."

Now I'm feeling more confident, I take a deep breath, to try and stick up for myself. "Miss Lomax—we're in a recession. Two years ago I was getting interns to help me, I had orders for shops here and in Japan, the Far East, for fifty necklaces, a hundred bracelets a time. But that's all gone now." I try to sound as though it doesn't bother me. "People are still buying jewelry, but not like they used to. And if they are they won't take a chance on some random girl they've never heard of. It's really hard." I sound as though I'm trying to talk her *out* of lending me more money.

"I can see that," she says drily. She leans forwards, so that a lock of her thin, brown hair falls over her face. "But if you'll allow me to say it, it seems to me you've been burying your head in the sand, Miss Kapoor. You've failed to keep up the repayments, you've not explained what's happening and why you're in difficulties, and most importantly you've failed to communicate with us despite many attempts on our part. And that makes you a bad risk in my book. You've got to face up to it. As it is, you'll probably lose the business if you go on at this rate."

You've got to face up to it. I stare at her, my heart hammering in my chest. "Right. Right."

She says, not unkindly, "I just don't understand why you've let it come to this." She sounds for a second like a concerned friend. I blink. I can't stand it if I start to cry. Don't cry.

I clear my throat noisily and sit up. "I don't understand either," I say softly. "I've had a lot of other shi—stuff going on. And it's been a hard time. Loads of my friends are going out of business. But I'm hopeful. I've got a new collection I've just finished designing."

"Really?"

"Yes," I say. This is a lie, but it's a hopeful lie.

"I've just got to get the cash together to get it made up. And take it to the shows. And I have to start doing the market stalls again. That brings in the money."

"I don't understand why you haven't been doing that all along," Clare Lomax says. "According to my notes when you opened the account you were selling at a stall at least twice a week, and always Sundays."

"I don't do that anymore."

"Why not?"

Why not? Vanity, greed, wanting to spend time with Oli, his jealousy at not having me on Sundays, believing the hype of Joanna, the PR person I hired, who told me I didn't need to stand in the cold on a stall next to lots of other jewelers all vying for attention and space. After the up-and-coming pop star was photographed wearing my necklace the orders started flooding in, and the website was launched a few months later. I listened to them, to Oli and Joanna, when they said I didn't need to do that anymore. And it was expensive—eighty quid a day for the stall, and the Truman Brewery near where I live has too many stalls anyway, and not enough customers, I told myself. I—Oli and I—decided I could live without it, that it'd be a better use of my time to take myself out of that scene, try and move up a level.

I was so wrong. I was wrong about that, about overpaying for the website, about the people I listened to, the way I changed my focus. Ben, in the studio next door, warned me but I didn't listen.

"You love the stall, Nat," he'd say. "You like meeting the people, it keeps you fresh. It's not good for you, sitting at home or in the studio all day."

I started trying to become a brand. A brand like the ones Oli promotes. He thinks everyone is their own brand and I'm sure he's right, but all I can say is, I was better off when everything was simple, when I could sketch in my book, pay the nice old man off Hatton Garden to make up my gold and silver pendants, and sit there in my studio happily making up the necklaces, cutting the chains, choosing the right pair of pliers from my set to bend gold and silver wire, researching suppliers, thinking up new ideas and just trying them out, listening to my iPod, and chatting to Ben and Tania, his girlfriend, who works with him. The trouble is, most of the time I'd prefer to be in their studio with them, instead of on my own. Everything's OK when they're around. There's a distraction, someone to talk to, instead of sitting alone amidst the accessories and pliers, staring into space, wondering what on earth comes next. It's so easy to pop next door and ask for a cup of tea, or bring them biscuits.

Ben never seems to mind. He's one of those open, friendly people who can work in Piccadilly Circus and still concentrate. He likes chatting and so do I. We like the same humor, the same old films, the same biscuits, we were meant to be office buddies, as we continually say. I think Tania is not quite so keen on me hanging around like a bad smell all the time while she's trying to mark up contact sheets or negotiate with a magazine. I think she knows I'm lonely. She wants to tell me to back off and go and do some work. And so I've started limiting myself to one knock on the door a day.

When I realize I've started thinking about it like that, I suddenly see that I have to control my loneliness—that crying all over Ben when Oli left, while Tania made some tea and went and got Jaffa Cakes (and she is French, so Jaffa Cakes are unfathomable to her, so I appreciated the gesture even more) is something you do once, because it's a crisis point, not every week, every day.

The new, strong, confident me looks at Clare Lomax to see if she'd understand this, the mind that has too much time to think. She wouldn't. I wouldn't either if someone else explained it to me. It's as though my life has veered way off track, and although I still can't quite see where it began, at least I can recognize this. I put my hands on the desk and take a deep breath.

"Look, Miss Lomax," I say. "I have really screwed up, but I can show you how and why, and how I'm going to change things. I know I'm good at what I do, and I want to work hard. I've just taken bad advice, and I know how to fix it." I look at her imploringly. "Please, please believe me. I've ignored you and I'm really sorry, but I've been an idiot, keeping my head in the sand. I'll get the money to repay the default loan payments, I can pay them with my credit card today. But please, please don't withdraw my overdraft facility. I just need a bit more time, but I'm going to pay it off."

She narrows her eyes.

"I am," I say. "I don't want it to be like this anymore. You need to trust me." I smile and I can hear my voice is shaking. "I know you've got no reason to, but I really hope you do."

I sit back in my chair and clutch the papers again.

Clare Lomax sighs. "OK, look, there's a way out of this." I hold my breath. "You will have to pay us back a regular amount each month and if you default just once more, that's it. We'll call in debt collectors. You'll have to cut back on your company expenditure. And I see you're married, right?"

"Yes."

"The flat is in both your names?"

"Just my husband's."

"So they can't take that."

"They can't take what?"

"You won't lose your flat."

My head is spinning. "Lose the flat? No, of course we wouldn't . . . would we?"

She says musingly, "Miss Kapoor, I honestly don't think you realize how serious this is."

"I do," I say, my voice practically begging. "Absolutely I do."

"Your husband's working?"

"Yes—yes, he is. But—"

"You're lucky," she says, pulling her papers together. "You can live off him for a few months while you sort yourself out. We'll draw up a payment schedule for the overdraft too and then work out a new way for you to go forwards with the business."

I nod numbly. Maybe I'll have to, but I don't like the idea. I want to get back together with Oli, but not because he'll pay for everything. I'd rather lose him, and the business, than feel that I'm taking him back so I can "live off him" the way Clare Lomax suggests. But I don't say anything. After all, what choice do I have? I've got to make this work for myself. I've got to change the way things have been. I quiver with purpose, I'm surprised Clare Lomax doesn't notice.

"And then we'll ask to see that you're conducting your business more profitably. So it's viable." She clears her throat. "Does that sound like a way forwards to you, Miss Kapoor?" She looks down at her pad. "I'm sorry. Is it Mrs. Kapoor then?"

"No," I say. "It's Mrs. Jones." I hate being Mrs. Jones, for all the obvious reasons. I shift in my seat again, and the papers in my pocket wrap around my thigh.

"Oh. Sorry." She isn't really paying attention.

"Don't be," I say. "It's fine. So—"

"I think we're going to be able to work this out," she says, pulling the keyboard out in front of her and swiveling round to face the computer. "Like I say, Miss Kapoor, things are going to have to change. The question is, are you willing to make those changes?"

"Yes, I am," I say, nodding, and this time I hear myself speak and it's clear, low, confident and I believe what I'm saying, for the first time in ages. "I really am."

Twenty-two

It is a cold day but sunny as I walk down from Liverpool Street towards the studio, hands in my pockets. I'm on the other side of the City, heading back to my beloved East London. Pushing past me on either side are bustling City workers in black and gray, enlivened only by the flash of a red tie or the glint of a gold earring. I shiver in the icy wind, walking briskly.

I hug the papers to myself, trying to keep warm. Now I'm out of it, the meeting seems almost funny, it's so awful. And one thing's clear: though Clare Lomax and I are not destined to be friends who meet in unlikely circumstances and form a lifelong bond, she's completely right. She could see it. Things need to change. I'll be thirty-one in May. I'm a grown-up, for God's sake.

Five minutes later, I am opening the door of the Petticoat Studios at the bottom of Brick Lane. "Studio" is a euphemistic name for the room I rent. It is basically an old sixties warehouse that has been roughly divided up into different spaces of different sizes. My aunt Sameena says that when she was over visiting relatives in the seventies, she'd come to Brick Lane and see row upon row of Bangladeshi men asleep on the floors. They'd wake up in the morning and go to work on a building site nearby, and their beds would be taken by the night-shift workers who'd come back as they were getting up. Now it has exposed brick and steel girders, and Lily the textile designer has stenciled huge patterns onto the wall behind the erratically manned reception desk. Being bohemian and cool does not necessarily mean the heating works or the loos flush all the time, I've found.

"Hello!" I say to Jamie, one of the two receptionists whose salary is paid for by our extortionate rental fee. Jamie looks up and moves part of her blonde fringe away with her finger. She is wearing a black velveteen hoodie with the hood up, and is flicking through *Pop* magazine.

"Hiya, Nat!" she nods perkily. Jamie is very perky. She's pretty and sweet and kind, like an East London version of Sophie Dahl. "How was the funeral?"

"Fine," I say, reaching into my pigeonhole and pulling out the post. "Well, you know."

"Oh, of course." She nods understandingly. "It's really hard, isn't it?"

I am in no mood for trite funereal conversations, and I'm in no mood for beautiful, sunny Jamie, whom I sometimes want to punch in the mornings, she's so upbeat. I smile and nod, then trudge up the cold, concrete circular stairs and unlock my studio.

It's only been two days since I was here, but it feels longer. It's very cold, and the big square windows don't keep in the heat, though it's always light. My own studio is about twelve square feet. It's all painted white. There are floor-to-ceiling shelves next to the window and an alcove with a safe in it, covered with a curtain, a red, lemon, and gray geometric fifties material from one of the bedrooms at Summercove. I keep my unsold pieces in there, and any metals I've bought. There's a small wooden table with an old, battered, paint-spattered radio, a kettle, and a few mugs on one of Granny's old trays, and the rest of the room is taken up with the workbench with all my tools on it. A hammer, pliers, drills, wire, and chain cutters, sharp knives, all covered with tiny pellets of old copper or gold wire, my apron which makes me feel super-professional, and my sketchbook, where I used to be constantly scribbling down ideas. I haven't drawn or written anything new in it for months.

Above the work table six big cork tiles are glued to the wall, onto which I have stuck photos—the one of Granny when she was younger; me and Jay at Summercove when we were five, squinting into the sun, both dark, fat, small, and serious; and Ben and me last year when we went as Morecambe and Wise to the Petticoat Studios

Christmas drinks. Tania didn't get it, but as she grew up on the Left
Bank that's excusable. No one else did either, though. Their average
ages are about twenty-three. The photo makes me smile every time I
look at it; there's such panic in our eyes as we realize what a mistake
we've made, and behind us are grouped our effortlessly trendy fellow
studio-renters in a variety of super-cool, fancy dress outfits, from
Betty Boo (Jamie, of course) to Johnny Depp as Captain Sparrow
(Matt, one of the writers in the writers' collective in the basement). I
never remember that about fancy dress: that you're supposed to look
brilliant, but gorgeous as well. I always just look insane.

Finally, there's a picture of Oli and me on our wedding day two
years ago at the Chelsea Physic Garden, he in a light khaki summer
linen suit, me in white Collette Dinnigan. We're in profile, black
and white, laughing at each other, and we look for all the world as
though we're in a photo shoot in *Hello!*. Sometimes, in the middle
of the afternoon, I'll glance up from my work and catch sight of that
photo, and I'll have to remind myself it's me. There are clippings
from magazines, lots of pins just in case I have ideas for things, a
cartoon from *Private Eye* about artists, and a Sempé cover from the
New Yorker which Oli had framed for me on our first wedding anniversary.

I have to call Oli now I'm back. We need to talk again. It's been
nearly three weeks, and coming back from Cornwall, from everything there and the meeting this morning, has made me see one
thing clearly: this state of in-between nothingness can't go on.

There are window boxes outside with pansies and geraniums
which have died. I need to sort them out now spring is nearly here,
take a trip to Columbia Road and buy some more. Cheaply, of
course. There's nothing to be frightened of. I can get on with things.
I want to channel my newfound, urgent sense of purpose, of the
need for action. But still there's something stopping me, I don't
know what. It's more than Oli. It's Granny's funeral, it's what Arvind
and Octavia both separately said, this casual crumbling of the wall
I'd always thought was around us all. It's the scant pages of the diary

I've read, enough to make me want to read more, desperately read more.

Where's the rest of it? Cecily didn't just write that first chunk, that much is clear. What happened that summer, after the boys arrived? I'm holding the post in my hand and I feel myself screwing up the letters as I screw up my eyes, trying to think. To go from never hearing her name mentioned, to being able to hear her voice so clearly that it's almost as though she's talking just to me, is incredibly strange. To go from thinking that your family is sane and happy, if distant, to realizing you don't really know anything about them at all—where's the rest of it? What happened afterwards, with my mother, with her, with all of them? I have to find out, but how? I have to find the diary. And I have to find some way of talking to my mother about it.

I put the post down on the table. The letters fan out by themselves. At least two are from the bank. I can stop ignoring them. There are two more window envelopes, which always means a bill or a reminder. And there's an invitation to a new trade fair, in June, in Olympia. I've been ignoring those for a while too: what's the point? But now, flushed with enthusiasm, I feel as though anything's possible. I realize that if I'm ever to make my own business work, I need to start designing again. Come up with a new collection that's so amazing I'll be on every fashionista's blog, sold in Liberty's in a year, and have my own diffusion line in Topshop by next year. But more importantly, get it right. Do it because I love it, not because I have to. So what . . . what collection? What will it be?

Then, as if someone else is telling me to do it, my hand steals slowly but surely to my neck. I feel the thin chain and Cecily's ring hanging on it. I walk over to the tiny mirror hanging by the fridge and stare at myself. There are dirty brown circles under my eyes.

The ring nestles against my skin, the almost pink gold soft against my skin. The twisted metal flowers are beautiful. I think about this ring, about Granny, about my dead, young aunt. And suddenly, I hear my grandfather's voice, as his dry fingers push Cecily's diary towards me: *Take it. . . . And look after it, guard it carefully. It'll all be in there.*

I take the pages out from my skirt and look at them, wondering what comes next.

"Nat," a voice calls outside. "Hey! I'm early!"

Of course she's early. It's Cathy, she's always early. Quickly, I shove the pages into my bag as Cathy pokes her head round the door.

Cathy is very short; I am tall. It is one of the many differences that brought us closer together, since we were eleven-year-olds negotiating the nightmarish, unforgiving terrain of the all-girls West London grammar school. She is holding up a brown paper bag.

"I went via Verde's," she says. "I bought quiche. Terrible morning. I think I lost someone fifty grand." Cathy is an actuary, she works in Bishopsgate, the financial district on the edge of the City which encroaches daily ever further into Spitalfields, bringing glass office blocks and Pret A Mangers into the once-ramshackle, historic streets. "I've got salad. And cakes. And some really expensive fruit juice." She comes towards me and kisses me on the cheek. "How are you, love?"

I lean down and hug her tightly, feeling her cold, silky, thick hair against my skin, her reassuring Cathy smell—I think it's a combination of Johnson's baby lotion and Anaïs Anaïs. She's not one to experiment with new things, our Cathy. If she's happy with something, she sticks to it. She found Anaïs Anaïs when we were sixteen and she's worn it ever since. She likes Florida and goes there every winter with her mum, to the same hotel in Miami. If Horrific Ex-Boyfriend Martin hadn't chucked her out and changed the locks three years ago she'd still be with him, which is worrying to me, as he was a bona fide psychopath. She doesn't like change.

She sets the bag down on my workbench and pats my hair. "I kept thinking about you yesterday. How was it?"

"It was OK. Awful, but you know what I mean." I kick my bag further under the table.

"What's that on your head?" She points to the purple bump on my forehead and frowns. "Did you have a fight with someone? Did your mum behave herself? Or did she try and snog the vicar and you got in the way?"

Cathy knows my mother of old. She remembers our parents' evening of 1991. She actually *saw* Mum with Mr. Johnson.

"It's fine." I laugh, though I feel a stab in my side as I think of my mother. I remember how jumpy she was all yesterday, see her distraught face as she remonstrated with Guy, waving me and Octavia goodbye, and hear Octavia: "*Do you really not know the truth about her?*"

"Just a bump." I don't want to, can't, get into that at the moment, not even with Cathy. "They're all pretty mad, my family. You know that."

"They are," Cathy says briskly. "It's a wonder you're not completely mental, Nat, I've often thought that. Or even more ment than you are, if you know what I mean."

"That's *so kind* of you," I say. "I want to know how you are, though. What's up with work? Why's it terrible?"

"I think my boss hates me. Genuinely hates me." Cathy is still staring at my head. "Look, forget about that. How was the meeting this morning?"

There's a noise in the corridor and my eyes dart to the door. I don't know why I should care; I'm paranoid about anyone, apart from Cathy and Jay, knowing how stupid I've been. Even Oli doesn't know the full extent of it. I hid it from him, just as he hid things from me. I don't want Ben, for example, to walk past and accidentally hear the reality of my idiocy. Why should I care what he and Tania think? I don't know. But I don't want him to feel sorry for me. I'm sure he already does, and I wish he didn't. I don't want him to know how stupid I am either.

"Um—" I put the cutlery and plates on the bench and reach for some napkins which I keep in my apron pocket. "It was pretty awful."

"Oh, no."

"No, it's fine," I hasten to explain. "I have to find a thousand quid now to pay back the defaulted loan payments. But I can put

that on my other credit card." Cathy whistles. "And I have to pay off
the overdraft, two hundred pounds a month plus interest. And they
won't, like, call the debt collection agencies in, or the police, or take
me to court."

"Ha-ha," says Cathy. She pulls her ponytail tight with both
hands, as though she's flexing her muscles. "Right."

"No," I say. "I'm serious. They were going to."

"Jesus," she says. She looks genuinely shocked. Cathy has never
been in debt, always pays her credit card off each month. She never
even gets the ticket gate beeping at her because her Oyster card's run
out. That's how organized she is. "I didn't realize it was that bad."
Then she asks awkwardly, "How did it—er, how did it get to that
stage then?"

"I know how it got to that stage," I say. I gesture to the one chair
and give her a plate and fork. "I've been a fool. Sit down. Eat some
of your food." I pour her a glass of apple juice into a navy, chipped
mug that says "Tower Hamlets Business Seminars." "Drink."

Cathy cuts some of the quiche away with her fork. "It's been a
hard time for you though, Nat."

"Maybe, but it's my fault. I haven't been doing it properly," I
say simply. "And I'm fucked as a result. If Granny knew she'd be
horrified—she was so proud of me. Man alive." I shake my head
when I think about Granny now, I think about her in the diary, her
impatience with Miranda, her daughter, as though she knew she was
a bad seed. Did she know?

No. I have to stop these thoughts, at least till I know more. "If
she'd had any idea I'd be leaving her funeral early to come back for a
business meeting to stop me being taken to court by the bank . . . if
she knew how much I've screwed it up. . . ." I think of her and how
much she loved me, how I felt that love all through my childhood.
It's hard to admit it but I plow on. "She'd be so disappointed."

Cathy is concentrating on her quiche on the plate. She says after
a pause, "I don't think she would be."

I laugh. "Bless you. But I think she would. She was really proud I
did fine art at uni. She was so disappointed when I didn't become an

artist, and she was OK with the jeweler thing because she thought it was arty. She didn't expect me to go bankrupt, did she."

"I think you're being too hard on yourself. It's really tough out there at the moment, apart from anything else," Cathy says. She swallows and clears her throat. "Not to be rude, but you know, I always thought . . ." She stops. "Actually, forget it."

"What?"

"Nothing."

I'm laughing. "Come on, Cathy! What?"

"I always thought she was pretty hard on you too, if you want me to be honest."

"Who?" I don't understand her.

"Your granny, Nat."

I scoff, it's so unlikely. "No, she wasn't!"

Cathy says slowly, "I just remember, when we went to Summer-cove, the summer after we'd finished our A-levels before you went off to college, she'd make you paint instead of coming down to the sea with me and Jay, and then she'd critique you. When she hadn't painted herself for like thirty years, and you were only eighteen!" She winces, as though she doesn't like the taste of what she's saying. "I think it was unfair. Like she wanted you to be something your mum wasn't. Or Archie wasn't. You know?"

That's so outlandish I goggle at her. "Cathy, it really wasn't like that!" My voice is rising. "I wanted to learn from her."

"I know, I'm sorry." Cathy is a bit red. "I just think sometimes she was using you to make up for disappointments in her own life. Please, I didn't mean anything by it. Forget it. I'm just glad you've sorted it out. You have, haven't you?"

I think of my already huge credit card bill; I've been putting things for the business on that too, of late, instead of putting them through the account. I am going to be very poor. These last couple of weeks without Oli to split the bills for food and cabs and toilet rolls have already taken their toll. I nod. "I have. It's going to be tight, but I think I have." I touch the ring around my neck. I'm going to start sketching tonight. I take another sip of apple juice and lean forwards, patting her arm. I am perched above her on the stool, she is in a low chair, so this is more difficult than it might be. "I'm sick of talking about me, though. How's tricks? Tell me. I haven't seen you for ages."

"Oh, OK." Cathy shrugs, so that the shoulder pads in her suit jacket shoot up, almost to her ears. "Had another date with Jonathan on Friday." I raise my eyebrows.

"Hey, how was it?"

Just then the door opens and a thick head of hair pokes round. "Nat?"

"Ben!" I stand up. "Hey, come and have some food."

The hair advances into the room, followed by its owner, my neighbor. He looks quizzically at the meager quiche, half-eaten, on the table, and the small salad next to it. "No, thanks. I'm on my way out anyway," he says, scratching his head. "Hi, Cathy. I just came to see how you were doing, Nat." He hugs himself. "It's freaking freezing in here."

Ben is wearing his usual uniform, which is a large woollen sweater. He has an endless supply of them, mostly bought from junk shops or markets, and they are all extremely thick. His hair is curly and long. It bounces when he's enthusiastic about something. I am glad to see him, as ever. I'm sure I have a Pavlovian response to Ben, because he represents company of some sort during the day, so it's normally lovely to see him. I'm sure if we went on holiday we'd fall out on the first evening. "It'll warm up soon, hopefully," I say. "Hey, man. Stay and have a cup of tea."

"I won't," he says. "Just popped by to say hi." He looks at me. "So you're doing OK?"

"I'll come by later," I say. "It was quite something."

"The funeral? Or the meeting?"

"Oh—both."

Ben nods. "Well, I've got a shoot this afternoon, but I'm not sure when. Come by, later."

"OK."

"Nice to see you, Cathy," he says. "Nat—see you in a bit. I want to hear about it."

I nod, and turn back to Cathy as the door closes. "I'm sorry about that. Blithely inviting him in when you're in the middle of telling me about Jonathan. Go on."

"He's so lovely." Cathy gazes at the shut door.

"Who, Ben? He's got a girlfriend," I say.

"I don't mean like that."

"Yeah, right."

"No, I don't. He's just lovely." She sighs. "Why can't all men be like him, eh? I don't get it."

I think about Ben, who I've known vaguely for years because of Jay, and his floppy hair and thick jumpers. I've never really thought about him in that way. "He's adorable. But he's a bit like a big sheep, don't you think?"

"What?" Cathy laughs. "You're insane. I think he's really cute. Those big brown eyes. That smile. He's got a lovely smile. If he had his hair cut . . . Wow, he'd be absolutely gorgeous. Pow."

She mimes an explosion with her hands. I sigh. Cathy has such weird taste in men. "Come on. Tell me. I'm sorry. You and Jonathan."

"Yes." She sighs. "It was odd. I don't get it."

"OK, so what happened?"

"OK. We had a good dinner. Good conversation."

"Where did you go?"

"Kettner's. I don't like it there now though, since the makeover. They've done it up like a whore's boudoir. It used to be so great."

I nod, a shiver running down my body. Kettner's, in Soho, was our favorite place. Oli and I, I mean: we used to meet there all the time when we lived on opposite sides of the city. Cheap, beautiful pizzas and a lovely champagne bar. Chintzy, seaside-hotel decor, old-fashioned service, and a pianist playing jazz standards. Now it's been "done up," the menu's been changed, and I think it looks awful.

Oli and I went there in November, and had a bad evening. Terrible, in fact. It was our first night out for a while and, to cut a long story short, it began when, during a conversation about the merits of our flat, I used the phrase, "because we might want a bigger place someday, if we have children," and it ended with me leaving the restaurant and taking a very expensive cab all the way home on my own. Oli wasn't ready for the "if we have children" conversation, you see. Apparently, being married for two years doesn't mean you're ready to even *talk* about it.

"Kettner's did used to be so great. But anyway. Did anything happen?" Ah, *did anything happen,* possibly the most-asked question in London.

"Sort of."

"Like what?"

Cathy shifts in her low chair, looking down at the ground, so I can't see her face. She is bad at the details. "Well, I mean, it was unsatisfactory."

"How?"

"Well, we had quite a lot to drink. And we kissed, outside Kettner's. And he lives in Clapham too, so we got a cab home. But it was odd." She wrinkles her nose. "We got to his and he could have asked me in, and we're in the back of the cab, you know—" she mouths the word *snogging*—"and we're kind of—" again, she mouths what I think is *doing stuff under each other's clothes,* but I don't want to check and interrupt the flow—"And he chucks a twenty-pound note at me and says, 'Oh, thanks for a lovely evening,' and then gets out!" She's practically squeaking in outrage at this.

"He chucked a twenner at you?" I say. "Like you're a prostitute and he's paying you in cash for letting him feel you up?"

"Exactly!" she shouts. "I mean, I think it was for the cab, but you know—wow, way to make me feel cheap!"

"Who paid for dinner?"

"We split." There's a silence. "I don't think that means anything though."

"Me neither. What does he do?"

"He's a . . . well. He's a dancer."

"He's a what?"

She takes a bite of her quiche. "He's a dancer."

"What kind of a dancer?"

"He's in *The Lion King*."

"He's a dancer in *The Lion King*," I say. "You snogged a dancer in *The Lion King*." I'm nodding. "What part does he play in *The Lion King*?"

Cathy still isn't looking at me. Her voice is shaking. "I think he's a giraffe."

We both collapse with laughter, and my stool rocks alarmingly. I steady myself with one hand.

"And you don't think he's . . ."

"He's not gay!" Cathy says in indignation. "He's bloody not! He says that's really irritating, that everyone always assumes he must be, and that it'd be much easier for him if he was!" She pauses. "Apart from with his parents. They'd disown him."

"Why? What's with his parents?"

"They're very strict Baptists. They think homosexuality is a sin." Cathy shakes her head. "They sound kind of awful. Very repressive. He grew up in Rickmansworth," she adds, as if the two are connected.

"Right," I say, though I now have severe doubts about Jonathan the dancing giraffe from Rickmansworth with the repressive Baptist parents. "Well, maybe he's just shy. . . ." I trail off. "How was the snogging?"

Cathy looks around again. "It was OK. You know? Sometimes it's just not that great. And we were quite drunk."

"But you like him?"

She stares into space. "Yeah, I do. He's really funny. And we have nothing in common. I like that. He's different from me." She shifts in her chair again. "Everyone at work's just like me. Always in suits. Serious. Reads the *Financial Times*." She pushes her lips out. "That's why I liked his profile, and when we were emailing. He just sounded really fun." She stops. Her voice is soft. "I just want to meet someone, you know? And it's hard."

I remember the last date I went on before I ran into Oli. A man with a signet ring and fat, sausage-like fingers, talking about himself all evening and how his friends thought he was "completely crazy, up for anything, me!" Yellowish blond thin hair, red face like a baby, eyes that looked anywhere but into mine, and I sat there in silence and thought to myself, *Perhaps he'll do, perhaps I'm being too picky, that's what everyone says.*

"I know," I say. "I know it's hard."

"Ha." Cathy looks at me. "Like you'd know."

"Oi," I say. She claps her hand over her mouth.

"Shit, Nat, I'm really sorry!" Red stains her white cheeks. "That's so tactless of me!"

I lean forwards on my stool and pat her head, which is all I can reach. "It's fine! Honestly, don't worry. I wouldn't know, anyway. I haven't been out there for ages."

"Do you think you will be, soon, then?"

"Don't know," I say, stretching my fingers out in front of me. "We need to talk. He keeps calling, he wants to meet up again. I just haven't wanted to see him."

"He wants to come back, doesn't he?" Cathy asks. I nod. "Of course he does!" she says, relieved. "You and Oli—you're together forever! I mean, you can't split up!"

"He slept with someone else," I say. "Don't you think that's a big deal?"

Cathy knits her hands together. Normally so sure of herself, she looks around. "Yes, of course it is. But if you're asking me if it's something to end your marriage over . . . I don't know. I'm not in it." She smiles, knowing it's a bad answer. "I can't make that judgment."

"Well, I am in it, and I have made that judgment," I say. "I just don't know if I can be with him again."

"Wow." Cathy opens and shuts her mouth. "Seriously? But your life—together."

"I know." My throat is dry.

"Weren't you going to start trying for a baby soon too?"

Now I am knitting my fingers together. I can't look at her, I don't want to lose it. I push down the sound I want to make, push it back down somewhere at the back of my throat. "No."

"Oh. I thought you were."

"Well, we're not. He doesn't want to. He said he wasn't ready."

Cathy flicks a look at me from under her lashes, and doesn't pursue this. Instead she says, "Do you think he's sorry?"

"Oh, yes," I say. "I think he's very sorry he's been chucked out of his nice flat with the big TV and all his DVDs and crap and someone who knows how he likes his coffee in the morning. I think he misses that a lot."

"Come on," Cathy says. "It's more than that."

I'm not sure it is for him, and I can't blame him either. Your relationship is in your home. Your home is where the two of you are for the most part. And your home is where you have your stuff and where you chill out after a bad day. Even after everything that's happened, our flat is still our flat. It's where I have my books, where my clothes hang in cupboards, where I keep the letters Granny wrote me, the postcards Jay sent me, the Zabar's mug I bought in New York with Cathy. I liked having space to put stuff, letting our things mingle together. In Bryant Court, Mum and I improvised almost everything. Her chest of drawers was the trunk she had at boarding school and our clothes hung on a wire rack she bought at a fair; the shelves in the kitchen were too narrow to store anything other than small spice jars, which was ironic as neither of us ever cooked and we lived on takeout or ready-meals and occasionally pasta. So our plates and glasses and mugs were all stacked in a corner, the cutlery in a large, patterned glass jar she'd got in Italy.

"It's a marriage, not just a home," Cathy says sternly. "For both of you."

We had a home together, the two of us, until Oli went and ruined it. But the thing is, I think I want that home, I want us to be together. I don't want to be out there again. I think I do still love him. That's the trouble.

Twenty-three

After Cathy leaves, I do some tidying up and sorting out. I put
things away, I arrange my tools in my drawer under the workbench.
I update my contacts folder on my laptop (a new state-of-the-art
Mac, which I convinced myself—helped by Oli, it's true—I had to
have for work, when any old computer would basically have done).
I email a few shops, some friends who are fellow jewelers to find if
they'll be at the next trade fair, in ExCel in May, and I get an appli-
cation form from Tower Hamlets for a grant. Though even this feels
wrong; I don't think I deserve the money.

What I need to do, I know, is keep on like this. Keep doing
things. Keep coming to the studio and actually making stuff, having
a plan, having tea with the others, instead of using this place as an
escape from the lonely, echoing flat, filled with Oli's stuff. I open the
unopened letters from the bank, putting them in a pile. I make a list
of things to do. And as I stand up and stretch, slinging my bag over
my shoulder, I put my sketchbook in the center of the table, so it'll
be the first thing I see when I come in tomorrow. Feeling suddenly
hopeful, I close the door behind me.

As I walk past Ben's studio I'm about to knock, but I can hear
him and Tania talking so I pause, listening for a second. I can tell
by the tone of their voices—slightly louder and higher than usual—
that it's not the kind of conversation you want to interrupt. Normally I'd knock anyway, or call out "bye" but perhaps I need to
stop hanging out with them instead of going home. Yes, I'm going
home.

I say goodnight to Jamie and as I have my hand on the door I open my bag, quickly, just checking. Yes, Cecily diary's still there, nestling at the top of my things, folded up inside my sketchbook.

One of the weirdest things about my "situation" at the moment is the labeling of it. Do I still say "we" when I'm talking about where "we" live or how long ago "we" bought the new flatscreen TV? It feels so odd, yet to say "my status-TBD-husband and I" is also weird. "We" live on Princelet Street, off Brick Lane, a couple of minutes' walk from my studio.

When I first left college I worked for two years on a stall in Camden Market and lived in West Norwood, so I know what a long commute is like. I was only there in the mornings, too—in the afternoons I'd do my own stuff—so it was nearly three hours of traveling for three hours of work, not a good exchange system. I had about fifty pence a week left to play with, if that.

We moved here after much negotiation. Oli flatly refused to cross the river, especially not to live that far out. He wanted to stay in North London. We compromised on East London, and it was one of our better decisions, because I can't imagine living anywhere else now. I have lived in West, East, and South and worked in North London, and this is where we both wanted to be. I don't know what "we" think about that anymore, but I love it here, and though East London isn't everyone's cup of tea, I wouldn't live anywhere else. I know where I want to be. Until a decade ago or so round here, Spitalfields, Shoreditch, Whitechapel, all of it was a real no-man's-land, abandoned since the days of Jack the Ripper, but now it is quite hilariously trendy. The slums they cleared people out of in the sixties, moving them into new-builds, are now Georgian terraces selling for half a million quid.

My road is not as posh as the great Huguenot weavers' houses on Fournier Street, which is now almost all private houses or museums masquerading as private houses, each front door now a tasteful olive, dark gray, or black, shutters immaculately reproduced in the original style and painted to match. Our street is one block up, a bit quieter, the houses a bit more dilapidated. If you half-close your eyes, you really can imagine some weaver hurrying back along the cobbled street through the mud and rain and opening the dark, sturdy front door to be greeted by a blaze of light and a warming fire. It feels less like something out of a film set and more like a place where people have lived and still live now. People like us.

I walk home that afternoon, past the guys pushing the empty rails from Petticoat Lane Market, past the sweet Victorian primary school where it is home-time. Children are flooding out in their blue sweaters, throwing themselves against their parents, jabbering excitedly to each other. Two little girls are in a minibus, kissing each other and playing with each other's hair, while an adult shovels more children in next to them. I stand and watch them, smiling, until one of the parents stares at me. Embarrassed, I walk on, pulling my scarf more tightly around me in the cold, hitching my overnight bag onto my shoulder.

I skid on a puddle and nearly slip. "Mind how you go," says one of the ever-present waiters who stand outside the curry houses all day, trying to entice passers-by inside. "It's cold, freezing, be careful, yes?"

It is freezing, I feel it now. I am sick of this winter. It's been neverending. It's almost March, and still so cold. I look up at the graywhite sky, heavy with cloud. The contrast with Cornwall is total, in fact. There are no trees on Brick Lane, only brightly illuminated signs, flashing LED lights, misleading banners ("Winner of Best Curry Restaurant"—where? when? according to whom?), comforting, spicy smells which make my confused stomach lurch with nausea and at the same time growl with hunger.

It is past five and getting dark. It is a night for staying in, for going to the Taj Stores opposite and loading up on poppadoms and chutney, it's a night for wrapping oneself in scarves and blankets and curling up on the sofa. I think how nice a takeaway from the Lahore Kebab House would be. If Oli was here perhaps he'd get it on his way back from work. If Oli was here we'd watch a few more episodes of *Mad Men* on the new flatscreen TV, and then I'd put my head in his lap and half-read a book while he watches the football.

I turn into Princelet Street, waving at another waiter, standing outside the Eastern Eye Balti House. "How was the funeral?" he says, bowing his head slightly as if acknowledging it. He wears a pale blue waistcoat and shirt. He must be freezing.

"It was . . . fine," I say, touched. I will never know how to answer that question properly. *It was . . . funereal, thanks for asking.*

"That's life," the waiter calls after me, nodding philosophically. "Life and death."

Just as I am getting into the flat, my mobile rings. I struggle with my overnight bag and my scarf, getting tangled up as I delve into my handbag to find the phone and press it immediately to my ear.

"Hello?"

"Hello? Darling? Where are you?"

It's my mother. I freeze.

"I'm at home," I say, after a moment. I dump my overnight bag on the floor. "Er—where are you? Are you still in Cornwall?" I stare at the bag.

"Yes," says Mum. "Off tomorrow evening."

"Um—" I don't know what to say to her. There's a silence. "So . . . how's the clearing up going?"

"It's OK," she says. "Fine. We're seeing the solicitors tomorrow, to sort out the foundation and the funding. Archie and I."

"Oh, yes. Is—is Louisa still there?"

My mother lowers her voice. "God, yes. Of course she is. I wish she'd just leave, to be honest, but no. . . ." She pauses, as though she's looking around. "She's still here. Pretending to be the dutiful daughter, even though she's not."

I am recasting everything in my mind, now: everything I thought I knew. I knew my mother and Louisa didn't get on that well, but I thought it was simply because they're so different. Now I don't know what to think. I don't know what actually happened that summer, after all, but I can tell Mum was difficult even then, based on just a few pages of her sister's diary. Does my mother know what they say about her? That behind her back people whisper about her, like those old friends of Granny's at the funeral, that they say, "You know, it was never proved, but Miranda . . . yes, that one over there, you know they always had trouble with her. They say she killed her sister. Oh, it wasn't an accident. . . ."

It occurs to me, as silence falls between us, that she does, always has done, that she has always known that's what they say about her.

Are they right, though? And if so, why? Why would she do it? What happened?

"I didn't ring for that, though," Mum says. "I rang to see how you are. Um—" She pauses. "I can't believe you didn't tell me about you and Oli."

"Look, Mum, I'm really sorry about it," I say. "I feel awful, but it was only three weeks ago, and I wanted to keep a lid on it until I knew what I was going to do—"

"Oh, Natasha, you always want to bottle things up," she says. "You never talk about things! You should have told me. It was awful, finding out like that. At the same time as Louisa! And *Mary Beth*. I mean—! When do we ever see Mary Beth? Who is she?"

I am not in the mood for her amateur dramatics, her sighing and hair tossing. "I had my reasons," I say. "I told you that. I'm sorry if you feel left out."

She pauses. "Well," she says, sounding slightly flattened. "Anyway— oh, darling. I don't know what to say."

There's a silence. I don't know what to say either. We can't help each other, my mother and I, we never have been able to. The ties that bind us together are so tight there's no room for friendship. We've put up with the cold, with crappy one-bed flats, with creepy landlords and no money, too-small winter coats, meal after meal of pasta or baked beans, watching a tiny TV with a coat-hanger aerial, and spending night after night in each other's company, always mak- ing out to our family and friends that the life we lived was bohemian, carefree, simple, and all the more tasty as a result. We don't run towards each other's company now. We don't really have anything in common, now we're both adults. Whoever my father is, he and I must be pretty alike. I often think we'd probably get on like a house on fire. My mother and I haven't really had that luxury. Instead we've tried to respect each other, and we don't go into any more of it than that.

Now, everything has changed, and I don't know what we do. Perhaps she's trying to be a good mother. And I don't believe Octavia, I don't believe my mother is responsible for Cecily's death. But then I'm beginning to realize I don't know anything.

"Look, I'm sorry I didn't tell you," I say.

She sighs. "It's fine, honestly, darling. I know it's been a hard time for you."

It's very odd, hearing her voice. "Well, it has for you, too, Mum," I say. "Granny's only just died."

"I know." She sighs again. "A lifetime and a week, a week and a lifetime."

"What?"

My mother gives a small laugh. "Nothing. I'm feeling a bit mad at the moment. Being with one's family will do that to one, won't it?"

"Oh, yes," I say.

"It's just hard, packing away the house, knowing we're leaving it empty, leaving all these memories behind." She sounds tired. "All these lovely pieces in the house, and I don't know what to do with them—whether Archie's right about it all. I'm sure he is, but—well, there's Louisa." Her voice hardens again. "Bossing us around."

"You should talk to . . . I don't know, someone who knows a bit about that stuff." I remember back to that scene in the kitchen. "Guy, perhaps."

"Guy Leighton?" Mum stops me. "No. I don't like Guy."

I remember how angry she was with him in the kitchen, just before I left last night. Only twenty-four hours ago. "Why not? He seemed quite nice. As if he knew what he was talking about."

"Well, he's not nice," Mum says. "He makes out he's nice as pie, all sticky-up hair and glasses. He's worse than the rest of them. No, I'm not having anything to do with him."

"But don't you have to, if Granny asked him to be on the committee?" I ask.

She clears her throat. "Believe me, Natasha," she says. "Guy Leighton is not what he seems. Just steer clear of him, if you can."

"What?" I say. "What does that mean?" I wind a strand of hair tighter and tighter around my finger. "What's he done?"

She seems to hesitate. "Well. He was a complicated fellow."

"Yes?" I say expectantly. "And?"

There's a silence. It's so long that after about ten seconds I think she must have been disconnected, and I say, "Mum? Are you still there? What did he do?"

"Oh." And then she sighs. "Perhaps I'm being unfair. I haven't seen him for years and years. It's a long time ago. Forget it!" She trails off. "I'd just rather do it at my own pace, and Archie agrees. Jesus." She breaks off, and suddenly says, "By the way, did Arvind give you anything? Yesterday?"

"Oh," I say. "Yes. . . . Sorry. He gave me a ring."

The instant I say it I know I shouldn't have. I know it's a mistake.

"A ring?" Mum says instantly. "What ring? Arvind gave you a ring?"

"Yes, Granny's ring, the one with the flowers." I hear her inhale sharply. "Sorry, Mum, I didn't think to tell you."

"Well, I wish you had." She sounds really cross, agitated even. "We've been looking through Granny's things today, and I couldn't find it." She hesitates. "Nothing else? He didn't give you anything else?"

I take a deep breath and lie. "No. Nothing."

I am wary of her now. I know what she can be like. And I feel, all of a sudden, as if we are playing a new game, one we've never played before.

"It would have been good if you'd told me, Natasha."

"I didn't realize," I say, nettled. "I didn't think it was your ring to give away. Of course, if you want it, I don't want—" It's still round my neck and as I touch it I know suddenly I absolutely won't give it to her. I know Arvind didn't want Mum or Archie to have it, though I don't know why. "It was in Granny's bedside table," I say. "He said Cecily wore it. On a chain."

Her sister's name feels like a heavy stone dropped into the sentence.

"She did wear it, I'd forgotten," Mum says. "Mummy said she could borrow it. She took it to school but then she lost it. We couldn't tell Mummy, she'd have been so cross. Cecily was distraught, I've never seen her so upset. We looked absolutely everywhere. It was a freezing cold winter, the coldest on record, that winter before . . . she died." She clears her throat. "And do you know where we found it?"

"No, where?" I say. The steam from the kettle is fogging up the kitchen window. I take a mug off a hook and put a teabag in it.

"The pipes froze solid and the sink fell off the wall in her dorm." Mum laughs softly. "When they took the sink away it slid out. She'd dropped it down the plughole and it was frozen in water. Like a stick of rock, with a gold ring in the middle."

"No way." That ring, the one round my neck. I smile.

Mum gives a gurgle of laughter. "It's true! But that was Cecily. Oh, she was funny. Such a drama queen. They all said I was—hah, she was! Such a prima donna. She swore she'd never take it off again. So she wore it round her neck on a chain. And then Mummy found out, and made her give it back. She was absolutely furious." She stops. There is a silence, and I hear a funny sound and realize she's crying.

"Oh, Mum," I say, instantly feeling guilty for taking her on this path, even if she was going there herself. "I'm so sorry, I didn't mean to make you cry—"

"No, no," Mum says. Her voice is really wobbly, as though it's been put through a distorter. "No! Oh, Jesus. I never talk about her, that's all. It's only . . . She was so young. It's hard now . . . when I think about then . . . and now. I wasn't very nice to her. I wish I could take it all back."

"Oh, Mum, that's not true," I say.

"You don't know," Mum says quietly. "I keep thinking about her, you know. Especially lately, with Mummy's death. I wonder what she would have been like now. She'd be middle-aged, not a girl anymore. She really was lovely. . . ." And then she makes a strange sound, half sob, half moan. "Oh, God," she says. "Cecily. No. Let's talk about something else. It upsets me too much."

"Was it really the coldest winter on record?" I say, after a quick think. I make the tea, wrapping my fingers round the thick mug for warmth, and go into the sitting room.

"The winter of '62/'63?" Mum sniffs loudly. "Oh, yes, darling. It snowed from December to March, Natasha. Two feet of snow outside. Three feet! There was no gas, no heating. We had to burn old desks at school, because we ran out of wood. We were snowed in for about a week."

"Wow," I say, sitting down on the slithery leather sofa. "A whole week?"

"I'm serious," Mum said. "We were all so cold, all the time. And I remember—gosh, it's all coming back now—" She trails off.

"What?" I say, intrigued, tucking my feet underneath me. I adjust the phone, hugging a cushion to keep me warm. The huge sitting room is always chilly.

"Our headmistress," Mum says. "Stupid bloody bitch. Do you know what she said to me and Cecily? In front of the whole school, at assembly?"

"No, what?"

Mum recites, as though it's a lesson. "'Girls like you with *darker skins* will feel the cold more than the English girls.' "

I'm so shocked I don't know what to say. "Really?"

"I hated that school, hated it. I was useless. They hated me too. You know, one of the mistresses at school, she made me wash my mouth out with bleach. Made me scrub my skin with it too. Said it'd lighten my dark hair."

"No, Mum."

Mum is such a drama queen, but for some reason I believe her.

"It's actually true. Hah."

"What happened?"

"I'd finally had enough when that happened." Her voice is dreamy, as though she's telling a fairy tale. "I went to ring up Mummy that evening in floods of tears, to tell her to take us away. But the phone lines were down," Mum says flatly. "And I had to stay anyway. There wasn't anywhere else for me to go. When I did finally get through to Mummy, she wasn't pleased. Said she didn't know why I always had to mess things up, that I deserved it. Oh, I behaved really badly that term. I nearly got expelled. Awful."

Yes, I want to say. I know all about what you did. About you and Annabel Taylor, about how you nearly killed her. A shiver runs through me. I don't know whether to be proud of her for her bravery, or afraid. My God. I realize I don't know her at all.

Mum says, "Then we got home for the summer, and . . ."

There's a silence.

"And what?"

"Well, that was the summer she died," Mum says. "August 1963."

"Oh. Of course. I'm sorry," I say. "So—"

"Natasha?"

I am completely absorbed by the conversation and her voice in my ear, but the noise, someone calling my name, somewhere nearby, makes me jerk upright and I remember. I didn't close the door.

"Hello?" I call suddenly. There are feet in the hallway, and I hear a sound I haven't heard for a long time: the clatter of keys being thrown onto the hall table.

"Who's that?" Mum says.

"Hello."

Oli appears in the doorway. I draw back.

"The door was open," he says.

I stare at him.

"Mum—look. I have to go."

"Is that Oli?" Mum says.

"Yes," I say, staring at him, at his trainers, his jeans, his smart shirt, his jacket, his face, his ruffled, boyish hair. This is my husband, this is our home. "I have to go," I say, as Mum starts to say something else.

"Why don't you come round next week?" she says. "Come and have some supper here."

"OK," I say, my hand on my cheek, not really listening. "Look—"

"Wednesday, darling. Come round next Wednesday?"

"Yep, yep," I say. "See you then. I'll come round on Wednesday. Yes. Bye."

I put the phone down and turn to him, my heart thumping almost painfully in my chest.

"Hi," I say.

Twenty-four

I've seen Oli once since he left. We had a drink two weeks ago at the Pride of Spitalfields on Heneage Street, down the road from us. We picked a "neutral spot," like characters in a TV soap. It was awful. It's one of my favorite places, a friendly, old man's pub, an oasis in the increasing Disneyfication of Spitalfields, and people kept saying hello. "Hi, you two, haven't seen you in here for a while, what have you been up to?"

Oh, this and that! I wanted to answer. Oli shagged someone else and I'm working on a new autumn/winter range of bracelets, thanks for asking!

Then, Oli was broken, quiet, weeping, wanting to know how I was. I said I needed time. Trouble is I didn't use that time. And now I am no closer to knowing what on earth comes next.

"How did you get that huge bump on your head?" Oli asks now, shoving his hands deep into his jacket pockets, his thin shoulders hunched. It is such a familiar gesture that I want to laugh. "What happened?"

"Oh. That." I keep forgetting about it. "I fell over. It's fine."

"You fell over?"

"Yep." I bend over a little bit, miming the act of falling over and he nods, as if this clarifies it for him.

We're both standing in the doorway, as though neither of us wants to be the one to control the situation, suggest a move somewhere else. I am terrified of offering an idea in case it's the wrong one.

God, it is so weird, seeing him again. I know him so well, better than anyone. I'm married to him. I love him. I loved him so much before this happened. When we were first together, five years ago now, I used to lie awake worrying about him. What if he got knocked off his scooter on the way in to work? What if he developed a terrible degenerative disease? What if I did? Why would someone give me someone, give me this happiness? To take it away, that's why. I would listen to him in the night, his light snuffling breathing like a baby, and stare up at the ceiling, praying that he'd be all right, praying that we'd make it, that I was worrying for nothing.

"Glad you're OK." Oli nods.

"Thanks," I say. "Nothing serious, honestly."

As if by mutual consent, we go into the living room. He looks round. There is no way to describe how bizarre it is, how we should just be chilling out on the sofa, not standing up awkwardly. It's our sitting room, it's both of ours. There's a big, red rug from a junk shop near Broadway Market on the floor, a rubber plant in a wicker container on the floor nearby, a blue corduroy sofa, deep and comfy, and the huge red and blue abstract print by Sandra Blow that we bought in St. Ives, the first time I took Oli to Cornwall. The wall by the door is lined with our books and CDs and DVDs. It's stuff like that. It's our home, our life together. It would be really hard to unpick.

"Do sit down," I say politely.

"Thanks," says Oli. He sits on one of the oatmeal low-slung armchairs, which look as though they should be in the lobby of a seventies LA hotel. He loves those chairs. He looks round the sitting room, his hands restlessly stroking the fabric of the arms. The rain has started again. There's a silence.

"Look, Natasha—"

"Yes?" I say, too quickly.

He stops. "Well, I wanted to see you. Find out how you are, all that shit."

I half-stand up. "Do you want a drink—?"

Oli waves me down, almost crossly. "No, thanks. So—how's it going?"

I touch the bump on my head. "Oh, fine, as you can see."

He sounds impatient. "I meant yesterday. I mean you. How you are. If you're OK." He nods.

Suddenly I can feel anger rushing into me. "Well—I'm not OK, no."

He looks a bit surprised. "Really?"

"Oli, what do you expect me to say?" I drop my hands into my lap and look at him, willing him to understand. "Of course I'm not OK. My business is on the verge of going under. My grandmother's just died. My whole family's going into meltdown—" I begin, and then stop, I'm not getting into that now. "And my husband's left me."

"You threw me out, I didn't leave," he says promptly, as if it's a quiz and he knows the answer.

"Grow up, Oli," I say, feeling a release of anger and riding it, loving the sensation of feeling something, anything again. "Is that all you've got? Still? '*You threw me out.*' " I am mimicking him. "You're such a fucking child."

He stares at me and shakes his head. "Nice." He looks as if he's about to say something else, runs a hand through his floppy brown hair, stops. "Never mind. I'm sorry. Shouldn't have said it, OK?"

"No."

"No, it's not OK? Or no, I shouldn't have said it?"

"Both. You pick."

It has become so easy for us to start sniping at each other, these past few months. I don't know where it came from. We know each other too well and take no pleasure in that familiarity. It's little things but they grow. I am bored witless by his alleged devotion to Arsenal. I don't believe it either, he was never into football at university or when we were friends in our twenties, and all of a sudden he's their number-one fan, along with every other media wannabe in his office. No chance he'd support Grimsby Town, for example, who happen to be the nearest team to the village where he grew up—no, not nearly sexy enough.

While we're on the subject, I hate the way he always orders pints now when he's with blokes. He doesn't like beer that much. He likes wine. He actually used to love cocktails, but he has to be seen to be one of the lads, to fit in with the metrosexual guys in his office who think it's fine to look at porn and find Frankie Boyle *hilarious*. I think that's pathetic. Be a real man. Have the courage of your convictions and order a damn Southern Comfort and lemonade, you big pussy.

I shake my head, ashamed I'm thinking these things, and I look at him. He has his arms crossed and his face is blank, as though he's shutting down, just as he always does when we have a row. Perhaps he doesn't want to push it, but I can't help it.

He changes the subject, wisely. "How's your mum?" he says. "Is she all right?"

Oli is very good about my family. He gets it. His father left his mother when Oli was eight, and she raised him pretty much by herself.

"Mum's OK. Ish." I wonder what's going on at Summercove tonight. I hope Mum is keeping it together and hasn't gone mad and attacked Louisa with a silver candlestick. Like in Clue. I smile, and then I think, That's not funny. I feel a bit mad all of a sudden. I look at him, at his face, the face I know so well. His glasses are crooked, his hair is sticking up on end. I smooth my skirt with my hands. "She's Mum, you know. A bit of a nightmare. But I think she's holding it together. I hope so."

Oli gives me a curious look. "You don't have to always hold it together, you know," he says. "Everyone gives her a hard time. I feel sorry for your mum."

I'm on my mettle. "You don't know what she's like."

"I do, because you've told me. Many times," he says, and then he bites his tongue, clamping his mouth shut. There's a silence again, and I can hear my heart beating.

"I'm sorry, I've obviously been really boring about it," I say snappishly. I hate the tone in my voice.

Oli blinks impatiently. "Come on, Natasha," he says, as if to say, You're being childish now. He jiggles his legs impatiently. "I probably don't know what I'm talking about. Your family is a mystery to me." He has his palms out in a conciliatory gesture and though I know he learned this on a negotiation training course a couple of months ago I nod, because he's right, though it irritates me.

"They're a mystery to me too."

"I'm sure they are." Oli smiles and shakes his head.

I wish I could confide in him, with an ache that surprises me with its intensity. I wish we were here and it was normal again.

I would tell him about the meeting at the bank. Work out what we were going to do about it, the two of us. I would tell him about the diary and what Octavia said. Maybe we'd sit at the table and read it together. I could ask his advice, talk about where we both think the next part is, whether Mum knows about it, what I should do. I would ask about his day, about the little things that have been bothering him: whether the ad agency was happy with the campaign they put together for a new brand of peanut, or the pitch they're doing for a big sneaker company, and how the new guy from Apple who's joined them is working out, and what he had for lunch that day, and whether he remembered it's his mother's birthday in a week's time, and . . .

We were so close, we used to joke about it. I hated it when the door closed behind him as he left for work in the mornings. I missed him all day. He made the demons go away and the happy, sane Natasha I wanted to be stay in the room. I was even glad when he had the stomach flu and was off for two days, isn't that dreadful? I didn't go into the studio for two days either, I stayed at home with him and we watched *Die Hard* and *Hitch,* his favorite films, and I made him chicken broth. We both longed for the weekends, forty-eight hours together, just the two of us, Oli and Natasha, walking down Brick Lane hand in hand, cooking up a storm in the kitchen, bickering over what shower curtain to get, what dish was nicest at Tayyabs, whether to watch *The Godfather Part II* again or *The Princess Bride*.

We were our own unit of one. Joined together to make one. Both from broken families, both looking for love and reassurance, both wanting to make a home of our own, a new family, a fresh start.

So how did it come to this? That he has slept with someone else, broken my heart, killed our dreams stone dead? That we can't say a kind word to each other, that we actually *dislike* each other sometimes? How the hell did we get here?

My eyes roam round the room, as though I'm searching for something to say next. I find myself staring at the photo of our wedding day, almost the same as the one I have in the studio. It stands proudly in a silver frame on the lowest shelf by the TV. We are smiling. I stand up and look at it more closely. There is glitter on my dress; it sparkles softly in the evening light. Oli follows my gaze, and we look at the picture together.

"Look at us," he says. "Funny, eh."

"I know," I say, closing my eyes, not wanting to look anymore.

"Where did it go wrong?"

When you fucked someone else. I pause, the quick retort on my lips, but I bite it back. "I don't know." I shake my head, look down at him, his hair falling into his face.

He nods, as if acknowledging what I haven't said. "I still love you," he says, "but . . . I just. . . . It's been hard." He scrapes his knuckles along the wooden floor, stretching his arms out from the low chair.

"I know that too," I say. "I don't know when it started being like that. Before—"

"I think it was a long time before," Oli says.

"Long time?" My eyes fly wide open at this. He puts his hands out again.

"Not a *long* time, but a few months now, you know? Because when it started, and for a long time, you and me, well—hah." He is smiling. "I thought we were the perfect couple. I think the problem is we changed. Both of us. And we didn't notice. I think we've become different people from the people we wanted to be at university, the people we were then, and that's the problem."

"Perhaps it has," I say slowly. He's right. He's changed. So I probably have too. "I haven't been easy."

"Neither have I." He smiles. "But it didn't used to matter, did it?"

"No." I smile back. "It didn't."

Oli looks into my eyes from across the sitting room, and suddenly the distance is nothing. "I loved everything about you, even the stuff I didn't agree with, the things I didn't understand."

"Me too," I say, clasping my hands in front of me and looking at him. "Ol, do you think that—"

"I don't know," he says simply. "I don't know where it's gone, and I don't know if we can ever get it back."

I take a deep breath. "You had a one-night stand," I say. "One night. You know—perhaps it's—OK. Perhaps we just agree to move on. . . . Perhaps we just say it's not the end of the world."

Oli puts his head in his hands. He gives a little groan.

Someone is shouting something outside in the street. I watch my husband, fear inside my head, in my heart.

"Oli?" I say gently.

"Oh, God. Natasha, that's why we need to talk. I didn't want to say it like this."

I swallow. "Why?"

"Come on. . . ." His eyes peer at me through his fingers, like bars on a window. "It wasn't a one-night stand. You must know that."

"What?" I rock on my heels. I feel as though he's just punched me.

"Chloe and I—it wasn't just once. It's more than that—it's, well. It's been going on for a while."

"But—" I shake my head. "No, Oli—"

"That's why I'm here, Natasha," he says, getting up, struggling out of the chair and standing in front of me. "I'm so sorry. I know this isn't what you want to hear."

I clear my throat, and when I speak, I am surprised by how calm my voice is. "You think—you think we should split up. Permanently."

Oli tugs his hair, hard, and then looks straight at me. "I don't know. Probably. Yes."

Twenty-five

"Hi, Nat. Same again?"

"Yes, please."

"Black coffee coming up, my dear. Sit back down, it'll be ready in a minute."

I sit down at the counter, watching the organized mayhem behind as Arthur, the owner, and his two cohorts juggle with beans, huge silver machines belching steam, frothing milk, and paper cups, as people stand patiently waiting for their orders to come through. I watch the world go by, the smell of fresh bagels from the shop next door wafting tantalizingly in, as Brick Lane slowly comes alive again. I love the early mornings here, before the tourists and the hungry hordes arrive, when it's just people who live here, work here.

I have been here since it opened at seven, sitting on a tall stool, staring out of the window, and trying to read the papers, but I can't. I haven't slept yet. It is just after eight.

"Nat?" someone behind me says. "Hey, I thought it was you."

I turn round slowly, and look up. "Oh, Ben. Hi."

Ben stares at me. I must look delightful, unbrushed hair, no sleep, bump on forehead, in an assortment of crazy clothes. I had to get out of the flat. "How weird." He stares at me. "I was just thinking about you. We didn't see you yesterday after lunch. Wondered if you were OK. Tania, look—"

He pats his girlfriend's arm and Tania looks up. She smiles when she sees me. "Nat, how are you?"

"I'm fine," I say. They both look me over.

"You don't look fine," Ben says.

"Natasha . . . ?" I look through the window. Oli is staring at me. He pushes open the door. "Where the hell did you go?" he says angrily. "I've been looking everywhere for you, you just ran off—"

"I didn't want to wake you," I say. I push my hand through my hair.

Ben and Tania are still staring at us, with increasing discomfort.

"Sorry," I say. "Oli, you've met Ben. And this is Tania." I wave my arm limpidly at them, as if it's filled with heavy liquid.

Ben steps forwards. "Hi, Oli," he says. He stretches out one thick, blue jumper-clad arm. "It's good to see you again."

"Thanks," Oli says, pumping his arm back heartily. "Ben—yes, it's good to see you. We met at that open studio night a few months ago, didn't we? You're a photographer, aren't you, I really liked your stuff."

This conversation is unreal. I want to pinch myself. "Hey. Thanks. Thanks a lot." Ben smiles at him, and turns back to me.

"Tania's Ben's girlfriend. She works with him," I say.

"Not anymore," Tania says hurriedly, as if she wants to fill the void. "But we used to."

Oli waves his hand to attract Arthur's attention. "Oh," I say. "I didn't know that. I'm sorry." How could I not have noticed she wasn't working there anymore?

"No, it's fine," she says, smiling.

Ben drums his fingers on the counter. "Look, we should go," he says. "Um—good to see you both. See you around, I guess," he says to Oli.

"Sure, mate," Oli says, not really listening.

"Nat—see you at the studio."

"Yes," I say. "See you—see you soon." I watch them go, Ben striding down the street, Tania next to him. It occurs to me then that they didn't order anything.

"Weird guy," Oli says. "Got a crush on you."

"No, he hasn't," I say, picking at a napkin.

"He has. He's the one who likes Morecambe and Wise, isn't he?" He laughs. "That hair, and those big jumpers . . . Weird guy."

"He's not weird," I say tiredly. "He's lovely. I've known him for years, remember. He's a good man."

A good man. That's what he is. I think it now, and I turn to Oli, turn and stare at him. Is he a good man?

"I'm starving," Oli says, patting his pockets. "I'm going to order some food."

Arthur's voice rises with pleasure. "Oli, great to see you again, it's been a while now. Where you been?"

Oli smiles and pulls out his wallet. "Working too hard, I guess."

"Neglecting your beautiful wife?" Arthur is shaking his head. "You want to be careful. I'll snap her up if you don't watch it!" He laughs and we laugh merrily back. "Same as usual?"

Oli nods. "Yeah. Same as usual." He comes back, and sits on the stool next to me. "I thought you might be here."

Before all this, we virtually lived at Arthur's, which is at the top end of Brick Lane. It's a little bit Brooklyn, New York wannabe, with simple wooden tables, chalked menus, and every third person owns a MacBook, but the food is delicious and the coffee is great. And Arthur is friendly and genuine, and it's locals of all ages here, not just tourists, and we could sit here happily for hours and read the papers. It's very lifestyle section. Our life together was, I've been realizing, very lifestyle section.

I nod. "Sorry. I needed to get out. You were still asleep."

Oli touches my hand. "Look," he says. "You can't just run away again. We need to talk about this."

"We talked about it last night," I say, knowing I am being ridiculous.

"We didn't!" Oli raises his voice and people look round.

"I just didn't want to talk about it anymore," I say.

"Well, locking the bedroom door on me and going to sleep isn't exactly—"

"I didn't sleep," I say. "I just—I didn't want to talk about it. Anymore." I couldn't. I got into our bed, staring at the ceiling until he stopped knocking, and then there was silence in the sitting room,

followed by snoring, and I lay there for the rest of the night, looking at nothing, not crying, not feeling anything. I don't know why,
even. Perhaps I was afraid of what I'd do if I let go, of all the tension,
the fear, the rage inside me.

"You shut the door, Nat. You locked it." Because our flat used to
be an office, it has locks on the doors. "What was I supposed to do,
just leave? Don't you understand what I was saying last night?"

"Yes, I understand," I say in a quiet voice. "You want us to split
up. Do you want a divorce?"

"I don't know. . . ." He runs his hands through his hair. "Oh, shit.
I don't know." He looks at his watch as he says this and I absolutely
know he's wondering how late he's going to be for work. Oli is not
a workaholic: it's more than that. He genuinely loves his job. Loves
the office, the environment. It's like a stage for him. He should have
been an actor. Last year, he missed his own birthday dinner because
he was working. "We need to talk, though. . . ." Oli taps my arm,
trying to get me to look at him, not out of the window. "You do see
that, don't you?"

I take a deep breath. "I don't see what there is to talk about, really," I say, my voice very small. I am so tired. "You're in love with
someone else, you want a divorce, and there isn't much I can do
about it."

Oli crunches up one of those shiny, brown napkins in his fist.
"Natasha. Don't you want to know why?"

"Not really," I say, trying to stay calm. "Because look at it from
my point of view. I was just going along thinking everything's fine,
and the next thing I know everything's crumbled around us, and I
don't understand why." I bite my lip, and I can feel the tears welling
up, water swimming in front of my eyes and then pouring down
my cheeks, almost as if it's unconnected with me. "I—I know everything wasn't perfect, but I love you, Ol. So I don't understand. . . ."

He makes a clicking sound with his tongue, and puts his hand on
mine. "Oh, God."

I wipe the tears off my cheeks with the back of my hand, but they keep falling, falling onto the pile of brown napkins, into my coffee. "I just—I mean, how long's it been going on?" I look at him, and see his eyes are full of tears too.

"I don't know. Not long. Since that night we had together."

"And you really—wow." I shake my head. "You're leaving me for her. For *Chloe*." I exaggerate her name.

"Natasha, babe—it's not like that."

"What's it like, then?" I say. It's so depressing, the clichés, the questions you've heard asked on TV shows and films a million times before. In a minute, he's going to say, I love you, but I'm not *in* love with you, and then I really will lose it.

At this exact moment Arthur puts the coffee and toast down in front of us with a smile. "Here you go, guys!" he says.

I turn my head away till he's gone, waiting for Oli to speak. He runs his tongue nervously, quickly, over his cracked lips, and he says, "What's it like? It's like, I think our marriage was over a while ago. And we didn't see it." I open my mouth, but he shifts his stool closer to mine and says, "I'm gonna say all this now, while I've got the chance, before you kick me out again. You're a hard woman, Natasha. You're a hard woman to live with. I don't think you love me, and you don't respect me. I don't know if you ever did." He has his hand on his heart and his face is only a couple of inches away.

"You think I'm hard?" I say in a whisper.

"Yes—no." Oli's expression is agonized. "Maybe it's because of your mum. Your family."

"They've got nothing to do with it!"

"Really?" Oli says. "Honestly? You've got this obsession with Cornwall, with the house and all of them, with your grandmother and all your family living this wonderful life that you can't replicate."

I tear the napkin in half. "That's crap."

He sighs. "Maybe it's your mum. Or because you don't know who your dad is. Maybe you need to find out. I just feel like you've grown this shell and I can't get through to you anymore."

"You think this is about *me*?" I can't believe it.

Oli's voice is hoarse. "I know what I did was wrong. I slept with someone. I lied to you about it, I carried on seeing her. Me and Chloe—it's different. It's new, it's clean, we don't have all this baggage that we bring to it—" He mimes a circle around the two of us.

Someone brushes past us, at our cramped window counter, calling out a farewell to Arthur. I lean in towards Oli. "Do you love her?" I can't believe we're sitting here, and I'm asking this question. Again, it's such a cliché. I hate it.

He nods, and says simply, "I think so, yeah."

"Right," I say. "Right then."

"But it's different. . . ." He shakes his head. His big blue eyes are full of tears again. "We can talk about work, we've got loads in common . . . but she's not you, Natasha. She's fun and sweet and she can drink me under the table, and she's lovely. And she thinks I'm great, and it's great." He says this without irony, and I feel a flush of shame at this. "But—I don't know—she's not you."

"No, she sounds much better than me," I say. "I'm amazed you're still here, to be honest."

He ignores this, and frowns. "That's the thing." He swallows. "You know something? I never even tried that hard to keep it a secret. I wanted . . ." He stops. "No."

"What?"

"No, I'm not going to say it."

"Go on," I say. I nudge him. "Be honest."

Oli looks at me. "I almost wanted you to find out. So you'd show some emotion. I wanted to hurt you. I wanted you to be hurt."

He looks at me with a kind of expectation, like, *That's it.* I get up, a tear running down my cheek. "I'm not listening to this."

He pulls me against him. "You're not leaving now. Dammit, Natasha!" Arthur looks over at us, blank surprise on his face. "You're so fucking afraid of anything dark or depressing or real, you can't admit it into your life at all. You can't even talk about it."

"I cried, night after night for you," I hiss at him, wrenching out of his grasp. "I bloody *fainted* at my grandmother's funeral. I don't sleep, I haven't for weeks. All I can do is think about you, about us, about where we've gone wrong. Everything *is* dark and depressing and real, *that's* why I'm crying about it! That's why I don't sleep! Ben asked me if I was OK the other day, how things were." My voice cracks. "He did just now! When do you ever *ever* say, What are you thinking, how are you?"

"All the time," Oli says. "You just don't want to tell me."

"Who are you?" I say. I push his hands away and stand there, looking at him. "I don't know you anymore."

"I don't think you do." Oli looks up at me, and his smile is ugly, his teeth gritted. "Because you saw what you wanted to in me, and you took it," he hisses. "You never saw the real me. You were looking for someone, I don't know, a daddy replacement? Someone your mum could fancy too? Someone you could live out your little sophisticated London I'm-not-like-my-mother fantasy with. You're so fucking *hard*, Natasha! You won't let anyone in!"

"That's not . . . true." I am speaking in a whisper.

"It *is* true! I feel like a fucking Italian, you're so unemotional! Why do you think I asked you for a divorce? To get a reaction out of you, let you know how serious I am about this! You keep everything to yourself, you put this appearance on all the fucking time that it's all OK! And it's not! You have to be in control, this goddess no one can touch."

"Shut up," I say. "Shut up, Oli, it's not true." I want to put my hands over my ears.

"You treat me like a little boy, Nat, like a stupid, little boy with a silly job. And I'm not." I am shaking my head, and he breathes in, his nostrils flaring. "I'm not, not anymore. Most people don't look at me that way. OK?"

"Most people like Chloe?" I say, picking up my coffee. I walk out into Brick Lane. He runs after me.

"I didn't mean it like that. I mean you're my wife, and you look at me like I'm a piece of shit."

"You *are* a piece of shit, that's why." I keep on walking, my bag swinging over my arm. "Go off to your meeting. Go away. I don't—I don't want to see you ever again."

Oli says practically, "Nat, you have to give them the mug back. You can't just walk off with it."

I realize I have stolen Arthur's coffee mug, but I try to brazen it out. "I don't fucking care." He raises his eyebrows; Oli knows as well as I do that I am the most bourgeois person in the world and I would no more go off with a mug than I would walk down the street naked.

"Fine," he says. "Fine."

Some men driving a white van are coming towards us as I stride down the middle of the road. "Natasha, move onto the pavement."

"No." I carry on, hating myself.

"Natasha, move!" Oli says. The men are beeping their horn. One of them raises his fist at me, like a thwarted cartoon villain. Oli runs across and pulls me off the road onto the pavement, grabbing my arm, and the mug flies out of my hand, bouncing and then smashing into thick pieces on the curb with a crunching sound.

"For God's sake," Oli says. "Nat, what are you doing?"

I'm sick of this.

I'm sick of hating him, of feeling like this, of the way our world has collapsed around us so quickly, when we should be building things together, not pulling them apart. He is gripping my elbows, glaring furiously at me.

"I'm sorry," I say. And I mean it. "I do put you down, I know I do. I don't know when it started." I shake my head, and I can feel my whole body shaking as I do. "I don't know how that makes you feel, it's like I don't care."

"How it makes me feel?" he says. "Knowing that you despise me? That you think you love me but you don't? You really want to know?"

"Yes," I say, taking a deep breath. "I want to know."

He says quietly, "I don't feel anything."

There's a silence, just the soft tread of pedestrians walking past us on either side and the wind whistling through the gray streets. I open my mouth, but nothing comes out. I nod.

"Yep," Oli says. "I don't feel anything at all." He looks at me, raising his eyebrows with a sad look of triumph. "And I don't think that's good."

He turns and walks away and I follow him, like a dog at his heels, along the street. "Where are you going?"

"I think I'm going to go to work now," he says.

"Oh—OK," I say. I'm terrified. "Are you coming back?"

"I don't know," he says, but he looks at me, and his eyes are blank. I want to run to him, hug him, but I don't know him anymore. That's when I realize.

"I just don't think you want to be happy, Natasha," he says. "And I can't help you."

I think back over the years, how I've known him for over ten years now, together for five of those. I think of my twenty-fifth birthday, at Jay's flat, where we got together, how he walked me back home, all the way to West Norwood, on a warm May Sunday morning. Of our wedding night, how we were so drunk we passed out and couldn't stop laughing about our hangovers the next day. How well I thought I knew him, and how I look at him now and I—I think we're completely different.

"We used to be a good fit," he says, putting his wallet in his back pocket. "I don't think we're a good fit anymore. Do you?"

"Yes," I say, but I'm lying, and he nods sadly.

"I think I'd better go now," he says, and he walks away down the street.

I watch him until he disappears around a corner. I don't know what to do next. What happens next. I turn and walk towards the flat, leaving the broken pieces of china in the gutter.

Twenty-six

When I get back to the flat, something is wrong. Oli has left the door open, and the skylight outside is also open. The wind has knocked over the coat stand, which has fallen against the hall table, shattering a glass. There are papers everywhere, takeaway menus, minicab cards, fluttering around, scattered on the floor. I bend down to pick the coats up, and I right the stand again, patting it as if it's a person, and I look around me at the mess left behind.

I have screwed everything up. I think about Granny's coffin being inexpertly loaded into the ground. About Oli's face when he first said, "I think I need some space." (What a cliché, what a fucking pathetic cliché.) Clare Lomax yesterday morning, telling me that she was extremely concerned about my "ability to sustain a viable business." Cecily's diary, Arvind's face, Oli's face, Ben being nice to me, my bedroom in our flat at Bryant Court, all of it is going round and round in my mind as I stare at our huge, empty apartment and I can't break the circle of thinking about it. I'm so tired of feeling like this, of wanting not to feel like this, of telling myself I'm being stupid—because I *am* stupid.

I keep trying to feel better, but these things keep punching me in the face. The collapse of our marriage: he's probably right, it was collapsing long before Oli's infidelity. The business going under. And Granny's death, and what it has started to uncover. Now, it feels as though something fundamental has shifted, as if all my efforts to make everything nice in my life are coming to nothing. My marriage is a sham, it's over. I can't make a living doing the only thing I'm any good at. And Granny is gone, the person whose approval I most wanted, whose presence I most often missed, she is gone.

Shutting the door, I start picking up papers, but then I stop and lean on the table and start to cry. I realize I can't stop myself. I turn around and sink to the ground, staring helplessly at nothing. The tears pour out of me, dripping like little streams onto the floor as I rock against the wall, hugging my knees. Everything is open, nothing can be concealed anymore, and it is terrifying. I cry and cry, for Oli and me, for the end of our marriage, for how happy I wanted us to be; how wrong I was, the life I've got ahead of me now—I can't see it, don't know what I'm here for, what I should do, in my self-pity can't remember anything worth working for. I cry for Granny and Arvind, for their lost daughter, for our weird, fucked-up family, for my difficult and strange mother, the father I don't know. The wooden floor is covered with dark circles, my tears.

I cry until there aren't any more tears left and I am sobbing softly, and after a while the roaring in my ears grows quieter and I look up and around me, expecting to cry again, but I don't.

It's very still. I hug myself again, blinking, my swollen eyes smarting.

It is strange, like coming to after an anesthetic. I blink again and wipe my nose on my hand.

A car honks in the street. I look at my watch. It's still only ten in the morning. It could be midnight. I stand up, staggering slightly, and I lean against the wall, breathing hard, as if I'm out of breath. I feel dizzy, but as though something is clicking into place in the stillness of the room. As if this is the bottom, I've hit the bottom, and now I can start to climb back out.

I stretch my arms out over my head, to ease my cramped back. I'm on my own, now. I understand that. Oli isn't coming back. He really isn't. I look round, and I roll my head back and forth. OK. I'll call Jay and Cathy. I'll ask Ben and Tania if they want to come to supper. Perhaps I should find some money from somewhere and go with Cathy to Crete this summer, she mentioned it a couple of weeks ago. If I'm not in limbo anymore, I can start to plan for the future, can't I? I think of the sketchbook in the center of the table in my studio. My fingers itch, something they haven't done for ages.

Is it possible that out of this something good might come? Immediately, doubt floods over me again, and I look helplessly around me. At first I see nothing. And then I spot Cecily's diary, sticking out of my still-unpacked bag in the sitting room. It's weird. In that peculiar brightness of an overcast day, against the brown of my bag, it is bright white. It is folded, and it looks as if it would like to spring out flat. I rub my eyes tiredly, go over and pick it up, and I stare at the pages once again.

"What happened to you, Cecily?" I ask out loud. "What happened, to all of you?"

There's no answer to this. But I feel better for having asked the question. I look around the big, empty apartment, and I don't recognize it. This isn't my home anymore. Perhaps it never was, not in the way Summercove was.

As I think this, I catch myself and it brings me up short. I glance down at those first few pages again, and stand still.

I remember the first time I took Oli to Summercove, being so immensely pleased that he liked it, that Granny liked him. Driving back to London, I turned my head away with tears in my eyes when he said he loved it. Well, of course he did. It's not difficult to like a beautiful house by the sea, is it?

I got that wrong. I got Oli wrong too. I got a lot of things wrong, it seems. Standing here now, I feel a fog start to lift in my mind. I've always thought Summercove was my real, spiritual home, the place where I longed to be for most of the year and where I was happy when I was there. I always liked the thought that Granny was the de facto head of a sprawling family, who didn't all get on perhaps one hundred per cent, but who, like me, loved being down there, felt it was the place where they could escape from all their problems. I felt that was where the heart of my family still was.

So it turns out I was wrong. I've never questioned it before, but I never questioned a lot of things, and apparently I should have done. I stand there for a long time, lost in thought.

Twenty-seven

I spend the rest of the day in the flat. I don't speak to anyone, I don't know how to ring up Jay or Cathy and say the words out loud. "We're splitting up." What happens next? Do we get a divorce? A lawyer? What happens to the flat, should we sell it, rent it, should I move out? The sun has barely come out all day, and it is dark by six. I have a glass of wine, and then another, and it goes straight to my head. And the more I think about things, the more I start to wonder, and the more I find myself thinking, just how blind was I? I think again about Oli's birthday last September, the fact that I'd booked us into the Hawksmoor for dinner, and he didn't show up till ten. The boys from work had taken him out for lunch, and in the evening he'd had to have a drink with a client. He was drunk, I knew it, though he tried to pretend otherwise. I'd been in the studio most of the day and then at home, waiting for the evening, waiting for him. I remember it now, as I pour myself another glass of wine and sit on the floor. I don't know if he was sleeping with Chloe by then, but in a way it doesn't really matter. The fact is, he didn't want to be with me. Because it wasn't an isolated incident, it happened at least once a week, more like two or three times before he moved out and I just accepted it. I didn't pretend to understand his job.

Was I so cold, so unresponsive, so uncaring of him? Am I really this hard, hard person, who's built a shell around herself so she can't get hurt? Is he right, have my family screwed me up so much? Should I try and find my dad? Should I confront my mum? Is Cathy right, did I want Granny's approval too much, did we all? It's so strange, these events at the same time: Granny's death, the end of my marriage. It feels like the end of things, and yet as this long, strange evening goes on, and I just sit there and think and think, my bottom sore from the hard floor, my eye keeps falling on the diary, and I sort of have to admit what I haven't really wanted to since I came home.

Perhaps Arvind is right. Whatever happened that summer in 1963, our family is poisoned, and one of them must know what happened, they were all there. But all I have is ten pages of a diary and that tells me very little. So the question is, what happened to the rest of it?

Just before nine o'clock, I stand up. I make myself a sandwich and drink some water, and then I pick up the phone and dial.

"Hello?"

I hesitate. Of course she's still there. "Louisa?"

"Yes. Who is this?"

"Louisa, it's—it's Natasha. Hello."

The voice softens a little. "Natasha! How are you, darling?"

Her voice is comforting, it makes you feel safe. For a second, I wonder if I'm just being stupid. I take a deep breath, feeling light-headed from the wine.

"I'm OK. OK. I was just ringing to see how Arvind is doing. Is he there?"

"He's here, but he's pretty tired—we were about to go to bed." Apparently Louisa does not think this sentence sounds weird. She says loudly, "Weren't we."

I smile to myself. "Fine, I'm sorry. I know it's a bit late to be calling. I only wanted to say hi. How's—how's it all going?"

"OK, you know," Louisa says. "Oh, yes. We got a lot done yesterday, and today, we're really clearing a lot out, and the solicitors have been very efficient too, you know, it's all going pretty smoothly." She clears her throat; she sounds tired. "It's so sad, though."

I feel a stab of guilt. "Why don't I come down and help you? I feel awful I had to skip off on Wednesday."

"Oh, no, it's absolutely fine, darling," Louisa says. "To be honest, Natasha, it's actually easier to just get on with it by myself." She pauses. "I mean, of course, your mother's done a lot, so has Archie, but the nitty gritty—you know, I'm an old busybody! I rather like sorting it all out." She's trying to sound light-hearted but I can hear that note in her voice again, and I'm not sure I believe her.

I wish I could go back and search through the house for the rest of the diary. But even my befuddled, tired brain knows it would look highly suspicious if I turned up again, so soon after leaving abruptly, to go through Granny's things. And that's not how I want to see Arvind again anyway, or the house. I feel like a criminal. So I say, trying to keep my voice casual, "Have you found anything interesting?"

"Like what?" she asks. "It's all being properly cataloged, Natasha. There are a lot of items that need to be valued, and Guy's coming down soon to do it. . . ."

"No, I don't mean it like that—" "With a sinking feeling, I wonder what Mum's been saying to her. "Just interesting things about the family, you know. Photos and all that."

"Oh." Louisa unbends a little. "Well, there are a couple of things. Let me think. Oh—yes! I've found some old clothes of Miranda's. All just bundled up in a cupboard."

I sit down on the sofa, hugging a cushion against my body. "How do you know they're Miranda's? I mean, Mum's?"

"Well, I remember she bought them with the money her godmother sent her. She'd never really been a clothes horse before, and suddenly she started turning up for dinner in these absolutely amazing dresses and things. And they're all there, just stuffed into a bag and hidden in the back of a cupboard. I'd forgotten all about them! And there's a hilarious picture of Julius and Octavia I found in a kitchen drawer, when they were children down on the beach, covered in sand and wearing buckets on their heads. Ever so funny." Louisa laughs heartily, and leaves a pause for me to laugh heartily too which I do, even though my heart is beating so fast it's painful.

"Oh, that's funny," I say unconvincingly. "Anything else?"

"No," says Louisa. "Franty, your grandmother, she was a very or-

ganized woman. There's hardly anything left, really. I think she got
rid of a lot . . . a lot of things."

I think back to my room at Summercove, which used to be my
mother's and Cecily's, and know Louisa is right. When I think about
it, it is rather odd. There is nothing in the wardrobe now—I know it
by heart—apart from an old backgammon set, some old books, and
a moth-eaten fur that Granny never wore. Certainly no diary. And
yet somehow this makes me even more convinced she must have
kept the rest of it somewhere. Out of sight. I take a deep breath.

"What about the studio? I went in, just before I left."

"Well, it is strange, having it open again, being able to go in,"
Louisa says. "I was never allowed to before. But no," she says, "noth-
ing there really either. So, you're OK then?" She changes the subject.
"All all right? I was worried about you, Natasha dear."

When I was thirteen, I was running back towards the house from
the beach and my newly long legs betrayed me, and I fell over, dis-
locating my shoulder in the process. The pain was excruciating, but
Louisa took me to the hospital as I wailed and screamed loudly, all
pretense at maturity abandoned. She waited with me for a doctor
for what seemed like hours, and fed me sweets and read out extracts
from her new Jilly Cooper novel to keep me entertained. I'm sure
she's forgotten it, but I never have. I don't want her to worry about
me, but it's comforting to know she cares. Like I say, she is a comforting person, and I feel really guilty about how mean I've been
about her, these last few days.

"Actually—Oli and I have split up. Permanently," I say.

"You and Oli? What?" Louisa makes a querying sound at the
back of her throat, as if she doesn't understand. "When?"

"Earlier today." It seems longer ago than that, this morning. Like
a morning from a week ago, a year ago.

"Oh, Natasha," Louisa says, her voice sad. "Oh, that's awful."

"It's OK," I say. "Really, it is. I mean, it's not, but—you know."

"My dear. Where are you, at home?"

"Yes," I say.

"On your own?"

"Yes," I say again.

"That's not very good. Do you want—should I get Octavia to come round? Keep you company? She's only in Marylebone, you know."

Yes, I want to say. Do send Octavia round. Her cheery face and happy modes of passing the time are just what I need. "Oh—that's very kind, but don't worry. I'm better off on my own." This is probably true. I'm on my own, for the first time in years. "I need some time by myself."

"Have you told your mother, or Jay, or anyone?"

"No, actually," I say. "Er—you're the first person. Sorry, I didn't mean it to be that way. I was really just ringing to find out how Arvind is and—I don't want to bother you with it all."

"It's not a bother," she says. "Darling, it's no bother at all. You poor thing." I have to remind myself that Louisa's not a fusser, though she so often acts like one. I wish again that I'd known her when she was eighteen, before she became this person who does things for other people all the time, when she was the pretty girl in Cecily's diary with a new lipstick and a scholarship to Cambridge, dreadfully ambitious and clever. And it occurs to me now that I've never heard her mention Cambridge or university or anything like that. Did she not go in the end? Where did she go, that girl? She's always pretended she loved her Tunbridge Wells life. What if she didn't? What if that wasn't the life she'd expected for herself?

"Look," she says, breaking into my thoughts. "Your grandfather's just about to go to sleep, and he's going into the home on Monday. I want him as rested as possible before then, it's going to be strange at first, I'm sure."

"It is," I say.

"I mean, I'd love to stay down here longer, but you know, I can't. I've been here for two weeks, and he can't stay here on his own, it is for the best," Louisa says, all in a rush. "Frank needs me back at home too, I don't like being away from him for too long either."

I can't believe she feels guilty about it. "Louisa, you've been amazing," I say, and it's true. "Please! What are you talking about?"

"Not everyone feels that way," she says. "I've been accused of—well, it doesn't matter."

"Do you mean Mum?" I say reluctantly, though this could easily apply to me, too.

"I'm afraid I do," Louisa's voice hardens. I wish I'd never asked. "I suppose there's no need to keep up a pretense at civility, now your grandmother's dead. She's made that quite clear, anyway."

"Oh, I'm sure she doesn't mean it," I say desperately. "She's very grateful, I'm sure."

"Natasha—" she starts. "Your mother—"

"Yes?" I say.

"Well . . . she's a complicated person. OK?"

"I know that," I say carefully. "She always has been."

"Yes, but—" She stops. "Never mind. There's no point."

Tell Octavia that, I want to say. I know what you're getting at. It's too late.

"Well, *I'm* very grateful to you, anyway," I say instead. "I don't know what we'd do without you."

"It's my pleasure," Louisa says simply. "I'd have done anything for Franty. She knew that. I loved her very much."

After I've said goodbye to Louisa I feel reassured somehow. At the very least, Arvind is all right. My mother is unpredictable, and I never know how she's going to react to certain situations. It's true, often those situations were connected with Summercove or the people there. When we were going, when we were leaving, who was going to be there, how long she'd stay. It's only now I remember that I said I'd go round for supper with her next week. I don't quite know what I'll say to her when I see her. About anything, really.

I make some tea, and I get into bed. It's cold. I hug the same cushion against me for warmth and comfort, and I take out a pen and write a list.

1. Get a lawyer?—Ask Cathy. File for divorce??
2. Flat. Mortgage? Move out?
3. Trade fair. x3 applications to diff. ones by end of week.
4. Call/visit x10 shops by end of week.
5. Jay: update website?

Fatigue gives me a curious focus and it's easy to write these things down. Closing my eyes briefly, I think about what else I need to sort out. I write:

6. Mum.
7. Find diary.

But I don't really know what to do about those two. I put the list by my table, so it's the first thing I see in the morning, and turn off the light. I sleep. I sleep for ten long hours, a heavy, velvety sleep, where nothing and no one troubles me, no dreams come to me, and when I wake up the next day and blearily blink at the dark room, I realize how tired I'd been. I feel new, different. I pull back the curtains, it's another gray day in London. But it's not so bad, maybe.

Twenty-eight

It has been such a long winter, it's sometimes felt as though it'd never end, but finally spring seems to be arriving. That cutting chill in the air that turns your hands red and numb and stings your face has gone, and though it's still cold there is something in the air, a sense of something new.

It's a cliché, therefore, to talk about new beginnings, especially as they don't feel very new, but by the time a couple of weeks have passed and March is well under way, things are already different. Outwardly, nothing much has changed: I am still alone in the flat, not really sure what comes next. But there's a difference this time. I keep making lists, and it helps. I've realized I have to keep myself busy, not just for my sanity, but for my business. As well as checking the post obsessively—no more ignoring letters from the bank—I have a filing system at the studio, where I carefully document every last piece of expenditure, and I like it; I feel virtuous, glad to be in control of this, at the very least.

I haven't been in the studio much. I've been out meeting people, having coffee with PRs for free advice, dropping in on old friends, fellow jewelers, designers, and people from round here who can help me, listening out for new shops and new shows that might help me. More green shoots. A company in China has been putting in a few orders with my friends, five-hundred-a-time T-shirts and hairbands, they might do the same for me one day, just with one necklace or bracelet and then I'm off again, and it'll be all hands on deck. Liberty have been scouting around for some new, edgy designers, so I hear. A couple of shops are looking for different stock, and I've been visiting them, leaving my card, dropping back the next day with a stock list and some photos. Even though I'd rather be curled up in bed, or slouched on the sofa in baggy trousers and four jumpers, I always choose my outfits with care, put on heels and blow-dry my hair, press my cardigan and skirt so I look neat and fresh. I'm asking these people to buy into me, as well as the jewelry I make. It's sometimes hard to have a smile and seem enthusiastic, but I just keep telling myself if I act as though it's a new start, perhaps it'll feel like that, after a while.

A week after that fateful morning at Arthur's, I pop into the studio after walking back from Clerkenwell, where I've had a meeting with a woman who sells vintage and new jewelry. I've been walking everywhere lately, my shoes in a cloth bag in my satchel. I kick off my wet, muddy trainers and lean against the counter, going through my emails. In amongst the spam and the special deals from wholesalers there's an email from Nigel Whethers, the lawyer Cathy put me in touch with.

> Further to our telephone conversation, I would be happy to meet with you to discuss your filing for divorce. I enclose a breakdown of costs. I look forward to hearing from you.

Seeing it written down like that, I realize I'm not quite ready to reply to him, not just yet. I let out a sigh, which sounds like a long *pllllllllllffffffffffffff*. A voice outside says, "*Pllllllllllffffffff.*"

"Ben?" I call. I run my hand over my forehead; it's clammy. "Is that you?"

"No, it's Ivor the Engine," the voice says. "Who's that? Thomas the Tank Engine? Is that you? I love the sound of your piston engine. Can I buy you a drink, handsome?"

"Har de har," I say, as Ben comes in. He shoots me a cautious, quick look, and then as it's clear I'm not in tears or rocking on the floor, he smiles. "You all right, sunshine? What's up?"

"Nothing much," I say, putting my sheepskin boots on. "Just got an email from a divorce lawyer, that's all. Kind of weird to see it there in black and white on the screen."

Ben puts two rolls of film down on the counter and leans next to me. "Sorry to hear it, Eric," he says. "That's awful."

"I'm Ernie," I say. "You were Eric." I point at the photo of us as Morecambe and Wise on the board. "Remember? You borrowed Tania's glasses and you couldn't see a thing?"

"Yes, yes." Ben rubs the bridge of his nose. Tania, like most people in East London, has black-framed glasses, perfect for "doing" Eric Morecambe and other assorted old-school comics. Who knew? He pats me on the back. "How are you?"

"I'm OK," I say. "I'm keeping busy. Think that's the most important thing."

"Sure is," he says. He drums his fingers on the surface. "Look, do you fancy going for a drink tonight?" There's a pause, and he amends what he's saying. "Not just with me. Er—it's me, Jamie, Les and Lily—we're going to the Pride of Spitalfields, do you fancy it?"

"Oh." I don't know what to say. "What about Tania?"

"She's busy. And—well, you know."

I'd forgotten; she told me that awful day at Arthur's, that she wasn't working with him anymore. I should have remembered. I just haven't seen them. I blush. "Of course, sorry."

But I feel awkward, I think because I don't want to go. The idea of going out and having a good time at the moment is a bit of a step too far for me. It's hard enough during the day, slapping on a smile and being professional. In the evenings I just want to eat and sleep. "Er—no, thanks," I say. Partly to avoid another long pause, I add, "You won't miss me. Or Tania, if Jamie's there. You can flirt with her to your heart's content."

Ben narrows his eyes and looks as if he's going to say something, but he doesn't. Instead he clears his throat. "I don't have a crush on Jamie, for the fiftieth time."

"You do," I say. "You show her your teeth whenever she hands you the post. And you say, 'Oh, thanks! Jamie!' Like she's just split the atom."

He pushes me. "You're just jealous I'm spending the evening with Les. He's promised to tell me all about his blank-verse poem set on the outskirts of Wolverhampton."

"No, seriously?"

"Yes," Ben says. "It reminds me of that bit in Adrian Mole, where Adrian starts to write a novel, called—"

"*Longing for Wolverhampton,*" I finish. "Absolutely." There's a noise outside in the corridor and we laugh, quietly.

Ben stands up. "No worries," he says. "I'd better go, anyway. Just wanted to check you were OK. Let me know if there's anything I can do. Anything in the flat needs someone tall to get at, or whatever. I know you're having a bad time. Just want to say I'm around. All right?"

I nod, my eyes prickling with tears. I'm surprised by them. "Yep. Thanks. Thanks—a lot."

"No worries," Ben says. "Bye, Eric."

"*Ernie,*" I call, but he's gone, and I go back to staring at the computer screen, then start checking my diary for a time to meet Nigel Whethers.

It's the strangest thing, but all the time, I've been drawing too. Walking through Spitalfields, watching the way the bare branches arch against the light in London Fields, the snowdrops struggling through the ground. Watching the buds on the trees, the pansies in the window box opposite that have flowered all through winter, the little sparrows that hop away from me along our street. It all feels new and exciting, all of it, it always does at this stage, and I know once I start working out how to make it a reality it'll be depressingly problematic, the designs will look flat and dull, and I'll have to discard many of them. But I can't worry about that now. I have to get on with it.

So after a couple of weeks go by, I'm surprised to find myself looking back and realizing that I'm coping. I like being by myself, if I've got work to do. I like the challenge of it all. I was never sure about hiring the PR and giving up the stall, and I know I should have listened to my instincts now. The bank thinks my husband is still around to bankroll things and so they're off my back for the moment. It's going to be tight, but I know what I'm doing each day and why I'm doing it. And that feels good.

I haven't seen Oli since last week, when I watched him walk away. We have spoken, though, briefly. "How are you?" "OK, yeah. You?" "Good, OK, yeah." He's going to come round sometime and pick up some more of his things, and we'll talk then. For the moment, the space is good. When I think about his face, laughing in the kitchen as I try to make scrambled eggs, or the hot, humid day we moved into Princelet Street, how we had sex in the kitchen, hurriedly taking each other's clothes off, amazed that we had done this, that we were living together, forever we thought, or even just doing karaoke together, singing Heart's "Alone"—his favorite song, Oli has a penchant for a ballad—sometimes I think I'm going to start crying, about how sad I am, how much I could miss him if I let myself. But that's not how it happened. He left, he has given me this month's rent, and moreover, he's loaning me five thousand pounds to pay back the bank, and for that, at least, I am truly grateful, as well as for the memories we have. I just—I'm just not ready to totally move on from them yet.

There are two things on my list I still haven't sorted: the diary, and Mum. Something is going on with her and I haven't faced up to it. I was supposed to be having dinner with her the week after Oli left for good. She canceled at the last minute, and hasn't been in touch since, though I've tried her every day. She's great at being unavailable, she's doing it now and I don't know why. Does she know I've got the diary? What Octavia said? Does she really just not care that much? I've called her again this morning, and there's no answer. "Hi, Mum," I said, my voice keen and bright. "Just at the studio, calling to say hello! Hope you're well. . . . Um, OK then! Bye."

Actually, part of the reason I'm cross is because I'm relieved. I don't like going to Bryant Court. I'd do a lot to avoid it, in fact. Since I left for college, twelve years ago now, I haven't been back much. I'd spend holidays with friends or my college boyfriend or at Archie and Sameena's in Ealing, or mostly down at Summercove. Bryant Court is my past, and I don't like it much.

It's not how small it is, or how dingy. It's not how the outside of the thirties block looks rather stylish and then you get inside and it's damp and musty-smelling, with an undertone of something rotten, and always too hot or too cold. It's not that when you arrive, you get the feeling Mum wants you to leave. It's all those things and more. It's the sense of detachment I feel from it—I lived there for almost twelve years of my life.

I look back on those years now and try and make sense of them. Was I just an uptight kid? Probably. But lately, when I look at my list of things to do, which I still keep by the bed, I see *"6. Mum 7. Find diary"* and I realize how far I am away from doing those things. More and more as the days go by, I find myself thinking about Mum and the flat and our lives together there, and how strange it was. It doesn't seem strange when you're in it. It's starting to, now.

Twenty-nine

A fortnight after the funeral, one Wednesday afternoon, I am in the studio. I have ticked several items off my to-do list for that day, and I'm feeling virtuous. I've called Mum: no answer. I've sent Arvind a *New Yorker* cartoon card to his new home, the one with the two snails and a remarkably similar-looking tape dispenser, and the first snail is saying to the second snail, "I don't care if she is a tape dispenser. I love her." I have spoken to Clare Lomax today, to let her know I've made my first monthly repayment. I've phoned a couple more shops about the possibility of them taking my pieces and I'll go and see them tomorrow. I've had two more orders today, and I'm extremely pleased. I need more to show them, though. And it needs to be great, really great.

As part of the new collection I have been trying to work on a new version of the jeweled headbands I did well with a couple of years ago, based on a photo I saw of a headband worn by a maharani of Jaipur. The bands are black silk, and clasping gently on to the side of the head are gray and the palest pink velvet floral shapes studded with diamanté. They can be worn to a wedding or a birthday party. They are really beautiful, at least they will be if I can get them right, but every time I try to add the diamanté it just looks tacky, amateurish. My fingers get covered in the glue, I prick my thumb twice on the needle as I try to sew them on, and eventually groan in frustration. I don't know what I'm doing wrong.

I start to sketch alternatives. I flick through the V&A book of jewelry that I have by my side. Ben and Tania gave it to me for my birthday last year. I get out my cardfile of postcards, pictures of different pieces of jewelry, different paintings and images that inspire me, everything from Rita Hayworth to a portrait of a very cross-looking Medici duchess, decked out in the most beautiful rubies. I jab my pencil into the soft paper and stop, looking up around me, blinking hard.

It's quiet here this afternoon. The writers' collective is meeting in the basement this evening, and they are always extremely raucous—apparently they have a lot to be angry about, and it often involves drinking a lot of beer. I can hear people pulling rails of clothes over the road in the market below but that's it. My eyes are heavy, with a sense of peace, but I'm not especially tired. My hand steals to my neck as I stare into nothingness and I realize I'm clutching Cecily's ring.

I've taken to putting it on every day since I got back, I don't know why. I like wearing it. It's unusual. Moreover, I like the fact that it was hers, and that Granny wore it all those years. I know nothing about Cecily, except from those pages of the diary, but I have this and I like wearing it.

I pick up my pencil and start sketching the ring from memory as I can't see it, nestled in the hollow at the base of my neck. The flowers are so pretty—simple and attractive. I join the tiny gold buds studded with tiny diamonds together, linking them together like a daisy chain, in a row. It is one of the most pleasing things I have done for a while, but I'm not sure I can execute it myself—it's too elaborate, and I may have to hire someone else to work it out. A section of it would work as a pendant, as well. A charm bracelet? Necklace? My pencil skates busily over the white paper, and the scratching sound echoes in the silence, broken only by the occasional noise from the street below. There's something there, I don't know what it is. The links . . . the flowers . . . Cecily's ring, perhaps I should use the ring as the centerpiece? My pencil is getting blunter as I push heavily down onto the pad, sketching, rubbing out, resketching. . . . My mind is clear of everything else troubling it. I love this, the fact that you can escape into your imagination, use a part of your brain that isn't affected by everything else in your life. I lost it for a while.

It's so good to have it back; even if what results is rubbish, just to know I still love doing it is the most important thing. And the voice in my head, sounding remarkably like Clare Lomax, that has been telling me I ought to give up the studio and save on the rent, is silenced. I need a place to come to, to work. This is my job, and if I'm going to take it seriously, I ought to have an office. If Oli's not coming back we don't need the flat, do we? I'd give that up before the studio. Somehow, that clarifies things for me.

And suddenly, as I am drawing furiously, there comes a soft tapping at the door.

"Natasha, are you there?" a voice calls.

I unfurl my legs, stiff and aching from the cold and from being in the same position for so long. I roll my head slowly around my neck, and it crunches satisfyingly.

"Who's that?"

"It's me," says the voice. "Mummy."

What's she doing here? The hairs on the back of my neck stand up; my hand flies to my throat. "Come in," I say, after a moment.

She peeks around the door, her dark fringe and long eyelashes appearing first, like a naughty child, her green eyes sparkling. "Hello, darling. My little girl."

"Mum?" I say, standing up. "Wow. I've been calling you for days. Hello! What are you doing here?"

"I was in the area," she says. "I wanted to see you. I've been rather un-*loco parentis* lately." She gives a tinkling laugh. "Awful joke. I'm sorry, should I have called?"

"No, of course not," I say, sounding ridiculously formal. My heart is beating fast, and my palms are slick. "It's fine. I've been wondering where you were. I haven't seen you since the funeral and—"

Mum frowns. "Well, I'm here now, aren't I?"

She advances into the room, arms outstretched. She looks fantastic, as always, skinny jeans tucked into brown suede leather boots, a thick gray cardigan-coat, and a long floral scarf wrapped many times round her neck and tied in a knot. Her skin is gleaming, her nails are beautiful, her hair is shining and soft. She wraps me in her arms.

"Poor girl."

She squeezes me tight. Her scent is heavy; it makes me nauseous. Suddenly I want to push her away. I'm repulsed by her.

I step back. She clutches my hands, then reaches into her large canvas bag. "Bought you a little something," she says, handing me a box of tiny, very expensive-looking cheese crackers in a beautifully printed box.

"Thanks," I say, bemused by this gift, which is so like Mum— there were months when we thought we wouldn't be able to pay the rent in Bryant Court, but she would think nothing of buying a free-range chicken from Fortnum & Mason for fifteen pounds and then not know how to cook it. I put the biscuits down on the little sink. "Have you eaten? Do you want some coffee—or tea?"

"Tea would be lovely," she says, and I suddenly realize what's been bothering me. She's nervous too. I don't think I've ever seen her nervous.

"Great." We are silent for a moment. We don't know how to do this. I look around for a distraction. Luckily, I remember Ben has borrowed my teapot.

"I'll get the teapot." I get up. "Back in a second." She is looking around the room, and she hums blithely in agreement when I say this. My hand is on the door and I say, "Mum—we do need to talk, you know."

Mum's expression does not change, but there's something in her eyes that I can't define. "Oh, darling, really?"

I realize this is a stupid way to begin. "Yes, really. Look, hold on."

I dash down the corridor and knock on their door. Ben flings it open.

"Aha," he says. "Hello there."

"Hi," I say. "Sorry to disturb you. Have you got my teapot?"

"Oh, right. Yeah, of course," he says. "Sorry, forgot to put it back. Hang on a second." He comes back with the pot and a teacake, wrapped in blue foil. "We've got one spare," he says. "Have it."

I take the teacake. "Thanks."

"Was going to drop by later. We're going for a drink."

"I can't," I say. "Mum's just turned up. Soon, though. I haven't seen you for ages."

"I know, you're busy," he says. "But it's good." He smiles, and I know he knows. "Just checking you're not rocking at home in a ball by the radiator." He scratches his curly hair and it bounces; I smile.

"Well, thanks again," I say. "I'm OK. I'm not going to start gibbering and weeping all over you."

"You're allowed to, you know," he says.

"You're so in touch with your feelings, Benjamin," I say. "I'm a cold-hearted bitch, however. So bog off."

He smiles, and then I hear Tania's voice in the background. "Hi, Nat. How you doing?"

In the back of my buzzing brain this confuses me. I thought she wasn't working with him anymore. Perhaps she's just popped over to see him, he is her boyfriend after all. "I'm good," I call back to her.

"See you guys later then," I say. "Coolio. Sorry about tonight."

"No probs," he says equably, sticking a piece of toast in his mouth. He reaches out and pats my shoulder. "Hey. You're not cold-hearted. You're lovely. Remember that. Keep your chin up, Nat." His voice is muffled as he closes the door, almost abruptly, and I'm left standing in the corridor. On the front of the door is written, in black marker pen:

Ben Cohen
Photographer & Male Escort

I've never noticed this before and it makes me smile. I'm still smiling as I walk back into the studio. Mum is looking at my drawing pad, the sketch of the ring and the necklace; she jumps guiltily.

"Oh," she says. "You gave me a fright."

"Sorry," I say. I fill the kettle up and then I take a deep breath and turn to face her. The unexpectedness of this encounter makes me bold. I haven't had time to worry about it. "So where have you been? I've been wanting to talk to you."

"Yes, I know." Mum runs one hand carefully through her hair. "Look, I'm sorry. It's been hard for me."

"You should have called me."

She smiles, almost sweetly. "Darling, you don't understand."

"I don't?" I say, looking at her.

"No, you don't. Sorry, Natasha."

"Try me," I say, opening my arms wide. "You've lost your mother, I've lost my grandmother. My marriage is ended. You're my mum. Why can't you talk to me? And why can't I talk to you? I'm not saying I'm a great daughter, but . . . where've you *been*?"

"Because . . ." She shakes her head, scrunching up her face. "Oh, you don't understand. You don't! I know you think I'm a terrible mother, but—" her voice is rising into a whine—"you don't understand!"

A kind of despair tugs at me—this is my mother, my mother. "Octavia said you were the last person anyone would ask for help," I say icily. "She was right, wasn't she?"

"Octavia? We're listening to what *Octavia* says now, are we? Right." Mum's eyes dart around the room, undermining the bullish tone in which she says this. "Funny, darling, I thought you and I were in rare agreement about Octavia. She's the last person I'd ask for help."

This is going wrong, all wrong. "She just said it, that's all. I'm not saying I like her, it's—"

Mum interrupts. "Listen, Natasha. She's her mother's daughter. And her father's. Hah. I don't care for their opinions, to be honest. Neither should you."

I'm standing behind the counter. She is facing me.

"Octavia said something else too," I say, nodding as if to will myself along, and her eyes meet my gaze. "Octavia said . . ." My voice breaks. "Mum, she said you pushed Cecily that day. You pushed her down the steps."

My mother's eyes widen a little, and she says, with a catch in her throat, "OK, OK."

She paces around, two steps forwards, turns, two steps back. I watch her.

"You think I killed her," she says. "Is that what you're saying?"

"They all think—" I begin, but she interrupts me again.

"Not them." She holds up her hand. "Not them, Natasha. You. Answer me. Is that what you're saying?"

I wipe my hands on my jeans. It is so quiet. Downstairs, a door slams. She is looking right into my eyes.

When it comes, the word slides out of my mouth quietly. "Yes," I say, not looking at her. "That's what I'm saying."

My mother doesn't react immediately. We face each other in the cold, darkening room. "Well, that's very interesting," she replies. "Very interesting. I guess I always knew this moment would come."

She says it lightly, as if it's of moderate interest, and hugs herself a little tighter, her head on one side. She looks so beautiful, but I am suddenly revolted by that cool, ravishing beauty, her cunning hooded eyes, her total lack of trustworthiness, and I remember how good an actress she really is, has always been.

"You knew this moment would come?" I say. I back up, stand against the wall, my hands on the cool, white plaster.

"Yes," she says. "When you finally went over to their side." She looks at her watch. "Nearly a month since Mummy died, and you've done it. I knew it."

"I'm not on anyone's 'side.' " I swallow. "It's just they say that—"

" 'They'?" my mother says, smiling. "Who are 'they,' please?"

"Well—" I stutter. "Octavia and—Louisa, and—the rest of them."

She nods. "Exactly." Her eyes flash a little as she sees my expression. "That's very nice. And my own daughter believes them." She leans back on the counter. "Louisa has no evidence, you know. This is a land grab, don't you see that?" She raises her eyebrows so they disappear into her tinted fringe. "They're all trying to ruin me, to make themselves feel better, now Mummy's gone."

I shake my head. "I don't think Louisa's trying to—to do any-thing, Mum. She just said—"

Mum's face is flushed. "Oh, if you knew what I know. . . ." She stops. She is almost laughing; her mouth opens without sound. Then she says, "What I've put up with, since I was a little girl, from all of them. You don't know what it was like."

I find that all my fear of saying these things I've never wanted to say has gone. All the thoughts I've been bottling up over the past weeks, over the past thirty years. "That's rubbish!" My voice is loud, harsh. "You're always trying to be horrible about Granny. All she ever tried to do was look after you."

Mum gives a weird shriek, something between laughter and hys-teria. "Her? Look after *me*! Oh, that's a joke." She shakes her head. "Yes, that's funny." She stops. She looks at a nail and cautiously bites the edge of it. Then she mutters something to herself, something I can't hear.

"Octavia said I should ask Guy," I say calmly. "She says he knows what happened."

My mother is pulling a smooth ribbon of her hair through her long fingers. She stops at this and laughs. "Guy again?" She bites her lip. "Oh, he's everywhere now, isn't he? He's really crawled out of the woodwork! Go on, ask away! I'd be interested to see what *he* has to say for himself."

"What does that mean?"

She is speaking so fast she can't quite get the words out. "Listen to me, Nat, darling. In all this, there's no one I hate more than Guy Leighton."

"Oh, come on, Mum—"

Her eyes are burning. "He's full of shit, always has been, and he hides behind some kind of nice-guy liberalism—I sell antiques, I live in Islington, I like Umbria more than fucking Tuscany." She is almost spitting, and the red spots on her cheeks are spreading. "He's fake. He's worse than the Bowler Hat. At least you know the Bowler Hat's a lazy fucking right-wing letch. Guy's worse. He's the biggest hypocrite of the lot." Her expression is twisted and her face is ugly. "I'm the one in this family that everyone hates and you know why? Because it's easier to hate me than look any deeper at them. She slipped, the path was slippery, fine, it wasn't my fault. But I still saw it. I saw her die, and she was my sister, and it ruined my life. No one understands that."

I don't know what to say to her, she's so full of self-righteous anger. She has that quality that a lot of people like her have in spades: I *have* to be right. Suddenly I find my courage. "Stop feeling sorry for yourself, Mum," I say. "Start taking responsibility for things."

She bares her teeth at me and lifts her head slightly. And she looks at me with such naked contempt I almost step back. This woman is a stranger, I don't know her. "Oh, you were always a self-righteous little prig, Natasha, even when you were little," she says clearly, an edge of cold anger in her voice. "God, I loathe that about you. All this—it's just so you can have a go at me, accuse me of being a bad mother and blame me for your own little life going off the rails. Isn't it?" And then her eyes fill with tears. "It's been hard for me," she says. "You don't know what it's like. They all hated me."

"Oh, Mum, they didn't." I am sick of this play-acting. "No one hated you. You just . . ." I trail off, I don't know what to say. You're just not very nice? You're a bad person?

"Mummy hated me, Cecily hated me." Her voice is rising, whining like a dog's, and it's horrible. She moves towards me and I step back again. "I was all on my own, with a baby, for years." She wipes a tear away. "You do have to accept me for how I am, darling. I'm not some fifty-something housewife with a middle-aged spread and a store card at Marks and Spencer." She shakes her hair a little, with some kind of assumed bravado. "I'm not that kind of mum. I'm different."

It's only then that I can feel myself losing it. It's the shake of her hair, the artificial way she's talking, the character she's constructed for herself—she claims it's for survival, and I am sure it's to cover something up. At any rate, I can feel rage bubbling just underneath me. "You've never been a mum at all!" I shout at her. "What are you talking about?"

"I tried to do my best by you. . . ." Her voice is like a whimper. "And then you went and got married, you totally rejected me. . . ."

I hear my voice screaming at her, as if it's someone else. "*Why do you think I got married?* I wanted to get away from you!" I am shaking, adrenaline is pumping through me, and I don't care anymore.

"Oli liked me!" she hisses, coming closer towards me. I laugh, as though this is the crux of the argument.

"Of course he did," I say, smiling an ugly smile, blinking slowly. "You're exactly the same, that's why. I can't believe how stupid I was, I married to get away from you and I went and married someone *exactly like you*." I put my hands to my burning cheeks and slide them up so I'm covering my eyes. "I can't believe I'm saying all this. This is not the point. We're not discussing me, we're talking about you."

"About me!" She laughs, eyes flashing. "What, with your cheating husband and this stupid, *freezing* studio with your necklaces no one wants to buy, just so you can get Granny's approval?" She rubs her arms with her hands, her eyes practically popping out of her head; it's so strange, how I really don't recognize her anymore. I see—for the first time, really?—that she is old. There are wrinkles round her eyes, her neck is saggy. I never really noticed before. "I just wanted you to do well for yourself. That's all I ever wanted, so you didn't end up like me, penniless, pregnant, abandoned by everyone, with no one to love you."

"That's not going to happen!" I shout at her. "I'm not you!"

"Oh, yes, yes. Of course." She nods sarcastically. "What a relief, you're not me."

"I've got a proper life, a grown-up life, it's not perfect, but it's OK. And I don't want you in it!" My cheeks are burning hot. I won't cry. "Stay away from me! I don't want you in my life anymore!"

We are facing each other, her with her arms folded. She registers no emotion whatsoever: my momentary loss of control is enough for her to assert herself again, and the mask is back in place.

"I know you're lying, Mum," I say softly. "I know it must be awful, but I know you did something bad that summer. I know you did."

"Well, I'm sorry you think that," she says, smiling the catlike smile again. "I wish there was a way I could persuade you otherwise."

"Did you know Cecily left a diary?" I say suddenly. "Have you seen it?"

"Well, that's very interesting," she says. "Have I seen it? Have I seen it? I could ask you the same question. But I know what I know, you see, and I don't know if I feel like telling you, now."

"You have seen it?" I say. "You—Mum, tell me." I drum my fingers on the counter, almost wild with desperation. My hands are outstretched. "Please, Mum. I have to know. Have you?"

She looks at me almost brazenly, like the bad girl at school who's just got away with something. Ignoring the question, she slings her bag over her shoulder. "I'd better be off," she says, as I blink in astonishment. "I'm meeting an old friend for drinks. I don't want to be late." She shakes her head, her hair making a slippery sound, like a stream, as it slides over her shoulders again. She walks to the door. "Can I say something?"

"Of course," I say.

"Natasha—one day you'll understand," she says. "I know you think it doesn't make sense now. But it will, all of it. One day."

And then she's gone, and I am left staring into space. I look up and out of the window at the street. I see my mother leave, fumble in her bag for something, and then take out a lip gloss and apply it. She walks off, tossing her hair again, as I watch her through the dirty window.

Thirty

I meet Jay at Ealing Broadway station, and we double back one stop, to Ealing Common. It's Sunday lunchtime, and when we get off the Tube the Uxbridge Road is jammed solid. We walk along the main road in silence, our steps exact. I keep looking up at the sky, expecting it to rain.

"Come for lunch at Mum and Dad's," Jay had said that morning, when I'd answered the phone the third time it rang. "Dad asked me to ask you. Mum's made loads of food." Jay has been away for work—he has a big job on in Zurich and had to go there almost straight after the funeral. So this is the first time I've seen him.

It's five days since my showdown with Mum and we still haven't spoken, but I bet she's told Archie everything, she always does. I get the feeling I'm being summoned to Ealing so he can waggle his finger at me and try and do his head-of-the-family bit. Well, he can try, I told myself as I sat on the Tube. I know all about you, uncle. You can try and act like the big head honcho, but it doesn't wash with me, not now I know you used to peek at your cousin while she was getting undressed, and your own sister thought you were pretty odd.

We don't talk much. There's a faint drizzle, it's misty and cold. Jay is silent, grumpy, I think he was out late last night. As we turn into Creffield Road, Jay's stride lengthens and I have to skip to keep up with him. "How was Zurich then?" I ask. "I missed you."

"Yeah, it was good." Jay is walking faster, his face set with determination like a mountaineer on the final stretch. "Fine. Hard work. Sorry I didn't call properly."

"It's fine," I say. "Hey. Jay—" I put my hand on his arm. "Stop a second. Stop!"

"What?"

"Before we get to your mum and dad's, I need to tell you something."

"What?" He shoots me a half-look, almost nervous.

"I split up with Oli. It's permanent." We face each other in the quiet suburban street. I am standing on a cracked paving slab; one side rocks when I put my weight on it. "It's not a big deal. I just wanted you to know."

"I know," Jay says.

"You know I split up with him?"

"Yeah." Jay carries on walking.

"Oh, right," I say. "Did—your dad told you then?"

"Yes, course. He spoke to your mum." There's a pause. "We're nearly there," he says. "I am so hungry, man."

We turn into the small driveway of Archie and Sameena's house. It's almost silent on their street; it always is. The occasional car rumbles past but otherwise all you can hear is the sound of birds. Jay knocks on the door.

"Aah." My uncle opens the door with a flourish. "You're here." He kisses his son, then me. "Natasha. Glad you could come. Good to see you."

He's in his Sunday relaxing outfit, which is nearly identical to his weekday work outfit: pink striped shirt with navy chinos. In summer they'd be khaki chinos. His hair is perfectly combed, his smile is welcoming, but he reminds me so much of my mother: there's something behind his eyes that I can't quite define.

We walk into the plush hall, with the gold-leaf mirror and the enamel card table, hung with beautiful old prints of scenes from the Ramayana. The cream carpet is soft and springy under my feet. Archie takes our coats and hangs them, then he turns to us and rubs his hands together.

"Your mother is making a feast today, Sanjay," he says. "A feast."

He ushers us jovially into the kitchen. Though I used to come here all the time, I haven't been here for a good few months, and I stare around me, impressed. "Is this a new kitchen?"

Archie nods. "Oh, yes. Look at the conservatory." We walk through the gleaming, ocher-colored, marble-topped kitchen and out through the French windows. There is a huge conservatory, with matching wicker furniture, china bowls filled with plants. Archie presses a button. "Natasha. Look." Automatic blinds slide up and down the glass ceiling. "Look," he says, pointing again, this time at the terracotta floor. "Under-floor heating." He smiles. "Amazing, isn't it?"

"It sure is." I smile back; his enthusiasm is infectious. Jay is smiling too.

"Dad, you're such a show-off," he says. "Nat doesn't care about the under-floor heating."

Archie's face clouds over. "Don't be rude, Sanjay," he says sharply. "Here's your mother. Go and say hello."

Sameena makes everything all right, she always has done. She bustles into the kitchen, putting the phone back on its cradle. "I am sorry. I was just talking to my brother," she says. "Hello, my darling children!" She gives us both a big hug. "How are you, Natasha? We are so glad you could come today, on such short notice. There is so much food!"

We sit in the conservatory. Archie has a gin and tonic and we both stick to Coke. Sameena shouts out questions to her son from the kitchen about his trip, what did you eat, what was the hotel like, was the work worthwhile? Archie tells him about the time he went to Zurich, to negotiate a new fleet of cars for "an internationally renowned hotel in the center of the city" and Jay nods politely and I watch them all, fascinated.

Because I haven't seen them all together for a while, and especially of late, what with the end of my own marriage, and because of my huge, horrible row with Mum on Thursday, they are even more interesting to watch than normal. Except for Bryant Court I probably spent more time here as a child than anywhere, at least one day a week after school, and often I'd stay the night. It was so easy for me to get on the Piccadilly line and come over that when I got to be about ten or so I'd do just that, if I knew Mum was going to be out late and I didn't want another night in by myself. The house has changed innumerable times over the years, barely a season goes by without Archie having something redecorated at vast expense, but Sameena and Jay have always been there.

During the school holidays, Sameena would often take me and Jay with her to Southall to meet friends, do the shopping for the week—it isn't far from Ealing Common on the Tube and the train. Sitting in the conservatory I watch her now in the kitchen as she prepares the food, making a huge feast for us all, handmade potato patties, crisp and sweet onion bahjees, fragrant fish curry, with huge plates of dhal and rice, the bangles on her wrist clinking together as she shakes the rice, humming a song to herself and looking out of the window. There are fresh, fat bunches of parsley and coriander on the gleaming marble counter of the beautiful new kitchen. Delicious spices fill the air—I'm used to them from Brick Lane but here they're better. Jay used to joke that I moved to Brick Lane so I'd be subconsciously reminded of Sameena's kitchen, and in some small way it's not a joke, maybe I did.

Why do I like it round here? Because often, Archie would be away for work and it'd just be the three of us. That's a terrible thing to say, but it's true. Sameena is not like my mum. She is a doctor at a local surgery, the kind of person you'd want in a crisis. She can talk to Arvind about home, tell him about Mumbai, a city he loves. She is an amazing cook, a proud Indian woman, and when I'm with her and Jay I feel Indian. It's not something I often feel—I'm a quarter Punjabi, and I grew up not really questioning where I'm from, because of not knowing about my dad. Summercove was what I clung to, where I wanted to be from. Watching Sameena now, as she pops a piece of spring onion in her mouth and tastes some sauce in a pan, it strikes me that I've always been welcome here.

"How is the business, Natasha?" Archie hands me a bowl of crisps. "I understand you've been having some problems, is that true?"

I don't ask how he knows. "Yep," I say, nodding. "It's been pretty bad. But I hope I'm on the right track now."

"The bank is involved, yes?"

"Yes," I say.

He frowns. "It won't look good if you don't respect your relationship with them. Be careful."

"I am," I say. "I've sorted it out. I hope."

I'm in no position to get cross about any of this, but I don't particularly want to discuss it. For the first time in a long time, I don't like thinking about work at the weekends, which I take as a good sign. It means I'm working during the week, like someone in an office, someone with a proper, organized job.

"Have you thought of getting Jay to take a look at the website again?" Archie says. "Maybe there's something there you can do." He removes his cufflinks and rolls up his shirtsleeves, sniffing the air hopefully. Something is sizzling, deliciously, in the kitchen.

"I'd be happy to," Jay says. "It's changing all the time, the way you reach the customer."

"Yes, that's true." Archie looks at me. "Natasha?"

"That'd be great," I answer. "Thanks, Jay."

"And maybe, have you thought of advertising in those free local-business newsletters? They have one in Spitalfields."

"They do," I say, acting surprised. They stock it in all the local shops and restaurants, it's about the area, who's keeping bees, who's got an art gallery opening, who's organizing a vintage tea party club night—it's very Shoreditch/Spitalfields. "That's a great idea. Thanks, Archie."

He's a good businessman, and he learned by himself—he certainly didn't pick it up from his parents. Archie nods, as if he's agreeing with me about his own greatness, which is probably true. "I picked up a newsletter in a restaurant last time I was over in the City, having lunch with an—well, I can't say who he is. Let's just say important client."

Sameena is standing at the door. She rolls her eyes. "Come on, you and your important client," she says. "Let's have our lunch."

We sit in the sumptuous dining room, with green watered-silk wallpaper, a glass dining table, elaborately cut crystal goblets—I remember when I was little thinking this must be what the table at Buckingham Palace was like. Archie munches slowly and steadily, like a grazing cow, not saying much. Sameena asks me and Jay how we're getting on, we talk about my jewelry, about the new places in Columbia Road. We plan a trip for her to come East soon. I ask about her family, whom she's just been visiting in Mumbai, her sister Priyanka who is having dialysis, her little nieces and nephews. She only sees them once a year.

"Were you lonely when you first moved here, Sameena?" I ask, thinking of my grandfather. "It's so far away."

Archie doesn't look up, but he's listening to her.

"A little," she says. "The weather got to me, you know?"

"How old were you?"

"I was young," she says. "Oh, twenty-five. We had no money, did we, Archie?" Archie doesn't meet her eye. He nods briskly. "We were living in Acton. In a tiny flat. I'd been to England but when I was a child, and I couldn't remember it that well. I'd invented what it'd be like. In my mind, you know? I thought it was palaces, very elegant people in tea dresses. Instead, it rained all the time, like this—" She gestures out of the window, at the faint patter that has started to sound on the conservatory roof. "Dog mess everywhere, cracked pavements, no one friendly. The old lady next to me, she was from Delhi, she would go to the shops in her shabby, old duffel coat, covering up her beautiful sari. At home she wouldn't have had to put her coat on and cover up her lovely colors, be drab. That's what I remember most of all."

Jay looks at her. "I didn't realize that, Mum," he says.

"Oh, yes," Sameena says, pushing a bowl of dhal towards me. "But you know, these things pass. And then I was very happy. It's my home, now. My home is with you. All of you," she adds hurriedly, looking at me. "You and your mother too, Natasha."

There's a silence. We all eat some more. Sameena glances at her husband.

"Are you looking forwards to going back for the launch of the foundation, Natasha?" she asks. "It sounds like a wonderful day. You know, they're calling people up about it already. And everyone's saying yes."

"I don't really know much about it," I say. "Mum hasn't told me a lot, and—well, Guy's the other trustee. I don't really know him either." I look down at my plate.

"We've been contacting people about it all week," Archie says. "Very notable people." He sighs. "It's going to be impressive, I think. Only two weeks to go."

"Do I need to do anything?" I say.

"Oh, no," he says. "Louisa's got it all under control."

I take a spoonful of sauce from the fish curry. It is delicious. The chili puckers my tongue. "I guess I still don't know why it's been so fast," I say.

"Our mother wanted it that way," Archie says. "Wanted it to start as soon as she died." He shrugs his shoulders. "She spent a lot of time planning for it. And you know, the Tate Gallery had already scheduled a major exhibition of her work, in 2011. Before she died. I don't think she wanted it to go ahead. It's strange."

"Why did she plan it out so much?" I say. I remembered how pleased she was, but also a little agitated. She won't be here for it now.

He sighs again. "I think she liked the idea that after she was gone, people could start to appreciate her paintings again, without her there. And you know, the foundation will help young artists too, like she and Arvind were helped. He was funded to come over to Cambridge, she had patrons when she was younger. People looked after them. I think she wants to help others, now—now she's gone."

Sameena nods. "Very noble. It's wonderful."

"Of course, that's where most of the money's going," Archie says.

"We shall see." He looks at me, and at Jay. "Her children, we get very little. That is what distresses me, on your mother's behalf. The lawyers say—" He stops, as if he's gone too far. "I'm sorry," he says formally. "Not suitable."

"No, go on," I urge. He frowns.

"Natasha, it's not your concern." I feel as though I've been slapped for being naughty. "She wanted you involved, she had her reasons, I'm sure. But for the moment you don't need to do anything. When the estate is settled, and we know what the money is, we'll be able to consider applications, and you'll be involved then, vetting the applicants, their suitability. Perhaps talking to people, visiting their studios. . . . I don't know."

"How ironic," I say. "Can I apply for some money?" I'm joking. Archie doesn't smile.

"You're going?" I ask him then. "Next month, back to Cornwall?"

"Yes, of course," he says.

"Have you seen Arvind?"

Jay shoots me a glance. *Stop asking these questions*. It occurs to me then that's why he's been in a funny mood today: he knows my uncle is displeased with me, and Jay, close as we are, is much more respectful of his parents than I am of my mother.

"I have not, no," Archie says. "We are going next week."

"Louisa's been down there," Sameena says, and I'm sure it's an innocent remark but Archie obviously doesn't want to hear it.

"Yes," I say. "She's been wonderful."

"She has," Archie says. "We are lucky."

Suddenly I can't resist. "Archie, can I ask you something?"

"Yes, Natasha?" Archie breaks another poppadom between his fingers.

"Why—well, why doesn't Mum get on with her? Louisa's been wonderful through this, organizing the funeral, getting Arvind sorted, the foundation. . . ." My voice is loud in the silent dining room. "I don't know what we'd all have done without her. And Mum—she thinks Louisa's after her in some way."

I know this is dangerous, but it is as close as I can get to asking

Archie about the diary, about what happened to Cecily, and I don't want to, here in front of Sameena and Jay, these people I love. I don't want to start throwing accusations around about my mother when I have no real evidence myself.

Archie breaks the poppadom piece in half again. "You just said it. Louisa and your mother don't get on. Never have done. That is all."

I want to laugh, inappropriate as it seems. That's only the beginning of it, I want to say.

But then he goes on: "Look, when we were growing up . . . it was a long time ago. We don't really talk about it much, because of the tragedy of my sister." He raises his head, and a lock of carefully combed hair falls in his face, making him look much younger all of a sudden. "The truth is—they were very different. You know? Louisa was—well, I found her rather insufferable at times. Always offering to help. Much better behaved than us, our parents loved her. Always doing well in her exams, good at sports." He stops and rubs his arms. He seems surprised he's saying all this, and then he plows on. "I was fascinated by her. So was your mother. She was everything we weren't. We weren't good at anything in particular. No artistic prowess, we weren't intellectual. No good at sports. We weren't blond, hearty. My mother was . . . disappointed with us. Always felt she'd rather Louisa and Jeremy were her children, not us. And Cecily, of course. She loved Cecily."

He trails off. I know he's telling the truth. He speaks in a low, clear voice, not very dramatic, just simply stating facts. The four of us are still. What he says and the way he says it, makes me so sad, but I can't reach out and touch him, I know that.

"That's why—" Archie begins, and then stops. He clears his throat and looks at Jay, then at me. "Well. Now that is why I have always been very pleased that you two—you cousins got on so well. That these things don't matter, these days. As has your mother."

"Have you spoken to Mum?" I ask him suddenly. I've called her since our row, several times, but once again she's gone completely off radar.

"Oh, yes," he says.

"Where is she?" I ask. "Is she around?"

"She'll be back in time for the foundation launch," Archie says. "Her work is important to her."

He raises his chin, and nods expectantly at me.

"We had a row—" I hear myself say.

"I know you did." Archie puts his napkin down. "Natasha, you upset her a great deal. I don't think you realize how much."

"She—" I begin, and then I stop. I look at Sameena and Jay, eating their curry in silence.

"She's your mother," Archie says. "You should respect her, no matter what."

"No matter what?" I say.

He looks at me, then at his wife and child. "Yes."

I can't push this anymore; I'm in their home.

The contrast between brother and sister strikes me again. Archie may be a bit pompous, but he's made his own life for himself, him and Sameena and Jay, and it's not like Summercove. I can see what he did—I tried to do it myself, with Oli, create a world different from the one I grew up in. I think of Archie with his parents, how he's never really present, like his sister. He turns up, bosses people around, shows everyone his flash new car or his nice new watch, and then he's gone. It's funny to read about him in those pages of Cecily's: the idea that he'd have gone to Oxford or Cambridge isn't really him at all. I don't know whether he took the exams or not, but I know he went away for a long time, went traveling, like Mum. He got a job working in a car dealership, in the mid-sixties when I guess it still had a modicum of glamor attached to it. Archie worked his way up; his business is now pretty successful. You'd know it, even if he didn't tell you. He lived all over the world, in Singapore, Tokyo. It was in Mumbai that he met Sameena.

I ask just one more question. "You don't know where she is, though?"

"No," he says. "As I said, she'll be back."

She's always flitting off somewhere, with no notice, and usually you're lucky to get a text. When I was about ten, she went to Lisbon for a week, and I only found out when she rang the school on her way to the airport and told them my aunt would be looking after me while she was away. . . . I remember this now in light of what I know, sitting at the Kapoors' table, as Sameena and Jay nudge each other and she laughs about something, and Archie helps himself to more mango chutney and I sit watching them. I feel very alone, all of a sudden. Archie got out, he got away from whatever it was. Poor Mum, dancing off around the world to find some freedom, some space, running away from her own thoughts, her own life.

Like I say, it makes me sad.

Thirty-one

On Thursday, the week after lunch at Archie's, my alarm doesn't go off and I wake up late. I lie in bed for about ten minutes, annoyed because the day is already off on the wrong foot. I have become very good at keeping myself busy with my lists and my actions and I know that lying in bed being annoyed isn't the way to keep myself from going mad. Do something, anything. I get up, shower, get dressed and clean the flat from top to bottom, tidying things up, putting some more of Oli's things away, dusting, scouring, scrubbing, singing along to the radio.

In the afternoon I head out for the studio, eager to stretch my legs, get outside. In the hallway I see the post has arrived, which even though it's nearly three is still something of a miracle. I pick up the bundle and sort it out, putting the post for the two other flats in our building into their rightful pigeonholes.

I know he's not coming back now, but some days events conspire to make it more difficult than others. This morning the post consists of a council-tax demand, Oli's Arsenal fanzine, one of his many gadget magazines, and a reminder to Mr. and Mrs. Jones that we have to renew our home contents insurance, which seems particularly cruel. There's also a small, thick, stiff envelope, with my name written in handwriting I don't recognize. I put the rest of the post in his pile—Oli is staying with his best friend Jason and his wife Lucy, nearby in Hackney, which is where he went before. He comes by the flat to pick his post up, just lets himself into the hall and goes again, we don't see each other. I open the envelope addressed to me.

YOU ARE INVITED TO THE LAUNCH OF
THE FRANCES SEYMOUR FOUNDATION
A CHARITY FOUNDED IN MEMORY OF FRANCES SEYMOUR
TO SUPPORT YOUNG ARTISTS
THURSDAY 9TH APRIL
2:30PM CHAMPAGNE RECEPTION & BUFFET LUNCH
3:30PM SPEECH BY MIRANDA KAPOOR, FRANCES'S DAUGHTER
3:45PM PRIVATE VIEW OF EXHIBITION OPENS

AT SUMMERCOVE,
NEAR TREEN,
CORNWALL
RSVP   RSVP@SEYMOURFOUNDATION.ORG
                    OVERLEAF: *SUMMERCOVE AT SUNSET* (1963)

On the back is a painting, one I have never seen before. *Summer-cove at Sunset* (1963) must have been painted from behind the white house, which is nestling against the black trees in the lane behind, the lawn and the terrace sloping gently towards the cliffs, the countryside lush and green, the gray terrace echoed by the gray-green of the lavender against it. There is a lone figure on the lawn, a tall man with a towel around his neck, walking towards the sea. It is very still, almost dreamlike; no feeling of movement in the branches or the lavender or the grass. The light is pale gold, casting long shadows. The man is striding but you feel he's been frozen mid-step by the artist, that they wanted to capture this moment in time.

I stare at it, in the fading afternoon light; I've seen Granny's paintings at Summercove, in galleries, in catalogs and books, but I've never seen anything like this before. It feels like a new approach, only it was one of the last things she ever painted. I turn the invitation over in my hand, letting the corners of the hard cardboard press into my palms. Who sent this out? Louisa, of course. It wasn't Mum, that's for sure.

It's been over a week now since Mum and I had our showdown, and I still haven't heard back from her. I don't know what comes next. This gives me another reason to be in touch, I suppose. Tapping the invitation thoughtfully against my hand, I walk towards the studio.

The sun is—sort of—out, a silvery sheen of cloud covering the sky but there are shadows on the ground and it's kind of warm, for the first time this year, over halfway through March. I am lost in thought as I walk round to Fournier Street and out at the back of the Hawksmoor Christ Church, its looming, sinister bulk casting the streets into shade. I need more time to think.

Cathy often says in her wise way that your life is made up of three sides of a triangle: home (where you live and how settled it is), relationships (friends, family, and of course romantic), and work (having a job, having a fulfilling job, one that doesn't make you cry every night or mean you're a sex worker). Cathy's triangle dictates that you don't have to have all three sides working to be happy, but you need two sides to be able to function properly. We used to discuss this in the long evenings around the time of Horrific Ex-Boyfriend Martin, three years ago—a psycho doctor who kicked her out of her flat and changed the locks, the week after she lost her job in her previous company. No home, no boyfriend, no job. No sides of the triangle: bad. But strangely, it was OK, because it was relatively easy to get two sides of the triangle up and running again. She got a job quite quickly, bucking the trend of my other friends at publishing houses or law firms or small start-ups who suddenly lost their jobs: it was obviously some kind of slow period in the actuary recruiting world. She stayed with Jay, who has a spare room in his flat, and whom she has known almost as long as me, and the weird thing is that we remember that period with a lot of happiness. We were out a lot, loads of us, drinking in Spitalfields and Shoreditch, there were great new bars opening up each week and it wasn't a stop on a tourist trail the way it is now. Oli and I were getting ready for our wedding, and finding the whole thing surreal and weird: Cathy and Oli and I all went to a wedding fair at ExCel, and had to leave after five minutes when the first stand we came across was a production company that will make a DVD of your wedding day set to a song

that is specially composed for and about you; it was next to a stand
that sold you fluffy toys with the pet names you and your partner
call each other embroidered on for you to give away to guests as
wedding favors. . . . We went to Summercove for a fortnight, the
four of us, and I remember we ate fresh crab nearly every day, with
pools of garlic butter and fresh bread. We helped Granny clear out
Arvind's study while he was away giving a lecture in Bologna, one
of his last trips abroad, and threw out a huge amount of papers. I
have since wondered what we threw out. . . . probably the secret to
happiness in the western hemisphere, or a cure for cancer, but it's
hard to tell when you're confronted with a box containing a copy
of *Woman's Own* from 1979, two packets of crisps that went out of
date in 1992, and assorted scraps of torn-up paper, which is what
it mostly seemed to be. I remember Granny so well that summer,
laughing over boxes, a scarf tied over her hair like Grace Kelly. She
would have been in her mid-eighties then and she still looked like a
star.

It seems a long time ago, that period in our lives. Rose-tinted glasses,
perhaps, but I look back on it now and smile. I clutch the invitation
in my hand, bending the hard card over into the shape of a tear.

At the studio, I put it on the little shelf by the safe. I stare at the
painting on the back, thinking. It is very still; starting to get dark
outside and the traffic seems distant. I shake my head. Where is the
damn diary? Where is it? I feel as if I'm no nearer to finding out.
I should have gone back to look for it and now I've made things
worse, not better. I feel like a failure. I've let Cecily down.

There's a knock on the door and a deep voice says, "Nat, hi."

"Ben! Hey," I say, and though it's hardly a shock to see him, I'm
particularly grateful for the diversion this morning. "I was just coming to ask you—" I turn round and stop, open-mouthed. "Wow.
Your hair! What happened to you?"

"I had it all cut off."

"When?"

"Last Thursday. You just haven't been in since then."

"I was out visiting shops and stuff. My goodness. Why?"

He rubs the top of his head ruefully. "Um—I decided it was time for a change."

"All your lovely curls!" I say. "And the stubble! All gone!"

He looks sad. "I know. My head feels cold." He is running his fingertips lightly over his scalp. I watch, transfixed, as his long fingers push through the thick, short stubble of his hair and move down towards his smooth chin.

"You look completely different," I say. "Strange."

"Oh, thanks," he says.

"No, I don't mean you look strange." I rush to correct myself. "It's strange, I mean. You look—it's like Samson."

"He lost all his strength and got murdered," Ben says. "You're making me think I should put a bag on my head. Is it that bad?"

"It's really not. In fact it's the opposite." I hear Cathy's voice, it seems ages ago, that lunch—*If he had his hair cut. . . . Wow, he'd be absolutely gorgeous*—and I can feel myself starting to blush. "You look great. Really—it really suits you. You look much better—not that you looked bad before. You always look good. . . ." I trail off. This is just pathetic.

His eyebrows pucker together and he frowns. "I don't know if you're trying to get yourself out of a hole or dig yourself into one," he says. "But I'll console myself with the thought that it'll grow out and I'll have my shaggy-dog hair again soon."

"Yes," I say, "but give this a chance. Honestly, it suits you." He nods and smiles.

"OK. I will."

"What happened to the jumpers?" I say.

"It's officially the first day of spring tomorrow," he replies. "Back of the wardrobe with the jumpers."

"Well, the new you is so handsome I daren't be seen out in public with you. You'll have young girls throwing themselves at you. You're like Jake Gyll-what's-his-name."

"Who?" He scratches his head again.

"Oh . . . no one."

There's an awkward pause, as silence falls over the bantering conversation.

"I was going to come and see you," I say eventually. We'd normally pop in and see each other mid-morning, for a coffee or a chat.
We are easily distracted, it's terrible. "What are you up to?"

"I'm doing paperwork." He sounds tired. "It's really boring." He
advances into the room and then he stops, looks down. "Nat, this is
beautiful."

He holds up a piece of paper. It's the design I was sketching last
week before Mum arrived, the daisy-chain necklace. I've left it there,
not quite sure what it needs, because I can't think about it without
thinking about Mum afterwards. "Oh, thanks," I say, blushing. "It's
nothing, it's just a rough idea for something."

"I think it's really lovely." He smiles, and I watch him, his bones
under his skin. He has a vein curling into the side of his temple, it
throbs as he speaks. "Really simple, beautiful, complex at the same
time."

"Oh, no, it's not." It's been so long since anyone's praised my
work that I don't know what to say. "But—that's really kind of you."
I'm flustered, and look around the studio. "Right. Best get on." I run
a hand over my forehead. "Sorry. I'm operating really slowly today."

"What's up?"

"I don't know," I say. "Just—stuff."

"Oli?"

"Well, yeah. Everything really."

Ben puts the sketch down and leans on the workbench. "It must
be really hard."

"I know. It's just I don't know what comes next. You know—
when do they ring the bell, say it's officially over?"

"I guess when you sign the final divorce papers," he says, and
then holds up a hand. "I mean, if that's what you want to do."

"Yes—" I shake my head. "I don't know. Probably. It's so—freaky
though." I pause. "There's a lot going on at the moment. Other
stuff."

"Like what?" Ben says. "Are you—OK?"

"I'm fine. It's family stuff."

"Heavy?"

"Pretty heavy. I found a—I found a diary," I say irrelevantly.

"Aha." Ben rubs his hands over his hair again. "Some childhood diary you don't want anyone to see? Or your diary of the studio and how you've got a crush on Les?"

Les is the leader of the writers' collective downstairs. He is a large, fleshy man who loves talking about his days in the Socialist Workers' Party and using words without pronouns, as in "Government needs to do this" and "Council isn't pulling its weight," just as wannabe trendy people say of the Notting Hill Carnival, "I'm going to Carnival this weekend." I know for a fact that he is from Lytham St. Annes.

I nod at Ben. "Yes, it's true," I say. "I am in love with Les and this is my journal of that love."

"Les is definitely More," Ben says, and we laugh, slightly too hilariously, as if to break up the atmosphere.

"No," I say, looking round again. I don't know why I feel as if someone might be watching us. "It's weirder than that. It's the diary my mother's sister was writing the summer she died. In 1963. She was only fifteen."

"Wow," says Ben. "That is heavy."

"Yep," I say. "My grandfather gave the first part to me at the funeral. It's just pages stapled together. But there's more, I just don't know where. I think my mum knows something, but when I asked her—" I trail off.

"I heard you guys shouting last week," Ben says simply. He pushes himself off the table and stands up. "Didn't Sherlock Holmes say when you have eliminated the impossible, whatever remains, however improbable, must be the truth?"

I smile at him. "That is correct. I just don't know what the truth is. . . . I feel like if I can only read the rest of it I'll know. It's like I've hit a brick wall."

"Sherlock Holmes is usually right," Ben says, brushing his hands together. "So what remains is, someone's got the rest of it, and they don't want anyone to see it, for whatever reason."

It's true, but strange to hear it out loud. "That's probably right."

"It's a mystery. It needs solving, and you shouldn't be sitting here stewing about it." Ben sticks his hands in his pockets and pulls out a tenner. I watch him, smiling. "Let me take you for a drink," he says. "A nice lime cordial."

I look at my watch. "But Ben, it's not even five yet."

"Exactly," he says cheerily. "We'll get a table at the pub." He sees my face. "Come on," he says. "Give yourself a break for once and stop worrying about everything. Let's get a drink."

Thirty-two

We go to the Ten Bells, which is one of my favorite pubs. It's on Commercial Street, in the shadow of Hawksmoor's magnificent Christ Church, and features on the Jack the Ripper trail, tediously, because two of his victims are known to have drunk there. It's been around since the 1700s and it's always really busy, but unlike other pubs round here it's not too touristy or full of City types, and there's a good laid-back vibe. Perhaps it's because the loos are absolutely disgusting. I think they do it deliberately. There is no way Fodor's or Dorling Kindersley could recommend a pub with bathroom facilities like that. We manage to squeeze onto a sofa squashed in by the bar and I check my phone while Ben gets the drinks.

There's a text from Oli.

Hi. Can I come and pick up more stuff tonight? 9ish? Be good to see you. Ox

Immediately I know if I don't reply right away I won't be able to think about anything else. It's not that I'm obsessing over him, it's just to keep myself sane. I text back.

Gone for drink with Ben so text me when you're near. In Ten Bells.

I put my phone back on the table as Ben reappears. "Hey, thanks," I say, slightly too enthusiastically as I take my vodka, lime, and soda off him. "This is great."

He glances down at the phone. "It's my pleasure. You need a night out I reckon. Tough couple of months."

"Maybe you're right. A gin and tonic," I say, changing the subject. "Nice."

He laughs. "You a fan of the gin and tonic then?"

"You don't see men drinking gin and tonic enough these days, in my opinion," I say. "It used to be a classy, Cary Grant-ish thing to do and now hardly anyone has one. They have *pints* all the time."

Ben looks amused. "Glad you're pleased."

"Well, I like a man who drinks gin and tonics," I say.

"Do you now." Ben gesticulates to an imaginary person next to him. "Waiter! Four more gin and tonics here, please!" The woman opposite looks at him as though he's a lunatic.

I laugh: Ben is really funny. Then there's an awkward silence, amongst the noise and chatter of the pub. I start picking at a beer coaster.

Ben watches me, and then he says, "So, tell me about it, then. The family stuff, I mean. What's the deal with them?"

"It's a long story." I stare through the great glass windows of the pub, out at the church, at the traffic roaring down Commercial Street. It has started to drizzle, and the light is already fading. "It's boring."

"It doesn't sound boring," Ben says. "It sounds pretty interesting, if you ask me. Fire away. It's a choice between this, doing my taxes, or watching the big match."

"Oh, what's the big match?" I ask.

"Absolutely no idea. I was trying to sound blokeish. Actually, there's a *Hi-de-Hi!* marathon on UK Gold I recorded last night."

"Hi-de-Hi!?" I fall about with mirth. "You're joking me."

"No, I'm not," Ben says. He is a bit red. "I love *Hi-de-Hi!*, it's my secret shame."

"No, I love it too," I say. "Really love it." Ben is the only person I know who has a genuine penchant for cheesy British sitcoms. "I kind of love *'Allo 'Allo!*, is that wrong?"

"It's sort of wrong, but I'm with you," Ben says. "You know, I

went through a brief phase when I needed cheering up when I actually used to record *As Time Goes By*."

"No way." I stare at him. "Me too."

He shakes my hand. "It is a fine program. Nothing wrong with it
at all in my opinion. Geoffrey Palmer is a comedy genius."

I smile. "Well, great minds think alike." Then I ask, tentatively,
"Do you also like *Just Good Friends*, with Paul Nicholas?"

Ben gazes at me. "Oh, Nat. You poor thing. No way."

"Oh, right." I am downcast. I actually have VHS tapes of it in
one of the cupboards at home but I'm not going to say that now.

Ben shakes his head, more in sorrow than in anger. "There is a
limit, you know."

"Sorry," I say. "Sorry."

"*Just Good Friends*? I thought you were a woman of taste." He
exhales sadly. "Right, let's move on. What were we discussing? Yes,
what I'd be doing if I wasn't here with you. So make it juicy. Tell me
the secrets of your family, which I'm hoping are that you're all half-
human half-wolf, or you've got Jesus's heart stored in a safe in the
vaults of your ancestral home." He widens his eyes. "Latin quotation
here. But I don't know any."

"No, I'm afraid not," I say. "Although there is a Knights Templar
society that meets regularly in the gazebo headed by Lord Lucan."
He laughs politely and there's a pause, during which I check my
phone again and say, "So is the football on tonight, or not?"

He looks at me as though I'm insane, and he's not wrong. "Er—
like I just said. I don't know. Yes? No? Probably?"

I can feel myself blushing, and it's so embarrassing. I scratch my
cheek. "I'm sorry," I say. "Just thinking Oli'll probably be watching
it if there's some big football thing on." My voice is too high. "He
might—he said he might pop over later, pick up some stuff."

"Oh, right," says Ben, and he looks out of the window as if he's
trying to spot him. "Have you seen him lately, then?"

"No," I say, too quickly. "But it's not a big deal. His things are
all still in the flat. It's fine if he picks them up. Just . . . I just was
wondering." I stop. "Sorry," I say, sounding more normal. "It's OK,

it's just everything's still quite weird at the moment and when I hear from him—"

"Yes," Ben says. "Nat, of course it is. I'm sorry." He pats my arm.

I have an overwhelming urge to put my hand on his, to feel human contact, but I stop and instead run my hands through my hair.

"So shoot, Kapoor," Ben says, changing the subject. "Back to the diary. Tell me all about it, my creative colleague."

So I tell him from the start. About going back to Summercove for Granny's funeral, and being given the diary by Arvind, about Cecily—what I know about her, that is—and what Octavia told me about Mum; and I tell him about how I've tried to talk to Mum about it and how awful it ended up being, and when I get to that bit Ben whistles. "Wow," he says. "That's a lot of stuff."

"I know," I say. "And what with me and Oli—I didn't take it all in at the funeral. I was so worried, about Oli and the business." I pause. "It's just now I've started really thinking about it all, and looking at—everything, I guess, and it's driving me mad."

"Like what?"

"Like . . ." I am searching for the right way to describe it. "I spent every summer of my life in the house in Cornwall. Mum used to drop me off there as soon as the holidays began and go off somewhere afterwards. I loved it. It was where I thought of as home. But it's where Cecily died. They were all there, that summer."

"Your gran dying, that must bring it to the surface," Ben says.

"Well, yeah," I say. I pick at the beer coaster again. "Arvind told me something, at the funeral. He said I looked just like Cecily. And it explained quite a lot. Why she was sometimes cold, off with me." I pile the shreds of cardboard into a pyramid. "I sometimes felt she didn't want to be there at all, like she hated us all, she'd chosen the wrong life."

Ben looks interested, and I am relieved; I don't want to bore him. There's a large part of me that thinks this is all in my head. "The wrong life? Why do you think that?"

"Don't know." I shrug. "I think it probably started after Cecily died, but who knows?" I chew my lip, trying to explain. "I can't explain it, but it was sort of like she was play-acting her own life a lot of the time."

"How?"

"Like she was going through the motions," I say. "As if she stopped being herself when Cecily died, when she gave up painting. She stopped being that person, for whatever reason."

"That can't have been easy for your mum, whatever the truth is." Ben stares into his drink.

"Well, that's true," I say. "And Archie's done OK for himself. Mum hasn't. She's never quite worked out what to do with her life. If she hadn't had an income from my grandparents, back in the day, she'd never have been able to survive." I give a short laugh. "Me either."

"What do you mean?"

"Granny and Arvind, they gave them both an allowance, when times were good," I say. "Not much, just enough to pay the rent. Archie used it to set up the car business, he provides fleets of cars for hotels and things, and he deals in classic cars too."

"Really? Wow."

"I know." I think back to Sunday lunch, the brand-new kitchen, the warm under-floor heating, the comfort, the security of it all.

"He's done really well for himself. He sort of left them behind."

"What about your mum?"

"Mum—well, I don't know. She doesn't really have a career or anything. I don't know why."

"I thought she worked at some interiors shop," Ben says.

"Well, yeah, but it doesn't pay much. It's in Chelsea, she knew the owner back in the good old days and she gets to hang out with posh, glamorous people all day and go on buying trips. Believe me, it's never been enough." I don't say what I want to, which is that one term at school she wouldn't buy me new shoes, because she said my feet were growing too fast and I'd just need another pair in a few months. It sounds ridiculous when you say it out loud, but it was kind of normal back then. "I guess she'll have some money from the sale of the house now," I say. "And she's got the committee too."

"What committee?"

I pull the invitation to the opening of the foundation out of my bag and show it to him. "Wow," he says. "That's fast."

"That's how she wanted it. Like she wanted people to remember her as soon as she'd gone. It's weird, when she was alive she didn't seem to care about all that, her reputation as a painter. Almost like, I'm dead now, you can start looking at me in the way I want." I shake my head. "That's what my uncle said too."

"Who's on the committee?"

"Louisa, Octavia's mum. She and Mum aren't exactly close." I pause and check my phone. Ben watches. "Me. And Guy."

"Guy?"

"He's the Bowler Hat's brother." He looks blank. "Louisa's brother-in-law. He's a nice guy." I snort at this unintentional pun; Ben shakes his head. "And that's it." I stop and raise my hands, to buy some time. Two girls behind us at the bar shriek with laughter, and I look over at them; they're both in vintage pin-tucked shirts, jeans, and boots, and one, who has her hair in a loose bun and wears an apple-green cardigan, has a beautiful gold necklace hung with about five different antique charms: a bird, a heart, a little apple. I take a mental picture of her.

Ben puts his drink down. "So, what about your mum? What are you going to say to her?"

I push the pieces of the beer coaster away and turn to him, admiring again—as I do each time I look at him—the new, hair-free Ben. "Well, perhaps it's the funeral, perhaps it's everything with Oli, and trying to keep the business together, but I've sort of realized I can't be that person in her life any longer. I just can't do it." I raise my shoulders and drop them again. "She makes me . . . Agh. Never mind."

"Makes you feel what?" Ben's voice is soft and kind. I find myself struggling not to cry.

"She makes me feel not very good about myself sometimes," I say in a soft whisper. "But that's—that's family, I suppose."

"No, Nat," Ben says gently. "It's not. Not in that way."

As I'm speaking, the iPhone buzzes and a text appears in a box, lighting up the screen. We both look down, force of habit.

Ben the beardy guy who fancies u?! Bell you laters. Ox

I snatch the phone up and shove it in my bag, but I know it's too late, that Ben has seen it already. I gabble, to say anything, anything.

"Anyway, I suppose, yeah. You start to realize you have to distance yourself sometimes, and that's just the way it is, I guess."

"Yes," Ben says. "I think you do."

I raise my head, look at him. Ben finishes his drink in one long gulp. "Ah, I'm going to get another drink," he says, standing up. A wave of embarrassment crashes over me. It's really hot in here, crowded with a yeasty, hot, old-man smell, and suddenly I wish we hadn't gone for a drink, that I was at home in my bedsocks on this cold night and didn't have to wait for Oli to turn up, whenever that might be.

But when Ben comes back, carrying a pint this time, he looks thoughtful. He puts my drink and some crisps down on the table. "Hope you like bacon. Tania loathed bacon crisps, I haven't had them for ages."

"That's my favorite," I say, ripping into the bag. "Thanks. So . . ." I eat a few more crisps, trying to sound casual, and I change the subject. "When we met in the coffeehouse that day a couple of weeks back, when Oli and I were . . . I didn't know Tania wasn't working with you anymore. Why's that?"

Ben looks blank. "We're still working together."

"She said she wasn't. I introduced her to Oli and said you were her boyfriend and you worked together and she said, Not anymore."

"Oh," said Ben. "Bit of a misunderstanding then. She meant we're not going out anymore. We're still working together, yeah."

He says it, as though it's not a big deal. I gape at him.

"You guys—you split up? I didn't know that."

"Well, yes." He scratches his shoulder, reaching behind with his arm and really concentrating, as if it's important to scratch it properly.

"But—you never said. How—when? When was it?"

"A month ago," Ben says. "Yeah." He looks down into his pint. "It's pretty sad."

"Was it—was it a bad break-up?"

He looks up and around the crowded pub but doesn't meet my eye. "It wasn't good."

He won't look at me. Even though Ben is pretty chilled, he's still a bloke. There's a lot of stuff you just don't get out of them.

"How long—" I begin, but he says quickly, "Yeah, two years. It was painful. But we get on, that's why we're still working together. It's weird sometimes, but . . . it's for the best, I suppose."

"Can I ask what happened?" I push the mess I've made with the new mat out of the way, embarrassed.

"Nothing really." He looks at me now. "Just that . . ." He pauses. "We were together for two years and . . . Yep."

" 'Yep'?"

Ben smiles. "Well . . . I've come to realize—we both did—that it's better to be alone than be in a relationship that's not right."

I nod emphatically. "Sure."

"And if you know you don't want to be with that person, that you don't love them anymore, it's best to do something about it sooner rather than later."

"You don't sound like most boys I know," I say. "Most of them stick with it but they behave so craply the girl eventually has to dump them."

Ben looks cross. "I hate the way people just assume all men are going to be like that." He mimics a busybody with a quavering voice, "'Oh, he's such a useless *man*!' Really pisses me off. Girls do it, mainly. Girls shouldn't do it. They shouldn't assign gender roles. They know what it's like." He frowns, so deeply that I laugh.

"Hello, second-wave feminist!" I hold up my hand. "You go, girl!"

"Everyone should be a feminist," Ben says. "I don't understand people who say, 'I'm not sure I'm a feminist.' It's like saying, 'I think I might be racist.' You get my mum on the subject. Wow."

Ben's mum is a professor of history at Queen Mary and West-field College. She is amazing—what my friend Maura who lives round the corner calls a Necklace Lady—one of those cool fifty-plus women with big, frizzy hair who wear draped jersey and huge, bold, signature necklaces.

"My mum doesn't believe in all that," I say. "Which is so weird, when you think about it. She acts like a young ingénue in a Jane Austen novel when any man speaks to her, all batting eyelashes and trembling voice. And she's tough. She raised me on her own, hardly any money, without a dad."

"Do you ever wonder who he was? Your dad?" Ben asks. "You never talk about it."

"A bit more lately, what with everything," I admit. "It's made me think about all that stuff more. Where you come from, who your family is. Etcetera."

"Just 'Etcetera'?" He smiles, and I think how nice it is to talk about this with someone, I never do.

"Have you ever thought it might be someone you know?"

"No, not really," I say. "I think it really is just some guy she never saw again."

"I know, but—" Ben puts his pint down and wipes his forehead. The noise in the pub seems to go up a notch, all of a sudden. "Your mum—I mean, you don't necessarily believe what she says all the time, do you?"

"I don't, sadly. Why?"

"Well, it must be something you think about. Half your family tree is missing. Where you come from, isn't it interesting?"

"I suppose so," I say.

"Like your grandfather—you've always been interested in his family, the Muslim side."

"He's not Muslim, he's Hindu."

"But I thought he was from Lahore, from Pakistan?"

"Yeah, but he's not Muslim. There were loads of Hindus there before Partition," I explain. Everyone always assumes Arvind is Muslim. I don't blame them, but his name alone should show he's not. "You're right, I'd love to go there. I am interested in it. But it's only a quarter of me, you're right. There's another whole half. Look at Jay," I say. "His mum's from Mumbai, his dad's half Indian—he's three-quarters there. Me, I'm only a quarter there. I used to wonder a lot about the other half."

"I would, if I was you," Ben says.

"I don't know," I say.

"If you ever want some help with it," Ben says. "Just ask."

"What, have you got a DNA database in your studio?" I ask.

He grins. "I mean it. Just—anything I can do. Just someone to talk to."

"Thanks," I say. "Thanks, Ben."

We smile uncertainly at each other in the crowded bar, and there's a pause, though everyone else around us is laughing and having a good time. Perhaps I should go. I don't want to, though. I glance at my watch, just as he says, "One more drink?"

And I don't say, No, I'll be off. I look at him, and I think about being at home, waiting for Oli to turn up or not, when I could be here, and I push my glass towards him, and I say, "Yes, please. Same again."

"Coming right up," he says, and we sort of know it's not going to be just one more drink.

Thirty-three

So we have another drink, and another, and it's seven o'clock and then it's eight-thirty, and we talk about a new commission Ben's just got, a photo-essay on a Countryside Alliance march taking place next week, and about my new collection, and about Les and the writers' collective with whom we are both obsessed, and about Jamie's love life—Jamie being the slightly more amenable of the two receptionists whom I think Ben has a crush on, mainly because she is beautiful, Sophie Dahl–style, but also fascinating because her boyfriend is an extremely short, pockmarked Russian guy, not obviously rich but we think he must be.

Then we have another drink and talk about what we're working on, and I point out the two girls at the bar and how one of them is wearing this beautiful necklace made up of different charms, and how I want to copy it, and Ben goes up to them super-politely and asks if we can take a photo of her necklace. And he manages to do it without sounding creepy, and the girls are really lovely, and he snaps away a couple of times because he has a little camera he always carries around with him. Then we have another drink, but somewhere along the line we've forgotten we got to the pub early, and nine-thirty seems deceptively early, and we're so pleased about this we have another drink. In all this time Oli doesn't call, and after a while I put my phone in my bag, because I'm sick of checking it every five minutes.

At ten-thirty we are both very hungry, and we know we have to go, and we stumble out of the Ten Bells onto the street, waving bye to the girls, who are called Claire and Leah and who are lovely.

The road is slick with rain and it is still freezing cold. It's mid-March, and this winter feels as though it will never end. We set off down Fournier Street; I'm just round the corner. As we walk, Ben hums to himself. He always does, I realize. I can hear him in his studio, sometimes, if the window's open. I don't think he knows he does it.

"What are you humming?"

He makes a noise like a scarily authentic trumpet. "'When the Saints Go Marching In,' " he says. "It's a good song to keep you warm. I'm cold."

"Me too," I say. He puts his arm round me and pulls me tight. He has one of those large, sensible Puffa jackets like security guards wear and it is nice and comforting. I lean my head against it as we walk, remembering how comforting he is, though we are walking slightly unevenly.

We're on the corner of Wilkes Street, and then I'll be home. Ben stops and says, into my ear, "Natasha. I'm glad everything's turning out OK for you. I really am."

"Thanks," I say. "I'm not sure it is, but thanks. I'm glad you think so."

"I was worried about you, for a while there." His breath is on my ear; it is dry and warm.

I stop, and he nearly trips over me. "Ah, that's nice. Why?"

"Well . . ." Ben says. "I just meant . . . Oh, shit."

"What?"

"I'm about to be rude. I've had a lot to drink. It's taken the edge off."

I close my eyes. "I've had six vodka lime and sodas. Possibly seven. Eight. Nine. Go on."

Ben says, "I meant you and Oli." He takes a deep breath. "I just didn't . . . didn't see you staying together. I know we only met a couple of times, but—just watching the two of you together, the way you talk about him—I always thought he wasn't good enough for you." He nods politely. "OK, I'll be off then. Off to bang my head repeatedly against a rock." He walks off and I follow him.

"I know," I call. He stops.

"What?"

"I know you think that," I say.

"Really?"

"Really," I say. "I know you didn't like Oli, Ben." He starts to protest but I carry on. "I'm not stupid. But he was my husband."

"OK." Ben nods and runs both his hands over his shorn hair, his kind face smiling at me. "You're right. I'm being a dick, Nat, I'm sorry. It's just I want you to be happy."

"But I was happy," I say. "We were happy, for a while."

"Right," he says, but there's a note of disbelief in his voice and for the first time I feel myself getting angry.

"We were," I said. "I loved him—I—I don't know, perhaps I still do."

When I say this out loud, I realize how long I've been wanting to say it.

"You don't deserve him," Ben says. He is staring into my eyes. "You should be with someone who wants you to be happy, Nat. Who it's easy to be with. Easy. Like . . . like it is with you and me."

He leans forwards. I don't say anything. I just move towards him, resting my head on his shoulder. It is so nice to be held by someone again after so long. He puts his arms round me, and I give in to it, sinking into his comfortable jacket and the comfortableness of him, how lovely he is, how kind, how handsome . . . how my head fits into the crook of his neck the way it's supposed to. The way it's supposed to.

I look up at him and he moves his head towards me just enough, so his lips are touching mine. And he whispers, so his lips brush mine, "You and me."

He pushes his mouth against mine, and I close my eyes, feeling the wetness of his tongue sliding into my mouth. He moves against me, and he sighs, and pulls me towards him; his lips are hard on mine, his fingers are on my neck, and it's as if I'm coming alive again, tingling all over.

His skin is so sweet, the touch of his kiss is so alarmingly exciting,

I push myself against him for a few glorious moments. I want him to pull me tighter towards him, to totally sweep me up, to carry on kissing me, feeling his hands on me, holding me close, it is amazing. . . .

And then my phone rings. I should ignore it, I should stop. But in the quiet street it is loud. As if I'm coming awake, out of a dream, I pull away from Ben, step backwards. I push him away, my palm flat on his chest, and snatch the phone out of my bag.

"Ol?" I say. I pause. "Where are you? You're—now? You're coming now? OK—um, yeah, that's—that's fine. See you in a minute." I put the phone away, my eyes still locked with Ben's. I wipe my mouth on the back of my hand and look at my fingers, as if he's poisoned me. He is staring, standing stock-still, in the shadow of the huge church, the cobbles shining in the moon and the rain.

"So Oli's coming over, then, is he?" Ben's voice is cold. "You're running off. He says, 'Jump,' you say, 'How high, Oli?' "

My stomach is churning, I think I'm going to be sick.

"I'm sorry," I say, breathing heavily, my heart pounding almost painfully in my chest. My hair is falling over my shoulders, around my face, and I back away, staring into his face. "I have to go, we should never—I'm so sorry . . . we should never have done this."

"Why?" he says. He's almost smiling. He reaches out to touch me, and ends up cupping my elbow in his palm. His hands are big and strong. "Natasha, you must have known this was going to happen."

"No!" I say, pulled towards him by his hand on my elbow, and by a huge desire to kiss him again. I shake my head at him. "Absolutely not, Ben, no!"

And then the doubt that can almost immediately cover the bravado of taking an action like this comes over him. "But—"

I put my hand underneath his and remove my arm from his grip. "I can't," I say. "It's too soon. It's too soon. Oli and I, we only just split up, and I don't know what's going to happen, and—"

"You do know!" he says, almost impatiently, and he steps forwards again, as if to touch me, but instead he clenches his hands into fists by his sides, his knuckles white with frustration. A passer-by scurries alongside the wall of the church, and we both turn. Ben lowers his voice. " Natasha—can't you see? He's never going to change, what are you waiting around for?" He trails off. "It's obvious, isn't it?"

I stare at him again. "That's horrible."

"Not horrible." His voice is low and soft. "It's because I want you to be happy. It's because—God, can't you see it? I'm in love with you, Natasha—I have been for a while." And he reaches up to his chest, and touches his heart with his fingers. I don't think he realizes he's doing it.

"You're what?"

"I've fallen for you. What the hell. I have fallen for you. Your smile, the way you bend your head when you're embarrassed, your long legs . . ." He opens his hands, his eyes burning into me. "How talented you are, and you don't see it, how tough you try to be, how sad you are, and how happy you deserve to be. You're so strong all the time and you don't always have to be. You need someone to look after you."

"Stop it, Ben," I say, and I'm trying not to shake. "Stop it."

"You deserve everything, Nat." He nods. "And you don't deserve him. You deserve someone much better."

"What? Like you?" I practically spit the words out, sudden anger coursing through me. "How dare you," I say. "Just because you're single again, and you don't like Oli, and you think you know me— you don't know me, Ben! We're colleagues, we're not . . ." I shake my head, looking for the right words. His eyes are still on me, searching my face. I think again how naked he looks without the beard and hair. Defenseless. I don't want to hurt him. "Look, I'm sorry. It's probably best if—I'm going to go now."

"Nat—don't go—" he calls. I turn and run up the street. He is following me.

"Please, just leave, just let me go!" I am almost hysterical. I turn onto my road, which is completely dead, and as I do I look back down Wilkes Street. Ben is standing there, watching me, a lone figure, dark in the yellowing lamplight. He turns and walks away.

My phone rings again and I pick it up, unlocking the front door.

"Yep," I say. "You're back already?"

"Yes," Oli says, his voice so familiar it beats a tattoo in my head. "Let myself in. Is it OK? 'S'not too late? For a visit?"

He's drunk. I'm drunk. I know what I'm about to do. Slowly, I shut the door and go upstairs, wondering where the hell that came from, whether it's always been there, and wishing, with a desire I tell myself is completely childish, that Ben were still here now, that I was in his arms, my head on his broad, comforting, safe chest, feeling his heart beating underneath. His heart.

Thirty-four

When I get upstairs, the flat is a tip again. All evidence of the tidying up I did that morning, so long ago now, is vanished. Oli is standing in the center of the room, his hands in his hair. He is swaying slightly. As I shut the door, he turns round. He's been crying. His eyes are full of tears.

"Natasha—" he says, and he pads over towards me. "Natasha. It's so good to see you, babe."

"Hi, Oli," I say wearily, putting my bag down on the hall table. Suddenly I wish he wasn't here, that I was alone. "What do you want? It's late."

He stands in the doorway to the sitting room, hands on either side of the door frame, pushing himself backwards and forwards. "I wanted to see you," he says.

"Has Jason kicked you out?" I ask. "Why are you here now? I—I don't want to see you," I say brutally. I think of Ben, walking through the wet, icy night, back home, alone. Instantly guilt rushes over me.

"Just miss you," Oli mumbles. He holds out a hand. "C'm'ere."

I take his hand, and he pulls me towards him. And I still want him. Oh, the smell of him: yeasty, beery, sweaty, but spicy too, something to do with his aftershave. His hair, so soft and floppy. His scratchy stubble on my cheek. He's my husband, he's the man I thought I was going to be with for the rest of my life. I know it's fucked-up, I know he's drunk, but so am I, and hey, isn't that what we should have done a while ago? Get drunk and just say what we think? With a mighty effort, I pull away.

"You seeing Chloe again then?" I ask. "What's going on?"

Oli doesn't say anything, he turns and goes into the bedroom. "No," he says. "Sort of—yeah. No."

I don't know whether to be pleased by this news or not, or even whether to believe it. I don't know what I think. I am really tired, drunk, my hair is wet from the rain, my feet are hurting, and I just feel sad, sad about Ben, sad about this. I should press him on it, but I don't want to hear what he says.

Oli flops down on the bed. "Look," he says. "Honestly just came t'get some more shirts and stuff. I know it's late, I know I've had too much to drink. I was out with the boys from work, and they all went off early, and I suddenly . . ." He looks up at me, I am standing against the chest of drawers looking at him. "I just really wanted to see you. To hold you. Sleep in our bed just once more. You know? No, you don't know." He struggles to stand up again and he mutters under his breath. "'S'Natasha, remember?" Then he says, "You hate me and you want me to go. It's fine."

Cold-hearted Natasha. I push him back down on the bed, just as I pushed Ben away, the same hand, the same gesture. "You can stay," I say. "It's fine. But nothing's going to happen. I'm tired."

"So am I," he says. He smiles. "I miss you. I saw *Mad Men* the other night, with—with Jason and Lucy, and they didn't understand what was going on. Kept wishing you were there."

As romantic scenarios go, it's not exactly up there with *Casablanca*. But it's Oli. He's my husband. And it's late, and we're both tired. I brush my teeth and hastily wash my face, and when I crawl into bed next to him, he's practically asleep anyway. He snuggles against me, holding me in his arms and I look at the alarm clock, blinking on the bedside table. 11:02 p.m. His hand is heavy on my ribcage. My eyelids are heavy too. In seconds, we are both asleep.

I have been dreaming a lot lately, vivid dreams about Summercove, something I haven't done since I was a little girl. When I was younger, at least once a week I would dream I was there. Perhaps Jay and I would be crouched on the beach, picking out shells, our bottoms wet from the sand as the sea crashed around us. Or we'd be on the lawn, chatting with Granny as she deadheaded the roses or picked the lavender. Or playing backgammon with Arvind, at the old table on the stone patio. Sometimes the sound of the sea would rush through my head so loudly I would rise into consciousness, a powerful sense of disappointment coursing through me, as I realized I was back in the flat in Bryant Court, dark and smelling of damp and fish, the dull light of a cold West London morning creeping in through the curtains.

I felt safe in Cornwall. I felt safe with my grandmother. She wasn't afraid of anything, and I think, more importantly, she understood her daughter. One summer, when Mum eventually joined us in Cornwall, Granny had found out—I don't know how—from Jay about the week in Lisbon, and more stuff, like the parties she'd have, how she used to leave me alone in the evenings, and she slapped her. Actually slapped her.

It was late at night, on the terrace; I was trying to sleep in my bedroom high above the house, but their voices woke me. I could hear them, whispering at first, then gradually louder.

"She's terrified, don't you ever leave her again," Granny hissed. "You selfish little—" I think she called her a bitch.

"Why don't you mind your own business," my mother spat back at her, and I could hear it in her voice, that she was drunk, her words slurring slightly. Mum didn't often drink much; she couldn't hold her alcohol, still can't. "Why don't you leave me to bring up my daughter my own way."

"I'd love to." My grandmother's voice was silky. "Believe me, I would love to."

"Listen. I don't need your help—you're the last person I'd go to for help on how to bring up-up . . . bring up their children." There was a pause. "I mean, we both know that. Don't we?"

The only answer was my grandmother laughing, low, heavy. "You're drunk, Miranda."

"I'm still better than you. Even after everything I've done. I'm still better. And I know it, and it kills you, Mummy."

Slap. A slicing sound, like the crack of a whip, in the dark. I lay there, completely still, terrified they would notice the open window above them, know I could hear them. . . .

When I open my eyes again, it's morning, or so I think, and I realize I've been in the middle of a dream about Summercove again, listening to Mum and Granny argue. I am instantly wide awake, clutching the sheets, rigid, as I remember where I am and who's with me. I give a little moan.

Oli stirs in his sleep, rolling towards me and scooping me up so he is curled against me and we are like two prawns. I can feel his morning erection through his boxers, poking against my thighs. He clutches me to him, and I turn my head to see his eyelashes fluttering. He makes a sound, like "Mmm?" but I slide gently away from him.

"Hey, hon," Oli murmurs. "You OK?" He's still half-asleep.

"Good," I whisper softly. "Just a dream." I kiss his ruffled hair, and curl into his chest, and close my eyes again, my hangover from last night kicking in. Just a dream, a false memory of something that you misremembered, you don't need to worry about it.

"Tha's all right then," he says croakily. He takes my hand and squeezes my fingers, kissing them gently, and then kisses my neck, my ear, as I lie against him, my head on his shoulder.

Oli moves my hand down his torso, so my fingers bump against his erection. It's done so seamlessly I'm almost surprised. He smiles, his eyes closed, pushing his thumb against my fingers, opening them up and guiding them so they curl onto his hard cock. "Good morning," he says again.

His other hand slides over my vest and then under, and he squeezes one of my breasts, his hands clutching my flesh, warm and sweaty. He sighs. "Oh, Natasha . . . babe . . ." He arches his back against my hand, trying to rouse himself even further. "Mmm," he murmurs again.

I am still half-asleep, can still hear the voices of my mother and grandmother shouting at each other. My brain is not fully in gear, not questioning everything, and so I don't think, I just carry on stroking him, loving the feel of him again, the warmth of the bed, of his body next to mine. It just feels good.

He stops and pulls the duvet over us, and at the same time he takes off his boxers and pulls my pajama bottoms down, sliding them off seamlessly, curling himself against me afterwards, so I can stroke him, and he can kiss my skin, rub me with his fingers. He pulls my vest aside again, nibbling on my nipple, and then he stops, and I stop, and he looks at me, panting, under the duvet. I want him. I know I want him.

"Come inside me," I whisper, and he grins, boyishly, and nods. "Lie back, babe," he says. With barely any preamble he's between my legs, rubbing his cock against me. He does this for a minute, and then wraps his hand round himself.

"Oh, Natasha," he says, his slight frame shuddering as he pushes inside me. "Oh. Oh." He buries his head over my shoulder, and I can't see his face.

Suddenly, everything's changed. I feel nothing. I am wide awake now, and it's different. Oli leans down to kiss me. His breath is stale, rank, his mouth is open, his eyes are half-closed. I can't do it, I can't kiss him, I pretend to arch my back and tilt my head. He puts his hands on my hair, pulling it, and I cry out.

"Yes," he says.

"You're pulling my hair, darling," I say. I look down, and see I'm still wearing my thick, green bedsocks, as he moves inside me. He hasn't noticed.

"It's so good, you're so good," he tells me. "I'm so close. . . . How about you?"

I want to shout with laughter at the idea that I too am on the verge of orgasming wildly after thirty seconds of sex, but instead I pull his fingers away from my hair. I just want it to be over. He puts his hands on either side of my head and pumps away. I count in my head. *One . . . two . . . three . . . four . . . five . . . six . . . seven . . .*

"Ooooh!" Oli comes, crying out, his voice high, rising at the end of his shout. He always shouts, incredibly loudly, I'd forgotten because it's been a while; in fact, it's been over two months since we had sex. He lies on top of me, panting. I can't feel him inside me. He's squashing me. I am thinking about this, and then I suddenly realize that the last time he had sex was with someone else. He has done this with someone else more recently than with me. Been inside another woman. Kissed her, stroked her, fucked her.

He pats my back, his hands moving gently across my skin, as his penis slides out of me, and his fingers are warm and soft on my spine.

"That was good," he says, elongating the last word. He blinks, smiling. "Thanks, darling. Thanks a lot."

He is so sincere, and his fingers are lovely, knobbling the bones in my back. I am going to be sick. I roll away as he's stroking my breast with his other hand, and I stand. Oli looks up at me, surprised. "I'm going to have a shower," I say. I walk out as he flops back onto the bed, his slimy cock like a slug against his pubic hair as if crawling away in disgust. I go into the bathroom and shut the door, and then I throw up.

Thirty-five

"So—what have you got on today then?"

Oli stands in front of me, decked out in a new change of clothes, showered, and shaved. I pull my knees up so they're under my chin, hugging myself. I desperately want him to go, but I say politely, as if we're old friends catching up, "I'm seeing someone about doing my stall again, and I'm meeting Cathy for lunch. Working on the new collection." I remember the photos Ben took last night, the girls in the bar with the lovely necklace. My stomach swoops, my head pounds. *What have I done?* On both counts, what the hell have I done?

We both pause, and neither of us says anything for about five seconds, which is a terrifyingly long time when it's a silence like this. Eventually, Oli says, "I'd better go—"

"Yes," I say, and I nod eagerly. "So—"

"Yes," Oli says. "Look, Natasha, about last night—"

"This morning, I think you mean," I say.

"Well, both," he says. "I was drunk when I rang you. I'm sorry. I know you were angry, and I know you didn't want me to come round, and I should have understood that."

God, he's clever, apologizing for it like this. "Look," I say. "Perhaps we shouldn't have done it. But—" I hold out my hands. "Oli, you know what? It was really good to see you."

Oli shuffles on his feet, as though he doesn't quite know what I'm getting at, what my move is, but I'm just telling the truth. The truth is, I'm lonely. I still miss him, it's surprising to me that I do. But then, if it was up to me this wouldn't ever have happened, and then

I realize we're back to where we were, two weeks ago, and nothing's changed. Except . . .

A jolt of memory passes through me.

Except I kissed Ben last night, and I don't know if that was an even bigger mistake. I rub my forehead, wishing . . . wishing I hadn't done it. Is that what I wish? Because Ben was one of the few good things in my life, a friend, someone who I could talk to about anything, who made me laugh, who got my family, my situation, my life. And now he'll probably never speak to me again, and I don't blame him. I blink and screw my eyes up, remembering what he said to me last night. I can't go over it again in my head, it's too—it's too painful.

"You OK?" Oli says.

"I'm fine." I clap my hands together gently. "I'm just a bit hung-over, that's all."

He doesn't ask how my evening was, or what's going on with my family, or anything else, and I'm not sad about this, I'm glad. He walks towards the door, takes out his phone and starts texting. I follow him, and he stops and says, "I'll see you soon, yeah?"

"Yeah," I say. I reach out to pat his back. But I don't. I stop. "Bye," I say. "And Oli—I think it's best if you arrange when you're coming round in advance next time," I add.

"Oh," he says, turning round in the doorway, his satchel over his shoulder. He puts the phone away. "Well, I might need some stuff next week, yeah?"

"Yeah," I say. "Just—call. Let me know."

"Sure," Oli says. He steps forwards to kiss me, but I step back. "So I'll see you then, then."

Another week of waiting for him to call, wishing he'd come round, wondering if we should sleep together or not. I know he won't think about it like that. I know he'll just pitch up and try it on if it's possible, not if it isn't. I say, "Wednesday's good for me. Come then. We should talk some more about what to do. About the flat. We should get an estate agent in, to value it." I want to mention the lawyer I've emailed about the divorce, but it doesn't seem right, not when I can see the bed over his shoulder where we just had sex. But I will, next week. I'll make a list, and put that on it.

1. Estate agent to value flat for rental/sales too.
2. Email lawyer about setting divorce in motion.
3. Tell Oli about it next Wednesday.

"You think we should? Start doing that now?"

"Yes, Oli," I say simply. "I need to sort out the money side of things, otherwise I'll be declared bankrupt. You're best off out of it." I roll my eyes mock-seriously.

"OK, fine." He takes my hand. "Bye, Natasha. Have a great day. I'm sorry for being a shit."

The door shuts and I stare at it, listening to his footsteps on the stairs, blinking with surprise and looking round the flat, as though it was all just another dream, something I invented. But it wasn't.

Cathy and I are meeting at the place with the thin pizzas on Dray Walk. I leave the flat a little early, at twelve, and pop into Eastside Books to buy myself a new Barbara Pym, after which I walk up the lane past the Truman Brewery. It's quiet round here in contrast to Sunday when all the markets are out, the vintage clothes, food stalls, and the stalls selling cheap cotton plimsolls and huge packs of batteries. (It's a sign that Brick Lane is going too far upmarket, in my opinion, that you can take your pick of stalls to buy beautifully branded Brazilian *churros* doughnuts, organic apple and pear juices, and hugely expensive chai teas, but you can't get hold of a simple onion.)

As I am about to turn into the studenty chaos of Dray Walk my phone rings. It is a number I don't recognize, and I am just debating whether to answer or not when I touch my screen by mistake and a tinny, vaguely familiar voice says, "Hello?"

"Hello," I say slowly.

"Natasha? Hello. It's Guy."

"Guy?" I struggle for a moment. "Guy—oh, hello," I say. My hand is on the door of the bookshop. "The Bowler Hat's brother."

"Yes, that I am," he says, sounding faintly amused. "Listen, did you get the invitation?"

"The invitation?" My mind is blank.

"To the launch of your grandmother's foundation."

"Oh, of course . . ." I'm embarrassed. "I'm sorry, I haven't done anything about it—I've been—busy," I say. "It's been—"

"Don't apologize." He sounds unruffled, as ever. "I know you've been having a rough time of it." His voice is kind. "Look, I almost called again to say don't worry about the foundation if things are hectic for you. I know they are. In fact, I even tried to text you. But I'm no good at texting, so that rather fell by the wayside."

"It's a skill, texting," I say.

"One I don't have. Like so many things these days. I despair, when I think what a forward-thinking young man I prided myself on being, and how I despised the older generation for being so complacent. Now I'm the old duffer who got an iPod for Christmas and can't work out where the on button is, let alone the rest of it. The iTunes, and so on."

"Oh dear," I say. "Can't someone help you with it?"

"Well, my daughter would, but she's gone back to university. That's my youngest daughter."

"Right." I didn't know you had any daughters, I want to say. And, Why are you calling?

There's a silence, and Guy suddenly stops, as if he's remembering himself. "Anyway, Natasha, look, I wasn't ringing to get you to explain my mobile phone to me. I was ringing to find out where you are this afternoon? I have something I'd like to talk to you about, and I'm not far from East London—I seem to remember that's where you live."

"Oh." I'm flummoxed. "Sure. I'm off Brick Lane—but where are you?"

"I'm in Islington," he says. "I am the antiques servant of the left-wing middle classes. Can I come and see you now?"

"I'm just on my way to lunch," I say. "Why don't I come and see you, are you around this afternoon?"

"Yes," he says. "Yes, I am. That would be a great pleasure. It is quite important we talk. Thank you."

He gives me the address—in fact I remember I have his card already, he gave it to me at the funeral. I hang up just as I arrive at the pizza place.

"Darling!" Cathy throws her arms around me, her head on my bosom. She has my arms in a straitjacket; I release myself gently from her grasp.

"How's tricks?" I say.

"Great, great, great," Cathy says, pulling out a stool for me to sit on. "I lost two pounds last week, *and* I finished *A Suitable Boy*. Not the same thing! Hahaha!" She slaps her thigh as if she's Robin Hood. "And Jonathan—well, I'm definitely sure he's not gay, even though he did this thing last night when he . . ." She stops. "Forget it. Let's get to that later. How about you? How's your tricks?"

"Weird," I say, pulling the menu towards me. "Bloody weird."

Thirty-six

Guy's shop is like something out of a fairy tale. Just off the increasingly corporate Upper Street is Cross Street, a higgedly-piggedly small road of shops, and Guy Leighton Antiques is halfway down. It is painted a kind of dove-gray, and in the pretty bow window is a rococo mirror, an old teddy bear sitting on a small wicker chair, and a heavy crystal engraved vase with a single dusky rose in it. I stare at the window, longingly. I want everything in it.

When I push open the door, an old bell jangles in a pleasing way. Inside, it's empty and silent. The distressed, white floorboards glow in the late-afternoon light, and as I look around, wondering what I should do next, I hear a voice say, "Hello? Natasha?" From a back room Guy emerges, pushing a pair of half-moon spectacles off his nose. They hang on a chain around his neck. He blinks, rather blearily.

"I'm not early, am I?" I seem to have caught him unawares.

"Sorry," he says, looking embarrassed. "I was having a nap."

"Oh."

"Quite nice in the afternoons, when it's quiet, you know. Put the radio on and have a doze—there's an original Eames chair out back I can't bear to part with, it's too comfortable." He catches himself. "Good grief. I sound like I'm ready for the old people's home."

This reminds me of something. "That's funny. I literally just left a message at the home for Arvind on my way here," I say, more to myself than to him. "He was out for the afternoon, they said. Do you know, is Louisa down there?"

"Yes, she is. She went down yesterday."

Archie was going to see him around now too. I'm not even sure Mum's been down since the funeral. "On her own?"

He misunderstands me. "Oh, yes. My brother likes an easy life." He smiles, rather sadly I think. I think of the indolent, good-looking Bowler Hat, so often to be found sleeping in an armchair or deck-chair while Louisa brings him tea. I frown at the thought. "She's a kind soul, Louisa, she loves to help." He scratches his chest and yawns. "She loved your grandmother, Natasha, Frances was like a mother to her. They were very close."

"Louisa had her own mother," I say.

"Yes . . ." Guy's expression is non-committal. "But I think Louisa loved it down there, and she wasn't a threat to your grandmother. Never was. Frances adored her, and she didn't have to raise her. And—well, Louisa just likes doing things for other people."

"I know." Fond as I am of her, I can't help rolling my eyes at this.

Guy ignores my expression. "Now, this is unpardonable, not offering you anything. Can I get you a drink, some coffee? Maybe some whisky? It's very cold outside."

"Tea would be great if you have it," I say. "Just plain black tea."

"No problem," says Guy, motioning me to come through to the back room with him.

The office is a small, chaotic space, overflowing with papers and books, some old and clearly antiques, others dog-eared paperbacks. There's a pile of old Dick Francis novels by the side of the worn Eames chair. Two dirty coffee cups sit on the floor and a fan heater purrs amiably beside them. There's a worn footstool too, upon which lies a sleeping cat, also purring.

Guy pushes the cat off. "That's Thomasina," he says. "Stupid thing. We thought she was a boy for ages, called her Thomas, and then she suddenly produces kittens, three of them." The cat straightens herself languidly and glides away.

It looks as if nothing's been changed for years. Everything in this shop is slow; the warmth is soporific, as is the smell of old, musty things, the rumbling sound of the heater. It is getting dark outside, and I wish I could just curl up in the chair and sleep.

"It looks very cozy here," I say. "Must be nice, if you're having a quiet day, to come in here and relax."

He gestures to the chair, and turns away to fill the kettle from a cracked, old sink in the corner of the room. "Yes, though lately it seems I've been doing a lot of napping and not enough selling of antiques. Not very good."

"It's a hard time," I say, sitting down.

"That's true," he says. "But I'm not keeping up. Not been going to the markets enough, getting new stuff in." He waves around the shop, and I see now that, while every piece is lovely, the space is bare. "We need more stock."

"You have some lovely things, though," I say. "It's a beautiful shop."

"Thank you," he says quietly. "Thanks. My wife used to keep it looking rather better than it does now. She had a wonderful eye for that kind of thing." He stops. "But she died five years ago, and I've let it go since then."

I'm sure Hannah was with Guy at Octavia's confirmation, but that was years ago. I'm sure I vaguely remember her, curly hair and a wide smile. "Well, I'm sure she'd be very pleased," I say.

Guy pours hot water into a mug. "You're very kind," he says. "But I fear she'd be angry with me if she could see what an old man I've turned into lately." He looks around and down, in disgust. "Reading specs, for Christ's sake! On a chain! Pah." He taps them gently with one finger. "Dozing in the afternoon, doing the *Telegraph* crossword and listening to Radio 3—if my younger self could see me now." He stops.

"No one wants to think they'll be doing a crossword and dozing in the afternoons when they're twenty," I say. "I wouldn't be too hard on yourself. When I was twenty, wow. I wanted to take over the world. I was very angry. I even took part in a sit-in."

"How admirable of you. What for?" Guy asks. He hands me the

mug and gestures vaguely towards a nearly empty pint of milk on a little fridge by the door.

"Do you know," I admit, "I can't remember. Something about students' rights. Or maybe animal rights."

Guy gives a shout of laughter and sits down on the footstool, smiling.

"So you sat in some student hall all night and you can't remember why?"

"I know," I say. "I think I fancied one of the blokes organizing it."

Jason, Oli's best friend, our best man, was a radical student leader straight from central casting: he even owned a khaki jacket and had a beard. "Now he's head of year at an exemplary secondary school down the road," I tell Guy, blowing onto my tea to cool it down. "He wears a suit to work. He and my husband aren't at all how they were when they were twenty. They used to want to change the world. Now they just want an app on their phones that'll tell them how to go about changing the world."

Guy looks at me, and he is sober for a moment. "Perhaps we're all guilty of that," he says.

"How so?"

"Oh, I was the same," he says easily, but his voice is sad. "Thought I had all the answers, like your friend there. I thought we lived in a stagnant, rotten country, run by elderly upper-class white men. And we did need to change, but I didn't do anything to help it." He smiles, but there is bitterness in his eyes. "I run a shop selling pretty old things to people. I live in the past now, and the country's still run by upper-class white men as far as I can see. Banks, government, committees—it's just that most of them are younger than me. Younger and richer."

I don't know how to respond to such honesty, and the silence is rather uncomfortable. After a few moments, Guy recalls himself.

"Rather maudlin," he says. "Too much time to think. Bad thing." He pats his knees and stands up, rather stiffly, for the stool is a long way down. "Time to explain why I asked you here."

He goes over to the corner of the room. "Now, Natasha, I have something to give you, and that's why I wanted to meet up. To—explain." He opens a cupboard door and turns back towards me.

He is holding a small, flat thing in his hand, and I stare down at it, not really thinking.

"Here," he says, holding his hand out to me. "Cecily's diary."

There's a thud and a squeal from Thomasina the cat. I have dropped my cup of tea, boiling water is everywhere.

Thirty-seven

It takes a few minutes to clean up, and I am very sorry. There is a painting that is probably ruined, as hot tea and watercolors don't mix, and I keep apologizing as I help Guy wipe down various cases and books and random antiques, but he is completely relaxed about it. As I am on the floor, mopping up the tea with a cloth, I say, "Where the hell did you get this?"

"Well—" Guy is immersed in a stain on the wall, and has his back to me. "It's—it's complicated."

I stare at the innocuous red exercise book, the white pages yellow with age. On the front is written, in the scrawling handwriting I know so well:

Continuing the Secret Diary of Cecily Kapoor.

"Did you take it?"

"No, I did not," he says firmly. "Your mother sent it to me. She took it."

"What?"

I am still holding a soggy ball of kitchen paper; my head snaps up.

"She posted it to me a few days ago. Said I should read it."

"But—" My anger is rising. "Why you? She can't stand you." I catch the tip of my tongue between my lips. "Sorry. She—she's just not your biggest fan, maybe."

"Yes," Guy says. "Right. I'd gathered that. I don't know why, to be honest. But I don't know why she sent me the diary either, I'm afraid. Well—I do know why. You ought to read it and find out."

I'm blushing, with embarrassment and anger. "Still. Where the hell did she get it in the first place?"

"It was in your grandmother's studio. She'd found it after Cecily died and kept it in there, all these years." He stops. "I did wonder, a few months after Cecily died—what happened to the diary? But I assumed they'd just put it away with all her things. I didn't think about it, really." His head sags. "I was too—I was thinking about other things."

"So Mum just took it." My head is spinning. "After the funeral? So she's had it ever since? Why did she take it? Why hasn't she said anything?"

"I haven't spoken to her. I think she just saw it and snapped," Guy says carefully. "She was in the studio with Arvind, and she spotted it. The pages you have must have become separated, somehow, just fallen out."

"Have you got the note?"

He pauses. "I didn't keep it. I'm sorry. I don't think she planned it out. I'm rather concerned about her, you know, Natasha. It's a lot to cope with, what she's been through. And she's completely disappeared now. I rang her after I'd—I'd read it, to talk to her. I've rung her several times, but she never answers."

"Typical," I say. My head is spinning. "She—I accused her of all these things, last week, and she just stood there. She didn't say anything. She didn't mention she had the diary, didn't say anything. And then she just sends it off to you—of all people, when she's told me you're the worst of the lot of them. She's—" I don't know what to say. "She is mad."

"You haven't read what's in here," Guy says. The lines on his face deepen, and a spasm of pain flashes in his eyes. "If she's mad—I can see why."

I don't say anything.

"Natasha, you don't know what it's like to lose a sibling," he says.

"I'm an only child," I snap at him. "Of course I don't."

Guy jangles some change in his pocket. "Yes . . . yes, I know.

Well, you have to understand. It's always been with her, this. It changed us all. I don't think—" He clears his throat, staring into the distance. "I don't think I ever really got over her death."

"Cecily's death? Really?"

"Yes," he says, and he looks at me now, his kind, gray eyes full of pain. "There's not a day that goes by when I don't think of her. It's strange. It was so long ago."

"Why? Cecily? But you didn't know her that well, did you?" I say. "You hadn't met her before that summer, had you?"

"No." Guy stands up, and he crosses over to the other side of the room, his back to me. He takes a deep breath, and then he turns around and stands up straight. He says, "You'll see. But—I saw her dead by the rocks . . . broken and battered." He passes his hands over his face, rubbing his eyes. "I brought her up from the sea myself, you know, that evening. I carried her in my arms." He's shaking his head. "We put her in the sitting room. Awful." He blinks and looks at me. "You know, until the funeral, I hadn't been back to Summercove since the summer she was killed. Died." He corrects himself. "Died."

My mouth is dry. "You think someone killed her. You think— Mum killed her?"

The silence is long, broken only by the sound of Thomasina's purring, her claws piercing the worn fabric she lies on. "No," he says flatly. "That's not what this is about, Natasha. It's not a whodunnit. It was an accident. Your mother was there, I saw it. But believe me, it was an accident."

"So why does everyone seem to think she did it?" I said. "There were people at the funeral, pointing at my mother, whispering about her. Octavia does, Louisa does, the rest of them." I shake my head. "I don't know what to think anymore."

"Perhaps it's been a useful diversion from what really happened." Guy's hand squeezes the coins in his pocket together so that they make a screeching, scratchy sound, and I wince. "Sorry," he says. His face is unbearably sad, old and sad. "You know, we were young.

The world was changing. We had our lives ahead of us. And then she died, and it altered everything. For a long, long time, I thought there'd never be anything nice or good in the world again."

He holds out the diary, his hands shaking. "Read it," he says, his voice cracking. "Find out what kind of person she really was."

"Who? Cecily?"

He shakes his head. "Read it."

We walk through the silent, echoing shop. It is almost dark now. I have my hand on the door; the old bell jangles loudly. "I'll read it tonight," I say.

"And call me afterwards?" His face is hopeful. "Don't talk to anyone else, will you promise me that?"

"Promise. Goodbye, Guy."

"Natasha—?" he says. "It's lovely to see you again. You look wonderful, if I may say. I heard from your mother that you and Oli have separated," he says. "I'm sorry. But it obviously suits you."

I think of the rumpled bed Oli and I had sex in this morning, the rain on the cobbles last night . . . Ben's face as I walked away from him. "That's unlikely. But thank you."

I smile my thanks and suddenly his expression changes, as if he wants me gone, instantly. "Well, I'd better get on—" He looks around the shop and I take my cue and go for the door again.

"Oh, let me get that." He comes forwards and holds it open for me, and then suddenly he leans towards me and kisses me on the cheek as the bell jangles.

"It's great to see you, Natasha," he says. He smiles at me and I smile back. "And—" He stops.

"What?" I ask. I'm standing on the threshold of the shop.

"You do look so like her. Cecily."

"That's what my grandmother used to say," I tell him.

"Well, it's a compliment," he says. "She was beautiful." He stares at me curiously. "We'll speak. Please, I want to speak to you once you've read it."

He shuts the door, suddenly. I am increasingly unsettled as I start off back home. I walk and walk, through the quiet Georgian terraces of Islington, down towards the canal, past the Charles Lamb pub, out towards Shoreditch. It is that curious time of day you get in spring when it is still light but feels as if it will get dark at any moment, that the day is over. It is dark by the time I reach the curious Victorian enclave of Arnold Circus and walk down Brick Lane.

I let myself into the flat. I make a cup of tea and sit down, thinking about my conversation with Guy. I look down at my lap, at the exercise book, so innocuous-looking in my hands, the schoolgirl handwriting and floral decoration around the border the same as a thousand others, before and since.

I open the diary, on my knees. The rest of the flat is dark, its cool loneliness is what I need. I feel my heart thumping, as if someone is holding it, squeezing it. I know once I start reading I won't be able to stop. Voices echo in my head as I open the flimsy red exercise book, looking at the carefully scratched patterns on the front. "That was the summer she died. . . . That was the summer she died. . . ."

And I read.

The Diary of Cecily Kapoor

Part 2

PRIVATE

25th July, 1963.
Continued!

Dear Diary, just us. I can write what I want, and no one need ever see it.

<u>So.</u> The Leightons have arrived. They are Frank, he is twenty, & he is training to be a surveyor. He is very good looking, tall & blond, & handsome. Rather pleased with himself, like a politician. He reminds me of Cyril in <u>Bonjour Tristesse,</u> except pompous. His brother Guy is nineteen. He is reading PPE (don't know what it is) at Oxford University, Brasenose College (like that word). He is quiet with hair that sticks up & glasses. He looks like an owl. Louisa is different now they are around. Normally she is so forthright, she thinks nothing of telling you when your brand new Fair Isle twinset looks moth-eaten, as she did to me the other day, or if your complexion needs carrots to wash it out. She said that to Miranda, & Miranda is veeery sensitive about her skin. She shouldn't do it, especially with Miranda, who we all know has a terrible temper.

Anyway we had a special supper tonight to welcome the guests & I was allowed champagne. Miranda wore a new dress, beautiful, black, thick, silky, taffeta-like. Apparently Connie (her godmother) gave her ten pounds. I find this annoying and I'm not even sure I believe that's where she got the money for them from. But it's strange, she did look very beautiful and she never has before. Sort of furious, all hair and frowns. But I heard Mr. Wilson the maths teacher say to Miss Powell once, "that one's going to be trouble" & she nodded & said "when she realizes . . . yes, I agree." I wasn't eavesdropping, I'm not a sneak, they were watching her chatting to the gardener on a sunny day & I was walking past & couldn't help. Perhaps that's what they mean. Because actually suddenly she is beautiful. Chic. As I say, ANNOYING!

~~Anyway~~ So back to Frank & Guy. It feels different, now they're here. Mummy likes visitors. Everything's perked up a bit. I was next to Frank at supper. He clears his throat before he speaks, & Louisa was staring at him the WHOLE WAY THROUGH the meal. He tried to impress Daddy, he called him "sir," which of course was a waste of time. Guy called him "sir" too but he talked to him about his books too, as if he was really interested. Another thing about Frank is: he kissed Mummy's hand after dinner! Which was so funny I just stared at him. But Mummy laughed, she said it was very charming, & she smiled at him & he looked rather embarrassed which at least took the ~~pompoisity pompousity~~ pomposity! off him a bit.

Jeremy told me I was being awful today but he was nice — I do like Jeremy, this is such a secret dear Diary. I looked it up at school this term & it isn't illegal to marry a cousin. Then I think about Archie peeping at Louisa & it makes me feel a bit sick. So I shouldn't think those things.

When I was waiting for Miranda to come upstairs last night, I heard Frank ask Louisa something, they were still up on the terrace chatting. I wasn't eavesdropping, it was right above me. I wish I hadn't heard it. But I pretended I hadn't & I scurried into my bed. I wish I could say it but I am too shy to write it down. He is not what he seems, that is all. It was a very rude thing to ask someone.

Bust: 20
Nose: 2 mins sorry.

Love always, Cecily

Friday, 26th July 1963

Today is Linda Langley's birthday. I wonder what she's doing. She had her hair cut before term ended, it looked marvellous & she said it was for her party. She lives in Bath, it's too far for me to

go for a party, not that she asked me. Bet her party is jolly good
though.

Louisa isn't speaking to the man with the Bowler Hat (ie Frank)
this morning. I bet I know why. It is bc of what I heard him ask her to
let him do last night which I am not going to say, it is too smutty for
the written word. The BH looks like he has rather loose morals, a bit
like Captain Wickham in <u>P&P</u>, good looking but FECKLESS — that
is a good word.

Apart from that it's fun having the boys here. Everyone is making
an effort. Even Miranda, who is so weird & shy & normally never
talks to boys, is suddenly talking to Guy & the Bowler Hat, &
parading around in her swimming costume, fluttering her eyelashes
at them. It's hard to believe this is the girl who ran off when Andrew
Laraby asked her if she'd like a cup of tea at the spring fete at Easter.
Mummy hates it, I can tell, she thinks Miranda is boasting, which
she is.

M. brought Jeremy's copy of <u>Private Eye</u> down to the beach
& showed off about her swimming, & she keeps having these silly
conversations with either Guy or B.H. She speaks to them in this
horrible arch way. She loves "That Was The Week That Was,"
apparently — hah!

Guy likes lots of strange things I've never heard of, he reads
American writers like Jack Kerouac & Martin Luther King who is in
jail, & books like that. Also George Orwell. BH just swanks around
looking pleased with himself. I tried to bring up the report of the trial in
<u>The Times</u> today as it was very juicy again, & there was such a funny
ad for British Rail with Tony Hancock which made me laugh, he is
pulling a silly face to a ticket inspector, but I was too shy in front of all
of them, & now they must think I am just a bit young & foolish & only
good at cricket.

Miranda on the other hand was so flushed with her success at being
sophisticated that she was horrible at tea, she said, "Cecily's a baby,
she only likes <u>Swallows & Amazons</u> & the <u>Lone Pine Club</u>." I HATE
HER!! Guy just said, "I love those books too, <u>Swallows & Amazons</u>

is my favourite." Miranda looked so stupid and then she started
pretending she likes them too because Guy likes them and she likes Guy.
It's obvious. He's not interested in her. I <u>wanted</u> to say what would you
know, you haven't read a whole book since <u>Just William</u> when you were
ten. Miranda has that effect on one. She brings out a nasty side of me,
more so than ever these holidays. I wish she'd go away. She didn't come
to bed till awfully late tonight and she was flirting with the Bowler
Hat all evening. She still hasn't come in, in fact. I'm waiting for her
right now.

Saturday, 27th July 1963

    Tired today. It is very hot, getting hotter. Mummy painted me
again. She snapped at Mary about the Eccles cakes we had for tea.
We went to the Minack Theatre & saw Julius Caesar. It was good, but
quite long about Latin politics. Louisa & B.H. had another argument.
Perhaps I will write a poem about it & it will be called, "Stop Having
Shrill Rows Outside My Bedroom Door." If he is so desperate to
do It with someone why doesn't he just go and ask Miranda? She's
behaving like she would.

    Haven't been doing my bust, etc. exercises which is bad of me dear
diary sorry.
    Love always, Cecily

Sunday, 28th July 1963

    Today was a wonderful day. It might be the best day of my life so
far, though I hope there are better to come. You know when everything is
perfect? & the air is sweet & people are sweet too.
    It has been so hot, so we went to St. Michael's Mount, in the
car, with the roof down. Miranda & the Bowler Hat stayed behind,
Mummy & Dad too. Jeremy drove us. He is a dear, Jeremy. But

perhaps he is a bit dull. I sat next to him & I realized halfway through
the journey — I don't know what to say to you next. Although he's
so nice to people. Tall & comforting & kind, when he hugs you it's
wonderful. But I feel awkward & silly when I talk to him & I don't
understand (or care about) rugby & I don't know medicine. We drove
past two huge billboards on the side of the road for the *News of the
World*, CHRISTINE'S DIRTY SECRETS one said. When I
asked Jeremy about the Profumo trial he blushed & got very awkward,
clutching onto the wheel like it was trying to get away. "Um . . .
ar . . . Cecily . . . Not very appropriate . . ."

    We parked by the fields because Marazion is a small village, full of
day-trippers. We bought pasties for our lunch & took them down to the
beach, where we sat on the golden sand & looked out to St. Michael's
Mount, & then we swam. I like it better out on a big beach sometimes
than our own cove back at the house. Our cove is secluded but sometimes
you feel shut off from everything. No one can see you. Marazion
beach had people with picnics & transistor radios, all playing "Summer
Holiday" over & over again. Secretly I rather like that song. It was
great to be out in the open, not cooped up at the house or in our tiny,
little secluded beach. It has been so hot & humid, today there was a bit
of a breeze & it was delicious.

    Guy & I walked across the sea on the causeway, to the castle. The
others couldn't be bothered to come. We talked about lots of different
things, I can talk to him about anything, he's v. calm but he's interesting
too and I like that. I didn't think you could talk to a man like that, I
have to say. Guy asked me what the exercise book was for & I told him
about the diary. He raised his eyebrows. "Are we all in it?"

    Me: Yes.

    G: & your darkest secrets?

    Me: Yes, but I don't really have any. (Except I do, squashing
my nose every night and bust exercises & not being quite sure what
intercourse is.)

    Guy: Tell me one.

    Without thinking I just said, "I want to be a writer." I wished I
hadn't, but he didn't say anything, just nodded & we walked on over to

the island and climbed up to the castle. It is very steep, along a cobbled path, but in the shade from the sun. The castle looms over you, it is very dramatic. After a minute G said:

"I think you'd be a jolly good writer, Cecily."

Me (holding my breath, because I found I really cared about his answer): Why?

G: Because you notice everything, & you see the world in your own way. You're your own person & you're lovely as you are. Don't ever change.

That's exactly what he said. I memorized it.

I think that is about the nicest thing anyone has ever said to me. Especially because I want to change everything about myself. I was embarrassed, but I didn't want him to see. I asked him about himself instead, what he wants to do when he leaves. He wants to be a satirist, writing for television or a lampoon like Private Eye. He would be ever so good at it, I think.

We walked to the top of the castle & we climbed to the viewpoints where you can stand & look out across past Penzance almost to our house, & the sun was glinting on the waves like diamonds. Everything looked still & peaceful from up there. I wondered about Miranda & Mummy & the others back at Summercove & what they were doing.

I talked to Guy about Miranda. I wanted to explain that she's not always this bad.

Guy said she's looking for attention. "Perhaps she doesn't get enough of it." I laughed cause EVERYONE pays her attention because she's so badly behaved a lot of the time. Then he said, "Why does she dislike your mother so much?"

I know they don't get on but it's not terrible, so I was surprised he'd noticed.

Me: She's just being difficult, that's all. Mummy can be tough with her, I suppose.

G: She's terribly jealous of you. Hadn't you noticed? That's why she's nasty to you.

I (laughing): Hardly. She thinks I'm a baby.

G: It's more than that. How old are you?

Me: Fifteen. Sixteen in November though.

G: Fifteen? Really? He shook his head.

Me: Yes why do I seem much younger than that? (I was crossing my fingers not.)

G: Sometimes, yes. A lot of the time . . . no. Fifteen, eh?

(He was silent for a moment & then he nudged me. I was blushing.) Perhaps she's right. Perhaps you're still just a baby then.

Me: You're 19! You're not much older. Just three years & a bit.

G: I suppose so.

I hope he was joking.

We came back via the moors & the day-trippers were just leaving the beaches along the way past Penzance: Lamorna Cove & the rest of them. We stopped off at Logan's Rock (the pub not the rock) for a lemonade & sat outside on the tables. The countryside was so beautiful, green and lush & heavy, so still & quiet. Jeremy, Louisa & Archie talked about what we would do this week. Guy & I didn't say very much. I sat next to him quite still. I felt the cotton of his shirt on my bare arm. I didn't move. He didn't move. We sat there while the others talked. I can't explain it but it was wonderful.

When we got home, it was late, after nine-thirty. Miranda was in bed. She pretended to be asleep but she'd been crying. I heard her when I came upstairs. I got into bed and I said, "Are you all right?" softly, but she didn't say anything. I don't think she is and I don't know why.

Monday, 29th July 1963

Miranda was sitting up in bed when I woke up this morning & she said, "You snore like a pig."

That is not very nice, I said with what I hope was dignity. I do not snore.

You do you're a horrible little pig. And then she walked past & threw her glass of water over me. I was still in bed & I sat up &

screamed, and then I said, "I'm going to tell Mummy what you've just done, you idiot, she is already furious with you."

M: Just go ahead & tell her, you little sneak. I tell you, she wants me gone anyway. She wishes I wasn't here.

Me (upset): Don't be mean about Mummy. You're always so horrible about her, & all she's trying to do this holidays is help you with what you want to do now school's over. . . .

I was trying to sound reasonable & mature, but this only made her crosser. DD, I thought she was going to hit me. She came over, looming over me & her face was like murder. M: "You have no idea about the real world do you darling? None at all."

Bits of spittle were falling into my face. She was gripping the bedstead with her hands, right over me. I thought she might actually spit at me or bite me. She is like a wild cat.

I dodged under her & stood up so we were facing each other. I was still in my nighty, she was dressed in her capri pants & a lovely black-&-white geometric patterned top.

Me: Where have all these new clothes come from?

M: Connie gave me some money, I told you.

Me: Well I don't believe you. Neither does Mummy.

There was a weird look on Miranda's face. She said:

No one ever believes me, do they. I try & I try to get better, and feel better & it still comes back to nothing. I get nowhere.

She said it in a really sad voice, & then she shrugged. I looked at her, diary, she looked different when she said it. So beautiful, so alive & like she fit everything for once. Like Mummy in her studio: another person, the real person somehow.

I remembered Guy saying it must be hard, being Miranda. I didn't ask him what he meant. But perhaps it is. Archie is the son, it's easy being the son. It's easy for boys, that's the truth. They can do what they want. If they make a mistake, or fail their exams, they go to agricultural college or train to be something boring. If you're a girl, you either have to be either useful or decorative. Like a lamp. I think about this a lot & it makes me angry. Mummy is the only person I know who does both, have a talent and be beautiful, and sometimes I think she doesn't like either of them.

Perhaps that's why Miranda's decided to be beautiful, this summer. It takes work, it's funny. Perhaps that's why Mummy's so cross with her. She doesn't like her being beautiful.

Oh, this is all rather long & confusing but I know what I mean.

I put on my dressing gown & said I was going to have a bath. She let me go but just as I was leaving she said, "Can I tell you one thing about Mummy, Cecily?"

Me: Yes.

M (in doorway looking pleased): If she's so wonderful, why was she up here yesterday, trying on my clothes, when you were out at the beach?

Me: What's wrong with that if she does?

I tried to pretend it wasn't anything unusual but it's odd, I knew that right away.

M: She's made me give her two of them. A coat dress I hadn't worn yet. And the cocktail dress.

Me: The black gros-grain one?

M: & that's not all she wants.

Me: What else?

She nods, & then she flops down on the bed. "You'll see." She's smiling up at the ceiling. "You'll find out. I hope it's not too late." & then she flounced out.

I have told this so badly, sorry DD. But I wanted to get it all down and so I'm writing this now before breakfast. I don't know what to make of it all. Things have changed, perhaps since the Leightons arrived? Since the weather got hotter? Since we grew up? I just don't know.

It is now evening & Miranda & I are sort of speaking but not friends. I keep looking at Mummy over supper, & wondering if it's true about her trying on the dresses. I just know it's not, that's all. My favourite advert in the <u>Illustrated London News</u> this week is: "Take No Chances with Facial Hair." The shop is 7 doors down from

Harrods. Extraordinary. Miranda is obsessed with her facial hair, maybe I should cut it out & leave it on her bed, but I don't think that would improve her mood.

Tuesday, 30th July 1963

I spent a lot of today playing backgammon with Dad again. I am now outside, on the bench under the apple tree on the edge of the lawn, writing up what we talked about, as he told me to. The lavender smells beautiful, perhaps Dad is right.

Since I came back home this summer I have been thinking about relationships. It is strange, being in love. I was so sure most of this year I was in love with Jeremy. And now I know I'm not. I do love him but because he is dear & kind & my cousin. So DD how will I know when the right man comes along for me? Maybe I won't recognize him, I'll think it's me being silly again? I hope not. This worries me.

Louisa & the BH are also strange to me. I assume they love each other? They are certainly here together & he is her boyfriend & I would hope they are, especially the way she raved on about him before he arrived. The only time I HAVE ever seen them alone together is late at night, when he asked her if he could kiss her breasts & lick them, which is what he did ask that night, in a silly boyish voice (yes that is indeed what he said. I have decided to be honest about such things. !!!! Why does he want to, and in this awful baby voice? So strange. They're just <u>there</u>, they don't do anything). They talk to each other in front of us, but I never see them go off for a walk by themselves, or chat together at the table, it's always with other people. He flirts with Miranda, it's disgusting ("You have the last piece of bread!" "No, YOU! You need to keep your strength up, I'm going to beat you at tennis this afternoon!" "Oh, really!" bleurgh like they're children) and he laughs with Guy or Archie all the time, never with Louisa. The people he hardly ever talks to are Dad and Mummy. I don't think he knows what to say to Dad, and I think he finds Mummy intimidating. In fact I think he has a bit of a pash for her. He blushes when she talks to him.

And Louisa is always hanging round pretending she's busy & being all bossy trying to organize things whereas in fact I know she just wants BH to go for a walk with her. Is that what being in love is like? Hanging around for someone? Seems rubbish to me.

Dad answers questions, but he never asks them. He is like a piece on a backgammon board: he will be moved around by you, but according to his own rules. He comes for meals & then goes back to his study, & I used to think what a fraud it is, that he is a philosopher who writes about people, & yet he must exchange less than 10 words to the 9 other people in the house.

I have been noticing things since I started writing this diary, one of them is that I don't mention Dad much. I don't talk to him. He's just there. Today after breakfast I asked if we could play backgammon again. He said "Yes, with pleasure, Cecily."

When Mummy said, "But you're sitting for me this morning," I said, "Please Mummy, just for today," & she looked at Dad & at me & she said, "Oh, all right then."

I like Dad's study but I never go in there. It is filled with books as you would expect, but it is not too much like a library, there are lots of blue pelicans & books on Indian art & paintings in there, & a low, comfortable chair for me to sit in. It smells nice too, Dad told me it is sandalwood, & he gets it when he's in London, because the smell helps him to work.

He won best of 3 & then I noticed the piles of paper at the side of the board for the first time, & the old typewriter, which Mrs. Randall uses when she comes to type things up for him, & I wonder (because I've been away for two months at school) how long it's been since Mrs. Randall came here so I asked him what the new book was about, which I never have before.

I'm so curious about what he's been working on all these years but I know this question really really annoys writers. So I tried to think of a subtle way to ask but I couldn't.

Me: So what's the next book about?

Dad: Do you know the story of the Koh-i-Noor diamond?

Me (pleased as never know answers to questions like this normally):
Yes, it's the one in the Queen's crown.

Dad (smiles to himself): Not quite. The Empress of India's crown.
Now the Queen Mother's crown. It is not the largest, nor the most
beautiful diamond in the world, but it is the most famous.

Me (anxious to prove I have some knowledge): Yes, we learned
about it at school, when we did the Great Exhibition in 1851. It was
presented to the British by the Indians & I saw it when we went to the
Tower of London last year.

"'Presented to the British,' " Dad smiles. "Very interesting. Do
you know what Koh-i-Noor means?"

It is v hot in Dad's study. I remember that even in winter & today
in the heat it was baking.

Me: No.

Dad: It is called 'The Mountain of Light.'

Me (slightly dim): That's what your book's called! So you're
writing about the diamond?

Dad wags his head, 1/2 nodding, half disagreeing: You know the
man who gave it away to the British? He was called Duleep Singh.
The British brought him to England. He was only 6, a little boy.
~~Maharaja~~. Maharajah. He never went back to the Punjab. He had
given away their greatest treasure. When 2 of his daughters returned
to Lahore, in the twenties, I remember it, people were fascinated. They
were the daughters of the last king of the Punjab, the crowds went wild.
But they couldn't talk to them. The girls had never learned to speak
Punjabi.

Me: That is sad.

Dad: Not really. You are my daughter, you can't speak Punjabi.

Me (looking to see if he's upset about it but I don't think he is, I
don't know): No I can't.

Dad: The diamond is in the Tower of London. You can go whenever
you want. So perhaps it is best left where it is, where many people can
see it.

Me: But it belonged to the maharajah. It should be back in India, shouldn't it?

Dad: Maharajah Duleep Singh was from Lahore. It's not part of India anymore.

There's a bit of a silence.

Me: Will you go back? You never have, have you?

Dad (shakes his head & looks down): No. It is a very different place.

Me: But you could now.

Dad: Maybe I will.

Me: Can I come with you?

Dad (nods and smiles): Would you like to?

Me: Yes please!

Dad (shakes my hand): Well, we will shake on it. This is our pact. When you are grown up, we will go together. I will show you my school, the bazaars, the Shalimar Gardens, Lahore Fort, built by the great Akbar. It is a very beautiful city, Lahore.

I feel sad then, that Dad has lived most of his life in another country. It's a part of me, and I don't know it.

Me: Do you miss it?

D: I miss my father, & my brothers. But they're dead.

Me: How did they die?

D: They were killed, after Partition. Many, many people died then. It was a terrible time.

Me: Who killed them?

Dad is silent, then he says: Ignorant men. They slit their throats. While my brothers slept. They killed my father when he tried to run away, in the night.

I've been trying to remember everything as accurately as possible as he said it, because I don't know any of this and I'd like to record it properly. But all I remember really clearly is his face as he said this. Awful. I just stared at him.

Me: I never knew that. Honestly?

Dad (smiles): Honestly. My cousin wrote to me of it. I was in London, in Spring. You were a few months old. I saw the letter . . .

very old it was, battered & the address was faint, the ink had run. . . .
And I knew. I had been reading the papers, I had tried to get messages
to them, to telephone the old school, the post office where Govind (think
that's how he said it) worked . . . then that letter came. I remember
walking to the door. It was on the wooden floor. Staring up at me. I knew
what was in it. I knew they had been killed. My cousin wrote about the
many trains pulling into Lahore Station. Filled with bodies. Hundreds,
thousands of them, slaughtered on the way up. Blood dripping onto the
tracks. The smell of it, in the heat.

Diary it was so awful just hearing his voice, monotone, saying these
terrible things, in this warm, quiet room with green outside the window,
blue sea in the distance.

Me: It must seem a very long way away.

Dad looks round the study, out of the window: It's a very long way
away. I do not know if I could even go back to Lahore, now. But we
could certainly go to the Punjab in India. To Amritsar, the Holy City of
the Sikhs, & the Golden Temple. Would you like that?

Me: Yes, I'd love that. When shall we go?

Dad: When you leave school, my little child. We will go then.

We talked for a long time. I looked down & saw <u>The Times</u> on Dad's
desk. Odd to think they started the summing up in the Stephen Ward
trial today. It seems so silly, so gossipy & . . . tawdry. When I looked
at my watch it was one-thirty, & no one had rung the bell for lunch.

"Alas, you cannot hear the bell in here," Dad said, which I thought
was pretty funny. That's why he's always late.

In the afternoon the others were playing tennis and going for a
swim but I went for a walk along the coast by myself. I felt all sort
of churned up, at what Dad said, about his brothers, my uncles, how
they died. That is a part of me, & I know nothing about it. It seems we
never discuss it, not because it is something bad, but because we are so
complete in our world here, I always thought.

We have a lovely house, we have money, we have Mummy & Dad,
the sea, & the knowledge that we are well-off & intellectually satisfied
with our lot. We have made our own way of life, the Kapoors. As I

walked along the cliffs, with the wind blowing my hair so it turned into little fluffy knots, I wondered then, WHY? Why does it feel like there is something missing, something wrong. There's Dad, in his study, so remote he can't hear the bell for lunch, and there's Mummy, in her studio, for hours on end. I don't think either of them looks out of the window. They don't go for walks on the beach or swim in the sea.

Later.

In the evening Mummy went to bed early with a headache, & Louisa helped Mary, she made chicken mousse, with salad & plum tart & clotted cream for pudding. It was delicious. Dear Louisa looked really pleased, we were all begging for more, & even Miranda said, involuntarily, "This is absolutely gorgeous, Louisa, thanks a lot."

Doesn't sound much but gosh dear diary, that is a lot coming from her at the moment. They smiled at each other & suddenly everything seemed a bit less . . . I don't know, again. I wish I wasn't so stupid & could find the words to describe it. But it's beyond me, obviously. Goodnight DD, I am finding you so helpful.

Love always, Cecily

Wednesday, 31st July 1963

After our long conversation, I dreamt I was with Dad, only he was a young man, in Lahore. We were walking through a bazaar together & it was very hot. I could smell sandalwood, incense, rich beautiful perfumes, & we were pushing red, pink, burgundy silk rugs & carpets out of the way as we walked. Then I woke up, & it is funny, for the first time I can remember I was disappointed to be here, in Summercove. Normally it is the place I long to be at most, my home, I dream about it when I'm at school endlessly, & when I wake up & I'm in my horrible dorm smelling of damp & Margaret snoring, I could cry. Like when you wake up thinking it's the weekend & then realize it's only Tuesday.

Today, me, Guy & Louisa went with Mummy to St. Ives to see her dealer. She tried to get the others to come along, & they were being too lazy & wouldn't go. Bowler Hat was going to come, but he was very irritating, humming and hawing about whether to, & in the end he dropped out. He wanted to sunbathe, which I suppose if I am being charitable is fair enough, it was boiling hot, but why does he have to take an hour to decide?

We were late to leave because something funny happened. Mummy was holding the door open for us as we scooted in, like an air hostess, & when the Bowler Hat finally made up his mind at the last minute not to come (I think he saw how cramped the car would be), she sort of swiped at him, like Scarlett O'Hara, only she stumbled a bit on the gravel (drive v uneven) & it was awful, she trod on his foot with her little heel. Nearly gave him a stigmata, Archie said. (Archie found the whole episode hilarious — but he loves pain & suffering, he is a fairly Base Person). He was hopping around in agony, & we had to give him a bandage. Mummy was so mortified, it was quite funny to see her embarrassed, normally she never loses her cool, ever.

She drove like a lunatic to St. Ives, I think it shook her up. But Louisa was wonderful, talking to her nicely about her show, though it only seemed to make Mummy crosser, somehow, oh ARTISTS. I talked to Guy, which is, DD, becoming one of my favourite things about this holiday. I feel like I could talk to him all day & night & never run out of things to say. I told him about my chat with Daddy yesterday, about going to India, about the Koh-i-Noor diamond.

Guy said: I saw it at prep school. We came up on a bus, we went to the Tower. I wore some chain mail. It was v exciting. When you're next up in town, we should go together & have a look at it if you'd like.

People are stupid sometimes. I said: "Guy, I'm at school. In Devon. I don't go up to town, ever."

He looked embarrassed as if he hadn't really thought about it properly: "Oh. Maybe in the holidays."

Me: Yes, that'd be lovely. . . .

Actually I don't ever go off to London in the holidays, unless we all go to visit Aunt Pamela. But I felt I could be honest with Guy. So I said, "Really Guy if I were to go out by myself in London, I should want to go to Soho, to sit in a bar & drink café crèmes (or is that a cigarette? Can't remember), not amble around with hundreds of tourists looking at the Crown Jewels."

Guy started to laugh, & he laughed so hard Louisa & Mummy asked what we were talking about. He held my hand up, like boxers do in the papers when they've won, & he squeezed it. "You win again," he said, & he kissed my hand, & then nudged me.

~~I sometimes think with Guy that~~

It's a bit of a pain, getting into the town, now more & more people have cars. There's a queue everywhere. It was annoying, & Mummy still had the roof down & we were in all the back streets & people were staring at us & I didn't like it. Stupid red-faced day-trippers with ices, staring at us, because of the big cream car & because Mummy looks like someone famous with her headscarf and big dark glasses. Suppose she is famous. But I felt like Little Lord Fauntleroy.

Mummy's dealer at her gallery is French, with a funny name— Didier & he is very nice. However his father was there too, a famous dealer from London who runs the gallery where Mummy's show will be. He is called Louis de something, & he was far too over the top, he kissed Mummy's hand too. He spoke to her in a very funny way. "Dear Madam," he called her. "Dearest lady, you who shine brighter than any other." Etc etc.

On the way back we stopped for petrol & heard on the radio that Stephen Ward has taken an overdose this morning. The judge began summing up the trial yesterday. He is in a coma. I feel sorry for him. But some of the things . . . ! Archie whispers "Vickie Barrett," whenever I go into a room, as she is the girl who said there were whips & chains & contraceptives lying around Stephen Ward's flat. Don't believe it but it's most alarming to think of.

Dear Diary, we had a lovely evening when we got back, quiche lorraine & salad & ratatouille except that Miranda flirted with Bowler Hat all evening, and it was pathetic. Why it was pathetic is because Miranda just gets hysterical, not sophisticated, and says racy things to him. It's not impressive, it's embarrassing, like Judith Fairfax at school who no one talks to & when you do she gets all silly and

overexcited and starts being embarrassing and childish. Even the BH
was looking a bit perturbed. Louisa couldn't really do anything. Louisa
is sort of diminished this holiday. I used to want to be her so much. She
was so strong & hearty, the blonde, beautiful, friendly Head Girl. Now
she's just . . . hopeful. Smiling brightly, wearing a nice expression in case
BH turns to notice her. Dear God, I really don't like him. Perhaps I
should try & have a word with Miranda. . . . She is downstairs still,
outside, I can hear her laughing with someone.

She is coming. I will put the diary away now.

Thursday, 1st August 1963

Yes, I did have a terrible row with Miranda. I wish I hadn't. Oh
God, DD, I wish I hadn't. I accused her of terrible things and she did
too, she was horrible. I shouldn't have started it, but she is so mad at
the moment. Esp now she has found her Beauty.

She came in last night after I put the book away & she smelt of
cigarettes. I will try & write it down briefly.

Me: Were you out with BH?

Her: MYOB.

Me: You're hurting Louisa you know.

Her: Shut up.

She hit me on the cheek. I knelt up on bed & hit her back. I caught
her by the hair & scratched her, I enjoyed it. I really did. It's awful. I
could feel a bloodlust in me. It was strange. I felt my fingers digging into
her scalp, she did the same to me. Then she let go. She said: I'm
not doing anything wrong.

Me: Yes you are.

Her: Cecily, you are a child, you know nothing whatsoever & I wish
you'd keep out of it. One day you'll realize. You are a little girl. A
hairy, ugly, silly little girl.

I wanted to hurt her too — the scratch on my cheek was throbbing
a lot. I said, "At least I've got a brain and a future & people like me.

Mummy & Dad like me more than you. Everyone does. Apart from the Bowler Hat, because you're letting him finger you."

(Fingering is sort of the worst thing I've heard someone let a boy do to them at school apart from intercourse, by the way.)

But as I was saying it it felt stupid. And now the words are out there & you can't take them back once they've been said.

Miranda said, "Tell me something I don't know."

And then she got into bed, didn't wash her face or take her clothes off. Just got into bed & turned her light off.

They found Stephen Ward guilty. But he is still in a coma, & he has no idea. Archie was poring over it at breakfast, & I was trying to read over his shoulder, instead of <u>The Lady</u>, which is awfully dull. It has adverts in it like "Are you fond of old people? Would you like to take an active part in their care?" or "A Doctor Explains How it is possible to grow an entirely Fresh New Skin." No no no & no.

Miranda went out early this morning with Archie & I didn't see them all day. I felt bad. I tried to explain to Mum in our sitting, how nasty I'd been (not all of it obviously). But she was annoying. She didn't really listen. I wanted her to tell me I'd been horrible and wrong & should say sorry. But she just sat there, painting away, the only sounds the slap of the wet paint on the canvas, scratching sounds as she blends it in, the sizzle as she draws in the smoke from her cigarette. I can only see the side of her head and shoulder. Oh Mum, be a mum, sometimes, please. Don't be the person Miranda says you are, who tries on our clothes and hates us for our youth. It's not true.

I apologized to Miranda that evening. She was asleep when I came in, I was sitting up late with Guy & Jeremy outside, it's been so hot. I said:

"I'm sorry I was so horrible & I didn't mean any of it, I just think sometimes we don't see things the same way."

She pretended to be asleep again. But I think she heard me.

Friday, 2nd August 1963

This morning seems such a long way away, it is so strange, so much has happened. Firstly, Miranda & I are pretending to speak to each other again, we were civil at breakfast, it was fine. I passed her the marmalade, she offered me the butter. I smiled. She sort of did.

Secondly, I sat for Mummy again. I can't explain it but it is putting me in such a bad mood. I didn't like it much to start with, now I really don't like it. It's hot & boring & my shoulders ache from sitting in the same way all day. My derriere hurts. Mummy sits & paints furiously, we don't talk anymore, & I more & more fear that it will just make me look like a horrible, ugly ghoul, which is what I think I look like anyway. It is depressing, that's all.

I was so glad to get out of there & to talk to Miranda again, & then all hell broke loose . . . oh dear God DD.

Louisa caught Archie again. Watching her getting dressed. AGAIN. And she — I think — broke his nose. Bashed her knee into his face when she opened the door. There was blood everywhere, anyway. It is disgusting disgusting, I can't really think about it. He tried to deny it, that's what's worse. Miranda of course defended him, though how you can I don't know, though I have to say even she looked a bit sick about it.

I looked at Archie, blood streaming down his face, swearing at Louisa, he was so nasty to her. Louisa was crying & the BH holding her & telling her it's OK. And Jeremy is saying, hey chaps, it's all going to be all right, in his rather bluff Captain Scott way. And Miranda starts uttering these threats. "Don't cross me, I tell you." The BH looked terrified.

I knew something was up. My stupid imagination but oh dear God, I hope I'm wrong about this. Miranda is my sister, I'm supposed to love her, & instead I am fairly convinced she is doing something really awful. And Archie gets pleasure from watching his cousin get changed. It's almost as bad.

Suddenly, in the midst of this Aunt Pamela & Uncle John arrive
and stand in the hall!

They are so stiff. I expect them to creak when they move. I'm sure
they thought something strange was up, & Mummy appeared and was
terribly flustered, of course. It was weird, having them standing there,
correct & smart in their London clothes. Makes me realize how isolated
we have let ourselves become these two weeks.

After lunch Guy and I went for a walk. Thank goodness for Guy.
We went to pick the early blackberries, tight, sharp, sweet little things,
all along the hedgerows up around the house & down towards the beach.
Just the two of us.

"Why do you think he's like that?" I asked him.

Guy thought about it for a while. He thinks things over, doesn't talk
unless he has something to say. I do like that.

G: Because . . . He is the only son, & that's hard. Your father is
a tough person to live up to.

I laugh: No he's not!

— because Daddy is so strange it's impossible to imagine anyone
else being like him.

G: Fathers & sons are tricky. Your father had a very different
upbringing, in a completely different place. He came to England to be
educated & he manages to snare one of the most beautiful women in the
country.

And THEN he says:

I read an interview with your mother a couple of yrs ago & did you
know 6 men had proposed to her before your father. & she chose him.
For whatever reason, he's a hard act to follow.

It's strange how when I talk to Guy I find these things out about my
family that had never occurred to me before, like I've been some silly,
blind girl not aware of what's right underneath her nose. It's like he
makes me see everything for the first time.

As we were having this conversation, we were standing on the cliffs,
me carrying the basket, & there was a lovely gentle wind blowing up

from the sea which was calm for once. It was very peaceful, almost too peaceful. Humid. A thin layer of cloud covering everything. Felt miles away from Summercove.

G: Anyway, Archie has a lot to live up to. I don't think your father puts pressure on him. I think everyone else does.

I ate a blackberry and I can still taste the juice now as it burst onto my tongue, sharp and sweet. We were silent.

"Prhaps you're right," I said.

Guy said almost as if he was talking to himself: I suppose the truth is, he's just a simple chap who likes cricket & girls & likes to think of himself as a bit of a smoothie. He doesn't know much about the real world & has two parents who are completely self-absorbed, & don't have the foggiest how to help him.

Then he's silent, & then he said, "My God, Cecily, I'm so sorry — "

Me: (pretending not to be shocked) It's fine!

Guy (very pale straight away): I'm — that's unforgivable of me — it's just sometimes I forget you're — Oh God. Cecily, please — God, what an ass I am.

He looked really upset.

Me: Guy, it's fine, honestly!

And he said, "Sometimes I forget you're one of them."

We were silent. My back was aching and I stretched my arms out, high above me. Guy said, "You're really not like them at all."

I turned to him and we stared at each other. It was strange.

"No," I said. "Perhaps I'm not."

We walked together not saying much. Just being next to each other.

And then later on, this evening, there were drinks & dinner. It was more formal, because of the Jameses. Mummy made me put on a dress. I felt different around him, all of a sudden.

Guy and I were standing by the French windows together. He suddenly touched my arm, & I wasn't expecting it. And DD, it felt as if . . . I have never had that before. Like electricity shooting through me, like I was alive, alive for the first time. I looked at him, & he looked at me, & . . .

I want him. I knew it then. I want him to kiss me. I wanted him right at that moment, his beautiful clear, gray eyes, his kind, handsome face, slow smile, sweet expression. I wanted to bite his lip, to hold him, for him to hold me. . . .

He said I was beautiful. We were silent afterwards, & then we were called into dinner. As I'm writing it now, the memory of it is lovely. Supper was awful, it's funny to think of it now, Miranda and Uncle John had a huge row. I was barely aware of it. Everything else that's going on, all these worries I've had about all of us, that Miranda's having an affair with the Bowler Hat, that Mum and Dad aren't happy, that we're not the family I thought we were, and I'm moving away from them — this feeling that I want to get away from Summercove, get away they just — they're not there when I look at Guy.

I'm in love with Guy? Yes, I'm in love with Guy. It should be scary. It's not.

I escaped to bed as soon as I could. I looked at Guy as I was leaving. He was just there, staring at me. I know he is watching over me. I know he loves me. I love him. So strange to write it! But it's so natural too. What will tomorrow bring?

I love you darling Guy. I always will.

Love always, Cecily

Saturday, 3rd August 1963

Darling diary,

I don't know what to do, how to write this, what to say, I am shaking as I try to hold the pen, because I can't believe what I've seen.

It's horrible.

I don't understand how people can do that.

I have been horrible to Miranda. I have got it all wrong, I am so stupid, I know nothing — oh my goodness, though, diary, is this how it happens, what it's like?

Today I went down to the cove. I have lost a sandal, & I thought it might be down there. I was walking carefully, so I didn't slip. I heard voices, when I got to the stairs. I should have turned back.

But I didn't. I could hear the Bowler Hat's voice. Gosh, I hate him. I hate what he is, what he stands for — that he can just do what he wants & get away with it? I HATE HIM.

I heard things, & I should have just turned & run away, I wish I had. But I wasn't sure, & I was sure my shoe was down there.

He was down there with Mummy. My mother. I stood completely still, I couldn't move. He kissed her, they took their clothes off, I saw him touch her, ~~then they began to~~ then I saw

I really can't write what I saw, & then I ran away.

There's no one I can talk to apart from you. I can't tell Guy, it's his brother. I can't tell Miranda, of course not, she must hate me. I hate myself, for thinking she would do something like this.

I heard the way Mummy laughed at him. Her voice, it was so — cruel. Cold. I almost felt sorry for him, & I hate him!

It's _Mummy_. I can't tell anyone. They wouldn't believe me. I hardly believe it myself. He was kissing her. He took her top off. She undid his trousers. I saw them. . . .

So I said I was feeling ill & I went upstairs and missed lunch. Mummy has been knocking on my door asking if I'm OK all day. I think I want to kill her, but I don't know what to do. Miranda has ignored me, that's fine. What shall I do? Oh God. What shall I do?

I don't feel grown-up anymore. I feel like I want to curl into a ball. I want to sleep. I know I won't be able to though. I wish I wasn't here anymore.

Sunday, 4th August 1963

I did not sleep at all. I am so tired.

And Mummy was vile about missing my sitting. I looked at her as she was being cross with me. Her green green eyes, so evil! Her skin is flushed with freckles and tanned, I know why now. All the times she's appeared smelling of cigarettes I thought she'd been working, now I know why she's behind this week all of a sudden with her work.

How did it start? When?

I don't know what to do. What shall I do?

Guy has been asking if I'm OK. I don't know what to say to him. I don't want him to ask me, I can't tell him, can't tell any of them. He must think I'm ignoring him.

I was sitting out on the lawn with him and all the others & the BH & Louisa were hugging each other & I just watched the BH. He saw me, & he looked uneasy. I thought, I can't stay here any longer, so I just went upstairs again & I'm here. The house is full, full of people. There's no space, no respite, except in my room. I act perfectly normally, I even reply when people ask me questions, & inside I am screaming, like a mad person. There are things I can't stop seeing in my head, like Mummy's face as she turned towards him, laughing, alive, full of cruelty, so beautiful. . . . I didn't know her, not at all, & she is my mother. I can't understand it. I keep seeing my sandal, bobbing in the water behind them, at the edge of the sea, & then nearly slipping & falling as I stand at the top of the steps, they are treacherous. Imagine if they saw me. . . .

It is strange, how you can appear normal to people. As if nothing's different. I am doing it, the Bowler Hat is doing it, Mummy is doing it. I don't want them to ever know. I should tell Louisa, I know I should. But I simply can't do that.

Perhaps it's not so bad, they will split up & she will marry someone else. And then I think no, something has poisoned us, this will stay with us forever. Mummy did this, she is behind it. She is my mother, I can't believe it. Am I being prudish? Have I been closeted away for too long? Is this quite usual, elsewhere? Do properly grown-up people act like this all the time?

If I didn't know, everything could go on as normal. But I feel that because I know it can't, now. If I wasn't here, it would be OK.

Monday, 5th August 1963

I have just reread the first pages of this diary. It's like they're from another lifetime. It is only two weeks. I feel like a different person. One thing after another, & it's as if I am watching myself do these things, say them.

Tonight I kissed Guy. I nearly had sex with him, in fact.

Funny, that we didn't, in the end, because I would have let him, only he stopped. I have never seen a grown man naked before. Now I have seen two, in three days. Guy, & his brother. I liked the idea that if I let him be with me, that he & his brother would have done some kind of double act, a mother & a daughter. Perhaps that's what happens in real life, perhaps I've just been innocent and stupid. But I am the only person who'd know that. Oh, DD, I wish I could be back at school, in my dorm with Margaret, Rita, & Jennifer. Being told what to do, when to do it, instead of this terrifying summer world I'm living in.

Most of all, I feel sad. Because before all this I thought Guy was . . . don't know how to put it, because it is ridiculous. But someone I knew. Someone I could fall in love with.

I still think that. But I also think it's too late, for him & for me.

It happened like this: Mummy, Jeremy, Uncle John, & Aunt Pamela played bridge after supper. Very demure. The Bowler Hat & Louisa sat outside with their cigarettes, listening to some jazz, he with his arms round her, both of them gazing up at the stars. She looked so happy, with her little pink & white face & fluffy hair. He was behind her, one hand on her shoulder, one on her rib cage, & he looked bored. I could tell he was trying to move one hand down, the other up, so he could touch her breasts, without looking indecorous. There was something . . . OH GOD, I HATE THIS.

Something so disgusting!! So vile & animallike about him, his leg splayed out, carelessly trying to touch L, when I know what he's been doing . . . it made me feel sick, & . . .

Anyway, I got up & said, "I'm just going to shut the gate." Guy followed me.

"Do you want to go for a walk," he said. It is a beautiful night, very clear, very warm. Stars everywhere.

We walked down the path, towards the sea. I wasn't even thinking about trying to impress him, now, I was just thinking about BH & his hands, & Mummy sitting upright playing bloody cards.

Guy said, "Cecily, are you all right?"

"Yes."

"Because — if you don't mind me saying it — you seem rather twitchy. I hope I haven't said anything. . . ."

I looked round at him, & he is looking at me, rather anxiously, & he looks so sweet, so reassuring, so kind, an island in the middle of this sea, like St. Michael's Mount. He's the one person I think isn't bad or stupid or evil or wronged or doing something wrong.

So, oh dear diary. I walked towards him — we were away from the house, almost at the steps by the sea. I put my hand on his chest. I looked into his eyes. I stood on tiptoe, & I kissed him. On the lips.

I didn't think about it, I just sort of knew it would happen.

He kissed me back. I kissed Brian Deans last year, the son of the history master at school, but this was different. There, I felt my tongue was getting in the way. Here, it was sloppy, but it felt nice. Guy put his hand on the back of my neck, & his tongue was in my mouth.

We sat down after a while, on the sweet, soft moss, with the crickets chirruping nearby, & the sea crashing in the distance & we kissed more, & then I wanted to touch him, & he wanted to touch me too. He smoothed his hands over my collarbone, & he touched my breasts, my stomach, & I took my dress off, & let him, & I touched him too, took his shirt off, everything really. We were naked, apart from Guy still had his socks on, & when I noticed that it made me laugh. We both laughed. We rolled next to each other, naked, & he held me, stroked me, & I touched him, it is so strange, a man's body, so different in a way. Much harder, less soft & full of places you can poke. And his penis was hard. I wanted to touch that too. Perhaps I am like my mother, a hard cold woman. Probably. I was quite grown-up about it. I felt very comfortable with him.

We were silent for a long time. I did hold his penis and stroked it and he loved that. & I kissed his mouth, his cheek, & whispered "inside me," but he shook his head, & he wouldn't. We lay on the moss for a while, holding hands. Just there, looking up at the stars. Summercove was a yellow light, fifty yards away. No one else was near. Just us two.

"I think I love you," he said. "In fact I know I do."

"Me too," I said to him. I stroked his cheek, his short, spiky hair, his beautiful, kind eyes, his lips.

It's true too. When I said it I meant it. Then I remembered the other things, back at the house. It all rushed back to me & I realized then I knew — it won't work out that way. I put my clothes on, & he followed me, & we walked back to the house.

Guy put his hand in mine, as we were walking. He stroked my palm with his thumb. And then he kissed my shoulder, very gently, as we got close to the house. I think I will remember that kiss for the rest of my life. Because it was almost perfect. Like Guy & me. Almost perfect.

Tuesday, 6th August 1963

I didn't sleep again. It rained in the night, just a bit, but it was noisy, thunder and lightning. It woke me up. I lay there thinking so much it was scary. Like a black wave washing over me. I can't ever see how this can get better.

This morning, Miranda sat down on the edge of my bed. "You know don't you?" she said.

I looked at her & she just stared at me. I thought how grown-up she is now. A different person. Both of us are. I nodded.

"How?"

I said I saw them together. She patted my leg.

"Me too. That day you were all out. It's like she wants to be caught. It's going to be OK. You and me & Archie, we'll grow up and get out of here soon. It'll be OK."

Me: But I don't want to. I just want everything to be the way it was before.

Miranda: Well, it's not going to be. Can't you see that?

Me: Why? Why do you think she's doing it?

M shrugs her shoulders, & I realize she doesn't have all the answers, of course not. "I don't know, Cec. Perhaps the same reason she tried on my clothes or she gazes off into space at supper or she spends so much time up in the studio. Perhaps she's just wishing she was young again."

"But that's so stupid," I said. "We spend all our time wishing we were grown-ups. She can do anything she wants."

"Maybe it seems like that," Miranda said. I wish she'd always been like this, calm and wise to talk to. I wish we could start over again.

"And why with him?" I say. There were tears in my eyes, like there are now as I'm writing this. "I don't understand why it has to be him."

"Because he's young & gorgeous and he worships her, you can see it once you know," Miranda says. "I used to think he was handsome, now I hate him. I hate her."

I sort of hate her too.

"Archie says she's done it before."

"No."

"Yes," Miranda says. "Sorry Cec." She leaned over and she patted my hand. "She's —— "

And we heard Mummy coming up the stairs. "It's breakfast, girls," she says, opening the door. "What are you two doing?"

She looks at us, stiff & upright on the bed. We look at each other. "Nothing," Miranda says. She gets up. "We're just coming."

"Miranda, I need you & Louisa to go to Lady Cecil's this morning, with a cheque for the Women's Institute."

M: We don't both need to go.

"Yes, you do," Mummy says sharply. She looks in the mirror, stooping a little. "She wants to talk to you about a job in London & I don't want you going on your own. You'll forget something, like when Mrs. Anstruther offered you the job at the kennels last year."

Now I can see it, I wonder why I never noticed before.

M: What kind of job?

Mummy says: Secretary in a lawyer's office. And don't say you're not interested. It's not as if you have anything better to do, is it? Darling, I'm only trying to help. Don't bite the hand that feeds you.

She goes out and we stare at each other again. "Miranda, what shall we do?" I started crying.

"You've got to keep calm," she says. "We can't talk here. Let's meet on the cliffs in a bit, I'll get Archie too."

"Don't worry," she says, and she kisses my head. "I'll look after you. You're my sister. I know we haven't always been the best of friends, Cec. But I'm your sister. I'll make sure it's all all right."

She goes out, & I stare after her. I've got her all wrong as well as Mum. She may be annoying but she's brave. She stood up to horrible Uncle John. She is willing to take the blame for her bad behaviour this summer, so that everyone thinks it's her flirting with the Bowler Hat. I'm proud she's my sister, I never thought I'd say that.

After breakfast when Mummy asked me about sitting, I just said not today, and I tried to wander off. My legs are all wobbly. She was ultra nice to me and then she gave me her ring. It is a lovely ring, she knows I've always coveted it. Why did she give it to me? I don't want it anymore, I felt that she was offering it because she knew, in some way? Or she could see I was sad and she was trying to make things better?

Perhaps I should tell her I know. But then Louisa will find out. Perhaps she should find out though? She can't marry him. I don't know. I must stay calm.

Miranda & I are going for our walk now. She's right, we should just get away from here, as soon as we can. But I'm so tired. I feel old, all of a sudden. Old and tired of all this. I will report back, darling diary. I know I can trust you. You will be here in the dark in the bedside table, waiting for me. I'll be back soon.

Love Always,

Cecily

Part Four

March 2009

Thirty-eight

It is cold and dark in the room, and as I look up, my neck, shoulders, and legs ache from the tense position I've been in over the last hour. The only point of light is the lamp next to me. It shines on the yellowing pages of the diary. Everything else around it is black. It is almost a surprise to me, when I put my hands up to my cheeks, to find that tears are running down them.

The shadow of my hands makes the light flicker on the brick walls, and I jump. It is very quiet, but the room seems to be crowded, with voices, people. . . . I shiver and stand up. I wish I wasn't here. I wish I was somewhere with someone I know. Someone who loves me, someone who I could turn to and say, my God, this is horrible.

I can't. I'm all alone, and her voice is echoing in my head.

I want to see her. More than anything, suddenly. I didn't know her before, so I couldn't miss her, and this is what's making me cry. I love this bold, intelligent, charming, eccentric, eager young girl, whose scrawling pages in front of me are so slapdash and immediate it's as if she's just run out of the room. I can see why Guy fell in love with her. I wish I had known her. I wish I could know what she might have done next, had she lived. There is something so hopeless about her last day alive; a girl worn out by the adults around her, by the life she had to live, and not even sixteen.

When she died, she left them all behind, and I realize, now, that they have been preserved like that, all of them—Mum, Archie, Louisa, Granny, Arvind—kept in a drawer along with the diary, not allowed to live the lives they wanted. Even Guy, who married someone else and got away from them, is a curiously reduced version today of the person he was in the diary. Poor, poor Guy. At the thought of him, my heart clenches and my eyes sting with fresh tears. Now I understand, now I know why he insisted I call him after I'd finished it. How must it have been for him, reading that diary after all these years, having tried to forget her, never having known why she died? To find out about his brother like that, to . . . oh, it's so sad. The whole thing is just so sad. I think of Mum. I wonder where she is. Oh, Mum. I'm sorry.

Memories start rushing back to me as I stand up slowly, my legs aching from sitting still in the cold, dark room. Of me on Granny's knee, teaching me to play the piano. Letting me sip her Campari and soda while she put on her earrings, dabbed scent onto her slender wrists. And her beautiful face viewed through the carriage window, waving enthusiastically at me as each summer train pulled into Penzance station and I thought—*I thought*—I was home, with my *real* mother, not living this sham life with a mother who forgot where my school was and didn't like birthday parties.

My granny, my favorite person in the world: was this really her, this woman who tries on her daughter's clothes, who sleeps with young men, who has to have attention and approval and glamor and beauty and simply takes it if she doesn't have it?

I look down at the diary. Yes, yes, it was.

And that furious, awkward, eccentric, and beautiful teenager, who has lived in the shadow of this ever since, suspected, mistrusted, abandoned by the people who should have most been looking out for her, was that really my mother?

Yes, I guess it was.

The ring, Cecily's ring, is still around my neck. She put it on the day she died. Granny wore it every day since, and suddenly it feels as though it's choking me, and my heart feels as though it's being squeezed. I rip it off my neck, almost panting. I switch the kettle on and stare at nothing. My breathing gets more rapid as I think it all through, and there are so many things that make sense. Like why Mum hates going down to Summercove, why she and Granny didn't get on, why Mum and Archie are so close, and why kind, caring Louisa is baffled by her cousins and their behavior, always has been.

And then there are things I just don't understand. Like how Granny could sit in a room with the Bowler Hat, knowing what they did. Like how Mum could stand it. And Arvind—does he know? Does Archie? Does Louisa really not know what her husband has done?

I think about the Bowler Hat, the way he's present and yet not really present at everything, this cipher. This empty, attractive casing of a man. Forty-six years ago, he was the same, just a younger, priapic version of that. I wonder if he connects the two, if he knows what he's done?

The kettle sounds louder and louder, the whistling steam rising up and moistening my face. I stare into the white-gray plumes.

How could Granny live there year after year, knowing she was as good as responsible for her daughter's death? Cecily herself said the steps were slippery, and they'd mentioned it a couple of times, so why didn't she or Arvind get them fixed? How could she let people think her own daughter might have been responsible for her sister's death? How could she . . . ?

And I can't think about it anymore.

I go into the bedroom. The chamomile tea tastes like cardboard. The flat is silent. I climb into bed. I pick up Cecily's diary again and flick through it—it seems the only real, concrete thing in my life. Words, phrases, jump out at me.

Mummy doesn't like Miranda being beautiful.

Dad has lived most of his life in another country. It's a part of me, and I don't know it.

We're not the family I thought we were.

I really can't write what I saw.
I think it's too late, for him and for me.
I think it's too late, for him and for me. . . .

I can't read the last couple of pages again. They're too painful. I stare at the diary, and the words swim in front of my eyes, and soon I slide into sleep, propped up by pillows.

Thirty-nine

That is Friday. On Monday morning, I wake up and I know I can't stay in the flat by myself anymore. It's not just the loneliness: I've been lonely for a while, I realize. It's that every time I look around there's something else to remind me of something I don't want to be reminded of. It just holds bad memories for me, as if sitting there in the darkness as I read Cecily's diary somehow released them all. I can't do it anymore. Perhaps I was holding on to some tiny hope that Oli and I might get back together again, but I know now that's never going to happen; this has clarified everything. We need to sort the flat out, and we need to crack on with the divorce. First things first, I need to get out of here. I ring up Jay, and ask to stay with him.

The great thing about Jay is he doesn't ask questions, and he doesn't fuss. He is waiting there when I turn up at his flat in Dalston an hour later, with a hastily packed suitcase. He gives me a cup of coffee and makes me some toast.

"I just don't want to be there anymore," I say. I wipe a tear away from my cheek.

"Why now?" he says. "I mean, you've been on your own there for a while."

I don't want to tell him about the diary. If I tell him, he'll want to read it, and he'll find out about our grandmother. Now I can see what Mum has been doing all these years, in her own way: protecting Granny's reputation, for the sake of others. We are sitting in his light, roomy, first-floor Georgian flat, just off De Beauvoir Square, and as I look out of the window I notice the trees have buds on them. There are no trees on my street.

"It just—got a bit much," I tell him. "It's pathetic, I know."

Jay makes a little sound at the back of his throat, and he shakes his head. "Oh, Nat. You poor thing." He shakes his head. "Oli. Wow, that guy. What a tool." He sees my expression. "Sorry."

"He's not a tool," I say. "It's more than that, it took me a while to see he wasn't coming back and it's over, and yep—now I know it, I just can't be there anymore. I needed a bit of limbo there, I guess. But it's over now. We need to rent it out and I'll move somewhere cheaper. I just needed to see it, that's all."

"Stay here," Jay says. "As long as you want. I've got the study, but I'm working in the Soho office mostly these days." I hold up a hand to protest. "Nat," he says patiently. "I wouldn't say it if I didn't mean it."

I know he wouldn't, and I nod. "Thanks, Jay."

"I know it won't be as nice as Princelet," he says. "The bathroom's got damp and it's well shabby round here, not like you're used to." He smiles, and I grin at him.

"Believe me, it's nicer," I say. I raise my coffee cup to him. "Thanks again. Seriously."

"No problem," he says. He pauses. "Dad rang me last night. You spoken to your mother yet?"

On Saturday and Sunday, I rang Mum. I rang Guy first, but then I rang Mum. No answer from either of them. I left tentative messages, but it's hard to know what to say. "Hi . . . ! I'd love to speak to you . . . ! I . . . I read the diary. . . . Give me a call . . . !"

What do I do next? I don't want to rock the boat. I can't do anything for the moment, so I smile at him, and try not to look mad.

"I left her a message again this morning," I say. "I'll call her again, later on."

"That's good," Jay says firmly. He is pleased. I am touched by his concern for her. It strikes me once again how craven I was, willing to believe what Octavia told me over what Jay believes. All he knew from Archie is that Miranda is above reproach, and he listened to what his father said. He may not agree with him one hundred per cent, but he's his father and Jay respects him.

He gets up. "Look, I'd better go to work," he says. "You know where everything is. Do you want me to help you get more stuff from the flat this evening?"

"That'd be great," I say. I chew my lip. "I guess I'd better call Oli, let him know too. We should start sorting it out. . . ."

"I bet he'll want to move back in," Jay says perceptively. "It's much more him than you, that place."

I think of the money Oli gave me as a loan. Because perhaps this would be the perfect way to pay him back, temporarily. Strange, strange, I think, that it was only Friday morning when I woke up and he was there with me, and we had sex, and then I knew, undoubtedly, that it was for the last time, and that it's over. It's over when you don't feel anything. It's over when you don't want to live there anymore. It's over when you want the other person to be happy more than you want them in your life. Sitting in Jay's living room, which is decorated—a loose term—with nothing more than slightly peeling oatmeal wallpaper, a few photos, and many video games scattered across the floor, I feel more at home here, on the comfy, worn blue sofa, than I have in my own home for a long time.

"You're right. He's welcome to," I say, and I mean it. "Thanks again, Jay." I lean forwards and pat his arm.

" 'S'OK, like I say," he says simply, getting up. "We're family."

I smile as I watch him go into his room and grab his stuff. I pick up the phone again and call my mother. The phone rings, and my heart starts thumping. But instantly, it's diverted to voicemail. I call Guy again too. Same thing. I sigh, and I go into Jay's small study and unpack my stuff. It's a meager collection of things: my sketchbooks, a pair of jeans, a couple of tops and cardigans, pajamas, a few knickers, a sponge bag with toothpaste and the like in it, and a little bag with Cecily's necklace. Right at the bottom, her diary.

Jay is whistling in the other room as he gets ready for work. It's just an ordinary day, I suppose. I feel as though everything has changed: more than that, that the world as I know it has fallen down around my ears. But you still have to go on, you can't just lie on the sofa staring at the wallpaper, tempting as that might be. I've done that too, and I know it doesn't accomplish anything. So I put Cecily's diary, my sketchbooks, and the necklace into my shoulder bag. Jay emerges with his backpack on.

"I'm going to the studio," I say. "I'll walk with you."

"Great," Jay says. He jangles his keys. "Tell me, how's my friend Ben? I was thinking, we should all go out one evening, don't you think?"

"Oh . . ." I say. "Yeah. That'd be great."

Jay looks suspiciously at me. "What's up? You two had a row?"

"God, no," I say, putting my coat on. I put my phone in my pocket, and that's when I see the text message.

Had to dash to Morocco unexpectedly for work! Know we need to talk darling. Just explained it all to Guy. He is around while I'm away. Perhaps you cld talk to him? See you for foundation launch? Do love you darling—Mum x

"It's from Mum," I tell Jay.

"How is she?"

"She's in Morocco. She's gone to bloody Morocco." She'd rather call Guy and tell him where she's going, Guy who she supposedly hates, than me.

We go down the stairs and Jay opens the front door. "Oh yeah, Dad mentioned she was thinking of going there," he says.

"She could have told me she was going," I mutter. I stare at the phone again, wanting to scream. Yes, I do want to talk to Guy, Mum. But I'd much rather talk to you. Stop running away from me.

Forty

When I reach the studio there is a new receptionist, a Breton-striped-top-wearing boy, very skinny, with a mop of curly hair on top of his head, shaved at the sides. He is wearing the obligatory thick black glasses that all boys and girls in East London must wear, from Tania to Arthur to Tom and Tom, the two gay guys who run Dead Dog Tom's, the hottest new bar in Shoreditch just down the road from the studio. I sometimes wonder what would happen if someone wore frameless steel Euro-style glasses in Shoreditch/Spitalfields—would an invisible forcefield shatter them?

"Hiyaa," he says, not looking up from his phone. "How're you."

This isn't a question, more a rapped-out courtesy.

"Hi. Where's . . . Jocasta?" I say. "Or Jamie?"

"I'm Jamie's like brother?" the beautiful boy says. "Dawson? She's not well today, her skanky boyfriend gave her food poisoning? So I'm filling in for her?"

I can't keep track of Jamie's love life. I thought she was with the dodgy pockmarked Russian millionaire and surely millionaires don't get food poisoning. "Oh, right," I say.

"Lily's having an open studio this afternoon, so she asked Jamie to get someone to cover for her." Dawson's eyes shift away from me, and then his face lights up. "Hey, you!"

"Hey," says a voice behind me. "Oh. Hi, Nat."

I swing round, my heart thumping loudly. There, in the doorway, is Ben, and again I adjust to the new person he is, shorn of hair. The person I kissed three nights ago. I stare at him, drinking in the sight of him.

"Hi, Ben," I say.

"Hey," he says, taking his backpack off his shoulders. He barely glances in my direction. "Hi, Dawson," he says. "How's it going? What are you doing here?"

He high-fives Dawson, who smiles at him and stands up, excited. "Ben, my man. Good to see you! Hey, thanks for those links! I checked out that photographer dude, he was amazing? That shit of those dead trees, and the foil—it was so . . ." He shakes his head. "So *relevant*, you know?"

"Good, good." Ben is nodding. "How's Jamie?"

"Good, she's good. Well, she's not, she's being sick every five minutes, but she's good otherwise."

Ben grimaces. "Oh, dear. Tell her I said get well soon, and she should definitely lose the boyfriend." He turns to me. "Hey."

I lean forwards. "Yeah. So—"

"See you later," he says, and turns away, making for the stairs.

I follow him. "Ben," I say, as we curl up to the first floor, out of earshot. "How—how are you?"

He nods vigorously. "I'm good, good."

"Look—" I take a deep breath. "I'm sorry about the other night."

A small muscle on his cheek twitches in Ben's lean face. "Yeah, no problem."

"I meant to text you . . ." I say lamely. "To apologize for running off like that. But I . . ."

I trail off. He is still as granite, watching me. Was it really Thursday that we kissed? It seems so long ago. He seems like a different person, tall and forbidding. He's hugging his backpack to him. "I didn't text you either," he says. "It's fine. Look, I'd better get on. . . ."

"Fine, of course," I say. I feel almost winded in the face of his hostility, it's like running into a brick wall. "See you—see you in a bit."

I go into my studio and shut the door, trying to breathe normally, but my chest is rising and falling alarmingly quickly. I lean against the door, listening to the silence, and then I shake myself down, go over to the counter, and get my stuff out. I write my list for the day, get out my sketchpad; sort out some more filing, turn on my laptop. I flick through the post. The details of my little stand at the trade fair in June have come through; I can see my position on the map, and it's OK. There's a sale on at the place I get my clasps, hooks, earring hoops. A letter from the bank, inviting me to a seminar on Small Business Management. I smooth it out flat and put it in my in-tray, thinking I should go. The last letter is from Emilia's Sister, the shop on smart Cheshire Street. They've sent through an order. An old-fashioned, paper order! It's like a novelty item, beautifully printed, and I stare at it in disbelief. They want twenty necklaces, thirty charm bracelets, some of the dangling rose earrings I'm having made. . . .

There's a knock on the door. "Come in!" I shout happily, and then look up. It's Ben.

"Hey," I say, putting down the order and picking up the broom which I use to sweep the floor. I brush it nervously. I don't know why I'm surprised it's Ben knocking at the door: it's always Ben. Always *used* to be. "What's up?"

He shuts the door. "Hi, Cinders. I just wanted to say sorry for being a cock."

I laugh nervously. "What are you talking about?"

Ben rubs one eye; he looks tired. "The last however many days, basically. I have been a cock. Shouting at you . . . Kissing you . . . Not calling you . . . Just now . . . Real cock behavior. I know you're having a bad time at the moment. I shouldn't have taken advantage."

For a brief microsecond I let myself think of his lips on mine again, the feeling of his skin, his tongue in my mouth. . . . I shake my head, smiling.

"You're many things, Ben Cohen, but you're not a cock," I say. "I should have called. Cleared the air."

"No," he says, smiling back at me. "I should have done."

"I behaved really badly. I'm the one who . . . who ran off. And I was drunk and hysterical. I'm sorry."

Ben laughs. "You weren't drinking alone, you know."

"It makes me feel better if you were as drunk as me," I say.

He pauses. "Let's say I was, and call it quits."

"Um—yes," I say. "Definitely."

I stare at him, unsure of what to say next—so, is it normal between us now? Is that it?

"So it's . . . it's OK?" Ben says, watching me.

"Yes of course," I say. I want to explain. "Look—me and Oli—when I ran off like that, 'cause he rang, it wasn't what you think." And then I stop. Because it is what he thinks. "I mean, you know. We're still married, we have to talk to each other. . . ."

There's a silence. I look up at him.

"I just want you to be happy, Nat," he says.

Suddenly, I desperately want . . . No, this is stupid. I'm leaning on the diary and the post, and I stand upright and brush myself off, as if I'm dusty. Ben blinks, as though he can't remember why he's here, and I think to myself again how tired he looks.

"Hey," I say, more than anything else to have some sound in the deathly quiet of the studio. "So, I found the diary."

I don't expect him to remember. "Cecily's diary?" he says immediately. "I've been wondering about that. Did your mum have it?"

"Yes . . ." I stare at him. "She did—how on earth did you know that?"

He shrugs. "I just guessed she probably would. Knowing your mum, even as little as I do. I thought it'd turn up sooner or later." His voice is kind of flat.

"That's amazing," I say. I smile, I can't help it. He knows us all, knows me better than I know myself. And he makes it sound so simple. "Well, yeah—she did have it."

"Have you read it?"

"Yes. Last night, in fact."

Ben gives me a sideways glance, as if he's reluctant to ask, but can't help himself. "So, what's in it? Is Jesus buried in your garden?"

"Um—" I take a deep breath, and it catches in my throat. I'm not sure how to explain it, and I can't think about it without thinking of the last page, of my mother and Cecily on the morning she died, sitting on the bed together, promising each other that everything's going to be OK. "It's—it's that thing of thinking you know someone and it turns out you don't." I try to explain. "Like you saying 'knowing your mum.' That's what's awful about it. I don't think I know her at all. I think all these years, we've all looked at her in the wrong way. She went through some bad stuff, and it turns out the people who should have been looking after her—well, they weren't. At all."

I am shaking slightly as I say this. "Have you talked to her?" Ben asks, fiddling with a bit of paper, shooting glances at me out of the corner of his eye.

I shake my head. "She's gone off for a few days."

"You need to talk to someone about it."

Not me. I can feel him, ever so politely, pushing away from me. "It's fine," I say. "I'm trying to get hold of Guy—old family friend, he—oh, it'll be fine. Just—stuff to think about."

I want to talk to him about it so much, though. I want his advice, as though it's back to normal in the studio and we're chatting about all and sundry the way we used to, before Oli's affair and Granny's death and before he split from Tania and everything got weird. I want to say, read this diary, I want to know what you think, what you think I should do, for God's sake, because I have no idea myself and it's freaking scary.

And I know I can't, because everything's changed, not least our relationship.

Most of all I want him to read the diary to get to know Cecily, to see what she was like, to hear her voice. I want more people to know her. Ben would get her. He'd like her.

"Look," he says, cutting into my thoughts. "I can't stay." He takes something out of his back pocket. "I just came to give you something."

"Oh," I say. "Right."

"I had these printed out for you," he says, handing me a manila envelope. "But I didn't get round to giving them to you. . . . They came out pretty well considering how much we'd drunk."

I tip the envelope open. "Oh . . . wow," I say, grinning. "I'd forgotten, thank you so much."

They're the photos of the necklace Claire, that girl in the Ten Bells, was wearing on Thursday, the necklace I've been working on adapting, using Cecily's ring and some of the duck-egg-blue laser-cut birds I'm waiting for today. I gaze at them with pleasure. He's had them properly printed, with white edges, and each shows the necklace perfectly. I flick through them.

"Thank you so much, Ben," I say, gathering them up. "They're—wow, they're just what I needed. You are great." I glance at the last one. "Oh. That's of me!"

I am raising my glass, my hair falling over my shoulders, and I am smiling, clearly one or two drinks up. He looks at it, and the muscle on his now-smooth cheek twitches again. "Oh. Yes, it is," he says. He pauses, just a second. "Yes—I thought you'd like one with Cecily's ring on it, to see how it looks next to the others."

"That's great, Ben, thanks so much." I come round to his side of the counter and squeeze his arm. "You're a great man." I look at him again. "With short hair."

He laughs, but there's a terseness to his tone. "Right. Look—"

"Thanks again," I say, as he turns to leave. Emboldened by this new, more friendly footing, I say, "Um—do you want to grab some lunch, or something? I'd love to tell you about the diary. Get your advice, and . . ."

I trail off. Ben looks down at the photos in my hand. "I don't think so," he says gently. "Nat, I think you kind of need to talk to Oli, or Jay, or someone, about that stuff first, not me."

Taking a little step back, I nod. "F-fine," I say. "You're right. But—honestly, Ben, it really is over with me and Oli. I've moved in with Jay. It was—he did come round that night, but he shouldn't have. It's over," I say, not really knowing why I say it. "It really is."

The tension in the room is suddenly palpable.

"I wasn't asking if it was or it wasn't," Ben says. He taps his forehead furiously with one finger, as if he's trying to release something in his brain. "Nat—I'm not stupid. You don't need any more complications in your life at the moment. Once again—I'm sorry I was a cock. We were drunk, I shouldn't have said that stuff to you, and everything else, that night. Let's just forget about it."

And everything else. I am blindsided. "Right, then."

"Glad you like the photos. See you soon."

He closes the door gently behind him once again, raising his hand as a farewell. I watch the closed door. I want to run after him, put him right, but what would I say? Yes, I slept with Oli, yes, we were drunk, no, I've no idea what's going on in my life, yes, I like you, I've always really liked you. But you shouldn't trust my opinion about anything. I don't.

I get my sketchpad out, tugging my hair and staring intently at the photos of the necklace. I call Charlotte at Emilia's Sister, to say how pleased I am about the order. I try Guy again: "Hi, Guy. Look, I read the diary—Mum's gone away, she said she'd told you, just wondering if we could chat? Give me a call."

In the afternoon, guests start arriving for Lily's open studio. I can hear sounds of chatter and laughter floating through the open window, down the corridor. I don't hear Ben leave; perhaps he's there too. When the charms arrive by messenger from Rolfie's, I thread them onto what I've already assembled, making up two, three, different versions of the necklace, trying each out with Cecily's ring. I make notes, I change bits around. I prop the photos up next to my stool and sketch on, waiting for someone to call me back, but the phone is silent.

Forty-one

The days pass by easily at Jay's. I fall into a rhythm there almost immediately. We know each other well, we can happily watch TV together or separately. Cathy can come round and hang out with both of us, just like the old days. Jay is laid-back about everything, to the point of being comatose sometimes, and I feel like Louisa, picking up his cereal bowls and dirty socks after he's left for work in the morning. I love it. I'm sleeping like a log. It isn't so cold, it's April now, and the days are warmer, the nights fresh, and it's quiet around our side of De Beauvoir Square, but a contented quiet, not the silence of an empty flat. We stay up late into the night watching films, taking it in turns to pick. Last night I chose *Tootsie*. The night before Jay made me watch *The Bourne Identity*, which I've never seen. I could have done without him making exploding noises at the exact moment onscreen that someone gets shot or blown up on screen, but otherwise it was great.

I used to wish I could live alone. Now, I am relishing living with my cousin. It's great to know someone will be there when you get back home. And even if they're not, that they'll be back eventually. With Oli, it got to a stage where even though he was there, he wasn't really present. There were so many things we couldn't discuss, didn't discuss: Should we move to a bigger place? When should we have children? Why are you never around anymore?

Anyway, it is with surprise one Saturday that I look round and realize it's April, and I'm going back to Cornwall the following week, for the launch of the foundation.

Yesterday, I had a call from Emilia's Sister. Charlotte, the owner, said she had to call, because they'd sold eight necklaces that Friday alone—that doesn't sound like much, but it's a classic Columbia Road shop, one that does most of its business on Saturday and Sunday, so that's pretty good news, amazing in fact. Earlier in the week, I found out I had a place at that business seminar I signed up for. It's in a couple of weeks. It's free, and as far as I'm concerned, I need all the help that I can get.

It's funny, but once you admit you've screwed up and don't know what comes next, it's easier to accept help. I have had my own business for a couple of years, and it's only now I realize how much I have to learn, look it square in the face. It's scary. But scary in a good way. I've been used, these past months, to scary in a bad way. A swirling mist of uncertainty, of misery and sadness that hung on my shoulders like a heavy cloak and which I could never seem to shake off. Every day it seems to get lighter.

Jay and I have lunch at a Vietnamese café round the corner from his flat. I'm meeting Cathy later, we're going to see a film and then for a bite to eat afterwards so I can hear about Jonathan, who has suggested they go away on a *Strictly Come Dancing* weekend featuring the stars of the show in a country manor house. He says it'll be good networking for him. (Cathy is torn between being totally convinced he must be gay and secretly desperately wanting to go, as *Strictly* is her and her mum's favorite TV program.) I want an early night, it's my first day back on the market stall tomorrow and I need to get there in good time, make sure I've got my act together.

After we've ordered, Jay says, "I spoke to Dad while you were getting the paper."

"Oh, yeah?" I say.

"He says Miranda went, like, last Monday. Ten, twelve days ago."

"I know, that was the day I moved in with you." I love how precise Archie is, he has all the information.

"Well, she's not coming back till Tuesday." He puts his elbows on the table. "Did you know that?"

"No," I say. I cross my arms. That's two weeks she's been away, why on earth? "Jay, I told you, I tried and tried to get hold of her before she went off to Fez, or wherever it is. I've called her, OK? I'll see her next week, when we go back to Summercove." I bite my lip.

"All right!" He holds up his hands. "Calm down. It's going to be weird," he says.

"I know. And kind of awful. Are you sure you won't come?" I ask, begging with my hands outstretched. He shakes his head.

"Nah. Don't mean to be funny, and I'll come if you really want me to, but I'm not invited. We should go down in May, you know? Before it's sold. Have one more weekend there. I don't want to be there with all those art people, all of that. Dad's dreading it."

He's right. I'm not much looking forward to it. Since I moved to Jay's, everything seems to be on a more even keel. Going to Cornwall is going to bring it all back again. I'm being a coward, I have to face up to it, really, have to ask the questions I don't have answers to. And it'll be good in many ways. I'll see Louisa. I'll see Arvind. I'll see the house, perhaps for the last time? Perhaps not. And I'll see my mum—although God knows if she'll turn up or not, even if she is supposed to be making a speech.

As for Guy, I haven't heard back from him, so I'll see him there too. I don't know what to say to him, either. I suppose I just have to wait till he wants to talk to me. I don't understand why he's gone silent.

"Is your mum going?" I ask hopefully.

"No, she'll be in Mumbai, won't she?" Sameena's sister is not well again, so she's going over to look after her family. "Like I say, Nat," Jay says again. "If you need me to be there, I'll be there. It's just hard with work and everything. I'd rather go when I can spend some proper time with Arvind, remember the house the way I want to, not with a load of posh people asking me stupid questions about Granny." The waitress puts two beers down on the table and Jay takes a big gulp. "I wouldn't know what to say to them, anyway, would you?" I shake my head. "It's private. Her being our grandmother hasn't got anything to do with whether she was a good painter or any of that."

Perhaps I'll never be able to tell him what our grandmother was really like. But as I watch him I think, what would be gained by telling him, anyway? How would it help him, to know the truth? It wouldn't. His father hasn't ever told him, and I'm not going to. He doesn't need to know. Jay has a family of his own, parents who love him, his own secure set-up. And yet again, I wish Mum was here, so I could say to her, I know you shielded us from the truth because it would have hurt us, and how much it must have cost you, and I am grateful. We all should be.

After lunch, we walk to the Central line Tube together. Jay is going into Soho to pick something up from his office before meeting his friends, and I feel like a wander, so I say I'll come with him. The daffodils are out in the square and the sky is blue. Finally, it feels as if spring might be on the way. The winter has been too long.

We walk to Liverpool Street. Jay is texting his buddies, arranging some complicated plan for this evening involving a club somewhere in Hackney, with drinks at some speakeasy beforehand. When we get to King's Cross, Jay shakes his phone, waiting to get reception as we walk through the cavernous station to change lines. The big, echoing corridors are full of people racing for trains, hurrying onwards, going back home. The strip lighting is harsh; I blink to try and see straight, thoughts crowding my head.

"Man, what's up with Samir and Joey tonight?" he says in exasperation, staring at his phone. "No one's around, this is shit."

"Hey, Jay," I say suddenly. "I'm going to get off here, OK?"

"What?" he says.

"I'm going to go and see Guy."

"Who? Oh, the Bowler Hat's Guy. Why?"

"Just—want to talk to him," I say. "I think he might help with some stuff."

"Like what?"

"He—it's just stuff about Granny's foundation," I amend lamely. "We're on the committee. Thought I'd do it while I'm in the area."

"He still hasn't called you back? Haven't you been trying him all week?"

I nod. "I won't be long. See you laters."

Jay already has his phone out, texting. "Sure. Laters, yeah?"

I love Jay when he's gearing up to be an East London wide boy with his brothers out for a night on the town. I keep expecting him to click his fingers together and shout, "Wicked, innit!" It's funny how he's so organized, sorted even, but still such a little boy in so many ways, and I find it endearing, whereas with Oli I came to find it disturbing. Perhaps it's because he really doesn't know he's doing it. Whereas I felt Oli had read too many lads' mags articles about how to behave like a child and get away with it.

I feel a curious lightening of my mood as I get off the bus on Upper Street a few minutes later. It's a nice late afternoon, the clocks have gone back and people are still out shopping. I head down Cross Street, walking with purpose.

When I get to Guy Leighton Antiques I stop. The blinds are down and there's a CLOSED sign hanging on the door. I peer through the glass; the shop is in darkness, but there's a light shining in the back room. I rap firmly on the door, rattling it slightly so the old bell jangles faintly.

After a few seconds, Guy appears, blinking. I watch him as he shuffles casually towards the door, trying to picture the young, charming, kind man Cecily fell in love with, the one so vividly alive in the diary. He's fiddling with his glasses, on the chain round his neck. He doesn't look up as he unbolts the door, and then he opens it.

"I'm afraid we're closed today—" he begins. "Oh."

He stares at me. His face is paler than ever.

"Sorry to drop by unannounced," I begin. "It's just I've been try-ing to get hold of you—"

His hands are still on the half-shut door. He opens it a little wider. "Natasha," he says. His eyes do not leave my face and I remember him saying I looked like Cecily. I feel uncomfortable.

"I wondered if we could talk," I say.

Guy is clenching the door and his knuckles are white. "Yes—yes . . ." He looks flustered. Um—so what do you want?"

The Guy I know (admittedly, not well) is normally calm, wryly amused, in control. This man is like a stranger to me.

"I don't want to disturb you," I say, thinking perhaps he was in the middle of something, or he's just woken up and is confused after a nap. "It's just—I read Cecily's diary, you said to call you when I had." I try to keep the desperation out of my voice. How could he have forgotten? "I've been trying to call you—and Mum—she's gone away."

"I know. She came to see me before she went."

"She came to see you?" I try to ignore the fact that my mother seems to be quite happy to contact Guy all the time over me. Here, take the diary. Here, I'm going away. I shift on my feet. "I didn't know what was in it—"

"I know," Guy says. "I know. It's terrible." But he doesn't move. His jaw is tight; his eyes are cold.

I swallow, because I think I am about to cry again, and I don't know why. Why's he being so . . . strange? "Can—can I come in? The thing is . . . I can't really talk to anyone else about it, you see—"

Then Guy holds up his hand. "I'm sorry," he says. "No, I can't. I can't do this."

"Do what?"

"This." He points at me. "It's—I'm so sorry. It's just too much. I should have realized. This family . . . It's—I'm not ready. I'm sorry. Go away, Natasha. I'm sorry."

And as I am standing in the doorway staring at him in astonishment, he gently closes the door in my face.

Forty-two

On this occasion, I leave time for the train. I am there so early, in fact, that I can walk the length of the magnificent interior of Paddington station, admiring the soaring Victorian poles of steel, the war memorial, the endless hustle and bustle on this beautiful spring morning. A brisk April shower has cleared and it is warm, sunshine flooding the station with yellow morning light. I even have time to get a bacon roll from the Cornish Pasty Company, which I used to go to religiously when I was younger, convinced that a pasty from there would bring me closer to Summercove. I eat it, hovering nervously in front of the ticket barrier, not wanting to spoil my smart new dress, and too scared to get on the train. Carriage G, seat 18.

Louisa sent the tickets to me last Friday with a note.

Have taken the liberty of booking our tickets there and back; no payment is necessary as this comes out of the foundation's budget. Please find yours enclosed. Look forward to what I am sure will be a memorable and moving day. Love from Louisa x

She sent it to Jay's address too, she knew somehow, with her organized ways, that I'd moved there. That's Louisa all over: always serving others, efficient, brisk, but still affectionate. I think back to the Louisa in the diary, the leggy blonde knockout still in thrall to her good-looking boyfriend. I sigh and ball my paper bag into my fist. Ten minutes till the train goes, and no sign of anyone. Perhaps they're all already there, waiting for me. I square my shoulders and open the carriage door.

I'm the first. The carriage is warm like the station and I'm hot in my coat, I can feel myself perspiring. I'm tired still from the previous night, and I just want to close my eyes and sleep. I put my overnight bag on the rack above and sit down in my seat at the table, looking around me. Both tables are all booked, the little tickets sticking out of the seats proclaiming the legend "London Paddington to Penzance."

It is coming up for two months since I was last on this train, going down to Granny's funeral. So much has changed since then that it feels like a lifetime ago, someone else's life, even. I take a sip of my weak, gray-colored coffee.

The automatic doors open with a whoosh and my head snaps up, almost of its own accord. The fact that I don't know who to expect gives the proceedings an unreal, almost filmic air of excitement. And there, bustling down the corridor, is Louisa. I stand up, squint at her, the way I did when I first saw Guy again, trying to imagine her that summer.

"Hello, Natasha dear," she says. She pats my cheek and then kisses it. I had forgotten how nice she smells. "Lovely to see you." She turns. "Frank, darling? Oh, where's he gone? Frank? I wanted him to—there he is!" she finishes, with relief.

And the doors open again to reveal the Bowler Hat, smart in a dark gray suit. He picks his way towards the table cautiously, as if afraid his height will cause him to knock out a light fitting. "Hello, Natasha," he says warmly. He puts his hand on my shoulder. "Good to see you." He kisses me too.

My blood turns cold at his touch. It's over two weeks since I first read the rest of Cecily's diary, and I haven't been able to face rereading it. I just can't. But words and phrases are burnt into my mind. *Rather pleased with himself, like a politician.* I look down to see its dull red color in my bag, bound loosely with an elastic band, bulging from the extra pages folded up inside. I want to take it out and show it to him, shatter his smug, self-satisfied veneer, make him crawl on his knees to my mother, to Arvind, to his brother, to me and all my family, for forgiveness. Especially to his wife.

But of course she doesn't know, he has never told her the truth, no one has. It's so strange, looking at him, noticing for the first time the liver spots freckling his pale, smooth cheekbones, the papery thin skin puckering around his eyes. I wonder what Cecily would say, if she could see him now. I stare at him.

Louisa sits down at the other table. "Frank, we're here," she says, patting his seat.

"Oh, right," he says dully. I notice it now, it's as if she's his mother and he's a child. I don't think they realize they're like this.

"I got some croissants in Marks yesterday in case we're hungry, Natasha, do you want one?"

"No, thanks," I say. "I'm fine."

"Are you sure?" She stares at me. "It's a long journey. You look rather tired."

"I am tired," I say. "I had a long night yesterday."

"Single girl, out partying!" she says, with an attempt at jollity, but she's trying too hard and her voice sounds a bit hysterical, as though she's sorry for me. "Good for you! Was it that?"

"Something like that," I say. I can't bear to go into it with Louisa. The truth is I just want to be off, for this day to be under way, so that last night can begin to be a dim and distant memory. Last night, and today. Once today's over, then the future can begin.

"Oh, Natasha. You're wearing that lovely ring." Louisa smiles, her eyes glistening. "It was Franty's, you know. She gave it to Cecily, the day she . . . the very day she died. Poor Aunt Frances."

I glance at the Bowler Hat but he doesn't betray any flicker of emotion. Does he feel guilt at all? Or is he just used to this, every day? It occurs to me that perhaps he must be.

Louisa says, "It is lovely. How sweet of you to wear it. Where did you get it from?" She asks this without rancor.

"Arvind gave it to me," I say. "So I felt I ought to wear it today."

"Well," she says, looking at the Bowler Hat and then at the croissants. "It's lovely that you are."

I want to agree.

* * *

I went back to the studio last night, to get it. I wish I hadn't, in a way. I wouldn't be feeling like this today if I had.

I'd left, about six-thirty, to go and meet Cathy and Jay for a drink, and halfway down towards the Whitechapel Road I'd remembered and turned back, with an oath. Work is really busy this week which is great, but I wasn't anxious to spend any more time in the studio where I'd been since eight that morning.

I've been working that out, these last few weeks. And "Cecily's Necklace," as I've called it, the charm necklace modeled on the ring and those charms I designed, has been reordered twice now, by Emilia's Sister and by PipnReb, and another shop, this time on Cheshire Street, has asked if they can stock me—*they* called *me*, not the other way round, which is amazing. Most amazing of all, someone claiming to be from Liberty came to the stall and bought a whole load of stuff on Sunday. It was only my first week there—I'm still in shock. It's the necklace with Cecily's ring, they all want it. It's like a sort of good-luck talisman.

So I was a little reluctant, therefore, to revisit the studio where Maya and I, the scary design intern I've hired, had been slaving away all day putting the necklaces together, but I knew I'd regret it if I didn't. Today is important, and I wanted to wear Cecily's ring for it.

Back at the studio, the writers' collective was having one of their readings in the basement, which normally meant a piss-up starting at about five; I'd managed to avoid it, but it was clearly still going on, and I could hear people chatting, laughing raucously, as I walked past. I didn't turn the light on when I got to my studio; it was still just light outside, and I dashed in to pluck the ring off the counter where I'd left it. As I was locking up again, I heard a noise down the corridor and looked down to see Ben coming out of his studio with Jamie, the Sophie-Dahl-like receptionist. They can't have realized I was there.

She leaned against the railing and he came forwards and kissed her, his hands on her face, her long, beautiful corn-colored hair glimmering slightly in the evening light. Two plastic cups, their clear sides stained with cheap red wine, were stacked at their feet.

I always knew Ben had a crush on her, even though he denied it. He was fascinated by Jamie's love life, we were always discussing it— even that night in the pub right before we kissed. Now I know why, I said to myself.

Luckily I didn't have to pass them to get down the stairs, they're at my end of the corridor. I just pretended not to have seen them and walked off. I didn't want to embarrass Ben. I didn't want to be embarrassed, is more likely the truth. But I *was* embarrassed. I burned hot at the thought of it, as I scurried away; why?

The last time Oli and I had sex, that awful, deadening Friday morning, we didn't kiss. I let him fuck me, and we didn't kiss once. So Ben is the last person I kissed, I guess, and that thought makes me sad for all sorts of reasons, most of all shame that I wanted him to mix himself up with me and my messy life. I think about him and Jamie together, and I nod. Yes, it makes sense. Of course it does. And I feel glad that, every time I've thought about him since, about how good that kiss was, about his face, his eyes, his friendship towards me, how great it felt to be in his arms . . . I feel glad that I pushed it away, never let myself give in to it. It just means it's easier now.

So as I hurried back down Brick Lane towards the pub, I tried not to feel sad, even though I couldn't help it. But, as I reasoned to myself, one hand on Cecily's necklace, it's only natural. I think I persuaded myself into love with Oli. We both did. I should be careful about doing the same again. Next time, it'll be forever. I've got to get next time right. Cecily didn't have a next time. I do.

My mind is drifting towards the latter stage of the evening, when I am recalled to the present, to the railway carriage, to the Bowler Hat, picking daintily over the croissant his wife has given him, long fingers taking up pastry flakes and carefully eating them. I look away, suddenly nauseated.

"The train leaves in five minutes," Louisa says, looking out of the window anxiously. "Where *is* your mother, Natasha? She can't miss this train, it'll be a disaster. She's making the speech!"

She looks at me slightly accusingly, but I remain calm. Before all this, I would have felt guilt on Mum's behalf. Now I don't. If I was her I wouldn't want to turn up at all, frankly. I don't even know if she's back—if she's ever coming back. I can see why she likes being away, now.

Once again, my head shoots up as the doors open again. But it's no one I know, a vast mum dragging two small children with her. She plonks them into the seat behind us, puffing at the exertion, her face stained red. I look at the clock. 7:26 a.m. My mind drifts again.

"What time is it?"

Cathy had asked me this question yesterday evening. "Nearly eight," I'd replied.

"Exactly. So you can't just run off. It's been an hour! I thought we'd meet Jay and check out Needoo. You know, the new Tayyabs. I've not been before."

"I'm sorry," I'd said, swinging my bag over my shoulder and standing up. "I've got to get out of here. . . . Sorry, Cathy."

Dead Dog Tom's was loud, crowded, hot, full of girls much younger than me. It's new and I'd been meaning to go for a while. But the moment I arrived, I knew it was a mistake. Not my kind of place at all. Asymmetric haircuts and big black glasses are one thing, but this was like an episode of *The Hills*, everyone tanned with perfect teeth, endless legs and beautiful hair—and that was just the guys. Cathy had just battled back from the bar with our second drink when I'd looked up and seen it.

"Why?" Cathy's face was a picture of childish annoyance, like a little girl who's been told she can't go to the zoo. She pouted. "I want to tell you about our weekend away! I think he's taking me to Southwold, we're staying next to Benjamin Britten's house, can you believe it?"

I touched her shoulder. "Cathy—it's Oli," I said. "Look—over there. He's—I'm sorry. I just, I just want to get out of here."

Open-mouthed, Cathy turned. She looked over to where I was staring.

There, his elbows on the bar, hands waggling intently as he talked fast and low, was Oli. He was saying something to a girl with her back to us. She had blonde hair, and was wearing a high-waisted tulip skirt, a puff-sleeved little shirt and tights with a black seam, and she was nodding at him.

"Oh, my God," Cathy said. "It's Oli! Bastard."

As if by some kind of magic alchemy the music stopped and the thunderous chatter abated for a few seconds, the way there is suddenly a strange lull in a noisy bar. Cathy's voice echoed around our corner, so loudly that Oli looked up and saw us.

Pushing himself off the bar, Oli stood up straight. He raised his hand as if in greeting and then, obviously thinking better of it, walked towards us, turning the handwave into a ruffle through his thick dark hair, which stuck up on end even more as a result.

"Cathy," he said, kissing her cheek. "Hi."

"Hi," Cathy replied, leaning up on tiptoe to kiss him. "Look, I'll—"

"I was just going," I said to him. "Honestly."

"I'll see you outside," said Cathy, vanishing discreetly towards the Ladies.

We stood on the pavement on Whitechapel Road. It was still light.

"Look, I'm sorry I haven't called," Oli said. He looked much younger. Dressed much younger, in a cardigan, jeans, sneakers. I held up my hand.

"No, it's fine. I haven't either. You got my email, about you maybe moving back into the flat, though?"

"Yeah," he said. "Yeah. It's a good idea. If you're sure?"

"Definitely," I said. "I don't want to go back there, honestly. How—how're Jason and Lucy? You still staying with them?"

A tiny hesitation. "Yep. They're well. You still liking Jay's?"

"Yeah," I said, slinging my bag over my shoulder. "Went back to the flat the other day to get some stuff, saw you'd been back too."

"Yeah, me too," Oli said. "Needed a few more things. I guess we should . . ."

"Yes, I guess we should," I said, not knowing quite what the next stage is with this. Instruct the divorce lawyer, say I'm going through with it? Proof of adultery, like in a creaky old thirties farce?

"Anyway," Oli said. "How've you been?"

"I'm OK," I said. "How about you?"

It was as if we finally had something in common we could talk about. The breakdown of our marriage and how we're both dealing with it.

"OK too," Oli said. "Up and down, you know. I miss . . ." He trailed off. "I don't know what I miss. I miss you, Natasha. I do miss us, being at our flat. I miss . . ." He scratched his head. "Ugh. It's— yeah, it's weird. Weird to think I failed. We failed."

I loved this Oli, the eager, kind person I fell in love with. I smiled at him. "I know. I think that's what I miss. What I wanted it to be."

He nodded, and our eyes met, as though we understood each other. He took my hand.

"Yes," he said. "I suppose there's no point in bullshitting any- more, you guessed it. That's Chloe in there. It's her friend's birthday drinks."

He was looking into my eyes, with such sincerity that it took me a moment to reconcile what he was saying with how he was saying it. And when I did I stepped back, gave a short laugh.

"Oh, wow," I said. "Right then."

"It's going really well again," Oli said. "That's why—hey, that's why I feel I have to be straight with you."

There was a roar of noise as the door opened and Cathy appeared next to us on the pavement. "So . . . ?" she said, looking from one to the other. "We off then?"

"Yes," I said. I turned to Oli. "I'll be in touch about the loan. I owe you—"

"Hey, Natasha, I mean it. Don't worry about that for the mo- ment," he said, nodding. "After everything, it's fine, it really is. I owe you, not the other way round. Plus, I know you need some time to get on your feet again."

I thought of the new orders I've had lately, of me skipping up

Brick Lane to drop the latest consignments off at various shops, of the meeting with the woman from Liberty. . . . I smiled at him.

"Not anymore. Honestly." I held out my hand. "Thanks," I said, looking into his deep blue eyes one more time. "Thanks, Oli. Have a—"

I wanted to say have a nice life. But it sounds bitchy, sarcastic, and in that moment, I really meant it. I did want him to have a nice life.

"Have a great evening," I said instead, and Cathy and I went off down the street together, and the rest of the night was thankfully without incident. But I didn't sleep when I got back, not a wink. I wouldn't have asked for either of those encounters, you know. But that's life.

7:29 a.m., and there's a sudden commotion, as the last people are flooding onto the train. I rub my eyes, trying to put last night out of my mind, and what happens next. This is what happens next, I tell myself, as the doors open again, one last time, and there's Guy. He doesn't look ruffled, like someone who's run to catch the train. He looks as if he's been casually waiting till the last minute, to avoid having to spend any extra time with us, I think to myself.

"Guy!" Louisa squeaks. "Thank God! We'd nearly given up on you! Miranda's going to miss it, I'm afraid!"

"I'm sure she won't," he says, putting his battered leather holdall next to my overnight bag. "Hello, Natasha."

"Hi," I say.

"Hello—hi, Frank," he says.

"Good to see you, Guy," Frank says, not really looking up from the *Telegraph*.

Guy kisses Louisa. "Hello, old girl," he says. "You look wonderful. Thanks for booking these. Sorry I'm late. I was being rather stupid."

"You're here now," says Louisa, practically weeping with relief. The train moves off, so slowly at first that I'm not sure whether it's moving or the platform is. "Oh, dear," she exclaims. "Miranda—she is awful—"

The doors burst open, and Mum rushes through. "My God!" she cries. "My God. These damned—this stupid Tube! I left Hammersmith over an hour ago! Would you believe it!"

She pulls strands of hair, which have glued themselves to her lip gloss, away from her face. She smiles brightly at all of us. Her pupils are dilated, her skin lightly tanned and perfectly clear. She could be my sister, not Cecily's. I stare at her, transfixed all over again by her. "Hello! Well, here we are. Off for a lovely day back at the old homestead," she says, sliding into the seat next to Guy, so she and I are sitting beside each other, only the passageway in between us.

"Hi, Guy," she says brightly.

He doesn't even look at her. Even in the midst of all this, alarm bells ring yet again; there's something there. Something else she's not telling us. What did she do to him to make him like this? "Yes," he says.

The train draws out of the station, and the early-morning sun hits my eyes. I squint. "Hi, Mum," I say, and I'm annoyed to hear my voice shaking.

She turns away from Guy and puts her hand on my leg, across the divide. "It's going to be OK," my mother says. "Promise."

Forty-three

Last time I was going to Cornwall, it seemed as if winter would never end. This time, it is glorious. We speed out of London and the trees are thick with new buds, sprouting like green fingers. There are even a few lambs in the fields, and white blossom smothering the black hawthorn branches. The countryside through the southernmost Somerset Levels is bright green, with a kind of alertness to it, as if everything is quivering with new life.

I stare out of the window watching the countryside unfold, coming awake again. I am the sole occupant of my table, as it turns out, but at the next table an uneasy silence reigns. The Bowler Hat reads the paper, Guy hunches over, writing notes on an auction catalog, and Louisa puts her reading glasses on and shuffles through a file of papers on the launch of the foundation. My mother is sitting upright, her eyes closed, but I know she's not asleep.

Somewhere around Glastonbury, Louisa puts her pen down. "Should we talk about what's going to happen?" she says. "I mean, I've deliberately kept this easy to manage, and of course Didier is really responsible for it all—"

"Didier?" I ask.

"Didier du Vallon," Louisa says. "He was Franty's—he was your grandmother's dealer."

"Darling Didier," Mum murmurs, her eyes still closed.

Louisa ignores this, and shuffles the papers again. I can see she is flustered. "Of course, it's primarily the launch of the foundation at the house today, of course." She blushes at her repetition and it is strange to see her so unsure of herself. Normally she's good at being in charge: organizing trips to the beach, scooting people into cars, sorting out the house, the funeral. "There will be a few art critics there, a few local papers, some local friends, you know."

"No national papers?" Mum opens her eyes. "I would have thought—"

"It's a six-hour journey to Summercove from London," Louisa says firmly. "And this isn't the retrospective we're announcing, anyway. You know that. It's too soon after Frances's death to have organized a proper exhibition: this is just a taster, the paintings Didier and the family had, and so forth. . . . That'll be in London, in 2011. Won't it?"

She looks at Mum for confirmation of this. Mum shrugs. "I suppose so," she says grandly. "Archie and I need to discuss it."

"Wonderful," Louisa says, slightly thin-lipped. "So, the schedule is as follows: One o'clock, arrive at Penzance, where Frank and I will pick up our hire car and go to Summercove—" She turns to Mum. "Miranda, Archie is picking you up, and you'll both go and collect Arvind from Lamorna House. OK?"

"Mm," says my mother. I really can't see how she can find fault with this. She's being incredibly childish. Guy is still pretending to make the odd note here and there but I know he's taking it all in.

"Great," I interject, smiling at Louisa with my usual "she's not normally like this!" smile, which won't work with my mother's own cousin of course, but sometimes helps. "Then kick-off is at—?"

"There are drinks, and then your mother makes her speech at three-thirty," says Louisa. "Just welcoming everyone, explaining the aims of the foundation as set out by her parents, and talking a bit about Aunt Frances."

Mum points to her bag. "Oh, yes," she says. "My moment in the spotlight."

Guy does look up then. He stares thoughtfully at her, then flicks a glance at me. I suddenly feel rather sick, as if the three of us are bound into this thing together.

* * *

When we pull in to Penzance a few hours later, my stomach is grumbling, so close to lunchtime. It is a long journey. There are fresh, frothing waves bouncing on the blue sea, St. Michael's Mount is glowing in a windy sunlit bay, and when we step off the train a warm wind—not tropical, but not icy—nearly knocks me sideways. I forget how windy it can be down here. When I was little, a gust of wind whipped my ice-cream out of my hand and into the sea at Sennen Cove, and I was so shocked I nearly fell in after it.

We make a strange band, the five of us, emerging out of the station. We are polite to each other but the oddness of the situation increases, as though we are inexorably tumbling towards the heart of something, the nearer we get to Summercove. The closest way I can think of to describe it is on Christmas Day, when you're all standing around in your best clothes, rather awkwardly waiting for something else to happen and it's a Thursday, and you suddenly remember that and think how odd it is. The Bowler Hat strides off to the car-hire place, and Guy goes with him. He has barely spoken a word the whole trip. I glance at my mother.

"When did you get back then, Mum?"

"Oh, late last night," she says. "We got delayed, a problem with some of the stuff we'd bought in a market in Fez. Fez is wonderful, darling, you must go there." Suddenly her face lights up. "There's Archie!"

I want to say, I don't bloody care about bloody Fez! What the hell are you talking about! I want to know about the diary, about you, about what you think of all of this! Jesus! H.! Christ!

But Louisa is with us and Archie is approaching, so I just say, "Hm, how interesting. Mum, can we talk later, please?"

She pretends not to hear. "Archie, darling!" She hugs him.

"Mum—" I say loudly. "You've been away for two weeks and there's a lot we need to discuss. You know there is. I said, can we talk, please."

Louisa looks over at this, and even I am surprised at the tone in my voice.

"Yes, yes," Mum says, over Archie's shoulder, and she steps back. "Yes, yes, yes."

She smiles and Archie looks at me, instantly defensive of anyone challenging his sister. They are side by side, the gray sea turning behind them, and for a second they are the people in Cecily's diary, and I can't help staring at them. They are so eerily similar, their green eyes flashing, their dark hair shining, the same height, the same expression. I can see now, what has kept them so close all these years, closer than any romantic relationship. It's Mum's face as she sees him approach. How good it is, I think guiltily, that she has had one person in her life with whom she can completely be herself, Archie too: he's never as stiff and awkward around her.

"Hello, Natasha. We'll see you at Summercove," Archie says loudly to the others—the Bowler Hat and Guy are walking back towards us, the former clutching a set of car keys in his hand. "We're off to pick up Dad."

"Byee!" Louisa says. "Don't be—" she begins, and then stops herself. "See you soon!" The Bowler Hat raises a hand in farewell. Guy gets in after him.

Just like February, I climb into Archie's car.

"Where is this place?" Mum says in her normal voice, the one she uses when she's with Archie and with me.

"Lamorna House? Just along the Western Promenade, before you turn off for Newlyn," Archie says. "He's doing well. I saw him yesterday. I brought him some food Sameena made. Lamb chops and butter chicken. He says it reminded him of home."

He stops outside a palm-tree-fronted esplanade, very English Riviera. He turns off the ignition and fiddles with his cufflinks.

"Listen," he says, turning to his sister and then to me. "He's fine, but I think he's a bit confused about things. Perfectly natural, and all that."

"About what kind of things?" Mum asks. "He never makes any sense anyway." She's not a great sentimentalist, my mother.

"You'll see." Archie gets out of the car and we follow suit. "We're not staying, someone should have got him ready, I told them when I came yesterday."

It's so strange, walking up the neat path and into the overheated home. There are large safety notices everywhere, bright signs about breakfast and afternoon activities, and paintings of vases of flowers. There are a couple of residents in the hall, two extremely frail old ladies pushing walkers, both clad in baby-pink knitted bed jackets, and one of them looks up and stares at my mother and Archie as we walk in.

"More foreigners," she says, with a baleful stare. "Why don't you go back to where you came from?"

Mum puts a hand on Archie's arm. "We're just looking for our dad," she says sweetly. "What a lovely jacket that is that you have on."

"I bet I know which one *he* is," says the old lady. "Through there."

"Charming," Mum mutters under her breath, looking down at the old woman. "Have a lovely day, won't you?"

"Stupid bi—" Archie starts shaking his head. He's flustered. "She can't talk to us like that. To Dad like that. I'm going to make sure she's not talking to Dad like that. Where is the bloody nurse, any-way?"

"I'm sure Dad wouldn't notice if she came back with a huge sign saying 'GO HOME' on it," Mum says. "Archie, she's old and mad." She turns back to the old lady. "We're from here like you are, by the way, madam," she says. "Not that it matters, but it's not very nice of you, to greet people like that. Bye."

The old lady, who is not as confused as one might think, purses her lips at this. I smile at my mother, impressed, as Archie pushes open a swing door into the conservatory, and we troop in. A group of men and women is grouped around the TV, the sun streaming in through the glass roof. There is a glare on the TV which means you can't see the screen. It is very hot. There is absolutely nothing here that makes me think of Arvind. It's the diametric opposite of him, in every way.

"There he is," Mum says, and her voice drops several octaves.

"Dad, hello, darling Dad." She swoops down on Arvind, who is sitting motionless in a wheelchair, a blanket over his legs. There is a photo album on his lap.

"Hello, Father," says Archie loudly. "It's Miranda and Archie, come to pick you up for the ceremony at Summercove."

Arvind doesn't move. Fear squeezes at my heart.

"And me," I add. I step forwards and kiss him. "Hi, Arvind."

In a clear voice, but still not moving, he says, "Cecily."

"Father, *no,*" Archie says, as if Arvind is five years old and has just tried to steal some sweets. "It's Natasha." He says this very loudly. I can feel perspiration breaking out over my body. "Look," he says to Mum. "They should have got him ready. I'll go and find someone, tell them we're taking him. Stay with him." He is shaking his head, and not even looking at Arvind.

"Ah yes, Cecily," Arvind says.

The sun is shining right onto us. I stare at him. I look down at the photo album. "Is that her?" I say.

It's a black-and-white photo of a girl leaning against a woman who has her arm around her. The girl is a teenager, long gangly legs, shorts, a shirt, and a big smile. She has a longish fringe, which falls into her eyes. Her face is heart-shaped. The woman hugging her is Granny.

"It's her," says Arvind. Mum is standing stock-still, staring at the photo.

"Yes, it is," she says. "I'd forgotten that. That's the day we got home from school."

It's deathly quiet in the hot room and we are the only ones speaking.

"I'm going to go and find Archie," Mum says. She leaves before I can look at her, tossing her hair out of her face, and she is gone, in an instant. I turn back to Arvind.

"How are you?" I say. "How are you settling in?"

"Hm."

"It seems nice here," I say, lying. There is a slight stirring in the background, as one of the TV watchers shifts slowly in her chair.

"Do you like cold porridge in the mornings?" Arvind asks.

"No."

"Neither do I. That is how I am settling in."

I don't know if this is an actual issue or not, as so often with Arvind. "Can't you have cereal?" I suggest, thinking what an Arvind-style conversation this is. I stare down at the photo again, greedily. I saw the sketch in Arvind's room, but I've never really seen her before. There were never any photos out at Summercove, apart from the one I saw Granny with, all those years ago. Paintings and sketches, yes. Family photos, no.

"Cereal does not agree with my digestion. But when you get to ninety, not much does," Arvind says, interrupting my train of thought. "To be fair to cereal."

"But you don't miss Summercove?" I instantly berate myself. What a stupid question, what a stupid thing to say, how could he not miss it, here in this overheated white-and-yellow prison smelling of antiseptic?

"No. I don't miss it," he says, to my surprise. "I am very happy here in most ways. As I say, the porridge, the cereal—these are things which need to be satisfactorily addressed. . . ." He trails off. "But up here—" he taps his head—"I have everything I need up here. Have you heard of a memory palace?"

"Sort of," I say. "You train your brain to remember things."

"That is almost it," he says. He closes his eyes. "You build a palace of memories. Each room in Summercove is in my head, filled with things I want to hold on to. I am not in the house anymore. It is in me.

"That's all I need. My old pupils write to me, I read books—thank God my eyesight is still good. I have my memories." He gently closes the photo album. "I can picture my bedroom in Lahore. I can see the Shalimar Gardens." He is staring out to sea. "The boat I took, from India to England, seventy years ago. I can remember my cabin. It had a stripe, painted green, across the wall. I remember the books I had on my trip, can see them on that little shelf, by the porthole—Boethius, John Ruskin, and Bertrand Russell you know, excellent fellow. And I remember Cecily. So." He puts his hands together. "Last time I saw you, I gave you the first pages of my daughter's diary. Tell me, did you find the rest of it, hm? Did you read it?"

I don't know how to answer. "Yes—yes," I say, as if admitting to something shameful. "Mum had it."

He nods. "I thought as much. I found the pages in my room, you see, after she'd taken me into the studio." He coughs, spluttering a little. "I thought she must have spotted it while we were in there. Put it away for herself. Dropped the first pages, not realized." He stops. "Yes, so she has it."

"I'm—sorry about all of it, Arvind." I don't know what to say. "It must be awful—awful for you."

"I haven't read it," he says simply. I flinch with surprise.

"What?"

"I know what's in it," he says. He smiles. "Perhaps I don't want to read it. Sometimes it's best to shut out the real world, you see." He taps his forehead again gently. "In the memory palace, I can choose what rooms to go into, you see."

My mother calls out to us from the doorway. "Ready?" she says, shattering the peace of the room. I turn, and her eyes are red.

"Ah." I push Arvind in his wheelchair towards the door. He waves a polite goodbye to his motionless fellow-residents. "The outsiders are outside. And it is written. Time for us to go back to Summercove once more."

Forty-four

Granny loved spring. She said spring made her happy. She hated autumn most of all, couldn't ever understand why people found it poetic and romantic. She said it was depressing, the sign that life was over. Spring, she always said, was why we stuck around, to see that life had survived during the long winter months. As we turn into the little lane that leads to Summercove and then on to the sea, I can see why. The branches are bursting with bright green new life. White apple blossom blooms in the orchard next to the house.

I think of her, starting another spring here, year after year, and then watching the summer fade away into autumn, the long winter nights, with nothing to do, nothing to occupy her, Arvind in his study, her studio locked away, only memories of what she did, what happened, and I start to understand a little better.

We roll almost silently down the lane in Archie's gleaming silver and red 4x4, so appropriate for Ealing, so out of place here, where it actually helps on the narrow, sometimes treacherous roads. He turns the engine off and he, Mum, and I look nervously up at the house, as if expecting some sign. Arvind is still staring straight ahead.

"They've done a good job, Didier's gang," Archie says to Mum, in the seat next to me. "Hope you'll think so. I think so." Why does he always want her approval? She nods.

"Good. I hope there isn't too much mess. You told him it goes on the market on Monday, didn't you? They have to have all their shit cleared out of here by then."

Archie nods, and I realize how glad they will be to see the back of the place, in some respects. How sad that is. "Agent says it'll go really fast," he says. "We spoke a lot while you were away. He says the price is absolutely realistic. And we should have some . . . left over."

"Really?" Mum says, as if she's only vaguely interested, but I see her hands tightening in her lap, clutching the sheaf of notes for her speech.

"Oh, yeah." Archie pulls the keys out of the ignition and turns to his father, as if remembering he's there. "Come on, Father. We're here now. Let's go inside."

It's Arvind's bloody house, I want to say to them. He's still here! Stop acting like that money's yours. I want to knock their heads together, and then I think, He doesn't care. He doesn't care and that's always been part of the problem.

It is strange to stand outside Summercove, looking up at the windows, with the memory of Cecily's diary still so clear. It hasn't changed much in all those years, either, it's not that kind of house, and so it is easy to imagine her, sitting at our room at the top, peering out of the window, dancing across the lawn towards the gazebo which stands at the edge of the garden, leaning against that wall there to have her picture taken. I clutch my bag, with the diary in it. It is now cloudy and the wind is still vicious, whipping itself against my hands and face.

We go inside, Archie pushing Arvind. The reception starts soonish. There are people already here, chattering, a few out in the garden, looking out to sea, sitting in the gazebo, enjoying the beautiful weather. I can hear Louisa in the kitchen, directing the caterers. We go into the long, bright sitting room, and I breathe in sharply.

It is not Summercove, the home I loved more than any other. That place is gone. It's as if it never existed.

Everything has changed. Gone are the comfy sofas, worn-out chintz armchairs, the fireguard. Gone are the shelves lined with books on art, travel, photography, the battered old TV in the corner. Gone are the original fifties wooden sideboards, the bright curtains and cushions that were so in vogue when they bought the house which have lasted, most of them, all these years. All gone, the contents of the ground floor either moved upstairs for today or taken away to the local auction house or up to London.

The curtain rail, even, has been unscrewed. The French windows, where Jay and I would sit on rainy days betting on raindrops racing down the glass, are closed and the cushions on the window seats removed. The room is white, devoid of any furniture apart from dining chairs placed strategically around it, and Granny's paintings.

They line the walls of the big room, fifteen or so, and below some of them are sketches. Above the fireplace is *Summercove at Sunset*, 1963, and I stare at it, having never seen it in the flesh before.

"Where did they find this?" I ask.

"It was in her studio," Archie replies. "She never showed it to anyone. That, and—this was there too." He points, and I swivel round. Next to the door, almost hidden in its shadow, is an oil painting of a girl, a girl I know very well now. *Cecily Frowning*, 1963.

It's the painting. I wonder whether Arvind still has the sketch. I hope so. She is sitting on a stool, watching the painter, her expression watchful yet slightly cross. She is wearing a pale blue cotton sundress, which sets off her dark hair and skin beautifully. One leg is tucked under the other, one hand holding the heel. She looks rather bored. I stand still and stare at it.

"My God," I say. "That's—it."

"I'm going to find Louisa," Archie says, looking at his watch, and he strides out. The door bangs behind him. We three are alone in the echoing room.

I turn to look at Mum. "She said she hated being painted, didn't she?"

"Absolutely." Mum nods. She narrows her eyes. "It's rather clever. The way Mummy got that absolutely right."

We stare at it together, neither acknowledging that we're talking about the diary.

"I wondered what happened to that painting," I said.

My mother moves closer towards it and peers. "Goodness," she says. "You do look so like her, Natasha."

"She does," says a voice beside us, and I remember Arvind is here too.

I do not move; I know that if I say the wrong thing, I could ruin everything. But I know now is the moment. This might be the only chance I get.

"Can I ask you something?" I don't use her name, or call her Mum, but she turns to me, slowly. "Why did you take the rest of the diary? Why didn't you tell anyone about it, about the truth? Why didn't you tell me?"

She looks at Arvind, then back at me. She folds her arms. "Oh, darling, it's complicated."

"I know it is," I persevere. I really want her to give me answers. She can't keep doing this. "Just tell me why though."

She shrugs, and looks at her father again. He nods. "Please, Miranda. Enlighten me." He gives a little gesture, as if to say, Go ahead.

"I knew Cec was writing a diary," she says, in a rush. Her fingers fiddle with the knotted tassels of her scarf. "All that summer. She wouldn't stop bloody going on about it. 'I'm putting you in my diary if you don't stop being so mean to me,' " Mum says, in a childish voice.

"Did you know about her and Guy? Is that why you sent the diary to him?" I wish it all felt as though it was falling into place, but it doesn't.

She blushes slowly. "I think I always knew, yes." She shakes her head. "It's not important, not at the moment. He had to have it though, I had to tell him. Anyway. I knew she'd written the diary so it had to be somewhere. I didn't think Mummy would throw it away. She wouldn't have done. Couldn't do it. So I had to find it. Because I knew—the day she died . . . she'd found out—about what she'd found out about—" Her eyes are burning into mine, imploringly. "I knew, you see."

"I know," I said. "I've read it, Mum."

"Well, we went for a walk. She says that. We were both upset—so tired. You have no idea what it was like. We had a row about what to do next. I said we should expose Mummy. Tell Daddy. She said absolutely not." She turns suddenly to Arvind. "Dad—oh, shit. I shouldn't have. . . ." She trails off, clamping her lips together. "Forget it."

"Please," Arvind says. "Don't protect me, my dear. I know what happened."

I must be imagining it, but it seems his tone is softer, kinder, for a moment, and the parent he could have been is apparent for a split second.

"You do?" Mum says. She runs her fingers along the mantelpiece, as if checking for dirt. "I never knew. Always, I thought I was the only one. And I couldn't tell. Look, look at us," she says, almost hysterically. She waves her arm round the empty white room. "Look at the—what this did to us, to our family. I—*Damn!* Damn her."

"Mum—" I go over to her, put my arm on her shoulder. "Don't." Someone drops something in the kitchen, I think it must be metal. It clatters loudly, recalling us to the present. I look at her. "What happened? Please tell me."

Mum glances at Arvind, and at me, and speaks softly, urgently.

"We fought. Not physically. I mean we shouted at each other. Oh, God. I—oh, she made me so angry! But I would never have hurt her. We were young, you know how sisters fight. We both had tempers, you know. . . . I wanted to tell Dad about Mummy." She looks again at Arvind and then carries on. "I—I wasn't getting on with her. I don't know if I ever did, really. I always felt she didn't like me." She smiles. "Always. What a strange thing to say about your mother. Isn't it?"

"Yes," I say. I look at her and wonder, quite calmly, whether she, my own mother, ever liked me. I don't know that she did. *The sins of the fathers*, Arvind said, and perhaps he's right. He knew.

"I wanted revenge, I suppose. Wanted to show her *I* was grown-up now, I could call the shots, all of that rubbish. She was always putting me down. And she had every right to, I wasn't—I wasn't—" She blinks, and two fat mascara-flecked tears roll slowly down her cheeks. "I wasn't a very nice person, back then. I was horrible to her that day. . . .

"Cecily said we could never tell. She got crosser and crosser. I did too. We were shouting at each other, at least I was shouting at her, she was just standing there at the top of the steps down to the beach, shaking her head. I think she didn't know what on earth to do. She was so young, you know. Fine time to lose your trust in the people you love most. She said I didn't know what love is, that I'd never know what it meant. I said she was just a silly little girl. And she smiled." Mum nods slowly. "I'm an idiot. I know why now. Hah! I know why. I can still see her face. She sort of stepped back, and—and . . ." Her voice cracks. "She just disappeared. She made this strange sound. 'Oh!' As if she was surprised. Annoyed. And then—she just . . . she just disappeared. . . ." Her shoulders heave, and she sobs.

"Oh, Mum," I say.

"I told them all this," she says, putting her hands in front of her face. "That she just stepped off and slipped, the stairs were dangerous." She looks up as though she wants my approval, there is the track of a tear on her cheek. "The police believed me. But somehow it never quite stuck with everyone else. I never knew why. Archie appeared immediately after it happened. Thank God. He ran down to the beach—he nearly slipped too." She stops and then she says, "Dad, someone should have done something about those steps a long time before."

Arvind says, "There, as in many other areas, we were deficient in our care of our children, Miranda." His thin old fingers tap his knees, worrying at the creases in his trousers. His face is terrible in its sadness.

She doesn't say anything immediately, and then she nods.

"All that time," she says. "It was so long ago, you know. And it's like everything's stood still since then."

"I think," Arvind says, "for your mother, it did."

I say softly, "How could you ever forgive Granny, Arvind? I mean—did you know?"

He is silent, for so long that I think perhaps he hasn't heard me.

"She had affairs, you know," he says. "Many of them. When we were first married, in London, before she had the children, afterwards. . . . She found marriage hard. Being a mother hard. We had no money, we were both trying to work as hard as we could. These days, I understand, it is perfectly fine to talk about nothing else. Then you couldn't, you know. Not a word. You had to be a contented wife and mother and that was that."

The old, black eyes are unblinking.

"She was glad when we moved down here at first, she said it was a fresh start, I think she hoped it'd stop her doing this. But she loved the danger. . . . I knew that about her. She didn't. She never really realized, and the risks she took got greater, and then . . ." his voice cracks. "And then Cecily died. And you know, she knew. She found her diary when she was clearing away her possessions. She read what Cecily, her own daughter, had to say about her mother's affair. She knew."

At the thought of my grandmother, a few days after Cecily's death, reading the diary where her own daughter finds out about her infidelity, I feel almost sick with pity, for her, for Cecily, for Arvind, for Mum. . . . For all of them.

"But I am glad Louisa has never known," Arvind says firmly. I look out of the French windows to see Louisa trotting across the lawn. "People make mistakes, terrible mistakes," he says. "But I loved Frances. I loved her. We understood each other. That's all that matters. That's why we stayed together, all these years. I understood what she'd done, and how she felt. I wasn't a perfect husband. A good father. My work always came first. It was easier, to lock yourself away in your own mind, you know?

"She understood what she'd done. We tried to be better people afterwards." He nods. "And some things are best left untouched. Left in the past."

Only if you learn to move on afterwards, I want to say. But you didn't, did you? None of you. And the ones who weren't involved spent their whole lives trying to make things better without knowing why, like Louisa, or going as far away from it all as possible and hardly ever coming back, like Jeremy. I look around the room, which is darkening now as the clouds out to sea scud over the sun. I don't recognize this place anymore.

The door opens, and I can hear the murmuring chatter that has been building all this time burst in on us, loud like a hive of bees. Louisa comes into the room.

"Miranda? Ready to face the music soon?" She looks at us. "OK?"

I see Mum taking in her out-of-breath cousin, in her slightly too-sheer white kaftan, red shining face, floral skirt, and fluffy blonde hair.

"Thanks, Louisa," Mum says, walking towards her. "Yes. I think we're ready. Aren't we?"

She looks at me and Arvind.

"Yes," I say. "We are."

Forty-five

Louisa has planned it all out, of course. The invited guests have been gathering outside, having coffee in what was the dining room, milling around the gardens, and now they all file into the sitting room until it is full. I identify people from the village, Didier and his wife, a few glamorous-looking men and women with the stamp of New Bond Street on them. Some stop to say hello to Arvind, sitting in his chair by the fireplace, and my mother next to him, flicking through her notes. She is pale, but seems calm. I am worried though.

When everyone is in, Louisa makes a loud "Shh" sound and the room falls silent. My mother steps forwards.

"Thank you for coming today," she says. "I am Miranda Kapoor, Frances Seymour's daughter." She pauses. "One of her daughters."

Someone shuffles in the crowd; a seagull cries outside. Then it is silent again.

"We are here to launch the Frances Seymour Foundation, which will support the work of young artists, and promote understanding and interest in all forms of art with young people today. I'll tell you more about this in a moment, but for now I'd like to talk to you a bit about my mother. Tell you about who she really was."

She looks down at her notes again and is silent. I bite my lip, nervous.

"You all know that Frances Seymour was one of the best-loved and most-respected artists of the postwar period. She found an instant rapport with the public, who loved her timeless, evocative, yet entirely modern paintings. I even have a statistic here from Tate Britain, which is that *A Day at the Beach,* one of her best-known

paintings, is the fifth most popular postcard in the gallery shop."
She smiles at this, and a little ripple goes through the crowd.

"What you don't know about her is who she really was, my
mother."

She pauses. I look around, past a couple of scribbling journalists,
at the members of my family. I see, with a jolt of shock, that Octavia
is here. I hadn't expected to see her and then I think about it and it
makes sense. Jay wouldn't come unless it was made clear to him he
had to. Octavia is that kind of person who has absolutely no reason
to be present, so of course she is here, standing next to her mother,
looking officious. She scowls impatiently at me, though that's actually her natural expression. Louisa is clasping her hands, her lips
moving. She is counting something in her head, and I wonder what
it is. The Bowler Hat is beside them, an air of quiet concentration
on his smooth features, Archie, hands in pockets, nodding as he
watches his sister. Arvind, as ever a mask of neutrality. And behind
me on the wall: Cecily frowning.

"Yes. Who she really was."

I stare at the painting, until I realize someone is watching me.
Guy. I meet his gaze, and again the voice of unease strikes up in my
head. He looks at me. He touches his hand to his heart, and then
switches his gaze back to my mother. I think of him staring at Cecily, in this very room, all those years ago, the two of them realizing
their feelings for each other, how scary it was, how wonderful. . . . I
can see her scrawling, black handwriting, flowering across the page,
the words so fresh and clear in my mind.

> Like electricity shooting through me, like I was alive, alive for the
> first time. I looked at him, & he looked at me. . . .

Mum is swallowing. She clears her throat. Stares at Louisa, at the
Bowler Hat. The silence is stretching, it's too long now, she needs to
say something. Don't, Mum. Please don't do it.

Next to me, an old, sweaty man in a pink checked shirt and ancient blazer, clutching a notebook, sighs under his breath. Still my mother waits.

I look at her imploringly, my hand on Cecily's necklace around my neck. Mum meets my gaze. Gives a little smile. And for the first time, I feel we understand each other, that we are the only ones who know what's going on.

"Frances Seymour was a difficult woman, but that is the territory with genius," she says. "She was beautiful, mercurial, enormous fun. She lit up a room. She opened her doors to anyone and everyone. You got quite used to coming back from school for the holidays and finding two Polish soldiers sleeping in your room, a penniless cellist and her son in the attic, and an ascetic priest with a long beard practicing the piano in the sitting room." There was a low laugh. "She was very understanding, as well. I remember when my brother and I were little, we said we wanted to run away and live in the woods. She came with us. She painted us huge Red Indian headdresses, and we camped out by the sea, ate sausages we'd cooked over the fire, and told ghost stories all night. When my father's book was launched, she had a special hardback edition bound just for him, with an engraving of Lahore, his home town, on the front." She pauses again. "And when my sister Cecily died . . ."

There's total silence in the room, and perhaps I'm imagining it, but a cloud of tension seems to hang, shimmering, over the assembled throng.

"She never painted after that." Mum clears her throat again. "She locked the door to her studio and didn't go back. Some asked why. If she felt guilt."

She looks straight at the Bowler Hat. I see Louisa turn to him, questioning. An arrow of pain shoots into my knotted stomach. *Don't do it, Mum. Please.*

"The truth is, she did feel guilt," Mum says.

Her head is bowed; her voice soft. I clutch my hands together so tightly it's painful.

"And," my mother says, "it's also true to say she shouldn't have. We can never know how much it cost her, to never paint again. It was her life. But she chose to give it up. She chose to punish herself that way. She thought she was responsible for my sister's death."

I stare at her.

"But she wasn't." For one second, Mum's eyes rest on me. And then she's talking again, her gaze sweeping the floor, the sense of occasion apparent again. "We will never know what she could have achieved if she'd carried on painting. We must just be glad we have what we do. And so in honor of my mother Frances, and my sister Cecily Kapoor, who never lived on to fulfill her potential, we launch this foundation. Louisa, my wonderful cousin who has organized today, and who is the backbone of our family, or Didier, my mother's very great dealer, have an information pack for all of you on the foundation and the upcoming exhibition at the Tate, which we hope will be in eighteen months' time. Thank you all for coming today. Thank you."

And she leans down and kisses her father, as the crowd applauds politely. Guy is nodding, clapping enthusiastically. Archie claps loudly, his hands raised high, smiling at his sister. She smiles back at him, and he nods. *Well done,* he mouths. Octavia is watching uncertainly, a frown puckering her forehead, and Louisa is looking at my mother, hugging a pile of brochures close to her body, with an expression on her face that I have never seen before.

Forty-six

The wind is still howling outside though it is sunny again. I talk to various people, old friends from the neighborhood, a couple of gallery owners who have shown Granny's work in the past, some of Mum's friends from Granny and Arvind's days in London. It's been a long, strange day. Archie has already said he will give us a lift back to Penzance to get the sleeper, Mum and I. The Leightons are driving back tomorrow. In happy contrast to my last visit to Summercove, this time it is work for which I need to be back in London as soon as possible. Maya, the intern, is slaving away in my absence making up necklaces and bracelets so we can fulfill all the orders, but it's not fair she should do all the work by herself.

I'm having an in-depth conversation about Granny's legacy with a journalist, a friendly woman in her fifties from a rather highbrow art journal. I am pretending (and failing) to sound as though I know what I'm talking about, when I feel a hand on my shoulder. I turn around and it's Guy.

"Hello," I say. "You off?"

"Yes," he says. "I'm driving back tonight. Left the car here last week. Came down in advance to finish the cataloging."

"Oh, right," I say.

"I had some things to sort out. Hey—I just came to say bye. Listen, Natasha. I'm sorry we haven't talked. Since you—"

"Excuse me," I say, turning back to Mary the journalist. "Nice to meet you." She smiles and moves off to greet someone else. I turn back to Guy, trying to sound jovial, scatty, breezy. "Phew. She was asking me about Futurism. I was out of my depth. Go on."

"Since you read the diary, I was wanting to say," he continues. "I've had a lot to think about, for my part. It's been strange."

"It must have been," I say. "I had no idea—you poor thing." I don't mean to, but I put my hand on his arm.

The muscles around his jaw tighten. He swallows.

"I was head over heels in love with her, you know," he says. "Reading it, hearing her voice again, it was almost unbearable, after all these years when I'd tried to put her out of my mind." He speaks so softly in the hubbub of the crowd. "It has been . . . very strange."

"I'm sure," I say. "I can't imagine what it must have been like for you, reading it now, finding out about Granny and all of that, now. . . ."

"Interesting." He smiles, his eyes still blank. "It's been—yes, interesting. There's no one else quite like Cecily. Never has been. I thought, at least. Now I'm not so sure."

He stares at me again.

"Guy—I really would like to come and talk to you about it," I say. I don't want to sound as though I'm begging, but I think it creeps into my voice anyway. "Just one afternoon. I know it must be upsetting, but you know—it's my family. I won't bother you again—"

"Your family," he says, as though he's considering this. "Your family. It is, isn't it? Look, Natasha, that's what I was coming to say. I was a prat, that's all. Come whenever you like. I'll be in touch if not. Have you spoken to your mother?"

"Mum? About the diary?" Someone pushes past me, and I sway a little on my feet. "Well, she's been away . . ." I say, and I trail off. He smiles.

"Of course she has. And she will be again soon, I'll bet." He takes a deep breath. "I'm sorry, but I do have to go. Listen, come round when you get back to London. Yes? And try and talk to your mother again." He hugs me. "Goodbye, my dear," he says. *Dear*. It's such an old-fashioned term. I like it.

So the afternoon wears on into evening and sooner than I would have realized it is time to leave. They have taken Arvind away already, around teatime. I have arranged to go and see him next month. People in the crowd were practically genuflecting as Archie wheeled his father out to the car. I kissed him goodbye and clutched his hand, and he stared up at me.

"Glad you came," he said. "Just remember." He half-sang, half-spoke. "'The flowers that bloom in the spring, tra-la, have nothing to do with the case.'"

I don't worry about my grandfather. It sounds callous but I don't. He learned how to file everything away in his mind a long time ago, and I wish I had that gift: I think I'm just beginning to learn it. Perhaps it's the nature of his job, perhaps it's being a foreigner in a strange country, never going back to the city you were from. Perhaps it's seeing your child die. Whatever the truth is about his marriage to Granny, it was successful in its longevity, which isn't important perhaps, but it is when you honestly believe, as I do, that they actually rubbed along pretty well together. Not very romantic, but perhaps that's real life. I don't think he was the best father in the world, and that's an awful thing to say about someone, but there are worse fathers, and like his wife he leaves an extraordinary legacy behind. I find myself wondering what we'll do when he dies, and then stop myself. Knowing Arvind, that won't be for another decade or so.

Clutching my bag over my arm, I walk down towards the sea one more time, the wind whipping about me. I think I will always remember these last few moments here, will remember the trees just coming into bud, the greenery everywhere instead of the bleached yellow and gray of August. Arvind is right about the flowers that bloom in the spring: cow parsley, hawthorns, and the beginnings of the apple blossom smother the lanes, and there are daffodils everywhere on the ground: these are not the flowers I remember from Summercove in the summer. For me it will still, always, be the place I spent the summer. Cecily's diary is in my bag, and I take it out and look at it. I feel I can read it again now, if I have to. I have stapled the first, loose pages, to the red cover, so it's all together again. I open the book, transported back into her world again.

I am writing this sitting on my bed at Summercove.

I look down to the sea. It is choppy. The path where Cecily fell is still dangerous, the rocks still slimy from winter. I peer down. I hear a voice, calling behind me.

"Natasha? *Natasha!* What are you doing?"

I turn around, and there are Louisa and Octavia, coming towards me. I sigh.

"Be careful, Natasha! It's very slippery!"

"I know," I say, walking towards them. The diary is still in my hand; I fold it under my armpit, hugging it to myself.

Louisa says, almost sharply, "Your mother's looking for you, Nat darling. Says it's time to go." She runs a hand through her hair. "Phew," she says, blowing air through her lips. "When will they go? I'm about to run out of rosé, and I wanted to keep at least a bottle back for myself. I'll need it, I tell you."

It's so Louisa, that; apparently rather bossy and straight, but in actuality a bit of a flapper, unsure of what to do next, and much nicer in her insecurity.

I run my tongue around my teeth; my mouth tastes stale, bitter. "Sorry to make you come looking for me," I say. "I was just—thinking."

Octavia is watching me, her arms crossed.

"What have you got there?" she asks, and she nudges my hand with Cecily's diary in it.

"Nothing," I say, immediately realizing that's a stupid thing to say.

"Come on, what is it?" she persists. Octavia is a burly, serious girl. I don't like the way she's looking at the diary.

"Natasha? You're there!" I hear someone calling. I turn. Mum is running down the path, her hair and her scarf flying behind her. The wind is blowing against her, it is strong now. She reaches us, panting. "We're going, Natasha," she says. "I've been looking for you everywhere—"

"Just a minute." Octavia steps in front of us. "I want you to answer something, Miranda." She points at my mother. "I want to know what you were talking about, during your speech."

"Octavia—sshh," says Louisa. "Please, don't make a scene."

"You were getting at something, I know you were," Octavia says.

"I said your mother was the backbone of our family. And it's true."

Octavia crosses her arms. "What a load of bullshit. I mean the other stuff you said. The insinuations about Franty, making out she was guilty of things—"

"I'm afraid you're wrong about that, Octavia," my mother says lightly.

"I know all about you—" Octavia says. "About the way you were carrying on that summer."

"*Octavia!*" Louisa says angrily. "Stop it!"

Mum holds up a hand. "No. Let her go on. I want to hear it. What do you mean?"

"You know what I mean." Octavia squares up to her, her mannish figure taller than Mum's. "You. Throwing yourself at my father, and my uncle! Your vile brother, perving over my mother. The two of you, bullying poor Cecily to death, just because she wouldn't go along with you—"

"Hey! Octavia!" I say, finding my voice. "You don't know anything! Shut the hell up!"

"No!" Her eyes are popping out of her head.

"You stupid girl," Mum says, baring her teeth. A strong gust blows her hair round her head, like a banshee. She looks terrifying. "Where do you get off, accusing me? You know nothing, darling. You don't know the fucking half of it, you have no—"

And then Octavia reaches forwards and whips the diary out from under my arm, with a movement so sharp and quick it's gone before I can stop her.

"Continuing the Diary of Cecily Kapoor,"

she reads. She looks up, smiling, as though she's won something.

Louisa's mouth drops open. "No—" she says, scanning the red cover. "That's her handwriting, that's Cecily's—" She stares at her cousin. "Miranda—is that her diary?"

"It is," Mum says.

"How—" Louisa's eyes are wide. "From that summer?"

"Yes," Mum says. She gently puts her hand on Octavia's wrist and strokes it, as though she's a cat, and Octavia's fingers slowly open. Mum takes the diary out. She looks at it, then at her cousin. "Yes, I've read it. It's pretty interesting."

"I bet it is," Octavia says. "No wonder you haven't told anyone about it, all these years."

"We only found it after Granny died," I point out. "OK?"

"What's in it?"

"Yes," Louisa says, shaking her head. But she looks terrified. And then she looks at my mother and steps back. "You know—I don't think I want to know. I just want to remember her as she was."

"Louisa, tell me something," Mum asks. "What do you remember about that summer? Before she died, I mean."

"Well—" Louisa looks wary. "Why?"

"It's Cecily's diary, not yours, or mine. She was writing what she wanted to write about. We were there too, weren't we? What do you remember?"

"Oh . . ." Louisa screws up her face. "I remember . . . 'Please Please Me.'" They smile at each other. "And my new shorts, Mummy said they were indecent, but I loved them. And the awful springs on Jeremy's car. I remember . . . oh gosh, how hot it was. Mary making lavender ice-cream the day we arrived, it was absolutely delicious. Archie . . ." She blushes. "Archie being a Peeping Tom. For years afterwards I'd try to avoid him. I always forget that's why, it got mixed up with everything else, didn't it? Oh, I remember Frank and Guy arriving, and how wonderful it was . . . at first. It all changed, after that. I don't know why."

"Everything did get mixed up," Mum says. She hugs the diary close. "I remember my new clothes, and my feet looking brown in the pumps I'd bought, and I remember how much I hated it at home, how I wished I could leave. I'd lie awake at night with Cecily snoring away and work out how I'd do it. Go somewhere where I wasn't the stupid one, the slow one, the lazy one. Be the pretty one, the fun one, the exciting one."

"But you were," Louisa says in amazement. "We thought you were absolutely it. We were so boring, Jeremy and I, compared to you three. You'd met everyone, seen everything, your parents let you do what you wanted. . . ."

"Funny, isn't it?" Mum isn't smiling though. The wind buffets us, stinging my cheeks. I am transfixed. "That's not how I remember it. At all. Look, it's all in the past now," she says. "It's gone. It's like the diary. It's her version, not mine, not yours." She clutches the diary close, drumming her fingers against it.

I hadn't thought of it like that. How if I were to read Mum's diary of the summer, or Archie's, or even Granny's, it might be different. I guess I'll never know the rest. They were all there that summer, they know what it was like, but even then there's still a lot they'll never really understand.

"I still think about her, I can still picture her so clearly," Louisa says. "Don't you?"

"Every day," Mum tells her. She looks so old, suddenly. Tears swim in her eyes. Whether it's the wind or not, I don't know. "She was lovely, wasn't she?"

They give each other a small, half-smile, as the wind buffets us. "She was," says Louisa. "It's not fair."

"It's not," Mum says. "But like I say, it's in the past now."

I find myself nodding. She's right.

"Well, I disagree. I think we should read it too," Octavia says.

"Why?" I ask her.

"Because we deserve the truth. All our lives, Mum's the one who's done everything for your mother and father. She's got nothing for it, she's never been thanked or rewarded—"

"What, you want money?" I ask. "Is that what this is about?"

"Octavia! Natasha!" Louisa hisses. "No, of course not."

"I'm just saying, I've grown up with it. I've sat there and watched Mum cleaning up, cooking, spending all summer here, her looking after *you*—" she points at me—"because *you*—" she points at Mum—"can't be bothered to come and see your parents. And no one ever says why, do they?" Octavia laughs. "They never say why we can't rock the boat. We just all pretend it's all OK."

I've had enough. "Octavia, you don't know what the hell you're talking about," I say. "You've got it all wrong! Mum's not the one who—"

And then something strange happens. The diary is in Mum's hand, and it suddenly flies out, eddying away on a huge, arching gust of wind, out over the beach, dropping abruptly like a rock into the sea. Louisa cries out, and Octavia scrambles for the steps, but my mother, with an iron grasp, stops her.

"No. Octavia, don't. It's too dangerous."

She turns them back towards the house.

"It's gone," I say, looking out at the tiny red exercise book, floating further out to sea. "It's really gone."

"Now we'll never know, I guess," Louisa says. She shrugs sadly, and looks up at Mum. "Miranda, be honest for once. There wasn't anything really horrid in it, was there?"

Mum glances down at her. "Absolutely not, Louisa. I promise."

"Good." Louisa nods. I don't know whether she believes this or not.

"And Louisa, you know, that thing with Archie?" Mum says. "Jeremy used to look at me all the time too. He was just better at not getting caught, that's all."

"That's not true."

"It really is," Mum says. "Like I say: just because you didn't see it doesn't mean it didn't happen."

"Why didn't you say anything?" Louisa demands.

My mother gives a quick, twisted smile. "Who'd have believed me?" She glances down at the shingley path. "Please, trust me. Just this once. It was a long, long time ago, all of it. You don't hate

Archie now, do you? I mean, you don't like him much, but it's all so long ago. All of it. So why don't we just call it quits?"

"You're bloody crazy," Octavia says.

"Yes, I am," my mother says. "I know it more than most people. Lousia?"

Lousia smiles her sweet smile. "Yes," she says. "Let's."

Mum's eyes shine at her for a second, and then she nods at me. "Darling, we should go—"

She takes my arm. Octavia storms ahead of us, not saying anything. Louisa calls after her. "Octavia?" She shakes her head. "Oh, dear," she says. "She's—well, a bit unpredictable." She smiles. "A bit like you, Miranda."

"Me?" My mother looks completely horrified at the suggestion that black-suited, clompy-shod Octavia and she are similar, and I chew my lip, trying not to smile. It's strange, but she's right.

The three of us walk back up towards the house in silence. We stand outside on the terrace, and Archie appears.

"About time," he says. "Come on, girls."

"Let me just brush my hair," my mother says.

"Mum, we really should hurry—" I say, looking at my watch. "The train leaves in less than an hour."

"So . . ." Louisa fiddles with her bag, peering right inside it as if looking for Aztec gold in there. "So . . ."

I lean forwards and give her a big hug. "Thank you for everything you did today," I say. "Well, everything. You should come into town some time. Come and see me."

She looks taken aback. "Oh, Nat darling, lovely. I'm sure that'd be—er . . ." She trails off.

"I'm very near the Geffrye Museum," I say. "We could go and look at nice almshouses and English furniture. Maybe wander down Columbia Road, there are some lovely places to have coffee there. And you could see where they're stocking my jewelry." Next to me, Mum looks uncomfortable. "I'd love you to see it." I feel that if I don't say it now, I won't have a reason to see her again. Yes. So I say, "I'd love to see you."

Louisa suddenly goes a bit pink. "I'd love that too." She pats my arm. "I'm so proud of you, Natasha. Your granny would be too. . . ." She bites her lip and looks away. "Goodbye," she says, and she grips Mum's arm too.

"Goodbye, Natasha," the Bowler Hat says.

He kisses my cheek and I stare at him. I don't feel rage, just cold dislike. I want him to suffer for what he's done but I realize there's no point, really. It would only hurt Louisa and that's not what any of us wants. He's not worth my time. Hopefully I won't ever have anything to do with him.

He doesn't go near Mum. "Bye," he says, raising his hand, rather flatly, as if unsure of what comes next.

"Ready?" Archie says. He opens the car door for his sister, as he always does. "I'll be back soon, Louisa," he says. "Sort out the rest."

"Thanks," Louisa says, her voice muffled again; and it's strange, I've never noticed it before, but it's true, there's an awkwardness between them. Whereas the Bowler Hat gets to stroll around carefree, and what he did that summer was much worse, and half of them—Mum, Archie, Guy—both my grandparents—know it. I sigh. That sums the whole crazy situation up, really. I mean, I know Archie can be annoying, but he's OK. He's Jay's dad, after all. He must have only just got back from dropping Arvind off, and here he is, driving us back to almost exactly where he's just been.

"Hop in, Natasha."

"Thanks," I say, feeling a rush of gratitude towards him, and I climb into the back. As we drive off I swivel round in my seat, just as I used to when I was small, to catch one last glimpse of the house, its white curves set against the sloping green and the sea in the background. In the front, Archie and Mum are chattering about something together, laughing, as if their spirits have been lifted already by going. I realize that, what with everything, I haven't said goodbye to the house, goodbye to Summercove forever.

Then it occurs to me that actually, I have.

Forty-seven

Just after seven the next morning, we pull in to Paddington. It is another beautiful spring day. Soft sunshine floods into the old, familiar station as Mum and I get off the train and stand awkwardly on the platform.

We look blearily at each other as the crowds recede. I swing my bag over my shoulder and she smiles at me, and tucks a lock of hair behind my ear.

"Darling Nat," she says. "My clever girl."

We're nodding at each other. We've made it. We've come out the other side. I feel as though I've been fighting my way through the darkness for a long time, the whole of the last year. Perhaps longer, when I think about it, as if my life had gone the wrong direction, with no input from me. The way Mum's did when Cecily died.

She grips my hand with her long, smooth fingers, so tight she's almost pinching it. She is sort of wild, her eyes are huge.

I pat her shoulder. "Mum," I say. "Shall we—do you want to go and get some breakfast? I know a nice place not far from here, by the canal."

She's nodding.

"We could . . . *talk*," I say, rolling my eyes, hoping she knows I don't like it much either, but that it'd be nice to chat. "Just . . . catch up and stuff."

Mum opens her mouth, smiling at the same time. And then she says, "Oh! . . . Yes. I'd—Yes, well, I'd love to, darling, but I can't."

"Oh. I thought you were—never mind, it doesn't matter."

"Jean-Luc rang me early this morning," she says, her eyes wide. "His wife's left him and he's in a terrible state. He just happens to have a booking for the River Café for lunch! So he's taking me. I really should get home and make myself presentable." Her smile is still bright, optimistic, sunny, and a little scary. "But it's a lovely idea, darling." She grasps my hand again. "Maybe some other time, hm?"

"Yes," I say, looking at her, into her clear green eyes so like her own mother's, so like mine. "Some other time."

"Which way are you . . . ?" She points towards the main concourse.

"I'm—" I point behind me, towards the Hammersmith and City line.

"Of course," she says. "Yes, well, I'm getting the District. . . ." We are still pointing in different directions. "Well, I'd better run," Mum says. She kisses me on the cheek. "Bye, sweetheart," she says, and she is dashing off down the platform, and I watch her go, and turn and climb the stairs to the Tube, the same stairs I ran down two months ago to catch this very same train, the one that would take me back to Summercove for Granny's funeral.

I sit on the Tube as it rattles gently east, away from the station, away from Mum, towards the center of London and another day. I don't know when I'm going to see her again; she has made the parameters very clear, and after everything that's happened, that she's been through, I know it's fine. I see Louisa hurrying off . . . Mum, hurrying off . . . I see myself saying goodbye to Arvind, packing up my marriage. And just as I think I'm alone, pretty much alone, apart from Jay, but without the rest of my family, a thought strikes me.

I cannot believe I haven't seen it before.

I stand up abruptly in the crowded Tube. The doors are opening at King's Cross. *Why didn't I think of it earlier?* Why didn't I see it? I run through the crowds, the same faceless sea of people hurrying from one place to another, back in to work, vanishing in the distance, like Mum, hurrying towards the exit. I speed up my pace.

Half an hour later, I am standing outside a door of a house in a pretty Georgian terrace. I knock firmly.

A girl answers. "Hi?" she says, looking at me. She is mid-twenties, with long, curly, dark brown hair, a touch of red in it. She is holding a half-finished cereal bowl and a spoon.

"Hi," I say, slightly out of breath, as I have run all the way from the Tube. "Hi. I'm Natasha. Is your—is your dad there?"

She looks me curiously up and down. And then she nods, and smiles. "Um—OK. Sure. *Dad!*" she bellows with unexpected ferocity. *"Someone called Natasha here to see you!"*

"Thanks," I say.

" 'S'OK," she says. She smiles. "Yeah—so maybe see you later," and she drifts off with the cereal bowl, back down the long corridor.

Guy appears in the hallway. He looks bleary-eyed, gray-faced. He peers, as if to make sure it is me. "Natasha?" he says, shaking his head. "When did you get back? What are you doing here?" It's not said unkindly.

"I wanted to ask you something," I say. I look steadily at him.

He meets my gaze. And swallows. "OK. Fire away."

"Guy," I say. "Um—"

He stares, and his eyes are kind.

"Go on, Natasha," he says. "Ask me."

I take a deep breath.

"Are—are you my dad?"

He gives a little jump, and it's as if some tension within him has been released. He sighs.

"Yes," he says. "Yes, I am." And he smiles, slowly.

"Oh," I say.

"I'm so sorry," he says. "I've been more than useless. But you're here. I'm so glad you're here."

I put my hand against the front door to steady myself.

"Why don't you come in?" he says. "Come on."

"Oh," I say, thinking of the girl inside, of how tired I am, how I want my breakfast, my bed. "Oh . . . well . . ."

"Come on," he says again. "I've been waiting for this for a while, you know. You're here now. Welcome."

And he puts his arm round me and pulls me gently inside, and he shuts the door behind us and the rest of the world.

Forty-eight

Guy's basement kitchen is a mess. He ushers me downstairs and sits me at the big wooden kitchen table, which is covered in newspapers and empty coffee mugs. He pushes some papers helplessly out of the way and gestures towards the cooker.

"Do you want some breakfast . . . ?"

I was starving, but now I have no appetite at all. "No, thanks. Can I have a coffee?" I say.

"Sure, sure." He rubs his hands together, as if pleased it's going well. He fills up the kettle cautiously, and I stare at him.

This man is my father. This is my dad. Dad. Daddy. Father. Pa. I've never said that to anyone before. I used to practice it at night in my room at Bryant Court, especially during the height of my *Railway Children* obsession. My daddy's away, I'd told myself. He'll come back soon. Mum's just protecting me, like Bobbie's mum is. Night after night, but he never came, and then I grew out of pretending. I watch Guy as he shuffles round the kitchen, trying to slot everything into place.

He's Cecily's lover. He's the Bowler Hat's *brother,* for God's sake—oh God, I think to myself. That means the Bowler Hat is my uncle and Octavia and Julius are my actual first *cousins,* not half distant relatives it didn't matter that I didn't like so much. And—he's my dad. Not much of one so far, I have to say.

The room is spinning; my head hurts. I get up.

"I'm sorry, I think I have to go," I say. "I don't know if I can do this right now."

Guy turns, his face full of alarm. "No!" he says loudly. "You can't go." He hears himself and then says, "Sorry. I mean, please, please don't go."

"I didn't have any idea . . ." I say. I shake my head, still standing there. To my surprise tears are flowing down my cheeks. I dash them away, crossly. "Sorry. It's just a shock—" I sink back into my chair.

"I thought she'd have told you," Guy says. "That's why I asked you yesterday, to come and see me. She promised she'd tell you. She really didn't?" I shake my head, stifling a sob. He grits his teeth. "God, that woman—I'm sorry, I know she's your mother, but really."

There's a pause while I collect myself.

"Don't be mean about Mum," I say. "Where were you, when she was bringing me up with no money, completely on her own?"

"I didn't know!" Guy shouts suddenly, and he looks about ten years younger, not this tired, washed-out old man I don't recognize from Cecily's diary.

"You didn't know?"

"Of course not, Natasha!" He looks appalled. "What do you think I am? I had no idea until she turned up completely out of the blue, two weeks ago, the day after I'd seen you at the shop. Out of the blue! First this diary arrives in the post, and then she arrives, no warning, nothing. At first I thought she'd brought another bloody diary for me to read, but it was this!" He's practically shouting. "She tells me this, and then she runs off to God knows where, and I'm left—I didn't know what to do! Do you understand? Next time she comes I'm not letting her in, I tell you."

His tone is so outraged, I almost want to laugh, but he's serious. He lowers his voice a little. "Natasha, don't you think if I'd have known before, I'd have . . ." He swallows. "I know I was awful when you came round last week, and I'm sorry. . . ." He bangs the teaspoon he's holding impotently against his baggy cords, like a child with a rattle. "I'd only just found out I was your father, and Miranda's nowhere to be seen, I don't know if she's told you or not. . . . And it was the anniversary of Hannah's death . . . it's always a bad day for me. Then you appear and—I'm so sorry." He looks so sad.

"I just—I wasn't ready to talk to you properly. To be the person you needed."

"Look, Guy," I say. "I don't need a dad, I've got by all these years without one. It's fine."

The kettle screeches away on the hob and he turns it off. I look round the sunny kitchen again with photos on the walls, poetry magnets on the fridge, cream ceramic jars marked SUGAR, FLOUR, TEA, COFFEE. In the corner, a cat stretches out in a basket. Radio 4 is on in the background. It's messy, but lived-in. Cozy. Upstairs, someone is moving about. When I was younger this was something like the sort of family set-up I dreamed of having.

"Do you believe that I didn't know?" Guy says. He comes over and slaps his hands onto the back of one of the chairs. "Does it make sense?"

I blink; it still sounds so strange. "You didn't have any idea? I mean—you knew you'd slept with her, Guy, didn't you? Are you trying to say she drugged you?"

He smiles. "Yep. I suppose this is when it gets a bit complicated. We'd been . . . well, over the years, after Cecily's death . . . you could say we sort of saw a lot of each other."

"You were fuck buddies," I say. His eyes open wide.

"What on earth did you just say?"

"Fuck buddies," I say callously. "Bootie callers. Friends with benefits."

"I have absolutely no idea what you're talking about." Guy moves back to the kettle, pours water into the French press and brings it over with two mugs, sitting down heavily in front of me. "It wasn't like that." He stares into nothing. "You have to remember, Natasha. She had a bad time growing up, but in the seventies your mother was . . ." He shakes his head. "She was absolutely devastating."

"The seventies were terrible for a lot of people, you know," Guy says, when we're sitting more comfortably, I've stopped crying, and he's calmed down. "No electricity. Strikes. Mass unemployment. Platform shoes and spotty punks everywhere. But you know, it was your mother's decade in lots of ways." He smiles.

"How do you mean?" I am fascinated, and I'm just enjoying looking at him, staring at his face, his hands holding the coffee mug. I tuck one leg under me.

"Oh, you know." He smiles. "You know. Her own brand of cod-mystical—er—you know, headscarf-wearing hippyness—it all flourished then. I just think she became more comfortable in her own skin."

I smile, because he's totally right, and it's so strange that he knows this. Knows her as well as he does. I prop my elbows up on the table, my chin in my hands, listening intently.

"I don't know what she'd been doing for the rest of the sixties," Guy says.

"She did some fashion courses," I say. "I know that. She used to try and make dresses years later when I was little, from those Clothkits sets. They were always awful." The burgundy and brown early eighties pinafore where one panel was back to front and the pockets were on the inside, for example. I shake my head, caught between tears and a smile as I think about her in the flat with her sewing machine.

Guy nods. "I seem to remember there was an upholstery course somewhere, she was always making cushions. And I know she went traveling, but I met her again when she was working at this boutique, I think in South Ken."

I remember her talking about the South Kensington shop. It originally sold awful kaftans and tie-dye prints, which in a few years gave way to Laura Ashley–style, rip-off, long, flowery dresses. She took it over and rechristened it Miranda. Of course she did. I have a photo of her standing outside the shop in skinny jeans and boots, a billowing embroidered cheesecloth blouse with huge sleeves, and a Liberty headscarf tied round her hair. She has her hand on her hip, her eyes are made up with black kohl and she is almost scowling. She looks like a sexy pirate. Something completely wild in her eyes. He's right, she looks devastating. I tell Guy this, and he nods.

"She was. We met at a party, in about 1973? I hadn't—I hadn't seen her for years. I'd been living in the States."

"Doing what?" I say. I'm so curious, I want to know everything. I look at him again. He's my *dad*.

He smiles. "Oh, not very much, I'm afraid. Writing in a rather desultory way for a paper, living in San Francisco. I was trying to be a journalist."

"Wow. Was it fun?"

Guy shakes his head. "No," he says flatly. "I wasn't very good. And I went away for the wrong reasons. I couldn't wait to finish at Oxford and . . . I left England immediately after I went down, to forget about Cecily. About what happened that summer." He stops, takes a gulp of his coffee. He is breathing fast. He purses his lips and says sadly, "I wasn't even there when Frank married Louisa."

"Really? You missed your brother's wedding?"

"It wasn't such a big deal then," he says. "Weddings weren't such a production, you know. Glass of champagne and some salmon mousse in a marquee then home by six."

He looks away. I don't believe him. I wrap my fingers round my mug, so that my thumbs are interlocked.

"Anyway, I was there till '73, and then I came back. . . . I'd been back a week, it was summer. Terribly hot. I wasn't sure why I was back, what I was doing. . . . I was rather a lost soul. And then I met your mother at this completely crazy house party in Maida Vale one evening. We . . . um." He trails off. "We had a brief fling. And then I went off again."

"Back to the States?" I ask. I'm not embarrassed. I am desperately curious. After all these years of knowing nothing, suddenly everything is out there, open, within my grasp.

"I was back and forth for a few years. There was a girl there—in San Francisco—things were rather complicated. I didn't know what I was doing, to be honest."

"So you carried on seeing Mum when you were here? And the girl over there?"

Guy heaves his shoulders up almost to his ears, and then drops them again. "Yes. But while it seems pathetic to say 'It wasn't really like that,' I try to console myself with the thought that it wasn't."

"In what way?" I take a sip of tea, warming my hands around the mug.

"Miranda was . . ." Guy's eyes light up. "She was very clear about what she wanted. And it wasn't a relationship. She was—you have to understand she was herself for the first time. She was making her own way in the world, she had a life of her own, away from Summercove, from your parents. She was the life and soul of every party. Absolutely beautiful. Coterie of men always around her, gay and straight. No fear. She swung on a giant chandelier once, in a dilapidated mansion off Curzon Street, and it crumbled away from the ceiling, and she fell to the floor." He is almost chuckling at the memory. "She didn't care. That was Miranda."

My skin is prickling, hot, all over. "What happened after that?" I ask. "Did you go back to the States?"

"Oh, yes, then back again to London. Few months here, few months there," Guy said. He swallows. "I was being pathetic. My girlfriend wanted me to stay there with her. She'd moved to New York by then. I couldn't make my mind up. Didn't want to settle down. Kept thinking . . . what if . . ."

He trails off.

"What if what?"

"What if Cecily hadn't died?" He looks up. "Would we have been together? That's why I couldn't settle down with anyone else for years afterwards. I always thought we would." He shakes his head. "I can't say that now, not after my years with Hannah and the children. *All* my children." He smiles, and he reaches out his hand, puts it on top of mine.

I let his fingers rest on mine, feeling his warm dry hand, his flesh, and I stare at him again in wonder.

"I wouldn't change that for the world. But I do think about it. I used to, all the time. You see, we never talked about her, none of us, after she died. I had no one to talk to about—about her. None of my friends had met her. It was so brief. I couldn't discuss it with my brother, with Louisa." He exhales. "I'm sorry. I find it very hard, even now. Reading the diary, it brought it all back."

"Did you know about Bowler Hat and—and Granny?" I ask. "Before you read the diary?"

Guy frowns. Two lines appear between his gray brows. He screws his eyes up. "I knew in some way," he says. "I've never trusted either of them. Don't get me wrong. I loved them both. I always will. But I—I think I didn't want to see what was going on. You have to remember how young we were, how naive, really. She tried it with me, you know."

"What? Granny?"

Guy nods. "Frances was a woman of many passions. She let it be known that she was available. Not long after we arrived, that summer. A hand here, a stroke on the cheek there. A look over the shoulder." He blinks. "I was so lily-livered. I'd have gone for it like a shot if I hadn't been so scared. Good thing I didn't."

I shake my head. I don't know why I'm surprised.

"Anyway," Guy continues. "I suppose, I suppose—yes, seeing your mother, it brought it all back again. But in a good way. She was wonderful. She was like Cecily, of course. But she *wasn't* like her. They're not that alike. So it was comforting, to see her again, and to be able to talk about what had happened." He looks awkward. "Not that she wanted to talk about it much. She was more interested in the present. Not the past. Always has been."

He shifts in his seat.

"You know, people always say she's difficult, she's crazy—well, I think they liked the idea that she was. It was easier for them to explain all these other things that didn't add up about that family. You know. The father never around, not very interested. The mother this great beauty, hugely talented but hasn't painted for years, the fact that the house used to be this mecca for glamorous young things and not anymore, the death of the younger daughter, the atmosphere that something's just not quite right—I think it was easier for people to look at Miranda and gossip than look any further. Does that make sense?"

That family. He talks about them as if they're nothing to do with him, or me, as if they're not my family anymore.

"Anyway . . . it was always very casual. We'd meet at parties, or we'd go out for some pasta when I was in town, catch up, and then she'd come back to my shambolic bachelor pad in Bloomsbury. . . ." He drops his hands into his lap. "She was rather wonderful about it." He smiles. "Then I'd go back to the States, or she'd find some other boyfriend . . . it was never official with us. Only ever a few times a year. There were always others buzzing around, you know?"

"I know," I say, feeling disloyal, but unable to deny it. "So you didn't think it was weird, when you knew she was pregnant?"

"That's just it," Guy says emphatically. "I never knew she was. I've thought it all through, these last few weeks. You see, I came back in '77. I was reporting on the Queen's Jubilee for an American newspaper. Your mother and I saw each other a couple of times that summer. Once or twice, if that, nothing much. We met . . ." He trails off. "Yes. We met at the French House. In Soho. The anniversary of Cecily's death, 6th August. I remember it really well. I was going to Ulster the next day, to report on the Queen's visit. It was going to be rather hairy, security everywhere. I was supposed to have an early night, but . . . we stayed up drinking, and talking. . . . Eventually we went back to her place. . . . I remember . . ."

He glances at me and falls silent. "What?" I say.

"Never mind," he says gently, and I realize there are some things I don't want or need to know, and it occurs to me that perhaps I was conceived that night, the anniversary of Cecily's death.

"Anyway, it wasn't anything out of the ordinary, us meeting up like that. We weren't in touch otherwise. And then I didn't see her . . . didn't see any of them, for another two years."

"Really?"

"Yes," he says. "No idea. I think Louisa mentioned that Miranda had had a baby, but by then I was married, we were having children. . . ."

"What happened to the girl in the States?"

"I saw sense," he says. "I married her. That was Hannah."

"Your wife?"

He smiles sadly. He has a melancholy smile, my father. "Yes. And I'm an idiot. We both were. It just took us a while to realize it. But all those wasted years, that's what makes me angry." He nods seriously, as if remembering something. "But we realized in the end. We were married in 1980, and our first daughter was born a year later, and our second in '86." He says slowly, "Hannah died five years ago. Five years ago in April."

I squeeze his hand gently. "I'm so sorry," I say softly.

"Thank you." Guy clears his throat.

"What are your daughters called?" I ask, trying to catch his eye.

"My daughters." His voice is warm. "My other daughters, you mean? Hah. Roseanna and Cecily."

"Cecily?"

He smiles. "You just met her."

I think of the lovely young woman at the door. "That's my half-sister."

Guy leans forwards. "Yes, it is."

"She looks like Hannah." I have very vague memories of Hannah, who had beautiful, long red hair before she lost it all, and who was American and funny and very kind. Guy nods.

"She does." He looks pleased. "I'm sure you've seen them before but you'll have to meet them, properly. They know about you. Cecily might not have known that was you at the door but she probably did. They know you exist. I told them last week. They're very excited."

"Really?" I can't imagine it, having been an only child my whole life. Siblings are a completely strange entity to me, I have no idea what it's like, having sisters. Being part of a family. "They're excited? Do they want to meet me?"

"All in good time," Guy says, noncommittally, and I know he's being diplomatic.

He stands up again. I look at my watch. It's ten o'clock. The house is very still, there's no noise from the street either.

"Do you want some toast or something?" Guy says from the sink. "I've been a shockingly neglectful host."

I shake my head, overwhelmed all of a sudden. I don't know what to say and I am very tired. "I'm fine."

Guy turns and looks at me. He walks over again, and crouches down, slowly—he's not a young man. He puts his finger under my chin.

"Did you know, I held you when you were about a year old?" he says. "I rocked you to sleep."

"No, really?" I look down at him, on the floor.

"Yes," he says. He pats my cheek. "It was Arvind's sixtieth birthday. A lunch, in a big old Italian restaurant near Redcliffe Square, where they still had their flat, do you remember the flat?"

"Very vaguely."

"Well, they invited me. Very kind. I admire your grandfather's work, I always have. So I went, I think I thought it was time to put all of the past with the Kapoors behind me. I was newly married, I was very happy. I went with Frank and Louisa, and yes—there was Miranda, with this little girl. It was the summer of '79, I think. You were very small—I wasn't sure how old you were."

"I'd have been about fifteen months," I say. "What did you do?"

"Well, your mother gave you to me to hold," he says. "You were falling asleep, so she chucked you onto my lap and said, 'There, sit with Uncle Guy for a while.' And you gave me this big, gummy smile and then you closed your eyes and fell asleep." There are tears in his eyes. "You had very fine black hair, sticking up everywhere. You were quite enchanting."

And he bows his head, and his shoulders heave, and he says very quietly, "I am so sorry, Natasha. So very sorry."

"What are you sorry for?" I ask quietly.

"For not realizing . . . for being so blind. And for everything else . . . for Cecily, you know . . . There's not a day that goes by when I don't miss her, wish we could have had one more day to-gether. You know, reading that diary—remembering it all again, these things I'd forgotten, how wonderful she was. And now you—you're here, standing here—" His voice breaks.

I pull him up so we are both standing, and he puts his arms round me and hugs me, and I hug him back, as tightly as I can. Not because now I've found my father, and everything's all right. More because I don't know if we can have a close relationship, if there's too much history already, and that is so sad, but also because he is a sweet, kind man, and I wish he were happier. He is not, and I wish there was something I could do about it.

"And what about you?" he says, releasing me from his embrace and stepping back. He takes a huge white handkerchief out of his pocket and blows his nose.

"What about me?" I say.

"Your friends—your life, your jewelry. I don't really know any-thing about it, though I've found out as much as I can. And," he says, drawing himself up with some pride, "I dropped by your stu-dio the other day, I remembered you saying it was just at the bottom of Brick Lane. They told me where I could buy some of your pieces, they were ever so helpful."

"Really?" I say, intrigued. "Who was it?"

"A very sweet girl," Guy says. "Terribly pretty, blonde hair."

"Oh," I say grimly. "Jamie."

"Yes," he says. "She was with a chap, hanging round at the desk. A photographer. He said he knew you too. They all seemed very nice."

"That's Ben," I say. "He's a . . . yeah, he's a friend of mine." I am really touched at Guy's making the effort. Then I think, How I wish I could talk to Ben about it all, and then I realize that's my fault. I need to stop being stupid about him, and knock this strange cool-ness between us on the head. We were friends long before we kissed, and we can be friends again. It was weeks ago. Three weeks ago ex-actly, in fact. He's been away a lot, with two big projects on, but I can't help feeling he's avoiding me too. I will call him tonight, see if he wants to come for a drink with me and Jay.

"Anyway, they directed me to a shop on Columbia Road," says Guy. "I bought two necklaces there for the girls." He points at Cecily's ring, as ever on its chain round my neck. "They reminded me of this." He smiles. "Lovely."

"I'm glad you like them," I say, a glow of pleasure washing over me.

"They're beautiful, but it's more than that," Guy says earnestly. "It feels a little like it's come in a circle, in some way." He shakes his head. "I don't want to sound mystical, I'm not really into any of that caper. But—Cecily had that ring the day she died. I remember it, I remember when Frances started wearing it, after she'd gone. And your mother's right, they all are. You do look like her." He smiles. "She was beautiful, but you are even more so."

"Oh, really, come off it," I say, embarrassed.

"And the way you've grown up, so creative, so wonderful— making things with your hands, those necklaces inspired by Cecily, and now your own half-sisters are wearing them. And they love them." He squeezes his hands, he looks so pleased and I can't help smiling. "Your grandmother was very proud of you."

"I'm not sure I want her to be proud of me," I say. "I don't really know who she was, anymore. I don't know how she could have done all that."

Guy says, "No. That's not fair, Natasha. I can see why, you're right. But she suffered every day for it. She gave up the one thing that made her happy, her painting. That was her penance, her punishment." He puts his hands in his pockets. "She was like Icarus, you know. She thought she could get away with what she was doing, and she flew too close to the sun. She didn't kill Cecily, you know."

"No, but she was happy enough to let everyone think Mum did, in some way," I say coldly. "She didn't care about her other daughter, about screwing her life up, about carrying on screwing it up. Not at all."

"You're right," he says, bowing his head. "You're right. But still—I don't think she was evil." He stops. "Just—she was a great artist. That's what they're like, I suppose. And she saw in you something special. I think, if it's any consolation, you gave her real pleasure, something to live for. And I think she knew I was your father."

"Really?" I say.

He nods. "Oh, I think it now. Didn't before. But the way she organized this whole foundation, the fact that you, your mother and I were on the committee—I'm sure she was trying to make amends, as soon as she died. So that when she'd gone we'd be thrown together, start afresh, as it were." Guy nods. "Start afresh, yes. All three of us, in fact." He puts his hand on my shoulder. "She was proud of you. And I am too. And so is your mother."

"Hah," I say. "Well."

"She is," Guy persists. "She's just never been able to say it. Give her time."

There's another pause. "Look, Guy," I say. "I am going to go now—just want to be on my own for a bit. Think this all through." I squeeze his hand. "Are you around this weekend? Maybe we could have a coffee?"

"Sure, either's good for me," he says. He holds my hand. "I'd love to meet Oli too, if that's OK?" He reads my face and says, "Oh. Oh, no, Natasha. I'm sorry. Have I put my foot in it?"

"No, not at all." I am impressed by his intuition, and then I think, Well, he is my father, I've got half his genes, and my mind is blown again by how strange this is, and yet how totally, almost unremarkably right it feels. I swing his hand in mine. "It's over with me and Oli, it really is this time." His face falls. "But honestly, it's for the best. I think I was looking for something, a family of my own, and it was a mistake."

"You don't need to look anymore," Guy says. "You've got me." He puts his arm on my shoulder. "I'm your family, Natasha. And soon Roseanna and Cecily will be too. We can take it slowly, you don't have to see me at all if you want. But from this moment on, for the rest of your life, that's a fact. I'm your family. OK?"

"OK," I say. He nods firmly.

"Shake on it? Will you trust me?"

I give him my hand again and we shake hands, smiling at each other in the sunny kitchen.

Epilogue

"Hey, someone's looking for you," Sara, the girl at the next stall, says to me when I come back from a coffee run. "Said he'd come back."

I am vaguely apprehensive today, and I don't know why. Something at the back of my mind is worrying me, which normally means I've been spending too much time on my own and I need to go down the corridor of the studio and find Lily or even Les, the leader of the writers' collective, if I'm feeling really desperate. Ben has been away in Turkey for ages for work, doing an upscale holiday brochure, so I can't even call on him. I keep going to knock on his door, or thinking of something funny to tell him, and he's never there. I text him, but he hardly ever replies. I miss him, I realize that now. He's always been there, and I thought it was great to have someone, anyone, next door. Now I know it was the fact that it was *him* next door that was great. I wish he'd come today. I'm selling some new pieces on the stall, and I've emailed a whole bunch of people, friends, contacts, asking them to drop by. It's my new range. Perhaps that's why I'm nervous.

I sit back on my stool by the stall, stroking the dull pink velvet cushions I have put the new bracelets I've made on. They are silver bangles each with a single charm, a fat enameled star with an initial, and the preorders are already fantastic. I've taken Maya on part-time, I'm paying her a wage, and I'm actually going in to meet someone from Liberty next week. I can hardly believe it.

Down here on Brick Lane, my stall inside at the Sunday Upmarket is busier than ever these days, since I sorted myself out, since spring came, and since I got Cecily's ring to inspire me. It turns out that Granny left me and Jay money in her will, £20,000 each, to be exact, and I need to spend it wisely. I can pay Oli everything back that I owed him, and clear my debts. I've bought some more stock, and I've spent some money dressing up the stall, having some business cards printed.

It's over two months since I turned up on Guy's doorstep. Three months since I kissed Ben. Nearly four months since Granny died and Oli moved out. It is starting to feel as if at some point these things might one day be part of the past, an archeological layer of my life I can look back on. But of course the roots are deeper than that. I was with Oli for five years, and though he and Chloe aren't top of my dinner party list at the moment, I can see a time when we will meet, at Jason's birthday drinks, for example, and it'll be fine. More than fine. I like him. I always did. We just shouldn't have been married. It's not an escape from the real problems in your life. It doesn't wipe the slate clean.

I sip my coffee, looking round the sunny room, swinging my legs.

"Hey," a voice says. "You're here."

I look up. "Ben," I say. I leap up and smile at him. "You're back!"

It seems like ages since I saw him. It's nearly a month, but it seems longer. His hair has grown back a little, not back to where it was when he was shaggy and comfortable-looking, like an old jumper, but it's not quite as skull-grazing as it was. He is tanned and lean, and there are red apples on his cheeks. His teeth are very white—I've always liked that about him.

Ah, it's good to see him, after so long. We've been funny with each other these past few months, and I wish we hadn't. And now he's here, and it's lovely. He's smiling widely and holding out his arms. I walk towards him and he hugs me.

"It's great to see you, Nat," he says. I look up and smile, and realize I am staring right at Jamie, who has been standing behind him. I step back.

"Hey, Jamie," I say. "It's great to see you too. Two of you too. Both of you! Hah!" I finish lamely, sounding insane. "Come on over! Check out my . . . stuff." I trail off, and they look at me politely.

Over at the next stall, Sara shakes her head at me, and then her attention is diverted. "Natasha?" I hear her say. "She's right here."

"Hello, darling," says a low voice in my ear. "Isn't this *wonderful*?"

"Mum?" I turn in surprise. "Hi—I didn't know you were coming."

"You invited me, didn't you?" She leans forwards and kisses me, and I smell her familiar scent, sandalwood and something spicy. My mother is channeling her favorite era today, in a beautiful cerise and turquoise silk maxi-dress and cardigan, and gold sandals. She looks younger than I do. I run my hands through my hair, awkwardly.

"Mum, you know Ben and—" I begin, but she interrupts.

"Ben! Hello, *darling*!" she says, throwing her arms round him, and I cannot help but roll my eyes at Jamie, who is standing off to the side, slightly self-conscious. I beckon her forwards, and she shakes her head, smiling.

"How *are* you?" my mother is asking Ben.

"I'm well, how are you? You look amazing, Miranda."

At this point my mother actually nudges him. I expect her to say, "Oh, get away!" and lightly tap his hand. "I can't stay long," she says, smiling broadly. "Jean-Luc's taking me to lunch! At Galvin!"

"Jean-Luc?"

"Oh, you remember, darling, he's a special friend of mine. Poor chap's had a terrible time, but he's left his wife for good now, and it's going marvelously."

I look at her and she does seem to be glowing, but perhaps that's just the bronzer and the new diamond earrings she appears to be sporting. Whatever it is, the coat of armor is firmly back on my mother, for better or worse. "Where is he?" I ask.

"Oh," she says, with devastating candor. "He hates this kind of thing. He's in a cheese shop somewhere."

"Charming," I hear Ben murmur, and I want to laugh, and I realize laughing is the only way to deal with it, because it really is kind of funny.

My mother leans forwards. "These are pretty," she says, her gaze sliding over my pieces. She strokes one of the necklaces with two fingers. "Cecily's ring, darling, it looks beautiful." She looks up. "These must be selling well, hm?"

"I've sold a hundred and fifty so far."

"Gosh." She nods. "And these are nice," she says, picking up the bangles. I forget how good she was at her job, with her eye for beautiful things and a sense of business that came from God knows where, and I think again about all the things she could have been if she hadn't been screwed up—or screwed herself up. She slips a bangle onto her slim wrist. The blue enamel glints in the sunny hall. "I love it," she says. "I'll take one." She pauses. "And the necklace too."

As I reach for some tissue paper to wrap them, Jamie taps me on the arm. "I just wanted to say hi," she says. Her blonde hair glows in the bright sun.

"Hi," I say, slightly confused, and I look around for Ben.

"I'm going, I mean, sorry. It all looks gorgeous, Natasha, I really love your stuff. I'm going to come by the studio tomorrow if that's OK and buy some things for my sisters."

"Sure—" I am pleased but a little bewildered. "Ben, I'll see you tomorrow then too?"

Ben and Jamie look at each other. "Bye then," Jamie says, and she scurries off, her head bowed.

Ben stares at me. "Nat, what—"

Someone taps my arm. "Oh. Look who's here."

The actual reality of sending out an email to all my friends and family becomes apparent as I stop hunting for tissue paper and look up to see Guy, Roseanna, and Cecily, walking slowly towards the stall. They look apprehensive, as well they might.

My mother's face gives nothing away. I clutch Ben's hand, not meaning to, and then release it instantly.

"Hello, Miranda," Guy says, and he kisses her on the cheek and sinks his hands into the pockets of his baggy cords. She kisses him back.

"Hi," she says.

I put the necklaces down and step forwards. "Hi, there," I say.

We've met quite a few times, but Roseanna and Cecily are still quite awkward with me, and I with them. We raise our hands to each other. They are both holding paper cups of coffee, and I feel a pang of tenderness towards them, with their skinny jeans and flats, long hair with jeweled clips, their stripy tops like a summer uniform. I don't know yet if they're anything like me. I find them fascinating.

My mother stares at them and points a finger at Cecily. "I recognize that necklace," and she smiles. "I'm just buying one too. So you're Guy's daughters," she says.

"Yes," Roseanna, the elder, replies. She gives a shy half-grin.

Then Mum turns to me.

"You're Guy's daughter too, I suppose," she says, and she smiles, as though it's a little social joke, and we all smile, and Guy and I look at each other.

Ben steps forwards. "I'll leave you to it."

"Oh don't—" I begin.

"Hey, I should leave you guys alone. I'm meeting Jay for a drink at the Pride of Spitalfields," he says. "We're—yeah, I'll see you later, Nat." He pats my back and he is gone before I can say anything.

So we are left, my mother, my father, my two sisters, standing around my creaking old stall, as people mill around us, and it looks totally normal, except it is anything but normal.

The two girls look down at the ground, and Mum and Guy smile at each other awkwardly.

"How's the shop?" Mum asks.

"Good, good," Guy replies. "The trip to Morocco sounds wonderful, are you off anywhere else?"

"Oh, Jean-Luc and I might be going to La Rochelle later in the summer," Mum says carelessly. "He has a house there." She waves her hand expressively to indicate something, whether Jean-Luc's presence nearby or the existence of La Rochelle, I'm not sure. "How—how about you?"

She bites a nail then, and I see it. She's nervous. She is nervous.

"Hannah's sister has a place on Martha's Vineyard," Guy says.

"We've always gone there for a week in the summer. It's beautiful there."

"Of course," Mum says. "How lovely." She looks at the girls. "You'll go too, um—I'm sorry, I don't know your names. How awful."

"I'm Roseanna," says Roseanna. "And this is Cecily."

My mother is completely still, a half-smile on her face, as if she's been turned to stone. Then she nods, and shakes their hands. "Those are lovely names," she says. "My sister was called Cecily."

"I know." Cecily speaks for the first time. "Daddy used to tell me you were the most exciting girls he'd ever met. He's always talked about you two. We've got a photo of both of you in the sitting room."

Mum looks completely at a loss. "Both of us?" She sounds unsure.

"Yes," Guy says. "Of course both of you. I took it, that summer."

"That's—that's lovely," she says.

"Well," Guy says after a moment's pause. "We should be off. Just popped by to say hello really, and to check you're still on for supper tonight, Natasha?"

"Sure," I say. "Jay would like to come, if he's still welcome."

"Of course," Guy says. Roseanna blushes. I frown. Jay has a thing for my half-sister. I am not at all keen on this idea.

They make their goodbyes and leave. Guy says, as he kisses Mum again, "It was great to see you. I'll see you soon, I'm sure."

He holds her hand briefly and then they are gone.

Watching them go, I turn to my mother, and I see she is watching them too, and her eyes are shining with unshed tears.

"Mum—?" I begin, not sure what to say.

"Yes?" She drums her fingers on the stall.

"What did he mean, see you soon?"

"He doesn't mean anything. That's Guy all over. Very sweet, but constitutionally incapable of making up his mind about anything. Not the boy he was all those years ago, that's for sure." Her eyes follow him as he leaves.

I know she'll leave in a moment, and be off again, and so I take my chance once more. "Were you in love with him?" I ask. "Is that it?"

Mum puts her bag over her shoulder and faces me.

"Yes," she says. She nods.

I hadn't expected her to be so blunt. After all these years of half-truths and secrets. My permanently evasive, slippery mother. "Right," I say, shocked. "I didn't know that."

"Of course you didn't. Well, I was. Not at first, but when we met again—yes. I spent most of the seventies in love with him, waiting for him to come back after another break-up with Hannah, desperately hoping he'd see how fantastic everyone else thought I was. I'd get friends to throw amazing parties in crumbling mansions just so I could show off and he'd pick me. Yes. And he always ran away again. I couldn't keep him." She says it perfectly matter-of-factly. "I knew I was losing him, I knew he wasn't really interested, I mean he was dazzled, but he didn't love me the way I think you have to love someone to be with them. I knew he'd go back to the States, patch it up with that bloody American girl again."

Then she holds out her hand for the necklace and bracelet, and I put them on her palm, wrapped in their paper sachet. "Oh, it's all ancient history now, darling." Her green eyes are snapping, phosphorescent in the light, and I know she's lying. "But you have to believe this, this one thing. When I found out I was pregnant with his baby, it was the happiest day of my life. That's who you are, darling. Half of each of us."

I nod. "He's lovely."

She swallows and shakes her head, as if she disagrees, but with a catch in her voice she says, "He is a lovely man. I'll love him. Always. Anyway," she says. "Off I go to find Jean-Luc."

"Mum—!" I say, light dawning. "But that's silly, can't you . . . he's very lonely. I know he'd love to find someone again. Why not you?"

Mum takes the necklace out of the bag and puts it round her neck, adjusting it a little so it sits right, on the cerise and blue silk of her dress, the gold chain settling on her smooth, caramel-colored skin. "Darling, I used to think that, you know. But it's too late for us. Far, far too late. Like I say, too much history. My whole life's been about history. It's nice to start again with someone else, that's the sad truth. But I'll never stop loving him." She opens her eyes wide. "He's your father, apart from anything else." And then she says, "That's the only advice I'll ever give you. Don't leave it too late. Don't wish you'd done something about it in ten years' time. Do something about it now."

"Now?"

"Now," she says firmly. "I really am going. Goodbye. I'm very proud of you."

Without a kiss, without any other farewell, she walks off. I stare, my mouth open, and sit back wearily on the stool, as if I've been awake for a week. I can see her leave, the bright colors of her dress like a peacock strutting through the sun.

"She's lovely, is that your mum?" Sara says from the stall next to me, where she's been watching everything, curiously. "You've got a big enough family, haven't you?" she laughs. I stare at her, and then I laugh too.

"I suppose I have. How about you?"

"Massive," Sara sighs. "But I don't tell them where my stall is, that's for sure. First time I had it? I had my two sisters come and tell me I was putting all the stuff in the wrong place. Nearly killed them, I did. That's families for you, eh?"

I laugh shortly. "You're telling me." I stand up. "Saz, can you do me a favor, can you mind the stall for five minutes?"

She nods. "OK, but you do me when you're back."

"Of course." I wave to her, setting off at a run. "I have to go somewhere."

I run out of the hall and downstairs past the stallholders, out into Brick Lane, bobbing and weaving my way through the crowds of people moving slowly down the road laden down with plants, bric-a-brac, drinks. It is hot, nearly midday. I dart around them, dodge down the back of people's stalls, inhaling the smell of burritos, coffee, weed, spices, and pollution that is in the heart of the city, a world, a lifetime away from Cornwall. As I run past Princelet Street I glance to my right at my old home, and I nearly stumble across an old Bengali man.

I turn into Heneage Street, only two blocks along. I am out of breath with ducking and diving and I stop to collect myself. There is the Pride of Spitalfields, tucked neatly away, with a knot of drinkers standing outside in the sun. One of them looks up at me, squinting.

"Nat?" It's Jay. "Did you finish early?"

I shake my head. "Can you give me a minute?" I say to him, still panting.

His companion is standing with his back to me. It is Ben. He turns to look at me. "Give her a minute," he says. "She's very unfit."

"No. You, Jay," I say in short bursts. "Give me a minute. I mean. Go away."

I gesture for him to buzz off.

Jay looks at me like I'm mad. "I'll get us another pint," he says. "What do you want?"

"She'll have a vodka, lime and soda," Ben says immediately. "And some water, by the looks of her."

I nod gratefully at him, and Jay disappears into the dark pub.

"Hey, Nat," Ben says, his voice friendly but a little guarded. "It's nice to see you again. Where's your mum gone?"

"Lunch with boyfriend," I say. I stand up straight, finally having got my breath back. "She said something to me. I thought I should come and say it to you. Because—" I breathe in, and then out. "Because it's important."

"Right," Ben says. He moves a little way away from the drinkers, so we are standing in the shadow of the houses. "What do you mean?"

"I mean—oh, well. Here goes." I take a deep breath. "Look. I know you're seeing Jamie. I saw you two together, one night."

"Hold on." Ben holds up his hand. "We're not together."

"Yes, you are."

"No, we're not. I snogged her, a couple of months ago, we were both a bit drunk. You saw us?" He blinks.

I feel like a stalker. "Yes," I say. "I came back to the studio and you two were there. In the dark . . ."

"Les had that reading in the basement, do you remember? You couldn't go. Jamie and I went, it was . . ." He shudders. "It was pretty hard work. All about a boy growing up with no fingers in Chatham and joining a gang. Jamie let me drink out of her hipflask."

Damn Jamie with her cool hipflask-toting ways, I think.

"There were drinks afterwards. . . ." He is staring at me. "We're not together, Nat. You of all people should know that."

"But you were there today! Together!"

"No, we bloody weren't!" His voice is rising in exasperation. "Is this why you were so weird, before I went away, the last few weeks? Man!" He looks furious. "Listen. I arrive, I look round, she's arrived! It's not out of the realms of comprehension we'd all bump into each other at midday at an event to which you specifically asked us to arrive *at midday,* is it?"

"Fine, fine, I get it." I clear my throat. "Oh. OK. So—you're not with her?"

"Believe me, it's at times like these that I wish I was," Ben says slowly. "But no, I'm not."

"Oh," I say again.

"What did you want to ask me?"

"It doesn't matter." I wipe my hand along my forehead. "Look— I'd better go back to the stall. . . ."

He catches my hand in his. He's smiling. "Nat, I'm joking. I don't want to be with Jamie. I mean, she's really sweet, but we're not at all right for each other. She doesn't like Morecambe and Wise, for starters. Now, again please. What did you want to ask me?"

I take a deep breath. I'm feeling completely light-headed, with the running, the sunshine, the events of the last hour.

"Well," I say. "Mum said I should go for it. So I really will now. Ben—I was wondering. Do you want to go out for a drink some time?"

His expression freezes. I watch him, my heart thumping.

"Are you serious?" he says. "Are you really, really asking me out?"

"Yes," I say. "Why, don't you—"

He turns his back on me, and my heart sinks, but he's putting his pint on the ground. "Come here," he says, drawing me into his arms. He kisses my hair, and then he bends his head and I raise mine to his, and we kiss.

"Yes," he says, after a moment. "I'd love to go out for a drink some time. When? Tonight?"

I stroke his cheek, his lovely lips, trace around the edge of his gorgeous, kind eyes. "I've got to have dinner with my new dad and half-sisters and watch while Jay tries to hit on them," I say. "It's complicated."

"No," Ben says, kissing me again. "It's very simple. So I'll see you tomorrow."

"Great," I say, a silly smile on my face. I can't stop smiling. "And the day after that?"

"And then maybe the day after that." Ben steps away and looks serious for a moment, then he smiles again. "I don't believe this, you know. I've been mad about you for such a long time. But I didn't know how to help you. I thought you'd never sort it out, get out of the life you were in."

I can feel his muscles under his shirt as he moves towards me and hugs me again. I think of Cecily's diary, where it is now, lying at the bottom of the sea, or perhaps washed up on another shore. "Cecily helped me," I say. "It's all because of her."

The door to the pub swings open again and Jay emerges, carrying a tray of drinks. He looks at us without any surprise, holding on to each other as if we've just found one another, and then gives us a small, pleased grin.

Ben and I kiss again, and I look up at the sky, opening out, blue and endless, above the narrow old streets, where Mum is having her smart lunch, where Guy and his daughters are making their way back to the tall, white house in Angel, where we are all, all of us, just trying to be part of one big happy family, whatever on earth that is, trying and often failing, and sometimes succeeding. "Thank you," I whisper, my face warmed by the sunshine. "Thank you."

Acknowledgments

For jewelry and business advice, I owe a huge debt of gratitude to Sarah Lawrence of the fabulous www.girlgang.co.uk: do check it out. For East London ways a big shout-out to Maura Brickell for her local tours and amaze times. Also thanks to the East London ladies, Cat Cobain, Leah Woodburn and Claire Baldwin, and Thomas Wilson and Pamela Casey, as ever, for the same and much more. Big thanks to Rebecca Folland for seeing me through the dark times, Anita Ahuja for help with Indian names, Nicole Vanderbilt and Maria Rodriguez for telling me to write it so very long ago ("Listen, chica . . ."), all at Curtis Brown (especially Liz Iveson and Carol Jackson) and of course Jonathan Lloyd (with special thanks to Marion).

Particular thanks to my parents, Phil and Linda, for their memories, support, and advice.

As ever, massive thanks to everyone at HarperCollins, in particular Lynne Drew for her editorial guidance throughout, and to my fabulous U.S. publishers, Simon & Schuster, especially Louise Burke and Kara Cesare.

A special shout-out to the members of Sleazy Velvet and a big HIYA to my nephew Jake.

Finally, my biggest thanks to Chris, for making me bread and for making me so happy.

Bibliography

There were various books I read during the writing of this one which were of great help and interest and for that reason I list them below, though I should of course make it clear that any mistakes are of course my own:

The Denning Report: John Profumo & Christine Keeler (Uncovered Editions, 1999)

The Pendulum Years: Britain in the Sixties, Bernard Levin (Jonathan Cape, 1970)

That Was Satire That Was: Beyond the Fringe, The Establishment Club, Private Eye and That Was The Week That Was, Humphrey Carpenter (Victor Gollancz, 2000)

Bringing the House Down, David Profumo (John Murray, 2006)

The Duleep Singhs: The Photograph Album of Queen Victoria's Maharajah, Peter Bance (Sutton Publishing, 2004)

The Maharajah's Box, Christy Campbell (HarperCollins, 2000)

Daphne, Justine Picardie (Bloomsbury, 2008)

Soho Night & Day, Frank Norman & Jeffrey Bernard (Secker & Warburg, 1966)

Cornwall: A Shell Guide, John Betjeman (Faber, 1964)

Liberty & Co. in the Fifties and Sixties, Anna Buruma (ACC Editions, 2008)

The 1940s Home, Paul Evans (Shire Library, 2009)

The 1950s Home, Sophie Leighton (Shire Library, 2009)

Love Always

Harriet Evans

INTRODUCTION

Love Always tells the story of Natasha Kapoor, a woman whose life is at a turning point. Her marriage is failing, her business is going bankrupt, and her beloved grandmother just died—leaving her large and complicated family to sell their family vacation home in Cornwall. In the midst of heartache and loss, Natasha finds comfort in reading the long-lost diary of her aunt Cecily, who died in a tragic accident when she was fifteen years old and whose death has never been discussed. Reading the diary, Natasha learns secrets that have remained hidden for more than forty years, and finds inspiration in the words of the aunt she never knew.

QUESTIONS AND TOPICS FOR DISCUSSION

1. The novel opens with Natasha's train ride from London to Cornwall for her grandmother's funeral. Looking out the window during the long journey, Natasha notices as they move "further and further west, the landscape is wilder, and though spring feels far away, there are tiny green buds on the black branches fringing the railway tracks." (p. 17) Consider the ways in which the change in landscape alters Natasha. Is she happier in Cornwall than in London? Why is Summercove so important to Natasha?

2. At the funeral there is a palpable tension between the family members. Natasha remarks "this is what we're like now Granny's not here. It's all changed, and I don't know how, or why." (p. 61) What has changed in the family dynamic now that Frances has died? What has stayed the same? What has changed for Natasha?

3. Compare Miranda and Louisa. How are they alike? How are they different? Do you sympathize with one more than the other? Who do you think Natasha sympathizes with more? Do her sympathies shift throughout the course of the novel?

4. Revisit the scene where Arvind gives Cecily's diary to Natasha. What do you think is his motivation for doing so? Why did he choose to share the diary with Natasha and no one else? What do you think he meant by the family being "poisoned"? Was he including himself and Natasha? Turn to pages 75–76 and discuss.

5. On page 76, Arvind says: "Freedom comes in many guises." In light of this quote, think about the unconventional ways in which the characters in the novel achieve a sense of freedom. Is the path to freedom through heartache? Consider Natasha, Miranda, Frances, Arvind, and Louisa in your response.

6. Were you surprised by Octavia's assertion that Miranda killed Cecily? Did you believe her initially? Why would Louisa and her family find Miranda at fault?

7. How would you define Oli's character? Do you see him as sympathetic? How does Natasha see him? How does Miranda?

8. "I know all men were created equal. But we're the only different people we know." (p. 136) Discuss the role of race in the novel. How does being half British and half Pakistani affect Archie? Miranda? Cecily? What role, if any, does race play in Natasha's life? In Jay's?

9. Consider for a moment the structure of the story. What effect does the diary and the leap back in time have on the story overall? Did you feel more connected to Cecily's story or Natasha's? Can you make any comparisons between the two women and their lives?

10. Discuss Frances's character before Cecily's death. Did you like her? What about after her death? Do you forgive Frances for what happened more than forty years ago? Why or why not?

11. "And then something strange happens. The diary is in Mum's hand, and it suddenly flies out, eddying away on a huge arching gust of wind." (p. 417) Do you think Miranda let the diary go on purpose? Do you think she let the diary go so that everyone in the family could continue to be protected from the truth?

12. Revisit the scene on pages 422–437 where Natasha realizes Guy is her father. Did you anticipate this to be the case or were you shocked? Do you think this event allows Natasha to be more open to love, now that she has discovered both the mystery of her extended and her immediate family?

13. In the end Natasha finally allows herself to be open to love and happiness. As she kisses Ben she looks up at the sky and thinks of everyone in her life "just trying to be part of one big happy family, whatever on earth that is." (p. 449) Did this moment in the story give you the feeling that Natasha's journey has been resolved? Has she found what she has been searching for? Why or why not?

ENHANCE YOUR BOOK CLUB

1. Harriet Evans's books are international bestsellers. Have your book club do a series on her. Read her two most recent novels—*I Remember You* and *The Love of Her Life*. What themes do you notice in her work? What message do you think Evans is sending to her audience? Which of these books was your favorite? The favorite of the group?

2. "Granny died in her sleep last Friday. She was eighty-nine. The funny thing is, it still shocked me. Booking my train tickets to come down to Cornwall, in February, it seemed all wrong, as though I was in a bad dream." (p. 7–8) Grief and dealing with tragedy, loss and heartache play major roles in the story. Have your group reflect on grief: what it means, how it impacts our day-to-day lives, how we move on afterwards or if we ever can. Have each member share a moment of grief or loss. Did your family grow closer in the wake of a difficult situation or tragedy? Do you think the Kapoors grew closer? Why or why not?

3. Turn to the opening pages of the book and read the first epigraph aloud to your book club:

   > We can never go back, that much is certain. The past is still too close to us. The things we have tried to forget and put behind us would stir again, and that sense of fear, of furtive unrest, struggling at length to blind unreasoning panic—now mercifully stilled, thank God—might in some manner unforeseen become a living companion, as it had been before.
   >
   > —*Rebecca,* Daphne du Maurier

Why do you think the author chose to include this quote as the opening of her novel?

Have a movie night with your book club and rent the made-for-TV-movie *Rebecca* (TV 1997), based on the famous gothic novel. What is the connection between *Rebecca* and *Love Always*?

4. On page 68 Miranda tells Natasha: "relationships aren't perfect. They're not. You have to work at them." In many ways, this moment indicates the version of Miranda we come to know by the end of the story—the woman who is willing to sacrifice her happiness to protect her family. Over a traditional Indian meal, discuss relationships, both in the novel and in your own life. What are examples of having to work at a relationship in your own life? In the story? Might Miranda have been speaking not only of Oli and Natasha, but her parents' relationship, or her relationship (or lack thereof) with Guy?